Nightmares Unearthed

Book Three in the Eve of Humanity Series

Brittany wants to know, when does a dream stop being a dream?
Nicole and Victor need to know, at what point is dead, dead?
They will get their answers… once their Nightmares are Unearthed.

A Novel by
Kevin Weisbeck

Nightmares Unearthed

An Owlstone Book

January 2025

Published as a Print-on-Demand book
through the Amazon Company,
for the author Kevin Weisbeck.

Cover design and Artwork
by Dan Huckle

First printing, April 2021

Dedication

I dedicate this book to the journey, because you don't just write a book, you rewrite it, and rewrite it… like a hundred times. Then you doubt what you have, read it, and rewrite it again. When you're finally done you walk away, but you're always wondering one thing…

…did I kill enough people?

Foreword

Nicole sat at the table staring at the empty cup. As good as Alzien coffee was, it was nothing compared to her memories of a dark roast Colombian. She took a second to check the numbers that were dialling down on the ship's overhead screen. In just under a week, Tranquillity2 would be finishing the trip to Earth.

A lot had happened in the near twenty years that they'd been gone. At almost thirty years, due to Tranquilty2's added travel time, Earth had gone through horrendous times. She let her memories drift to Elizabeth and to their daughter, Brittany. It tempered the fact that they had also been through a lot.

When Elizabeth had been shot, the decision to leave Earth became an easy one. The planet needed to work this out. But before departing, they had left a pup ship for the Chinese to explore. That had been a mistake. The United States, Canada, and the United Kingdom immediately attacked Shanghai. The bombing was relentless until there was nothing left of the craft, or the city.

Crippling trade sanctions came next, and while Nicole initially felt horrible for China, she soon learned that they had been playing their own game. There had never been a Shenti Lui or anyone else looking out for the people of Asia. The government's plan was to ram the Alzien system down the people's throats until the technologies were handed over. Then, that system would be sabotaged from within. Before long, the people would be begging for the old system. China would use their people to justify backing out of their commitments to Alzie. It had been a calculated move, and it had played out perfectly. These flags should have been seen.

Picking up the cup, she got to her feet and poured another coffee. A quick check on the crew's vitals was next. Normally the main computer did this, but she had set the exit time of her hibernation two weeks early. Reviewing the last five years of Earth's news seemed more important. She returned to the table and watched an American live news feed on the big screen.

As expected, the front and centre news was that of the new economic and trade systems that were still being adjusted. After decades of war and suffering, a mutual agreement had been made. It had ended both old and new economic systems.

China was losing traction with their allies. It started as the war was winding down. Russia disagreed that China should be in charge, and they weren't the only ones. With that, the derailing of China's push for power had begun.

Nicole, an economist at heart, had spent some time studying the shifts of power and money. While the once rich traded their bank accounts for a wealth of special privileges, the average citizen slowly slipped deeper and deeper into levels of dependency. They were corralled into mega cities and had their freedoms stripped. Forced subservience would make it easier for governments to manage them.

Mandatory health passports had also ensured compliance. Imagine speaking up against a government that had the ability to restrict travel, employment, housing, groceries, healthcare, and entertainment. It wasn't right and caused ongoing protests.

She took the headset off and slid her fingers through her hair as she looked down at the latest statistics. Earth's transition had taken its toll. Billions had perished at the hands of war, sickness, and starvation. Anxiety and desperation had many of the survivors looking through their telescopes for help. When were the Alziens coming back? Could they fix this?

Putting the headset back on, she flipped to a Chinese news feed, followed by a few Russian ones, eventually landing on one from England. They had just signed a trade deal with India. China would be the next one to write up an agreement. These were baby steps.

Earth, albeit no longer at war, had a long road ahead of them before any form of success could be declared.

Chapter one

B rittany looked out from the cab as the downtown core of Beijing passed by. Her thoughts had slipped back to a recent trip to the United States. She'd spent the last three weeks getting to know her Earth-father, Jenny, and Jenny's kids. Her father, Greg, and his wife were an exciting pair to spend time with, and the visit was good, but Jenny's visit was a lot more interesting. This woman was the cool aunt, the kind that treated her like an equal. Brittany hadn't seen too much of that from her father, or anyone else on Earth. To them, she'd always be Elizabeth's daughter.

Happy to be back in China, she was already missing Jenny's daughter, Melanie. The girl had recently turned seventeen and she was in boy crazy mode. Dating was definitely a different ritual here than on Alzie. The two of them had gone out to the mall a few times and flirted, but it was a foreign ritual. Brittany preferred to focus on one boy at a time and Melanie's brother, Mathew, had caught her eye. She imagined herself curled in his arms, but did he even like her? And was there something in the way he talked to her?

"Oh. Stop here for a second, please," she shouted as her hand reached for the door handle of the taxi. "Right here."

The cab driver had fallen into a trance, manoeuvring the busy streets like a robot. It was the only way to safely drive in this country. He snapped out of the driving fog, did a quick shoulder check, and cut off a blue sedan before rolling up to the curb.

It was hard to tell if it was the musky smell of the cab or the fact that her favourite restaurant was on the right side of the street, but suddenly, Brittany was hungry for Mrs. Lee's shrimp fried rice.

Although the pungent smell of this dish was almost choking to the nose, the taste was out of this world. She never tired of it. "Wait here. I'll be right back."

He nodded as she fled the car like a bank robber, less the mask. Pinballing her way through the busy crowd, she tried to decide between the dry garlic ribs and the honey garlic beef as a second dish.

"Mrs. Lee!" she cried from the doorway of the Golden Palace. "I'm home and I'm starving."

An elderly Chinese woman looked up from her newspaper and smiled. She was a bigger woman, and to Brittany that meant she was a good cook. Her sons were also on the portly side, another dead give away that she knew what she was doing. "You home girl. That good. You miss my rice?"

"More than you know. There's nobody like you in the States. Can I get some rice, sweet and sour pork, and that beef broccoli stuff? Oh, and a couple of those future cookies."

"That's Fortune cookies."

"Right."

It was great to be back. The Chinese had set them up in a great apartment and even though they'd only been on Earth a couple of months, it had quickly become home. The United States might have been more central, but this was all about the politics. China and the US were still working through the post-war relations and the diplomacy was needed... keep your friends close.

Mrs. Lee carefully filled the cardboard boxes and set them in the bag with a few extra egg rolls and the fortune cookies. "You need your veggies. Where you mother?"

"She's around somewhere. I just got back from the States, meeting friends and my father. I've got a cab outside, but I had to see you before I got home." She smiled ear to ear as she stuck her nose up to the bag and took a deep breath. "Now that smells like home."

Mrs. Lee walked her to the door and gave her a hug. "You such a good girl. You say hi to your mother for me. You tell her she not to be stranger."

"I will, as soon as I find her. Thanks again." She returned the woman's hug and bolted out the door. Halfway back to the cab, she was knocked down. Cradling the food like a football, she got back to her feet.

The cabby had watched her leave the restaurant and had seen her fall. Being old school, he believed that women weren't to be pampered. It wasn't a feminist thing, more an inferiority thing. Brittany had felt his eyes on her as she pulled herself up. She knew it wasn't personal.

The cab carried her down the bustling streets until she could see the high-rise through the dingy window. Hopefully, her mother was hungry. The car stopped and Brittany grabbed the luggage and the food. She thanked the cabby with a wave, walked through the lobby, and headed straight for the elevator. Now in the building, she needed to get to her suite before Chuck found her.

He was a nice enough boy, but she'd heard rumours that he wanted to ask her to some dance. Her fondness was with Mathew, albeit a relationship evolving at a snail's pace.

Swiping her thumb against the up button, she watched as the numbers above the elevator doors began to drop. Her head anxiously rocked from right to left hoping the doors would open soon. Then she could make her escape. The guy was hovering somewhere. He always was.

The elevator gave a ding and the doors opened. She gave a last quick glance over her shoulder and muttered, "made it."

"Hi, Brittany. Made what?" Chuck asked from inside the elevator.

Her heart sank. It was like there was a tracking device on her. "Chuck, so good to see you."

"Going up?"

"Yep. Since down would take us to the parking lot and I don't have a car."

"Good one." He wasted no time. "Hey, we have a staff party this weekend. You can go with me… if you like?"

Her eyes widened. "Oh, I think I'm busy. I'd have to check with my mother and get back to you." She watched the light climb through the numbers until it got to her floor. Again, he was a nice boy, just not her type. Like the cab driver, he was old-school Chinese.

"I'll ask your mother and get back to you," he barked. "It'll be great. Lots of punch and dancing. I hear they're getting a band."

"That sounds exciting." She had heard Chinese bands and hoped her sarcasm wasn't too obvious.

Ding! The elevator doors started to move, and she slipped her delicate frame through them before they were fully opened.

"Thanks Chuck." She started down the hallway. "Have a good one. We'll talk later."

He looked puzzled. Have a good what? He shook the comment. "I'll get back to you after I talk to your mother."

The suitcase was dragged through the doorway and left there. She started for the kitchen. Safely inside her apartment, she could shake the last few minutes like rain off an umbrella. "Mom! You home?"

The silence wasn't a surprise. Nicole, her mother, had been ridiculously busy. Returning to Earth had kept her on her toes. In the last two months, she had settled her and Brittany into their apartment, done no less than twenty television appearances, and met with every World Leader in ten different joint meetings. She had solved three major trade issues and set up a task force to start sharing Alzien medical advancements. She'd only spent twelve of the last sixty nights in the apartment.

Brittany had spent thirty-five nights in there, bouncing back and forth. Most of it, she could have lived without. There were the stuffy political dinners and the numerous television appearances.

A sudden burst of light filled the room. The crack of thunder immediately followed, shaking the walls. The power went out and the emergency lights flickered twice before coming on. Shadows quickly formed throughout the apartment.

"Shit." She set the food down and started for the drawer with the candles. "Hey, Mom. Are you home?"

Chapter two

Victor woke up consumed by the darkness. He took a minute before looking over to the nightstand. The clock read 3:16 am, just as he'd expected. He could have looked right away or waited another couple of minutes. It wouldn't have made a difference. It was the number that he'd seen so many times after waking from bad dreams as a child, and lately as an adult. This time it was somehow different. He hadn't been dreaming, or if he had, he didn't remember. Regardless, he knew the clock would read 3:16.

Outside, the wind howled as it usually did on the islands. The Indian Ocean was famous for its persuasive winds. He sat up in his bed, swung his legs around, and set his feet firmly on the floor. Then he clasped his hands to his face and tried to shake the dream he couldn't quite remember.

And was he being watched? He looked around. If a lifetime of living off his instincts had taught him anything, that was if you felt you were being watched, you usually were. But here on his estate, there was no chance of him being observed or threatened. He had some of the best security known to man, and why not, he had trained them all himself.

Victor got up and headed for the bathroom. He had to remind himself that those days of shoulder checks were in the past. He now owned his own country and ran a somewhat reputable business. He'd reached a somewhat amicable agreement with his enemies in the United States. He'd stay away from them, if they stayed away from him. It was a win, win. Nobody needed a war.

Small claws scratched at the door.

"Not now, Morgan."

Morgan was a cat that had strayed onto the grounds from town. It was all black and it somehow knew life would be better if she lived on the compound, and it was. Not an animal lover, the years had softened Victor. He'd allowed the cat to roam the grounds and even kept it fed when the mice were scarce.

The cat eventually pushed the door to the bathroom open with its nose and jumped up onto the counter. "Meowwww."

"What? You feel that too?"

"Meow."

"You've got good instincts." He finished his business, stepped over to the sink and turned on both taps. "What do you think is coming?"

The cat didn't answer. Instead, it arched his back, jumped over to the window and hissed.

Victor rinsed the soap off his hands and grabbed the towel. "What have you got?"

The cat's tail bushed up as it continued to stare outside.

"That's one hell of a reaction, even for you." Victor leaned over to have a look.

Outside, the ocean crashed up on the shore and the moon lit the crests of the waves. It also shimmered off the wings of the birds. Thousands of them filled the branches of the trees, the grounds, and the rooftops of the other buildings.

The cat looked back at Victor, as if hoping for the explanation it couldn't find on its own.

"Not sure, Buddy," Victor shrugged. "But I'm pretty sure this isn't a good thing."

Chapter three

The Pup ship landed at the base of the dig sites in the main canyon of Mars. Nicole had landed there many times in the past. Each time she'd found the visits enlightening. The fact that her good friend Virgil had taken over the expedition was no surprise. He was a master when it came to finding and engineering a means to buried treasures. And the best thing, at least for Nicole, was that he knew of her secret agenda and was willing to discretely help her with whatever fact-finding he could. Mars held a bounty of information.

After Elizabeth's passing, Nicole had looked forward to going back to Earth and Mars. The man with the birds had taken a stronghold in the back of her mind. Could Elizabeth's death be reversed? Could there have been a mistake, one they'd be able to correct? Was he a man of God?

She'd studied the bible and had a million questions about it. Interpretation was everything and that book left little in the areas of black and white.

And what about the Ledger, or that book with the image of two planets colliding. And then there was that gaudy necklace that she'd found on Mars, so many questions and so few answers.

Virgil had called her and said it was important. She used that call as an excuse to escape her schedule, not knowing what to expect. He had mumbled something about hollows and underground chambers. She had tried to get more from him, but the telecommunication reception from Earth was poor. Repeaters would be set up to alleviate the delay issues, but the system was still in the early stages of development.

Her space suit fought her as she struggled to put it on. Exhausted by weeks of globetrotting, the weight of it taxed her until the craft depressurised. From there, a noisy gondola carried her up to the opening of the cave and as it did, she thought of Brittany, Jenny, and her kids.

Melanie and Mathew were good kids, and she was fairly certain that Brittany had a thing for the boy. That wasn't the worst thing that could happen. Jenny had brought these kids up properly. She'd trust him before Brittany.

Rolling her shoulders, Nicole reminded herself how nice it was to get away. Being penned up on Earth had worn her out. It wasn't like she had wanted any of this. Her goal was to find the man with the birds. Never one to be hard-wired for acceptance, she truly believed that this man, and all his stupid birds, could change Elizabeth's fate, couldn't he?

The gondola stopped with a jerk, almost knocking Nicole to the floor. At the entrance, she punched in the code to pressurise the room. The light went off, letting her know it was safe, and she stripped out of the bulky suit.

Virgil met her at the second set of doors. "That was a quick trip."

"You can't imagine how nice it is to get away. Mom's been running me ragged. With the main ship heading the communication project, the workload from those scientists has been shifted to guess who?"

To Virgil, she looked more worn than usual. "That's one of those rhetorical question, right?"

"It is," Nicole chuckled. "It's good to see you again. What have you got?"

Virgil didn't say a word. Instead, he gestured for her to follow as he turned and headed for the Scan room. Nicole knew, by this reaction, it had to be good. The man preferred showing verses telling, because nothing explained things better than a first-hand account.

He kicked on the screen's backlights and several scans appeared on the monitor like x-rays. To the average person, these images resembled a freaky combination of inkblots and ultrasounds. To Virgil and Nicole, they were scientific works of art.

8

Nicole took a minute before speaking. "Are these the hollows you were referring to?"

"Yes. I saw a unique pattern to them."

She also saw it. Although he had spent more time using this equipment, Nicole had an eye for seeing things in the labyrinth of black and white. "Many of these hollows seem to be adjoining." Her eyes turned to his. "Is that what you see?"

Virgil nodded. "Affirmative. I'm not sure what that means though. Could be nothing."

It was a curious find. "There are buildings back on Earth that are adjoined due to the climate. They're called 'plus fifteens' and join the building so people don't have to weather the cold when travelling through the city." It was a fact that she'd remembered from her stay in Calgary.

"How cold does it get for them to need these?" Virgil asked.

"With the wind chill it can dip colder than minus fifty. That's the Celsius measure," Nicole explained.

"Why do they allow it to get that cold?"

"Earth doesn't have climate control."

"Do you think they had temperatures like that on this planet?" Virgil asked.

"Who knows. Adjoining buildings might be a sign. This could also be a mall. Earth has those things too. Hundreds of stores, all under one roof. It's quite convenient. You really should take the time to see it some day. Brit and I will take you shopping. You'd have fun," she promised.

"Earth?" Virgil thought about it for a second, but had no interest in shopping, or people. His life had been all about tunnels and desolate areas. The people he worked with had similar interests and he could always talk shop to them. What would he say to an Earthling? "I'll take a rain check."

"Come on, you'd love it. It's a lot different than Alzie. The food alone would sell you on this planet." She reached into her bag and emptied a handful of candies on the counter.

"What are these?" He fumbled through the wrapped trinkets.

She grabbed a chocolate and carefully unwrapped it. Then she squeezed his cheeks, causing his mouth to open, and it was popped in. He started to chew and his eyes lit up like firecrackers. "Mmm, what is this stuff?"

"It's candy. Some are chewy, some crunchy, and others like the chocolate, just melt in your mouth. You can share or hoard with the others. It doesn't matter to me. It's just one of the tastes of Earth."

Virgil swallowed and looked for another one like the last. "Well, I must say, this does make me curious."

"These should too." She reached into her bag again and pulled out a few comic books. There was nothing like it on Alzie and the whole idea of books having hand-drawn pictures fascinated him. The stories were even more intriguing as they reached out at crazy fantasies about space. She had grabbed a few Batman comics along with a few Superman, and Justice Leagues.

"Read them and let me know how you like them. The story continues in a new book every week, and I can send them to you if you like." Suddenly her phone rang, and she looked down to see the number. "It's Brit. I'll have to take this."

The call was brief, and she watched as Virgil thumbed through the magazines. His eyes danced over the pages until the call ended.

"How's Brittany?"

"Brittany is Brittany. She's back in Beijing driving somebody else crazy."

"Tough going?"

"She's in a blaming phase. As for these comics, they have hundreds of different stories, and these are just a couple of the more popular ones. Come to Earth and you can check them all out for yourself."

Virgil scratched his head and turned the page as another candy found its way into his mouth. That one was chewy. "What is this guy? He looks like a bat. He is a man though, right?"

"The whole story is that he fights crime, and he uses the costume to hide his identity. It also gives him superpowers."

"Superpowers? I like that idea." He was hooked. "Yeah, I'll take a trip to Earth, but you'll have to show me around and keep an eye out for me. I mean it would be so easy to get lost in a world with six billion people. I can't even imagine. They must be shoulder to shoulder."

"The numbers aren't even close to that anymore and it's not like you couldn't move on Earth. There are many areas where you can walk for miles without seeing anybody. Just like there are areas where you can't walk down the street without tripping over people. It's very diverse, but that's part of its charm." She looked up at the screens and got back to business. "This hollow is right below the caved-in high-rise. It's probably for parking or something. I wouldn't waste too much time on it unless you're bored."

"What about this one?" he spoke with a mouthful of toffee.

"That's a good call. It looks like a building full of something. Might be a few treasures in there. Maybe a storage area, or an office. It's hard to say by looking at these shots. Have you done the angled scans yet?"

"No. I wasn't sure where you wanted me to concentrate our resources."

Nicole pointed to the dark hollow at the right of the screen. "This one is talking to me. I'll get you to focus on that one first. It looks accessible and I like the idea of it having contents. Who knows, it might be an art gallery, or they might have a box of comic books."

Virgil's eyes lit up. "Imagine what their stories would be."

"You know Virgil." Nicole was trying to bait him. "I'm due for a vacation, and Brittany should be home for a while. You could stay with us for a week. Margaret can handle this place."

Virgil thought about it and was almost sold when he popped a mint into his mouth. "Oh, this is good. Sadly, I must decline. I need to tunnel into these hollows. Once I get these black spots figured out then maybe." He held up a comic. "But you will keep me supplied?"

"Not a problem." She grabbed a candy and popped it in her mouth. "I have a question on another topic. You've been here a while. Have you seen Frederich?"

"You mean your ghost?" Virgil felt a shiver run the length of his spine. "I saw him briefly, but then he faded away. What do you think he is?"

"An apparition. Does he give you the freaks?"

"There are no such things as ghosts."

"I'd say we've got one upstairs."

Virgil shook his head. "If you say so."

"I should have brought you a Casper comic. It's a cute little story about a friendly ghost," she laughed. "You'd love it."

"That's quite okay. Anyway, he's your ghost, not mine. I'm going to make prints of these for you and then I'll set everything up for a cross scan."

"Yes, do thirty-five and seventy-five-degree scans. That should show us the easier hollows to access. We just need to be careful when we tunnel. Remember that this is volcanic dust and rock. It caves in easily."

"Actually, it's surprisingly, like sandstone, but I'll still web the walls as we go."

The webbing, he referred to, was the material they sprayed on the walls and ceilings above where they worked. It hardened like steel and gave them a safe spider web like structure to support the soil's weight.

"Well, I'm going to check on Casper," Nicole joked. "If I don't return soon, come looking for me."

"Don't count on it."

He wasn't kidding.

Chapter four

Morgan jumped down from the sink and scampered over to the French doors at the far side of the bedroom. She wanted outside and Victor knew she'd yowl until she got her way. Other cats would have been terrified by the spectacle of so many feathers, but not this one. She wanted to feast. Too bad she wouldn't find this menu to her liking.

On his way to the door, Victor stopped at the nightstand, opened the drawer, and took out a 9mm handgun. It didn't do as much damage as the larger magnums, but if used right it could drop somebody all the same. He gripped it as if he was shaking hands with a friend, and why not? This gun had saved his life many times.

"Meow." The cat paced the carpet by the door, a little agitated that this was taking as long as it was.

"I'm coming. I've never known a cat this eager to get its ass kicked by a bunch of birds. You know they're going to kick your ass, right?"

"Meow." Which still meant hurry the hell up. There'd be an ass kicking all right, but it wasn't going to be hers.

Victor opened the door and watched as Morgan sprinted for a large tree. The birds immediately took flight and the cat jumped up and swatted at as many as she could. She was empty-pawed when she landed, and a little miffed at becoming a spectator.

Both Victor and Morgan watched from the backyard as the birds formed the cloud. It was a spectacle that Victor had seen far too often, something the cat had never witnessed. Both took a few seconds to watch.

When it was over, the cat returned to the door. That was when Victor noticed the envelope. It wasn't as thick as the ones in the past, but he knew what it was, and who had dropped it off. He looked across the grounds.

Moonlit shadows hid in corners, under trees, and in distant doorways. None of them were made from the man he was looking for. The Birdman was nowhere in sight.

Morgan raced past him, not looking back. She'd chased many a bird in her days, but none like these. These birds weren't right.

Chapter five

The apartment was a beautiful one and yet it was modest for someone of Nicole's importance. She'd never expected lavish. It was important to prove to the people of Earth that they were equals. The only thing that Nicole spoiled herself on was her collection of artworks. She had filled the apartment with elegant and ornate objects from around the globe and beyond. The tribal Voodoo and black magic ornaments from Africa topped her compilation.

As expected, Brittany found a note stuck to the fridge with a Star Trek magnet. She pulled it off, grabbed a glass of chocolate milk, fumbled a fork out of the silverware drawer, and scooped up the bag of food with her free arm. Juggling everything, she headed out onto the balcony where the moonlight made reading a little easier. Everything was set down on the small glass coffee table in the corner. Then she curled up into the comfy lounge chair and reached for the food.

Prying the top open with her fork, the rice was dug into first. She washed it down with a swallow of milk as she looked out over the city. The last remnants of sun had been consumed by darkness. With her mouth full, she opened the note and started to read:

Hi Honey...

Not sure if it was today or tomorrow that you said you'd be coming back. I left for Mars this afternoon. Virgil has found a few things and wanted to share. I'm thinking of bringing back a few more artifacts for the apartment. I'll say I'm studying them. Think we need a few things for around the fireplace. What do you think? Room for more clutter?

Did you get a good visit in? How was your father?

There are leftovers in the fridge but stay out of my ice cream. Almost forgot, Chuck called and wants to take you to some staff party. You should go. Confirm with him and let him know when he can pick you up.

I'll be back in a couple days. Stay out of trouble...please!!!
MOM

As she finished reading, a large drop of rain landed in the middle of the note. It was soon followed by a second. Brittany looked up to see even darker clouds creeping in from the other side of the building. It was time to go inside. The note was crumpled and tossed off the balcony.

The clouds opened up before she could get everything rounded up. Moving the food inside to the counter, she watched as the puddles began to form on the deck as the rains pelted the world outside. Getting soaked in a summer rain wasn't the worst thing to happen to her, but if she was going to get wet, a soak in the tub would be better.

She made her way to the bathroom and started to draw her bath. The room was a cosy one with an old fashion tub. The taps were adjusted with her box of rice in hand until she got just the right temperature.

Taking another mouthful of food, she added an extra long drizzle of lavender bubble bath to the water. A fresh towel was tossed on the floor beside the tub. The running water began to foam up and she made her way back to the stir-fry in the kitchen. Unlike Earthlings, she hadn't been conditioned to dislike broccoli. It was delicious with the button mushrooms, snow peas, and those little, tiny corn on the cobs. Her fork dug for several helpings before she closed the boxes and put them in the fridge. The empty milk glass was left on the counter before heading back to the bath. She disrobed while she walked.

Brittany let her battery-operated toothbrush scour her teeth as she stood naked in front of the mirror. She set it down and took a second look at her curves, or lack of. "You really need to catch up."

The recent trip to the United States had created a few insecurities. Everyone her age had mountains growing out of their chests. She was built more like the Chinese, ample, but by no means anything to brag about.

The water was warm, and it welcomed her like the emptiness she'd been feeling lately. Leaning back, she covered her face with a wet washcloth and started to drift. The visit with her father and Alexis had gone better than expected. The two of them were doing wonderful things with the restructuring of California. He was a nice man and Brittany understood what her mother had seen in him. What had he seen in her?

As the bath water cooled, so did her interest in soaking any longer. It was time to towel off. Maybe she could find a good book and crawl into bed. The wet towel hit the floor and was replaced by a comfortable terry robe. Still a little damp, she headed for the kitchen and tossed a bag of popcorn in the microwave. Nothing happened, as the power was still out. Her second choice was a bag of chips. A handful of books adorned the corridor next to the kitchen.

"Damn, I've already read these ones." She ran her fingers over the spines of the books before moving on to her mother's room.

She spotted it the moment she entered the room. Her next read would be the journal that Nicole had been working on. Documents from Mars had been acquired and she was in the middle of piecing everything together. Brittany thumbed through it and grabbed the gaudy neckpiece that sat beside it on the nightstand. She put it around her neck. The thing felt oddly alive next to her skin, emitting pulse-like vibrations. On her way to the bed she grabbed a couple candles, poured herself another milk, and emptied the bag of chips into a bowl.

Her down-filled comforter weighed heavy on her legs as she propped herself up against the pillows. It was the weight that always made her feel safe. She did a quick check to make sure she had everything. There was her mother's book, chips, milk, and the phone. Before she started reading, she called her mother.

Nicole answered right away. "What's the matter?"

"Nothing, Mom. Just wanted to let you know I'm home and yes, I had a good visit with everyone. Dad said I could stay longer next time, if I wanted."

"That sounds odd. I mean, he hardly knows you."

Brittany didn't respond.

"I'm going to stay here for a couple of days. Virgil found some underground hollows and we're documenting the upper floors of that high-rise."

"Is it a big building?"

"More a complex, or some kind of mall. This building is quite unique when compared to the others."

"That's the one I was in before?" She remembered being dragged on a brief tour of the dusty building a couple weeks ago. It was run down but had an entire floor of cool items.

"It is."

"And you've checked out the rest of the building?"

"Not all of it. There're about twenty floors in total. Some are rooms like a hotel and there are stores and offices. It's a real multifunctional building. It's practical and in fairly good condition except for the core of lower floors."

"What are the hollows?"

"We, or Virgil, found them. They'll be accessible, but only after a little excavating. There's possibly one right under the high-rise. It's likely just a parkade, but I still want to check it out. So far, we can't find a stairway down to it, but it's there. We'll start tunnelling soon. It's hard to say what we'll find. Two of these hollows are rather large. It would be nice to get at those ones first."

Brittany yawned as she listened on the other end of the phone. Her mother was having fun, and it was great to see the passion returning. It could result in a bit more freedom for her.

"Just be careful, Mom. I know how crazy you can get."

"I don't get crazy. We'll talk more when I get back."

"If you say so. See you later."

"Be good and eat the leftovers in the fridge. They're just a day old. Love you."

"See ya soon."

"Hey Brit, is everything okay, really?"

"Don't worry about it, Mom. I can handle my shit."

"Do you have a lot of shit to handle?"

"Have fun in the dirt and I'll see you in a few days."

The call ended without her telling her mother about the book. She didn't need the Debbie-downer lecture. Besides, what harm could there be in reading the journal? One day everyone would be reading it. She set the phone down, started in on it, and stumbled over the first sentence in disbelief. "What the heck?"

Chapter six

The Gift of Distinction

The 'Gift of Distinction's' origin is not so much a place in history as it is a journey travelled time and time again.

Brittany stopped for a moment and reread the line. She thought about calling her mother but quickly came to her senses. Confused, she forged on hoping to find clarity. Instead, she stumbled through the first few pages. Eventually, the empty chip bowl was moved to the floor, and she shifted to get more comfortable. The pages, as difficult as they were to understand, seemed to be conceptual.

Man was not meant for existence until the Creator made it so. This Gift of Distinction had been used to construct a world of elements. These elements, the body, would supply the food, the warmth, the water, and could adapt as needed. Only after these elements were created was man welcomed into his domain. Man's welcoming that could last an eternity, as long as he obeyed the Creator. Man ruled and watched over his kingdom, but sadly, kept falling to the temptations of idolizing his own self worth.

Because of that, man was humbled time and time again. Bad behaviour was rewarded with the ability to process guilt and shame. To keep his empire whole, man now needed to use discipline, to which was not accustomed. Discipline, although given the tools to master, is not man's strongest ability. It also leads to his other greatest weakness, denial.

Man was given the Gift of Distinction, which was also given to all other living things. All creation would be given this blessing to recreate life with a miraculous act. This would sustain all existence. The act would begin and end with a heightened emotional state so that all would understand the importance. Control would be needed to regulate this act so that the world might survive overindulgence.

The Gift of Distinction is given in two forms, Reality and Conception. All that is, exists in the realm of Reality, whereas all that could be, exists in the realm of Conception. Conception can create Reality, but man can only live a current existence of a thousand years. Although multiple existences can occur, they must exist as one origin.

Soon, the Gift of Distinction would allow man to govern his own fate.

Brittany shook her head. It was getting tougher to follow, but not impossible. Maybe, Brittany thought, living to a thousand years could be attained if the planet revolved around its sun quicker. What if a revolution around the sun, or year as we know it to be, only took a tenth of the time? Then what we consider a year would be ten of theirs and our lifetime could be a thousand of their years. But could there have been a planet with life and an orbit like that? The story had holes. There hadn't been enough papers brought back from Mars. Hopefully, the recent box of documents retrieved could fill in the missing gaps. She took a sip from her glass and carried on.

The Gift of Distinction to man is not his own creation. His is that of a partner for the purpose of procreation of life. They would have their own creations. They will be given emotions to struggle with and these struggles will result in pain, suffering, and euphoria. The ability to learn from these emotions will be taught starting with good. They will build alliances called a family and grow as a whole... as a tribe. There is strength in this form of a union, but it should never be stronger than the union of man and the Creator, as He provided his light to see the way, clean air to fill his lungs, and the food to fuel his body.

In time, some tribes would reconcile for food, for education, and for services. While some tribe members would become known for their abilities to construct answers to life's challenges, other members would excel for hunting and survival. Stealth and a keen understanding of their prey must be learned for their success.

While fortunate tribes would construct large dwellings and used their ingenuity to stockpile vast amounts of food and wealth, other tribes would struggle and built armies to pillage what they need. Survival will be innate.

War will be the invention of weaker tribes to balance the resources of the successful. To be successful at war, you need large armies. We now find ourselves on the verge of self-annihilation. Overly aggressive tribes have been forced into a defensive role of procreation to replace their losses. The quality of these creations are lacking... even flawed at times.

Brittany put the journal face down, so not to lose the page. She quickly slipped out from the covers and crossed the room to use the bathroom. She imagined the tribes fighting over food. It was no surprise that this would happen, kind of inevitable even. This had happened on Alzie, and this was happening on Earth, although Earth was getting things back under control.

And these were only the documents her mother could decipher, the ones from the book with the picture of two planets colliding. Virgil, and a handful of others, had been a huge help. They'd all spent countless hours trying to rearrange and manipulate the language into something they could understand, an estranged Latin.

What about the older documents, those loose pages found with the amulet? Pages and pages of symbols had eluded understanding. What were those documents, and what story did they tell?

She crossed her arms tight over her bare chest as she sat. The apartment was cool, raising goose bumps on her skin. Standing and pulling her panties up, she headed for the sink and washed her hands. Her toothbrush was quickly run over her teeth one last time. It was getting late, and she figured she'd be nodding off soon enough. She dropped the toothbrush in the holder and headed back to the warmth of the bed. She'd read until she fell asleep.

Running her fingers over the words, she had to wonder if her mother had realised the acronym for the 'Gift of Distinction'. Did that mean this Gift of Distinction could be God? If so, did that mean religion, or the theory of creation, had originated on Eve?

This was why her mother had wanted answers. If this were true, then why wouldn't the Alzien culture have taken on this philosophy? Why didn't they have religion, when Eve and Earth did? Brittany curled up and thumbed ahead until she saw another section that caught her eye.

In time of tribes with opposing visions, unique languages and beliefs would form.

With unfavourable numbers, we've found ourselves reaching to our technologies for answers. We've used our intelligence to further our development. We cannot let our tribes fall to these barbarians. Recently, we've developed abilities that our enemies don't possess. We've also learned to disappear from our foes, but sadly, we cannot disappear from an unforeseen and inevitable fate.

Will the evolution of these abilities be our Armageddon?

Abilities, Brittany wondered. The word echoed in her mind. She and her mother had abilities. Was that what these people were talking about? She started to skim ahead, but the pages were wordy. Her eyes were getting tired of her mother's handwriting and beginning to play tricks on her. Parts of what she read suggested that these tribes could do what her mother could do. How was this possible?

With a mighty yawn she shook her head and tried to refocus, but the words spilled into black lines. That was okay. She'd had a long day with all her good-byes, the travelling, and being run over on the sidewalk. It was time for her to put the book down and call it a day. Then a few more words jumped out at her.

It is the comforts of home that tether us to the ones we love, as it is this love that forces us from our belief in the Creator. To survive, roles are taken that we normally wouldn't choose. Such despair will lead our civilisation to the Creator's return. Rules were given and a covenant was formed. Refrain from the worries of time, of the inequalities between man, and of the doubt of the Creator's ability to provide. We were promised that no man shall go without food, breath, water, and the ability to create his own life through life.

But to man, this is not enough.

Brittany's eyes closed for a good two seconds. She didn't want to stop reading but couldn't continue. This was quite the story. Why hadn't her mother shared this with her? Could these people actually render?

Brittany wanted to read on, but it was late and there was no stopping the inevitable as her eyelids gently closed.

That was when the first nightmare began.

Chapter seven

As Brittany slept, her mind wandered to a little dirt road. It looked like it hadn't been travelled in years. The overgrown weeds grew without opposition down the slightly humped centre. What she noticed next was that her hand was locked in somebody else's. She studied the young man while she walked. Who was he? Easy on the eyes, she felt that she knew him. Perhaps he was an old forgotten friend? She tried to jog her memory, find him in there somewhere. His grip was loosening so she tightened it up.

They didn't talk. He seemed to be in a hurry. She followed along at his side and took in the scenery. Where were they? It was a heavily forested area with water to the right of them. This was a large body of water, yet not big enough to be considered a lake. It was more like the forest had flooded. Her hand left his and she found herself moving towards the water's edge. Looking out over the calm pool, she concluded that it was some kind of bog or swamp, and it likely went on for miles. Trees towered out of it and the water was shallow.

She looked back for an explanation, but he was gone. Her face scrunched as she looked around. Who was this mystery man and why did he leave her here?

Turning back to the bog, she found herself being pulled into the water. It wasn't a physical pulling, but more just a willing of sorts. Not wanting to fight the feeling, she kicked off her shoes and got her feet wet. Her pants soaked up the water as she walked out until she was waist deep. Then she looked back to the shore. A handful *of steps had put her fifty yards from where she'd stood. How was that possible?*

Confused, she looked around to catch her bearings. The shoreline was changing. The road and lush forest had given way to dead trees. Light green moss hung on these trees like grapes.

"Hello?"

At least the water was warm. An underlying urgency got her walking again. Even though common sense told her to go back, she wanted to carry on. Birds started settling in the trees around her. They were black, small, and soon numbered in the thousands. The constant chatter from them made her look away. She had seen these birds before, but where?

And where were the algae or spooky slime of a pond? The water was clean, clear as tap water and yet she couldn't see her feet. Without thinking, she squatted down, cupped her hands, and drank from it. It was delicious. She let herself gracefully fall forward until her body was floating face down. Without panic, she allowed this for what seemed like minutes. Why wasn't she breathing? It was like she didn't have a need for the air.

Brittany awoke with a gasp. Half-awake and fumbling for the covers, she awkwardly knocked the journal to the floor. She tried to clear her mind, tried to shake the fear of falling back asleep, but suddenly there were voices, voices in her head dragging her back.

Dilapidated buildings edged the road like weeds as she ran past them. Children were in front yards, singing and playing as if she wasn't there. The songs they sang sounded familiar, as did the language they sang it in. She'd heard them before. Maybe Nicole had sung them to her when she was a baby.

The fence pickets were leaning like little white drunks holding each other up, and each home was a carbon copy of the one beside it. This must have been a housing project. Again, she felt herself being pulled. She didn't fight the direction. Someone here wanted to talk to her. How did she know? And how did she know it was a woman? Brittany made her way down the street, side-stepping garbage and abandoned toys. She stopped in front of a broken house that was slightly different from the rest.

26

This old house had a clean yard and flowers growing in the flowerbed. Somehow, they had sprouted from the hardened dirt in a haphazard manner of colour. It was a nice change from the rest of the block.

Taking a few steps into the yard, she looked down at the welcome mat in front of the door. The words were worn, but the message was alive. At one time this place had warmed her heart. It was the very warmth you felt from a freshly made-up bed, or a favourite childhood dish cooked by someone you loved.

Brittany poked her head in the door. She spotted the cross hanging on the adjacent wall. It belonged. She belonged.

"Hello, Mom?"

Chapter eight

Morgan watched from the foot of the bed as Victor finished packing. She was hoping this didn't change the feeding arrangements that she'd grown so accustomed to. Victor was more concerned with the new list he'd received. He had hoped those killing days were done, that his friends in space had taken care of that damn Ledger. That had obviously not happened.

He took the list out of the envelope and looked at it again. Not much of a list, as there was only one name on it. The problem was that the name made no sense to him and the address didn't exist. He stuffed it back in the envelope and pushed it in the lining of the suitcase.

"You ready, Boss?" Don asked.

Victor zipped the suitcase closed and stepped back so the man could take it. "As ready as I'll ever be. You've got the plane ready?"

"Yes. I've also cancelled your meeting with Mr Dawson and set up our next two drops. Do you think you'll be longer than a week?"

"I have no idea."

"Do you need anything other than the…"

Victor knew he was fishing for information. He wasn't very good at it. "I'm sorry I can't tell you more, and no I don't need any security. I just need Jake to fly the plane."

"You know you're important, don't you? No other crew, no security. People are going to talk."

"Then you cover for me. You know how this works."

He paused. "How do I explain letting you run off like this?"

"Tell them, I'm the Boss and you didn't have any say in this. You know how to run everything, and the boys trust you as much as they trust me. You won't have any problems. Besides, I'll eventually come back."

It was a hard statement to spit out, but it needed to be said. "And if you don't?"

Victor appreciated the man's honesty. "Then you, Molly, and the boys own a country, my friend."

"Why are you going? What could be more important than this? You have an empire to run."

"I also have a promise to keep and pissing off this guy is the last thing I want to do."

"If he's holding something over you, we'll go to war with him. We aren't afraid."

"We'd never win." Victor put a hand on his shoulder. "This guy is an old friend and an ally. I need to do this, for him. It's gonna be okay."

The man grabbed the suitcase and started for the door. "If you say so, Boss. Should I wake Molly? She'll want to know."

"Let her sleep."

"Meow."

"Oh, and speaking of bosses, make sure dingle-shit gets fed on time. I don't want to come back to a hairball barfed up on my pillow." He gave the cat a quick head scratch. "There, I told him. I can't be held responsible if he forgets."

"Meow?"

"Don't sweat it, Morgan. Nobody's going to forget you."

Chapter nine

A bead of sweat made its way down Brittany's neck and trickled down her chest. She wiped at it with a clumsy hand. What the hell had just happened? Had Mrs Lee's rice been bad? She grabbed for her stomach but didn't feel nauseous. A shiver ran up her spine as she thought about her mother. What was she doing in that old house? This was a dream, not a stupid premonition, but it sure felt like one. It was as if it had happened, and the house was real.

She tried to shake the nonsense by swallowing the last bit of chocolate milk. How weird were those dreams? They were like the ones you had when you were fighting a fever.

Brittany picked up her glass and made her way to the fridge. What was the date on that milk?

Halfway, she realised that she was still in just her panties and wrapped a free arm around her chest. Could anyone see her, maybe from an adjacent high-rise? She picked up the pace as she finished the trek to the safety of the windowless kitchen. The milk still had a week, so she topped up her glass.

Almost scared of her bed, she took her milk over to the couch. For now, she just wanted to sit and catch her breath. The gaudy stone necklace still rested against her skin, and as much as she wanted to take it off, she couldn't. She loved it and it loved her. There was a synchronicity. It understood her.

After watching the better part of an hour-long infomercial on no stick frying pans, she got up and headed back to bed. The dreams weren't that threatening after removing herself from the moment.

Hooking her t-shirt with her big toe, she kicked it into her room while she walked.

The crisp linens felt good against her skin as she tucked herself back under the covers. She was over the dreams, and yet she still fought sleep. Sadly, she'd lose that fight as the nightmares returned.

Horseback riding? This was a better way to spend the day. A beautiful thoroughbred carried her down a trail toward a smaller town. Again, the area seemed familiar and yet she knew she'd never been there before. Knowing this was a dream, it was time to take control. She would imagine what was up ahead.

There should be a little ice cream hut around the next corner. It came into view and the lady inside stepped through the doorway and waved at her.

Brittany waved back. "Morning Mrs Bernaldo."

"Morning. How's my favourite girl?"

"I'm fine." She smiled as she rode on. "One for one. Actually, I'll take an extra point for knowing her name."

Down the street, there was a convenience store named Benny's and the sign in the front window said they sold live bait for fishing, but she already knew that. "That's two for two," she whispered to her horse.

Brittany made a checkmark in the air with her finger each time she saw something she knew. The horse carried her down to the end of the street and into the woods. This was an okay dream. There was nothing weird about it, and yet she still found herself waiting for the other shoe to drop.

Her horse, familiar with the trail, meandered through what resembled an overgrown walking path. At one time, it may have been a busy little area, but the years had put an end to that. When the trees thinned out, Brittany found herself looking at a mountain lake with a beach as sandy as a Mexican resort.

She trotted her horse to the edge of the treeline where a beautiful lodge filled her eyes. What purpose did all this have in her odd collage of dreams? And the fact that the sun's heat felt so real against her skin, how was that possible?

Sweat had her long hair sticking to her neck, so she loosely twirled it up in a bun. That heat also had her looking to the lake. A welcoming dock protruded into the water. Since the horse was already ankle deep and drinking, she decided to dismount.

Feeling a little lightheaded, she took a seat at the end of the dock and rubbed her eyes. Even the wood felt warm against her shorts. Again, this was a place she remembered, but how. Had her father taken her here for vacations? She'd only met him a few weeks ago.

She looked down at the water as she swung her feet, kicking at it with her toes. The water was cool to the touch. Because the water was clear, she could see down to the bottom. There was something shiny in its depths.

Brittany grabbed the edge of the dock and leaned forward to get a better look. It creaked beneath her small frame. The sun's light danced off the ripples of the water, hindering her view, but she could see something on the lake bottom. Whatever it was, it was also throwing flashes of light at her.

Suddenly, her grip broke free from the dock. It wasn't that she had slipped, more like a pair of hands had shoved her from behind. Much colder than imagined, she sucked in a lung full of water. Thrashing for the surface, Brittany felt the strong grip of the hands again. They were holding her under. A blurred outline of the man was all she could see.

Her struggle eventually ended, and she could feel her body calmly drifting downward. The last thing she remembered before waking from the dream was that the shiny object, the one that had first caught her eye, had been around somebody's neck.

Brittany gasped for breath. Her hands clutched at her throat, and she coughed as if she'd truly sucked in water. Calming herself, she looked for the comforter that once covered her. It had been kicked to the floor. A moonlit sky flooded into her room, casting shadows that look like trees, mountains, and reaching arms. She tried to shake her grogginess, but knew the nightmares weren't finished with her.

"Whose hotel room is this?" she muttered to herself. She felt an uneasy urgency to leave and quickly ran out. In the hallway she found an open stairwell and started her descent. Although she

couldn't place anything, everything was familiar. Hell, everything in these dreams had been familiar. How many floors would she have to go down to get to the lobby, and was there a lobby?

On the main floor, Brittany found rows of little shops. This was a mall. Wandering from shop to shop, she looked for something to guide her through this dream.

An elderly store clerk spotted her. "Can I help you, Miss?"

"I'm not sure. What is this place?" Her question fell on deaf ears as he tried to get a better look at her eyes.

Uncomfortable with his stare, Brittany looked away. "Never mind."

He grabbed at her arm. "You're one of them, aren't you?"

Brittany felt his weak grip and pulled herself free. "What are you doing?"

Suddenly, the man started yelling for security. He tried to grab at her again, but she shoved him aside. The fight continued until he fell into a display.

It was time to move. She could hear him screaming something about her eyes as she made her way back to the stairwell. What was wrong with her eyes? Taking the stairs two at a time, she headed for the room she was in before.

There was a couple walking towards her. The man's eyes wandered straight down to her chest, and he smiled. Brittany looked down. Until now, she hadn't noticed, how huge she was. His girlfriend had also caught the strayed glance. Her words were sharp and cut into the meat of his excuses like a chainsaw through a never-gonna-happen wedding cake. Brittany just stood there semi-amused as they walked off screaming at each other.

Holding out the neck of her shirt, she stared down her top. They weren't hers. Her shirt snapped back into place when she let go. Then she reached for a handful of hair. It was blonde.

Her instincts led her back to the suite where she had started the dream. Now she wanted a mirror. Had these dreams been guiding her through these adventures as someone else? Who was this person?

She ran for the bathroom and before she could turn toward the mirror, a man burst into the apartment behind her.

"Hey!" he shouted. "What the hell is going on here?"

Brittany didn't recognise the voice as her eyes popped open. He seemed as real as the glow of the morning sun that was filling the room. Hunched over on all fours, she wasn't in her bed anymore. She looked down at the carpet to see all the blood.

So much blood.

Chapter ten

The air left Nicole's lungs in a cough. She'd never noticed how damp and musky the room was before, likely because there'd always been distractions. Past visits had been hurried and she'd never been here alone.

Again, she thought about how nice it was to be so far away from the hustle and bustle of Earth. Too bad her mother hadn't stayed back in Alzie. The woman worked hard and everyone around her was auto-enrolled into that same work ethic. That was fine for the other scientists. They were teaching the advances of DNA manipulation, and of the different energy sources used on Alzie.

For Nicole, it was simply exhausting. Lectures, labs, and countries quickly blended into one. Granted everyone treated her like royalty, but if she had to eat anymore exotic food, she'd likely barf. Chicken fried rice was what she craved, or perhaps a good burger, maybe a steak. Half the dishes she'd ingested didn't even resemble food. Was it chicken, or was it fish?

Without warning, Frederich knocked her back to reality. "Miss Nicole. Such a pleasure to see you."

The man stood there, looking as dapper as the last time she'd seen him. He always looked like he was hosting a ball... or perhaps a funeral.

"Mr Frederich. The pleasure is mine."

"What can I do for you today?" He was all business. Clasping his hands behind his back, he cocked his head slightly to the left and leaned forward. "I haven't seen you in some time."

"I haven't been in the neighbourhood lately." It puzzled her that he knew it had been years since their last visits. Was time a thing in his realm? She shook the thought. "So, what's new?"

Frederich stood there, puzzled. "I'm not sure I understand."

"I just came up here to talk." She quickly realised that social conversation wasn't a thing here. "Kill some time?"

"That doesn't sound very productive."

"Nope. It's not productive at all. It falls into the category of relaxation."

"I've never tried that. I conceive one should always remain prolific. Anything less is a waste of resources."

Was he kidding? Her last few weeks had been work, eat, and sleep. Prolific sucked. "Overloading isn't any good. I need to take a couple of days to recharge."

He nodded. "Those are your emotions. Rid yourself of them and you'll become much more efficient." He smiled like he had solved all her problems.

Nicole frowned. "Sorry. I'm stuck with those. Blame Earth. I'm probably keeping you from something." She could sense the growing anxiety, standing here talking about nothing, doing nothing.

"My apologies. I fear I'm coming across as rude." He studied her reaction, hoping he'd got the terminology correct.

Nicole laughed politely at the comment. "Not to worry. We are what we are. It truly is pointless to fight it. I've enjoyed your company, but I should let you get back to whatever. Until next time?"

"Yes, next time." With an uncharacteristic half-smile, he was gone.

Again, she was alone in the room. A sinister thought suddenly put a smile on her face. She couldn't help herself. It was time to go shopping.

Her apartment had been filled with all kinds of gifts from various countries and both her and Brittany loved them all. Mars had given them a couple of trinkets, but now she had the opportunity to nose around for some top-of-the-line swag.

Her flashlight cast shadows around the room as she walked from glass case to glass case. She wondered what she'd say if

Frederich returned. Talk about getting caught with a hand in the cookie jar.

The struggle with her morals only lasted for a second. Then she found and unrolled a dust-covered painting, a painting far too exquisite to be left under the blanket of age.

This particular piece had obviously been forged from passion and sorrow. The painter had obviously survived the volcano, only to live through the aftermath. He had captured the pain and suffering that these people had gone through before they died.

On the canvas, drifts of dust crept up the sides of buildings while a lone little girl stood ankle deep in ash. Her face was filthy, and she looked like she'd just crawled out of a coal mine. Her only friend was a teddy bear that she clutched in her hand. The eyes on this girl were a little bigger in proportion, but it worked. A lone tear ran down her cheek, cleaning away the dust as it made its journey to her chin. The only colour in the painting was the blue in her eyes and that clean path of skin.

Nicole could feel her heart aching. Hopefully, Brittany wouldn't mind it in the apartment. It was soulful, but quite a dark painting. It captured what these people must have gone through in the final hours. Nicole quickly rolled it up as she headed back down to the labs.

"What have you got there?" Virgil asked as he handed her the copies of the scans.

"I'm taking this." Her words were a little shakier than expected.

"Information about Eve?" His voice almost cracked with anticipation.

Nicole quickly caved. "Virgil, I'm stealing a piece of art. It has no use for my studies, and it really shouldn't leave the site, but I want it and I'm taking it!"

"What is it? Let me see what you're so upset about."

The canvas was rolled out and Virgil scratched his head. "This could be Mars, or perhaps it is Eve," which he knew was a stretch. "You should take it home and study it. One just never knows."

She didn't catch his wit at first. "You think?"

He smugly popped a chocolate into his mouth. "Could be as important to your studies as these candies are to mine."

"It's just that…"

Virgil cut her off. "You don't have to explain your actions. You've put in countless hours, not only on this project, but on others as well. Now you've snapped and become an art thief. Personally, I think you could have found better, but it's all in the eye of the beholder. I predict a steady flow of comics and candy coming my way."

"That's funny, and a very Earthly way of thinking." The corner of her mouth hinted a smile. "Are you sure you're okay with this?"

"I'm okay."

"Thanks. I'm gonna set up a bed and get some shut-eye. We can go over those scans first thing."

"That sounds fair." He gave her an awkward hug. "And don't worry about the painting. These items don't have any relevance to our project."

Nicole rested her head on the pillow and was asleep before her eyes were closed. It didn't matter that the cot was stiff and the pillow filthy. A bed was a bed.

She slept through the loud rhythmic droning of the magnetic scanners. If anything, they helped her sleep, that is until Virgil shook her awake.

"Nicole!" His voice was frantic. "Your mother just called."

Nicole struggled to prop herself up by an elbow. Her eyes were partially glued shut with sleep and her back felt like she'd been sleeping in the back seat of a golf cart. "I swear that woman is going to kill me! What does she want now?"

"It's Brittany. She's been taken to the hospital."

Chapter eleven

Nicole felt the weight lift when her little girl's eyes opened. "Brittany! What were you thinking?"

Brittany turned to her mother's voice. She wasn't in her bedroom. Was this another dream? Then the fog began to lift. "Mom? What are you doing back?"

Nicole pulled her daughter close. "You had us all scared." She pushed Brittany back and stared into her eyes. "What would ever possess you to…"

Brittany stared back. "To what, Mom? What's going on? Where am I?"

"Some guy brought you in, saved your life," Nicole explained. "You tried to commit suicide."

"Suicide? What have you been smoking?" But in the back of her mind, she had remembered the dreams. She'd remembered the odd places and the man's voice in the apartment. None of it had made sense. She also remembered the blood. Was it hers? "Talk to me. What happened?"

"You don't remember?" Nicole took Brittany's hands and gently turned them over.

Clean white bandages were wrapped around her wrists. "This is bullshit. I never did this! You have to believe me."

"But…"

"You know I'd never do this. I was having some weird dreams. I mean they weren't just strange, they were bizarre. There were places that I've never seen before but felt super familiar with. I saw something in the water and then someone was trying to drown me.

It felt real." Her eyes widened as she looked away. "I would never do this!"

Nicole held her tight. It had been a tough twelve hours. She had a hard time believing what they had told her, that she'd been found with her wrists slashed after slamming a stand-up mirror against the wall. It was assumed that she'd knelt down, picked up a broken shard, and proceeded to slice into her wrists. Thankfully, someone heard the noise and decided to investigate. When he found her, she was lying in a puddle of her own blood.

"It's okay, Brit. You're alive and that's all that matters." She had Mr Hong to thank for that. He had talked Nicole into banking some blood, just in case of an emergency. This wasn't the emergency they had expected, but it had turned out to be a lifesaving decision.

Just then the door opened, and the doctor walked in. "We're awake. It's good to see you back." He took her pulse and then grabbed a light to shine in her eyes." The sight stopped him. "Do you wear contacts?"

"No. My eyes are a perfect 20/20," Brittany boasted.

He smiled and went to the chart. "Says your eyes were blue when you were admitted. Now they're brown. Any idea as to why?"

Nicole spoke up. "Had to be a mistake on the chart. Her eyes have always been brown."

"Except I'm the one who filled out the chart. And they weren't just blue. They were a brilliant sky blue. We never see eyes that bright in China. I didn't make a mistake." He looked to Nicole and shrugged. "Either way, she needs to stay here a couple of days and talk to one of our counsellors. They can help her get through whatever's troubling her."

"Not happening. Tell him, Mom. I'm going home. Tell him!"

"I'm not sure what happened, but you're safer here than anywhere else, and your safety is everything."

"Seriously. I'm stuck here?"

"I'll be staying here with you."

"Then we can do this at home. I'm not gonna let some shrink judge me."

Nicole looked to the doctor. "Can we have a second?"

"Definitely."

Nicole watched the doctor leave and then zeroed in on Brittany. "What's going on? You're not even home one night and you're having weird dreams, attempting suicide, and what the hell is going on with your eyes?"

"He's delusional. You know I don't have blue eyes. And why would I need someone to tell me not to do what I'd never do in the first place."

"Something happened. Why were you having those dreams?"

"I don't know."

"Nightmares don't induce suicide attempts. And why were you reading my journal and wearing the artifact? That thing is not a toy."

"I know that now. What the heck is that stone?"

"I don't know yet, but I'm beginning to think it's more than just a key to a box of crazy papers. How much of my journal did you read?"

"I just started the Gift of Distinction part." She paused for a second and then continued. "You do know what the acronym for 'Gift of Distinction' is, right?"

Nicole thought for a second. It was God. How could she have missed it? "Wow, that's a little weird."

"Oh, and there was something about a war in your journal and special powers."

"The artifact is related to that in some way."

"As a mind control device?"

"Perhaps. Tell me about the dreams and describe these places."

Brittany started with the swamp story and moved on to how the store clerk had stared at her eyes. He'd said she wasn't one of them. And everyone in the dreams were familiar, and yet she knew none of them. And then there was the cross on the wall.

Nicole knew that most dreams were first person. To be a part of someone else's dream was remarkably odd and troubling. It was an indication of schizophrenia, and although this was a viable possibility, the more likely option was the artifact.

A nurse entered, holding the necklace. The gaudy stone hung like a pendulum. "This is very interesting. I think it belongs to you."

She held it out and Brittany almost crawled under the sheets. Nicole thanked the nurse and took it from her. Then she gave Brittany a peck on the forehead. "I'll get this home. You stay put and I'll be right back. Don't do anything while I'm gone, okay?"

"Just get rid of that thing."

Nicole left and Brittany began to relax. She took a drink from her Styrofoam cup and played with her bendable straw. Eventually, she put it down. Her eyelids were heavy, and she let them droop and eventually close. She'd only planned on resting them for a few seconds.

The dreams had other ideas.

Chapter twelve

Back in the hotel room, Brittany was still in the bathroom. This time she managed to turn toward the mirror before waking up. The mirror reflected a beautiful young woman. As cute as she was, not seeing her own reflection ran a chill up her spine.

This girl had to be about twenty years old. Brittany's curiosity soon got the better of her and she reached for a handful of breast. They were real and she could feel her hands on them. And then there was the blonde hair, arrow straight and running the length of her back.

But what really caught Brittany's attention were the cobalt blue eyes. They were as brilliant as the doctor had described. She stared into them looking for anything abnormal. There was nothing.

Brittany brought her hand up to her face and ran her finger over her cheekbone. Then she puckered her full lips. "You're gorgeous. Who are you?"

The shirt was quickly lifted, exposing her torso. She spun in the mirror looking for tattoos, scars, or beauty marks. Then she emptied her pockets. Maybe there was an ID or something. Again, she found nothing other than some coins and a balled-up tissue.

On the counter, a pill bottle sat beside the sink. Could there be a name on it, maybe an address? There was nothing.

"Come on girl. Help me out."

She was still holding the pill bottle when the door of the suite opened. Brittany froze. She quietly listened from behind the counter. It had to be security or a peace officer. She looked around for a hiding spot. There was a hamper and a shower, but they *wouldn't do. With only the one door, she was trapped. A man's voice bellowed out at her from the other room. This was an oddly familiar voice.*

"Cassandra! Did you leave the apartment earlier?"

Brittany woke up on the floor of her hospital room.

"Ah, shit."

The tiles were cold against her face and faintly smelled of urine. She thought back to her dream and wondered where she knew that voice. Almost able to place it, she tried to wake up before the next dream sucked her back in. There was no way she was going to let herself drift off again. Why was she lying on the floor?

Lifting her head, she turned to the door. Her arms were uncoordinated as she propped herself up and crawled across the black and white tiles. Halfway back to the bed, she spotted the empty pill bottle. It had rolled under the bed. She picked it up and held it out in front of her. Squinting, she strained to read it, but it was no use. Her eyes couldn't flush away the confusion.

She pulled herself part way up the bed, fumbled for the nurse's chain before falling back to the floor. It snapped out of her hand and landed on the bed out of reach, but that didn't matter. The triangle shaped light was now lit.

There was an old, discarded tissue that had cuddled up against two dust bunnies hiding only a few feet from her face. She tried to focus on it.

It didn't work.

Chapter thirteen

B rittany remembered nothing other than pulling the string to summon help, and that old tissue. An instant later the nurses were whisking her away on a gurney to have her stomach pumped. In all the chaos, Brittany agonised to remember the name of the girl in the hotel. Every part of her world was flipping around in her head like numbered balls in a bingo cage.

Nicole arrived to an unimaginable confusion. Scrambling for answers, all she was told was that it was an overdose on pills. Where the drugs came from, or what they were, remained a mystery. The pills, and the bottle, were like nothing they'd ever seen before. Nicole summoned her mother and when she arrived, they waited in Brittany's room.

"What's this all about, Nicole? It has something to do with that artifact, doesn't it?" her mother snapped.

"It might." She dropped her head. "I thought the artifact was perhaps a key to a box. Maybe there were more papers."

"But it was more?"

"Oh, it may be much more. I've been researching it as you know, and we've combed the Martian building and found some disturbing information. We think we've uncovered a story of revenge."

"Revenge?"

"One of their scientists lost his funding." Nicole lifted her head and stared down her mother. "Apparently there were people that had a gift. They could disappear from their enemies!"

Her eyes remained locked on her mother. She saw the fear, and the guilt, and waited for a response. "They could render, because like me, they were unique." She paused. "Like Brittany."

Her mother said nothing.

This was a talk that Nicole had put off far too long. "What have you done? Elizabeth and I weren't born, were we?"

"You don't understand?"

"I've always known I was unique, and that Elizabeth was too, but then she died. Did she have an expiry date? Do I? And please tell me we weren't conjured from that Ledger."

"No. You and Elizabeth were... created."

"Created? Like something you might make out of Play-Doh?"

"No. I carried you to term. Elizabeth was also carried to term."

"Then what were we?"

"I don't know. I wasn't the brain behind this. Elizabeth's father was. Your father and I couldn't have a child. Suddenly, I was told that I could. He had made two of you... a redundancy protocol."

"Did he use technology from the Ledger?"

"Only he would know that."

"And of course, he's dead." Nicole dropped her head into her hands. "I don't know what to say. On one hand, good job. Truly an amazing feat, but on the other hand, did you ever wonder about the side effects. I mean, I figured there had to be something going on when I talked to Mr Hong. He had told me that Elizabeth's DNA showed no signs of origin."

"What did you tell him?"

"Nothing. I thought he was crazy, but now the pieces are starting to fit. I was the only one that could give her blood. It's been like that our whole lives. I think you need to come clean."

"It's a long story and I made promises."

"Are these promises more important than your daughter and granddaughter? Because that girl is anything but normal right now." She took her mother's hand. "You owe her."

"I swore to Elizabeth's mother that I would never reveal their secret."

"You've got a granddaughter fighting for her life. I think that commitment died when they did."

"Joe and Vanessa, Elizabeth's parents, were on the verge of some major breakthroughs in science. He was so gifted at what he did. They had advanced to the point of being able to create strands of DNA from scratch and were able to replace and manipulate them at will. He'd already mapped everything about our DNA. That was when they, or he, got the idea to create a human embryo."

"Where would they get such an idea?"

"It was a bet between Joe and your father. He only bet them as a means to push them. You know how that works. Scientists have always challenged each other."

"I was a bet?" Nicole couldn't believe her ears. It was bad enough she wasn't real, but a bet? "I understand why you didn't want to tell us."

"Doing what we did was reckless, and that was another reason why we didn't say anything. As happy as we were, we weren't proud of what we did. Six months later, a work transfer separated us from Joe and Vanessa. That was probably a good thing. We needed the break from each other. I was ashamed, but it didn't stop me from falling in love with this little girl growing inside me."

Nicole sat there with her mouth slightly open. "I thought we were normal kids. We thought our DNA was slightly altered for the mission to Earth, and that our rendering was a fluke, not a side-effect."

"There's more. When you and Elizabeth were reacquainted, Joseph and Vanessa weren't the same couple. They were distant with us and with each other. They hid it from you kids, but Vanessa and I used to talk.

When Elizabeth turned sixteen, they had a horrible fight, and he decided to leave. He wanted Elizabeth and threatened the unspeakable, exposing her. She was his lab rat."

Nicole hadn't remembered that. "What happened?"

"Her mother made supper one night, when Elizabeth was staying over at our place. She had poisoned the food. We lost them both that night."

"Why would she have eaten any when she knew what it was?"

"His death would have been investigated. Elizabeth's secret could have come out. She didn't want to take the chance. She loved that girl and took her secret to her grave. A couple days later I found a letter in my dresser. It was an apology and legal direction on adopting Elizabeth as my own. She'd thought of everything."

Nicole sat quietly until the physician came out. She couldn't read his expression. He looked concerned. "How is she?"

"She's been sedated and might be a little confused when you talk to her. She's awake, and you both can go in."

"But she's okay, right?" She looked to her mother and smiled.

"She'll be fine, but we've strapped her into her bed. I hope the restraints are okay with you. I figured you should be warned. They're never a pretty sight."

Nicole's mother had expected that. Crazy had to be treated like crazy. "That's fine. Can we see her now?"

"By all means." He led them into the recovery room.

Brittany looked over as they entered. "Hey y'all. Hi Grams."

Nicole grimaced at her slur. "Y'all? How are you feeling?"

"In a wurd, I'm scared shitsless." She paused at how her words came out. "I did it again, didn't I?"

"It's okay, Honey, but that's why they have you strapped to the bed. Tell us what happened?"

"I dreamt I wurs in dat hotel again and I looked in da mirror. Mom, it wasn't me. It was some girl named Cassandra. I think she's in danger. I think maybe I was her in each of da dreams."

"What is she talking about Nicole?" her mother asked.

"I'll fill you in later. What else do you remember, Honey?" She reached out and took her hand.

"Mom, if I knew I'd tell ya. Why am I trying to kill myself?" She started to cry. "I can never sleep again, can I?"

Nicole's mother spoke. "You're safely strapped in. Besides, we'll stay here and keep watch on you."

"You know I can render out of these in a second." She tugged on the straps.

"No, you can't!" Nicole snapped. "Promise me you'll stay put. These straps are for you. You can render, but I can guarantee you this Cassandra girl can't, so stay put."

"Okay."

"And, uh, we're going to move you."

Brittany scrunched her nose. "Nah. I don't mind this room. We can stay."

Nicole's mother, interrupted. "You don't understand. You'll have to live on another floor, a floor that is more geared for your state of mind, so that you don't have to have these restraints."

This enraged Nicole. "Thanks, Mom, but I can handle this." She turned to Brittany. "What your tactless grandmother meant to say is that you'll have to be on a floor better suited for your needs, and your safety."

"Oh… you mean a psych-ward or nut house. Wow." Brittany looked away.

"Brit. It's for your own good. You won't find pills lying around, or mirrors to break. These people are trained in dealing with these situations."

"Yes, but I'll have to live with a bunch of nut jobs?" Brittany's head lowered. "How about if I promise to never sleep again?"

Nicole stared down at the straps. "Sorry, Dear. You'll be safe from the dreams."

Brittany knew she was wrong as she remembered the pill bottle from the dream. These dreams couldn't be stopped.

Chapter fourteen

The nurse swiped her card allowing the heavy metal latch to snap open. The woman swung the door to the side and held it for them. Brittany inspected the entrance as she walked through and glanced back at her mother. "You know this can't hold me."

Nicole apologised to the nurse before shooting Brittany an angry stare. There was no way a comment like that would fly here. It would only make things worse. "That's enough."

"Just saying. So, which one's my cell?" Brittany panned the open area. All eyes were on her. She was the freak among the freaks. They came out of the cracks and shadows to check out the new girl. Some hid behind small windows and others at the end of the long hallway. Each one was watching her become a part of their world, a world that few ever got to leave.

"We put you, with Chyou. She nice girl and the two of you get along."

"I don't get my own cell?" Brittany felt an honest panic as they made their way down one of the hallways. "I don't mean to be rude but…"

"We call rooms," the big nurse corrected. "We have limited bed space. It should only be couple of day. Chyou's done well. We just wait on the paperwork for her, go home. Her being here is plus, for Miss Brittany. You learn routines and she introduce you to residents."

"Residents." Brittany thought that that was a cute name for a prisoner. She produced a polite smile for her mother. "Sounds a little too permanent, if you ask me."

Nobody responded and the silence became awkward. They stopped in front of room 202W. This would be home. The inside of her room wasn't much different than her last one, except for the bars on the windows and the lack a mirror and medicine cabinet in the bathroom, making it fairly impersonal.

Brittany took a seat on the bed nearest to the door and looked over to the other one by the window. It had to be Chyou's bed. A couple of freshly folded shirts and a book were nestled against the pillow.

"Um, are we allowed to wear street clothes?" Brittany asked.

"Some yes, some no," the nurse offered. "You wear clothes if, pose no threat to you or others. Sadly, most pose threat."

"How?"

"If you try hurt yourself, clothing hinder saving you. Easier to open gown. Cutting off pants or shirt take time. Also, we had residents trick visitors, help them escape." She paused and let Brittany absorb what she'd said. "You have sweater, but no pullover... no buttons. We cut them off. You have favourite?"

Nicole bit down on her lip, closed her eyes, and took a deep breath through her nose. This was going to be harder than she thought.

Brittany looked down at her wrists and sighed. "It's okay, Mom. This won't be that bad. I'm safer here, and you're stuck here with me." She smiled. "I need that white sweater of mine when you get a chance. You know the one?"

Nicole nodded. She knew the sweater. It was a beautifully knit, knee length sweater that had buttons the size of dollar coins. "Anything else?"

"Whatever they'll allow to make this place home. Maybe my knee length toe socks." She shrugged. "Can I get these things right away?" She spun around to flash her bare bottom. "It's a little drafty in this gown."

Her mother shook her head as she stared.

"It's okay, Mom. I'll be okay. That necklace is at home, right?"

"It is." Nicole gave her a hug.

"Go, take a break. Grab my sweater, and when you get back, we'll do supper. I'll introduce you to any friends I make." She playfully pushed Nicole out of her room. "Love you, now go, have a bowl of ice-cream, and hurry back. My ass is freezing."

Nicole left and didn't look back. On the elevator, she wiped a tear from the corner of her eye and opened her phone. It rang twice before Jenny answered.

"Hello?"

"Hey, it's Nicole. Could I get you to come to China?"

"What's going on?"

"I just left Brit. She's in the hospital. She's had two failed suicide attempts." She waited for the response and got nothing. "Jenny, you there?"

"You are kidding, right? Our Brittany?"

"Yeah. I'm having a hard time dealing with the whole thing. None of it makes any sense to me and I'm close to losing it. I'll send one of the Pup ships for you if that's okay?"

"Not a problem. We'll be ready."

"Thanks. Did anything in her last visit seem weird?"

Jenny didn't even hesitate. "Her and Mathew were awkwardly hitting it off, but I'm not sure if there was anything to write home about. If there is, I'll drag it out of him."

"I wouldn't pursue that one. It was probably harmless."

"Okay, but I'll still grill my kids until I see you. Want me to call her father?"

Nicole wasn't sure. He deserved to know, but she didn't want him here. He wouldn't understand and could cause more grief than comfort. "Hold off on that one. I'm not sure he's strong enough to deal with this. I've got to run. I'll call you when the pup ship is on its way, and hey, thanks."

"We'll be waiting. Keep your chin up, and I'll see you soon." She hung up and gently set the phone down.

Brittany was sitting on her bed, fiddling with the bendy straw in her plastic cup when she noticed Chyou walk in. "Hi."

Chyou stopped in her tracks. "Oh my word! It's you."

Chapter fifteen

C hyou was a drab looking young woman, twenty going on sixty. Brittany took one look at her and immediately wanted to run a brush through her hair.

"Hi." Brittany gave a half-hearted wave. "You must be my roommate."

"I can't believe it's really you," Chyou repeated.

"Do we know each other?"

"You're kinda out-of-this-world famous." She looked down at Brittany's wrists. "You don't strike me as a slasher?"

"Is that what we call it? You should tell the nurses that." She waited for Chyou's response, but it didn't come. "So, what's your deal?"

"Daddy issues. My father's been... an asshole since I can remember." She rolled her eyes like it was no big deal. "Mom used to blame me, so I assumed everything was my fault. I stopped talking. That wasn't a socially acceptable behaviour, so I ended up here."

"Really?" Brittany tried to imagine.

"I had nothing to say. The schools sent me for counselling, but I'd just sit there."

"That must have been horrible." Brittany scrunched her face.

"I'm past it. The world is full of bad people. I can't let them destroy me. It's strange how we can be manipulated to shut down like that, don't you think?"

Brittany had a million questions but wasn't sure about the etiquette. "Um..."

"Ask," Chyou said. "One thing you'll learn here is that we don't do awkward. Like I know you're an Alzien which means you can render. Let me ask a question. Why, when you have everything, and these abilities, would you want to end your life?"

"It wasn't a suicide attempt. Now you answer one. Why are you doing the whole old lady act?" She motioned at the clothes. "You're what, thirty? You look like you're seventy."

Chyou felt that comment land squarely on the chin. Her head dropped. "I'm twenty-three."

"Oh shit. I didn't mean..."

"That's okay. I still have a few issues. I've always dressed down... way down. I'm not a fan of the attention."

"That's an issue we need to address."

She shrugged. "Back to you. Wrists say suicide. You say not. What happened?"

Brittany looked down at them. "I didn't do this."

"What then? You got a homicidal cat with a pocketknife living with you?"

"I'll tell you my story, but after that, we're doing something with your hair, and that wardrobe."

Chyou listened as Brittany told her about the dreams. The stories went on for a while, so she started shampooing Chyou's hair while she talked. A nurse supervised, and even supplied a couple of hair elastics. Chyou sat on the bed and reluctantly soaked up the attention while Brittany talked and brushed.

Soon, her story was finished. "What do ya think? Do I belong here?"

"Definitely! It all sounds certifiable."

"Seriously? I never did this."

"Were you the only one in the apartment?"

"Yes, but..."

"Then you did it." She turned to face Brittany. "I wish more people could spend a month here getting their lives sorted out. I know you think of this place as a punishment, but it's not. It's an opportunity."

Brittany pondered that while she wove Chyou's hair into a stylish French braid. Maybe this girl was right, and she was looking at this the wrong way. She just hated the idea of being called crazy. Could they help her figure things out? "Do you believe my story?"

"Why not? It's not like you've had an ordinary life. That means you shouldn't have ordinary problems."

"That makes sense. How do I get everyone to listen? My own mother looks at me funny."

"Don't worry about what they think. Just tell the story and stay true. Do that and everything will fall into place."

"I just wish they would listen."

"Your mother is listening, trust me." Nicole entered the room with Brittany's sweater. "I brought a bag of belongings."

The nurse promptly grabbed the bag and proceeded to rummage through it.

Nicole ignored the woman and gave Chyou a head nod. "I see you've made a friend."

Brittany finished braiding Chyou's hair. "Mom, this is Chyou. Chyou, my mother."

Nicole politely extended her hand. "I see my daughter talked you into a make over."

Chyou shook the hand and smiled but didn't say a word.

Meanwhile, Brittany dumped the bag out on the bed. "Ah, here we go." She grabbed a handful of cosmetics and held a set of eye shadows up against Chyou's face. "We'll play with this stuff later."

"Play now," Nicole said as she started for the door. "I have to talk to your counsellor."

Chyou waited until Nicole had left. "Which one did you get?"

"Mrs Xiang," Brittany offered. "How is she?"

"She's good. She was my counsellor and I'm leaving in a couple of..." Chyou stopped talking as she looked past Brittany. There was a man standing at the door, watching them. "Can I help you?"

"Sorry to interrupt." The man started to back away. "I was just looking for somebody."

Chapter sixteen

Nicole sat with Mrs Xiang hoping to control the meeting, but sadly, she quickly found that wasn't the case. This ward was Mrs Xiang turf, and she wasn't about to downplay what had happened.

"I'm sorry, but I'm worried we're on different wavelengths. You don't seem to be looking at these suicide attempts in the same light that I am. Why do you think that is?"

Nicole slowly leaned forward in her chair. "Don't get me wrong. I'm definitely concerned with Brittany's well being, but I don't think they were a result of her mood swings or personal problems. She's not suicidal."

"And yet..."

"What about the guy that brought her in? What's his story?"

"He was just somebody in the right place at the right time."

"Pretty convenient, if you ask me."

"It was, or your daughter wouldn't be alive right now."

"You know what I mean. This guy finds her, brings her in, and doesn't hang around. I think there's something to that, because, like I said, Brittany is not suicidal."

"She's slashed her wrists and overdosed on pills she found." Her eyes wouldn't leave Nicole's. "I disagree."

"Her situation is unique. You can't hold her to the same standard like you would..."

"Like what... another human?" Her stare didn't waver. "Please try to accept the fact that maybe, just maybe, your daughter might have issues that she can't deal with."

"Like?"

"Like losing her mother, or maybe, she feels a little odd with the fact that she has friends that can't render like she can. She's different here. How could she tell you that? And what about her father? I hear she met him recently. How'd that go?"

"She was fine."

"Look, I agree that her situation is unique. She's unique, and she's been dealing with it well for years, but isn't it possible that coming to Earth has triggered something?"

Nicole was instantly angered, but only because this was the same advice she would have given. True, her little girl was well adjusted, but there were a lot of things going on in her life. She thought back to Brittany reading her mother's diary. That was an eye opener and yet she seemed fine with it.

"Nicole, I believe everything will be okay. Your daughter is not broken beyond repair, but we need to find out why this is happening. We need to work together on this."

"You're right, and thank you." Nicole got up and shook her hand.

"We'll have a casual meeting later, after Brittany has settled in. It was nice meeting you. I appreciate your popping by."

Nicole was politely walked out of the office.

Halfway down the hallway, she stopped. There was a set of eyes on her. She could feel them. When she turned, two nurses were leaving the nurse's station. It wasn't them. Off in the distance, she noticed the man in the waiting room smoking a cigarette. He was staring.

She didn't recognise him at first, but once she did, she couldn't help herself from running toward him. The man wrapped Nicole up in his arms. They were as strong as she remembered. After a few seconds, he released his grip. Nicole continued to hold on tight. She dropped her head on his shoulder.

"I've missed you," she half-sobbed."

"Then..." He kissed the top of her head. "You really need to get a life."

Nicole smiled as she let go of him and took a step back. "You look good, Victor."

"You do too." He dropped a brow. "You haven't aged much."

"I'm a few years older."

"You don't look it." His eyes stared into hers before unapologetically dropping to take in the rest of her. Not much had changed.

Nicole took that moment to do the same scan on him. The arms, the hair, and that face looked pretty damn good. "Thanks again for freeing our scientists. I hope you didn't get hurt."

"Got a couple of souvenirs out of it." He pulled his shirt open a bit to show the scar on his shoulder. "I'll have to show you the other one some other time, if you know what I mean."

Nicole imagined the worst and cringed.

"No. Not there. I took one in the hip."

"Glad to hear." She moved in for another hug. "What are you doing here, at the hospital?"

"Long story," he answered.

"You got time for a coffee?"

"For you?" He returned the hug and then held out an arm. She took it.

They started walking toward the coffee machine and Nicole gave his arm a squeeze. "I can't believe it's you. What's new in the wonderful world of Victor?"

"I own a set of islands off the coast of Burma. They're a challenge."

"That's pretty cool. How big is it?"

"Just over three thousand square miles." He pulled out a pocket full of change, sorting the Chinese renminbi from the Corvus coins.

"Whoa. That's big enough to be its own country."

"It is. I even have my own private jets. They're not as fast as your little spaceships, but they work well enough for me." He paused for a second. "I'm a little surprised that you haven't tried to contact me, after all we'd been through. Is everything okay?"

"It's not like I haven't thought of you. I've just been very busy." She paused. "Do you still do favours for damsels in distress?"

He chuckled as he dropped a couple coins in the machine. "There's my girl."

Chapter seventeen

With coffees in hand, Victor and Nicole made their way to a quiet corner of the waiting room. They remained on Brittany's floor but had a lot to talk about and needed their privacy.

"I wasn't sure how to get a hold of you," Nicole confessed. "Are you still in hiding, or did you patch things up with the American government?"

"Sorta yes, sorta no. I'll never be allowed on American soil." He took a nervous drink from his coffee. "I was glad to hear you decided to stay in Beijing. Have you talked to Mr Chen?"

"Briefly. Because we're spending so much time with the United States, we didn't want China to feel left out. I heard China took a bit of a beating while we were gone. They're still rebuilding Shanghai."

"China had it coming. They were using you guys to get in on the ground floor. It was a power move. With that one little spaceship, they could have used the technology to take over the world."

"We never thought they'd..."

"Don't blame yourself. Your plan was doomed no matter which side you took. There was already a plan in play and most countries were being bullied into what they called a Great Reset."

"We'd run across the term. What was that?"

"It was a plan a lot like yours, only with the rich running the planet. Your Shenti Lui..."

"What about them."

"Actors. They were running the banks, stock markets, and investment companies, basically using the people's money to manipulate them."

"I'd heard something about that, but how?"

"Imagine you had a monopoly on the stock markets. You own the banks and the media, so you can tell the people what ever you want. Most people believe the news. The world is too complicated for them, so they have no choice. You bump up the house prices, so the people have to buy condos. You bump up gas prices and the people can't afford to travel. Bump up inflation and throw a bunch of government incentives and the people become dependant. Now, like a pet, you're just taking up space and doing what you're told."

"The people would never go for that."

"They did, especially after they introduced a virus that crippled the economy."

Nicole knew all about that virus. "Is that what happened?"

"The virus locked the planet down and caused chaos. Everyone looked to their leaders to get them through it. Sadly, they didn't know that they were the ones behind it all. Economies predictably tanked, and a Great Reset became the only way out."

"Why call it a reset?"

"Because calling it the ultimate manipulation might have ruffled feathers. The governments bought the people's debt, and it came with a price. You had to stay on the government's good side. Speak against them and you'd lose all your rights, not that you truly had any."

"That's BS."

"You don't even know the half of it. They're hiding most of it from you."

"Like what?"

"The whole world is divided into zones, national ones and municipal ones. When you travel from one zone to another, you pay a toll. If you plan on staying in that zone for any length of time you also pay a displacement fee. Between that and gas prices, most people simply stay home."

"Brittany never paid any fees when she went to the United States."

"Being Alzien comes with its privileges."

"It sounds sinister."

"It is. That's why everyone was so upset when you showed up with a similar plan all those years ago. You were trying to fast-track what they'd taken decades to put into place. Shame on you."

"Our plan was different. We weren't creating zones and..."

"Don't kid yourself. Same shit, different pile. Maybe not as corrupt, but it still meant an end to freedom."

"But people seem happier."

"They fought back, and thanks to them, we're back to a gold standard. That means the economy is stable. But don't kid yourself, the people are still being oppressed. Even though a good part of the corruption has been put to rest, it still hides behind the laws and what's considered best for the people."

"You're saying there's still corruption with the current leaders?"

"If you mean food shortages in zones that act up, yes. It happens all the time. At least we have people helping people on the ground. That's a miracle in itself. It seems the elitists have been pushed back behind the fence for the most part. In time we might get to that system you guys talked about, but it won't be today, or next week."

"Are we talking years?"

"Decades, if I'm being honest." He shrugged. "Hey, off topic, who was that girl in your apartment?"

"What?" The question caught her off guard. "How do you know about that?"

"I was the one that found her and brought her in."

"That was you?" She set her coffee down and dropped her shoulders back against the chair. "No offence, I mean thanks for saving my daughter, but how'd you know to be there?"

"Relax, I'm not psychic. I was there to see you. I was caught up with work, decided to swing by and look you up. At the door I heard this loud crash, so I knocked, a few times. Then I kicked it in and found her by the broken mirror." He stopped and put his hands down on the table. "Did you just call her your daughter? When were you going to tell me?"

"Long story. Elizabeth was pregnant when we left. Before she died, she asked me to raise Brittany. Greg's the father."

"Greg? Really?" He ran his fingers through his hair and stared at her as if it might help him understand. "So… she's not…"

Nicole didn't understand at first. She started to laugh out loud when she realised what he was asking. "Oh! Oh, no. She's not ours, if that's what you were thinking."

He shook his head. "Right. No, I didn't think that…"

Nicole cocked her head. "Uh, kinda looks like you did."

"Well, we did… you know." He shook the thought of fatherhood. "Hey, I'm sorry to hear about Elizabeth. I honestly thought she was going to be okay."

"She died giving birth. Nothing made sense that day. We have technologies that can…" She took a deep breath. "Her death never should have happened."

"It wasn't a natural death?" Victor asked.

"No, and I have a theory."

"A theory? Do tell."

"When Elizabeth died, there was a bird by the window. It was a…" She tried to remember the type.

"A sparrow?" he offered.

"Yes." Nicole nodded as if she'd come up with it. "Soon there were thousands of them. I'd never seen these birds on Alzie before. I swear."

They blankly stared at each other for close to a minute before Victor broke the silence. "I don't think my guy oversees your birds. I think he has a region, or a boundary."

"But you don't know that for sure."

"Hell, I'm not sure of anything. He doesn't answer to me."

"Could you find him and ask him anyway. Find out if he took Elizabeth's bird and gave it to Brittany. It's the only thing that makes sense. Greg was a creation, so he wouldn't have had one. Maybe the birdman used Elizabeth's bird to balance the books."

"Balance the books? You said you didn't have birds. Now you have them. I'm confused."

Nicole shrugged. "Hey, I don't know how it works either."

"What would I ask him, that's if I could even find him?"

"Ask him if Alziens have birds. Ask him if he could make an exception to the bird rules and bring Elizabeth back. It was a mistake, a dumb technicality. Ask him if he'd please stop fucking with me."

"It's been quite a few years since her death. How would you even bring somebody back from that? What would that do to her, or you and your daughter? The ripples would be... Think of everything that has happened since she died."

"I don't care."

"Think about what you're asking. What if that meant losing your daughter."

"I need you to ask. Can you do that?"

Victor thought about the envelope in his pocket. He might see the man, could ask, but it was wrong. Elizabeth was dead.

Nicole took his hand and gave it a loving squeeze.

"Let me see what I can do."

"Thanks, Victor."

"Any idea why your daughter would have done what she did?"

"She thinks it has something to do with these dreams she was having while she wore that..." Then she remembered that he knew about the necklace. "It has something to do with that gaudy necklace. You know the one."

"Oh, I remember it. That damn thing was around her neck and pulsing when I found her, like it was alive. You aliens don't do easy, do you?"

"Isn't that what you love about us?"

"And here I thought it was that thing you did with your hips."

"You've been thinking about that a lot, haven't you?"

"I should go." Victor decided to end this before they got carried away. This wasn't the time, and he was older and mellowed by the years. He got to his feet. "You're pretty tough to forget. And don't worry about the birdman. I'll find him and get back to you."

"You know where he is?"

"More like he knows where I am."

She got up, hugged him one more time, and handed him an Alzien phone. "Keep in touch. Can you do that for me?"

"You can count on it."

Chapter eighteen

Back at the room, Nicole stopped in the doorway. A small miracle had been performed. "Chyou? Is that you?"

"Hello."

"Hey, Mom. What do ya think? She's looking pretty damn good."

"She sure does, and please watch your language." The worn-out request came out more like a desperate plea.

"Oh, oh. Looks like your mother had the talk." Chyou had seen that look before. "They're all like that after talking to Mrs Xiang. It's the reality bites expression."

"Are you okay, Mom?" Brittany asked.

"I will be."

Chyou continued her diagnosis. "Your mother's caught up somewhere between denial and confusion. It'll pass, but I should leave you two to talk."

Brittany sat down and patted the bed with her hand. Nicole took the invite. "Mrs Xiang claims you may have issues that you're not dealing with. She thinks there may be things that I don't even know about."

"I disagree. You know everything about me. I'm an open book."

"I've dragged you across the universe to meet your father."

"Okay, but that's not a reason to kill myself. What else have we got?"

"You lost your mother, your father's an Earthling, and I hear that Mathew recently made a pass at you. Where should we start?"

"I never knew my mother, so it's hard to miss her. Besides, you've always been the one. This universe trek is a huge thrill. Dad is a man I just met and nothing more, and as far as Mathew goes, I know he's just as confused as I am." Her smile broadened. "I think this place will be fine. I'll play their game as long as it keeps me safe. And for the record, these dreams don't warrant suicide, but there's something about them that's tied to me. We'll figure it out."

"I agree. Now what about that supper?" The afternoon was waning, and Nicole hadn't eaten yet.

"Hospital food will be served in an hour. Chyou says it's fairly good." She smiled, knowing her mother was thinking take out. "I need to accept their rules. We can share a table with Chyou."

Disappointed at the thought of dry meatloaf, or whatever it was in China, Nicole knew this was going to be an adjustment, for the both of them. "A cafeteria supper might be fun."

"And you won't have to do the dishes."

"Shall we grab a table?"

Brittany took her hand.

The dining room was smaller than expected, but the wall of windows more than made up for any claustrophobic fears. Brittany found the place cosy. Sure, the beds were institution style, but the atmosphere was on the homey side. It helped, having her big sweater, with or without the buttons. They looked over to see Chyou and somebody sitting by a window and joined them.

"Hey good look'n. Mind if my Mom and I roost with you guys?"

"By all means. This is Manchu. He's not much of a talker, but he's good people."

The boy was in his late teens. He was a handsome young man, with a face that was soft. A deeper pain filled his eyes, like a puppy that had just been scolded.

"Good to meet you Manchu. How ya liking the girl's new do?"

His answer was a simple head nod.

The odd silence was broken by Chyou. "What? I'm scorching." She elbowed him and they both smiled. "Manchu, do you know who these two people are? They're like celebs."

He shook his head, gave them each another glance, and shook his head again.

"I'll give you a clue. They came here from another planet, and they can do some pretty cool things like disappear and reappear."

Brittany flashed him a movie star smile.

Nicole, on the other hand, rolled her eyes. She'd rather forget what they were. "We're just like you guys."

Manchu inched closer. "You're from Alzie?"

"Yeah." Brittany returned his stare and felt the connection.

"That's cool. Maybe we can talk later?" Ignoring the others, he got to his feet and shuffled off to his room.

Brittany watched as he got up and left. "Uh, that would be... What just happened here?"

Chyou waved it off as if it happened all the time, but as soon as he was out of earshot, she blurted, "I can't believe it. He talked to you?"

"Is that a big deal?" Nicole asked.

"He's been here a couple years with next to no progress. I'm his closest friend in the world and I've only heard about twenty words out of him."

Brittany felt bad. "I'm sorry. Am I overstepping?"

"God no. He needs help. I'm ecstatic."

That put up red flags with Nicole. "What's his story?"

"Please, keep an open mind. Nobody really knows what happened, and he'll stay here until he spills, but they found him soaked in blood, a crumpled heap in the corner of his bedroom. He hadn't eaten in days. The neighbours called the cops because of the smell."

Brittany's heart was pounding. "What the hell..."

"He was the only survivor. The whole family had been murdered, except for Manchu and his father. The man was out of town on a business trip. The police figured that Manchu was lucky to be alive, at first. When he was taken to the hospital, they realised that he had no injuries. All the blood was from his mother and two sisters. One plus one, right?"

Nicole's expression remained a forced neutral. How in the hell was Brittany safer here? "How long did you say you've known him?"

"About a year. I'm the only one he speaks to. He's a science nerd. It took a lot of one-way conversations until I finally hit on that. We, or I, talked about spaceships and he was eating out of the palm of my hand. I grabbed him a few science fiction books and he read them and wanted more. That's why he finds you so fascinating."

Brittany sat and listened to Chyou's stories. Did she want to get close to this guy? He was a murderer, and his family no doubt, yet he seemed gentle, like he'd be the first to climb a tree to save a kitten. "Has he ever snapped or given you any reason to be afraid?"

Without hesitation Chyou answered, "never!"

The conversation ended there, and they waited for the food. It was meatloaf and plain rice. Thank God for gravy.

Mrs Xiang entered the room and zeroed in on them. "Ladies."

Brittany offered her a seat. "Is it normal to always feel like I'm in trouble around you?"

"That's an interesting question," Mrs Xiang replied. "We'll have to talk about that."

Brittany looked over to her mother. They were both a little stunned at this woman's energy.

"Put in effort and we won't have a problem. I only have one rule, that there is no blame, just progress. It's not a race to get better. You're here because we're worried about you. This is a safe environment to find out what fuelled the attempts."

Brittany was okay with that, but she didn't feel safe. She had powers and these dreams knew it. They'd have to watch her like a hawk. And it wasn't like she was a prisoner. If push came to shove, they couldn't hold her, and everyone knew it.

Darkness came shortly after supper and with it, the night. Nicole tucked Brittany into bed and left to get a coffee.

Brittany's head hit the pillow and she fell asleep thinking about Mathew. She had hoped for a peaceful sleep, but the dreams wouldn't be denied.

Chapter nineteen

Thе water, that Brittany was in, was neither warm nor cold. It was distant, like she was floating. Weightless and without working her muscles, she tried to open her eyes. They were already open, but everything was blurred. There was an outline of somebody. That somebody was above her, above the surface, and they were tugging at her.

Suddenly, her vision cleared. The man had pulled her up out of the water. The brightness of the sun beat down on her, but it wasn't warm like it should have been. It wasn't anything. Her body lay limp on the dock as the man leaned over top of her. She tried to scream. She couldn't.

"Oh my. She's not breathing," a woman's voice cried out from the shore.

Not breathing she thought. That wasn't right. She tried to concentrate on taking in a breath. Again, she couldn't. How could that be, unless she was dead? Other voices joined them. What were they saying?

"Somebody, go for help! Tell them we have a drowning victim at the Maramount Lake Resort."

Another voice added, "Tell them to come in from Winfield. It'll be quicker."

As he blew, her lungs were filled with air. This was attempted several times, then he put his head on her chest. His hands quickly found her breastbone and he thrust down several times before stopping. Her lungs filled with air again. She didn't count the thrusts this time. She was too weak to care.

Again and again, her lungs filled, one long breath after another. There were chest thrusts, but they weren't working. She could feel herself fading. An obscure peacefulness was taking over. An eerie silence flooded over her as the man pleaded for her to stay with him. But her time was up.

I need to render, she thought to herself.

Brittany sucked in as much air as she could. Her eyes popped open, as she tried to orient herself. The morning sun was shining down on her and the window that it had been coming through looked strangely familiar, as was the bed. This was the loony hospital. She quickly propped herself up and looked for her mother.

Startled at Brittany's sudden movement, Nicole bolted upright in her chair. She had slid it down to the foot of the bed and covered up with part of the sheet. She'd only planned for forty winks.

Her voice was groggy. "Hey, Britt. How'd you sleep?"

"I died. I was at the dock again and they pulled me out of the water. Somebody tried to resuscitate me, but it didn't work. I tried to render, and it wasn't me thinking like that. It was her." She tried to slow down but couldn't. "She wanted to render!"

"That's impossible. Whoever this girl is, she knows nothing about rendering." Nicole was awake now. "It had to be you thinking that."

"It was all so confusing. I was struggling with the fact that my heart wasn't beating. Some man was blowing air into my lungs. It was kinda peaceful, dying, and yet it was way too weird." She tried to shake the feeling.

"Are you okay?"

"I'll be fine. You think it was me wanting to render?"

"I can't see it any other way."

"I suppose." She pulled herself out of bed and wrapped herself in her sweater. "You must be sore, all bent up in that chair."

"I'm okay." She rubbed her neck and stretched out the kinks. She'd slept in worse conditions.

"Hey. No suicide attempts. That's a good thing, right?"

"Yes, but a vivid dream where you lose your life isn't what I'd call the road to recovery."

"Yeah, well I can't have you sleeping at my feet like a cat. You'll be a cripple in no time. We need to start trusting these people." She grabbed her hand and pulled her mother out of her chair. "Come on cripple. Let's get a bite to eat. Hopefully, I'll remember more after a snack."

They'd only taken a couple steps before Brittany stopped. "Grab a pen. I do remember something." She watched as her mother went into her purse. When she was ready, Brittany blurted out, "Maramount Lake Resort. That's the name of the lodge and it's close to a place called Winfield."

Nicole wrote it down. After breakfast, she'd pick up Jenny and research all cities called Winfield. She could narrow it down from there. With any luck this town would have a mysterious past.

Chapter twenty

Victor stepped off the plane and watched as two men crossed the tarmac with a tire on a rim. Neither one of them looked like they worked at the airport and yet the tire looked like it belonged to one of the planes.

"They will sell it back tomorrow," the woman on the tarmac offered. She had noticed the confused look on his face. "The Haitian airport has a budget for this."

"But..." He stopped. Say too much and she might figure out who he was. The mission wasn't to correct the injustices of this place. He was there to meet a woman, and not just any woman. They had met many years ago. She had come to him with something she'd picked up in Russia, that and one hell of a story.

The price had started at two million dollars, for a necklace with a very gaudy purple stone. With the Alziens gone, the item was worthless. That had brought the price down to a million, then one hundred thousand, and finally five hundred American dollars. But worthless was worthless and she ended up with an ugly souvenir.

Four days later, the woman was killed in a gunfight over a job description. Victor saw her take three bullets in the chest before she could make it to safety. It had been one of Victor's men who had shot her. She was simply in the wrong place at the wrong time.

Although it wasn't Victor's fault directly, he still felt bad for the woman. He made sure her funeral was paid for. Two weeks after she died, he could have sworn he saw her in the street, walking with a goat. It wasn't her he recognised, as much as it was the damn necklace she was wearing. He shook his head. It couldn't have been her, maybe a twin. The country was full of cockroaches.

Now, all these years later, he wanted to find her. He had to know for himself. Was she still alive, did she have bullet holes in her and if so, how'd she cheat death?

"Sir?" the woman asked. "Are you okay?"

Victor watched as the men rolled the tire through a cut in the fence. "I'm good."

In the parking lot, a brown Chevy pick-up truck sat in the nearest stall. Two men with guns strapped to their armpits were leaning against it. He walked up to them.

"Hey Boss," the one said.

Victor rolled his eyes. "Don't call me that. You know I don't want that target on my back."

"Sorry, Boss." He slapped a hand over his mouth. "To the Bat Cave?"

The Bat Cave was Victor's safe house. On the northern edge of Port-au-Prince, there was an acreage on the beach with a gated house. It was a four bedroom with servant's quarters and a helicopter pad that was only used for pickleball. Victor didn't need the attention.

"We can head there after we find the woman. Have you had any luck?"

"We found her. Are you sure about this?"

"It's my call, right?"

"Of course, it is. Hey, and ain't nobody gonna tell you how to spend your time when you're here, but if the people find out you saw her…"

"Has she been shooting off her mouth again?"

"She says you should have bought that necklace when you had the chance. Says she saw your death. What kind of crazy is she talking about?"

"Exactly. The woman is crazy." He got behind the wheel of the truck and the two men joined him in the cab. The truck fired up, sputtered, and revved as he stepped on the gas. "Now, where is she?"

"Hang a right at the stop sign."

Victor drove for twelve minutes before stopping a block away from where the two men had told him the lady would be. "Out."

"What? Why?"

"I don't need help."

"How come?"

"Because of the questions I'm going to be asking her. I don't need you thinking I'm crazy too."

"A little late for that," the man laughed.

"Out. I can always get crazier."

The two exited the truck and started for a small café. "We'll see you at Bernie's when you're done."

"Don't wait up. I'll see you at the Bat Cave when I get there."

"Tonight?"

"Tonight, tomorrow… whenever."

The road took Victor another two hundred feet before he killed the engine. There was an apartment building, beaten by the last hurricane that had rolled through. Curtains hung from a few of the windows, flapping like war-torn flags. She was on the ground floor.

"I've been wait'n for you," she said as he walked through the doorway. "Heard you were look'n for me."

"Hey, Rose." He took a seat in a chair at the kitchen table across from her.

Rose Madden was the name she was going by, but it wasn't the name she'd been given. She never knew her real name, and it didn't much matter. The dress she wore was one she'd worn most of her life. The fabric was thin and through it he could see two of the three scars that had been left in the aftermath of the shoot out. They always stood out on the darker skin.

"I don't have it anymore. You missed your chance."

"Not sure I even want it."

"Then why are you here?"

"I wanna know how you survived. I mean, I saw you get all shot up. My guy couldn't hit the broad side of a barn if he was in it and the door was closed, yet he got you three times. Sorry for that." He leaned forward and put his hands on the table. "How'd you do it?"

"I don't think I did anything." She took a puff off her cigarette. "I think I died and was resurrected. I lost about four days, and it was the necklace that brought me back. I swear."

"You know that's impossible, right?"

"Ain't nothing impossible, as I see it."

"So, you were dead for four days?"

73

She didn't say anything.

Victor shook the question. "Then what?"

"Ever do LSD?"

"I was young once," he replied. "Why?"

"This was ten times worse. For four days I had the strangest dreams. I was people I didn't know, in a land I'd never been to. None of it made sense. I woke up in the mortician's crypt with that dang thing still around my neck. I had to knock to get them to let me out. Over the years, the nightmares have faded. I've replaced them with sleep. It took a long time, but I sleep good now."

As much as it made no sense, Victor believed her. "Where is it now, Rose?"

"I was robbed a few years back. Kid took my watch, some groceries, and that necklace." She took another drag off the cigarette. "Can't say I miss it."

"Well, I need it. "

"Then I guess you need me." She crushed out the cigarette. "And my fee is a million dollars."

Chapter twenty-one

The front of the pup ship opened and Jenny exited the ship with her two kids. She was a sweetheart for coming on such short notice. Melanie, her daughter, and Mathew, her son, looked a little lost. While Jenny and Melanie greeted Nicole warmly, Mathew was another matter, being brought against his will.

Nicole gave Mathew a sideways stare. "Am I missing something?"

"He's not taking any of this well. How's she doing?"

"No attempt last night. That's a plus, but she keeps having these dreams. I have no idea where they're coming from. It's as if she's acting out somebody else's life. Last night, she died from drowning. We got the name of the place where it happened, so I'll be checking it out."

Jenny tried to understand. "And how are you holding up?"

Nicole shook her head. "Coping."

"You look like shit," Jenny uttered. "Have you slept?"

"Caught forty winks at the foot of her bed."

Melanie edged forward. "Can we go to the hospital? I want to see her."

Nicole nodded. "Of course. You guys can take the car and surprise her. I know she'll love to see you. I'll render back to the apartment and get it cleaned up. You'll stay there with me tonight if that's okay? I'll get you your own rooms for tomorrow."

Nicole appeared in the living room and went straight to the computer. She tapped away at the keys, spelling Winfield, and the search came back with several cities, most of them in the U.S. and Canada. She quickly jotted down the locations. Alberta, Canada had one between Calgary and Edmonton, but with no lakes around it. She quickly ruled it out. Central Kansas had a Winfield, but again eliminated for the lack of a lake resort. Marion County had a Winfield in Alabama and there was one in Australia, but the two best choices fell in Colorado, and in the Okanagan Valley, in British Columbia, Canada.

In Colorado, it was a ghost town up in the Rocky Mountains. They had all the lakes you could ever want. The other option, a small town in the Okanagan, was also full of fishing and camping resorts. That town was large enough to have their own ambulance service. It would have been the one dispatched in case of a lake resort emergency.

Nicole picked up the phone and dialled.

An elderly woman answered. "Hello?"

"Hello. I'm phoning from China, and I'm looking for a Maramount Lake Resort. Have you got anything like that in the area?" There was silence and Nicole felt uneasy. "Hello?"

"I'm sorry, Dear. We don't have any active resorts by that name around here, but we have three abandoned lodges. I know that Edwards Lodge was the name of one of them. I'm trying to recall the names of the other two, but I... I just can't remember."

Nicole felt a tingle of excitement with the idea that one of the other lodges might be the one. "I know this sounds a little crazy, but was there any history to either resort, like a drowning or something?"

"Is everything okay?" the lady asked, trying to remain diplomatic. "That's an odd request."

"I'm investigating a cold case."

"You're a detective? How exciting." Interest had been sparked. "We've had several drownings at the one resort. Damn it, I wish I could remember the name of that place."

"The Maramount?"

"I'm sorry. It's not coming to me."

"That's fine... uh." She paused, hoping the woman would offer her name.

The lady needed a second to clue in. "Oh sorry. It's Cassandra."

Nicole almost dropped the phone. "Thank you, Cassandra, and maybe we'll see you." She could hardly wait to hang up and pour herself a drink.

Not a fan of hard alcohol, she needed her nerves calmed for her next task. She downed the scotch and poured another before heading toward Brittany's room.

She pushed the door open with her drink in hand. The site of the far corner forced Nicole to finish the drink with a guzzle. Walking past the dresser, she set the empty glass down and dropped to her knees in front of the overturned mirror. The wooden frame had almost been completely dislodged from its stand. It had taken quite the angry wallop.

Shards of the mirror were slowly placed into the wastepaper basket. Then, Nicole filled a bucket with soapy water, found a cleaning rag, and proceeded to mop her daughter's blood from the carpet. The sight of the pink lather brought tears to her eyes.

When she was done, she gathered the cleaning supplies and basket of bloodied mirror pieces. Her heart pounded in her chest as she poured herself another drink. The glass was a tall one and she was hypnotised by the ice cubes as they swam around in it, that is, until she noticed a trace of blood on the back of one of her knuckles. That caused her to start up the computer again.

She had to find this lodge, before it was too late.

Chapter twenty-two

Two blocks from Rose's place, the neighbourhood changed from mere poverty to all-out slum. Piles of garbage littered every intersection and parked along the street, there were more cars without engines than with. Victor made his way up the sidewalk on foot. Eyes lit up from the shadows, gauging him to see if he was worthy of a mugging.

Victor stopped at the entrance of an apartment when Rose held her arm out. The security door had been removed and the buzzers on the wall didn't work. Rose stepped across the threshold and waved him to follow.

"If he's here, you owe me a million dollars."

"No, Rose. If he has the necklace, you get a million dollars. I couldn't care less about the guy himself." He did a routine shoulder check. "What's his name?"

"Benny something. He's a cracker."

"Great. And you think he still has it?"

"Thing's too ugly to sell."

"And yet he took it from you."

She brought her hand up to knock on the door of room #127.

Victor stopped her.

He turned the doorknob and slowly swung the door open. Poking his head inside, he looked for signs of life. There were two guys passed out on the couch, a woman in the corner sleeping in the fetal position, and a person of unknown gender lighting a cigarette with the toaster.

"Are any of these creatures him, Rose?"

"No, and you be nice, Victor. I don't need these people pissed off at me. I still have to live here."

Victor made his way over to the bedroom. There were burlap sacks covering the window, and two people in the bed. It was hard to tell if they were alive or not.

"Benny?" Victor called out. He turned to Rose. "Is this the guy?"

She moved in for a closer look. "That's him."

Victor pulled the covers back revealing two naked bodies. One was Benny and the other, some blonde that hadn't seen food in years. She woke up first and reached for a t-shirt. For some reason she felt it necessary to cover up the mosquito bites. Then she grabbed a shoebox and left the room. Benny never stirred.

Rose gave the man's ankle a tug. "Get up, Benny. You have company."

Benny slowly stirred. "What the fuck?"

Victor picked a pair of jeans off the floor and threw them at him. "Get dressed. We need to talk."

Benny eyed Victor from head to foot. This guy, standing over him, was twice his age, but twice his size. He slipped one leg into the jeans. "If you're robbing me, look around. I ain't got nothing."

"You have one item that I'm interested in." Victor took a burnt knife off the nightstand, closed the door, and jammed it into the doorframe. They didn't need any heroes trying to break in and save Benny. "I'm looking for a necklace, big purple stone."

Benny stuck his other leg into the jeans and stood up. He zipped, reached for his cigarettes, and lit one that had already been half-smoked. "What you want with that damn thing?"

"Just want it. You still got it?"

"Hell no. I couldn't wait to get rid of that thing. I hate voodoo and that necklace was full of that shit. It creeped me out."

"It saved my life," Rose announced.

"Me fuck'n too." He stared at her, afraid to hear her story.

She asked him. "How?"

"I was wearing that thing, so damn ugly."

Rose asked again. "How'd you die?"

"Overdose. I was double dipping, heroin and meth. I knew better, but hey, you only live once... or so I thought. I swear I died. I heard my heart slow down and stop."

"How long were you out?" Victor asked.

"My boss says I missed six days of work so I must have been out for close to a week, except I wasn't out. It was so weird. I was tripping, like really bad. It was like dreams that weren't dreams. My body was in other people, and they were doing weird shit. I was along for the ride." He finished the cigarette, flicked it to the floor and went for another.

Rose had hoped for the offer of one but didn't get it. When he put the cigarettes down, she asked, "What were the dreams?"

"Like I said, weird shit. Places I'd never been to and an explosion in the sky."

Victor pulled out two cigarettes, lit them both, and handed one to Rose. "And none of it made sense to either of you?"

"Bits and pieces, but no." She took a long drag. "Why do you want that thing so bad, Victor?"

"Trying to help a friend." He turned to Benny. "Where is it?"

"I sold it to this guy."

"How much," Rose asked.

"Guy gave me fifty thousand gourdes and two grams of heroin." He said it as if he was proud of the trade.

Rose worked it out to about eight hundred American dollars. "You idiot. This guy was gonna give me a million for it."

"Gourdes?" He blinked twice.

"American Dollars," Rose answered.

"Hell, for that kinda dough I'll take you to the guy."

"You think he still has it?" Victor asked.

"Oh, he has it. He wears it when he gets high, says it talks to him. He'd never get rid of it."

"And who is this guy?"

Benny hesitated. "Antonio Gomez."

Victor sighed. "Seriously?"

Benny shrugged.

Of all the people in Haiti, this guy was the only one who gave Victor the heebie-jeebies. He pulled his phone out of his pocket and phoned the General. The man wasn't actually a general, but he headed the Haitian Military.

"Hey, General. This is Victor. I need a favour."

Chapter twenty-three

Melanie and Jenny surprised Brittany as they entered the dining room. She was learning how to play crib with Chyou. Mathew trailed behind his mother and sister, keeping quiet.

"Whoa, I can't get rid of you people," Brittany joked. "Man, it's great to see you guys. What brings you here? Me?" She got up and went in for hugs.

Melanie's was first, but only because she stepped in front of her mother. "What the hell are you doing in here? We're gonna talk tonight. What's up with you?"

"That wasn't me! I'm possessed or something." She started to spill. "Some girl named Cassandra has me under some spell. She visits me when I sleep. Last night I drowned. It was all so strange." She gave Mathew a shy wave. "Hi you."

"Hey." He dropped his eyes.

"Okay. Enough said." Brittany rolled her eyes. "Hey, I'd like you guys to meet my new friend, Chyou."

Jenny stepped forward and held out her hand. "Thanks for looking out for her."

Chyou gave it a polite shake. "My pleasure. She's a good kid."

Brittany took Melanie's hand. "Come, I'll give you the tour."

Mathew had seen enough and started for the exit. Jenny started after him. "Sorry, Brit. We'll be back later."

Melanie watched as her mother and brother slipped out of sight. She looked to Chyou and Brittany. "We should talk."

"I have to run so you two will have to talk without me," Chyou said as she started down the hall. "It was nice meeting you Melanie. I'm sure I'll see you later."

Brittany waited until she was gone. "What's up with your brother?"

"He's feeling sorry for himself, like this is his tragedy. He needs to pull his head out of his ass. There's more to this world than just him." She took a seat on the bed. "So, fill me in on everything. Who is Cassandra, and why does she want you dead?"

Brittany sat beside her and conveyed what she knew, which wasn't much. Then Brittany told her how Nicole had crippled herself sleeping in the chair.

"How about I take the night shift? I'm younger. I can sleep in the chair. I've slept in a lot worse."

Brittany chuckled as she remembered two weeks ago getting drunk in Jenny's back yard. Mel had sucked back a bottle of wine and slept in the flowerbed. The ants loved her, and Brittany took enough pictures to wallpaper her room. Her grandparents, Tom and Claire were less than thrilled.

Mrs Xiang heard them and leaned in the doorway. "Brittany your session is in an hour, okay?"

"But Mom's not here."

"That's fine. You can introduce me to your friend. It's all introductory stuff. I want to see who you are."

"Cool."

"How long have you both been friends?"

"Maybe a month, and it's kinda part-time because of the distance. Why?"

"You look like you've been friends forever. You two ever have any problems?"

Melanie thought for a second. "Nope. Thick as thieves. Her and my brother aren't talking anymore, but that's no big deal."

"What's going on, Brittany?"

She flushed. "Personal stuff."

"All the more reason to talk about it."

Brittany looked at Melanie and then back to Mrs Xiang. "Nobody better hate me after this, or I will snap." She paused and looked to Melanie again. "Your brother and I were kissing, and he unbuttoned my blouse. It was awkward."

"Then what happened?" Melanie asked.

"He gawked at them like they were deformed. I mean, I know there nothing to look at, but still, it was a dick thing to do."

"He was probably in shock."

"Doesn't matter, now that he thinks I'm some sort of emo-suicidal freak."

Mrs Xiang put a hand on her shoulder. "You and Melanie need to talk to him, help Mathew understand. He probably sees someone very special to him trying to end her life and there's confusion. He's feeling guilt, anger, betrayal."

Brittany scratched her head. "How so?"

Mrs Xiang explained. "Boy meets girl. Boy cares for girl. Boy upsets girl and girl tries to kill herself. It's all his fault."

"Surely he's not that stupid."

Melanie knew better. "This is my brother, remember?"

"Do I need to talk to him about this?"

"Not much to talk about?" Melanie joked, "and I'm so gonna be a fly on the wall. I wouldn't miss this."

Nicole entered Brittany's room with Jenny and Mathew. "I hear I missed your session. I'm sorry, Brit. I thought it was later. How'd it go?"

"It went well. She's nice. Melanie and I did all the talking. So, how'd your day go?"

"There's a resort in a little region called the Okanagan and there has been more than one drowning there. I just got back from the place, took the pup. We'll have to go there in order for you to see it. It's in British Columbia."

"How, when I'm stuck here?"

Nicole thought for a second. "At night. I've seen it so I can render you there." She ignored the stares from Jenny and Mathew. "What? We check it out and we're back. It'll only take a minute."

Jenny broke the silence. "You *do* know the rules, don't you?"

"We need answers. I can't worry about rules right now."

Melanie agreed. "How can I help?"

Chapter twenty-four

The aroma of Jack's coffee filled the morning air as he cast his line into the water. The weekend ritual was a great coffee, a quiet mountain lake, his boat, and a fishing rod. He had twelve hours to enjoy his solitude. Then his wife would expect him home for supper.

She often had his favourite meal ready for him. Predictably, it would be some form of chicken with mashed potatoes. He'd been spoiled like that ever since the doctor diagnosed his mild chest pain as a heart attack. Work had taken a back seat to play, and his wife had learned a dozen different ways to cook chicken. He took another deep breath as he enjoyed this new freedom.

The sun had finally climbed into view and was quickly burning off the chill of the morning mountain air. The mist had faded from the lake, exposing the still calm water. Slight ripples formed around his boat and slowly began their long journey to the shore. He watched them as he waited for the next fish to nibble on his line.

Often, he was skunked, but that didn't matter. Whether he brought a fish home or not wasn't important. There was always a good story to tell. Several weeks ago, a mature Bull Moose went for a swim across the narrow end of the lake. Last week it was a black bear in a tree.

For that reason, he started bringing his camera. You never knew what you'd run across and today was no exception. He raised his camera and started to focus on the two figures that had just appeared out of nowhere.

Brittany watched as the man in the boat started to snap picture after picture. "Mom, I think we have company."

Nicole had also spotted him. "Yeah. I'll bet he wasn't expecting us. Well, does any of this look familiar?"

Her ponytail swung from side to side as she shook her head. Part of the old lodge still stood, and she headed for it. She leaned down and tried to get some kind of vibe from touching the concrete.

There was nothing, so she looked back toward the lake. The scene was beautiful, but was it her lake? The mountains and fields framed the water like a picture, and the man in the red boat was that splash of color it needed to make it a postcard, but where was the beach?

Brittany made her way back to the lakeshore to check for a dock. Nicole's gaze never left her daughter as she searched for anything familiar. Neither of them saw any rotted posts in the water, but that didn't mean there wasn't one back in the day.

Jack caught their eye as he came to shore. "Name's Jack and I've seen some pretty peculiar things on this lake, but I think they've all been topped." He stepped out of his boat into the ankle-deep water before pulling his boat up on the shore.

"I'm sorry if we startled you." Nicole had learned her gift of rendering was a bit much for most people.

"No, it's great to meet you. Mind if I take a picture? The wife will never believe this story."

Brittany found it ironic that he had asked after shooting so many already. "Sure." Never shy of the camera, Brittany had always hammed it up. After a couple of clicks she stopped him. "I have a question."

Jack dropped his camera to his waist. "Shoot."

Brittany giggled and looked down at his camera. He got it, and also gave a chuckle. "What was this place?"

He cleared his throat. "I used to come here as a kid. My father took me fishing. We'd get up before the sun and the boat would be in the water before the fish woke up. This place shut down about forty years ago. It was the same year I went off to college. I became a chartered accountant, working seven days a week and this place became a forgotten treasure. Life has a way of doing that to these places."

"Had anybody ever drowned here?" Nicole inquired.

"There were three different incidents that I remember. Two of them were old men like me. Blame it on fishing derbies that focused on drinking… tragic, but inevitable. The third was a pretty young woman who drowned just off the shore."

That had Brittany's interest. "How old was she?"

"About twenty if I remember right. Such a cute young thing."

"What happened to her?"

Jack's gaze drifted off for a second while he recollected the story. He had told it so many times. "It was the usual start to a usual day. She was spotted in the water and pulled out by a guy who wasn't supposed to be here. He'd just driven up on the spur of the moment. He said his secretary had mentioned what a wonderful time her kids had here, the week before. These lodges relied on word of mouth, you know."

Brittany didn't much care for his long-winded way of telling a tale. "So, what happened to her?"

Jack looked at her like she wasn't paying attention. "Well, she died of course."

"No, I mean how did she die?"

"Drowned." His voice remained calm.

Brittany struggled to find a different way of asking the same question. "Was it foul play?"

"Yes, it had to be. She was a brilliant swimmer, two awards for record breaking swims in the Okanagan Regatta."

Nicole wondered. "What's that?"

"Big race around these parts. Starts in Peachland and ends up at Rattlesnake Island. It's about a mile."

Brittany felt a shiver. "Rattlesnake Island? Gross!"

"No. No. There's not too many snakes there anymore."

"All it would take is one."

"A mile's a pretty long swim," Nicole noted. "So, it was murder?"

"Had to be. She wasn't the type to drown just offshore."

Brittany pushed for more. "And they found her by the dock?"

"Dock? There's no dock." He looked at her oddly. "No, she was found right over there."

Brittany started in the direction he was pointing. "Are you sure about that?"

"Oh, I'd have remembered if there was ever a dock here."

Brittany looked out over the water and then back to her mother. Nicole was wearing the same deflated look. "Thank you, but I'm gonna head back." She disappeared.

Nicole thanked the man and followed her daughter's lead.

Chapter twenty-five

Brittany tossed and turned for most of the night. She had trouble falling asleep after returning from Canada. Melanie stayed by her side and wrestled with the idea of going for a walk, but walking wasn't why she was there.

Meanwhile, Nicole couldn't sleep and spent the night searching for more resorts. She arrived at the ward the following morning. Melanie and Brittany were already enjoying breakfast. "Hi girls."

"Hi, Mom."

"The eggs are good here, if you're wondering," Melanie added as she stuffed the last bite into her mouth. "I'm going now. I'll be back tonight."

Brittany nodded. "I'll walk you out. Back in a second, Mom."

"Sure." Nicole nodded in a way that Einstein might have nodded to his wife after doing a night's worth of calculations on relativity.

Partway down the hallway the girls ran into Manchu. Melanie elbowed Brittany for an introduction.

"Hi Manchu. This is my friend Melanie. She came to visit me from the States."

He gave her a brief glance and quickly dropped his eyes to the floor.

Melanie noticed a hint of a smile before it vanished.

Manchu took a step back. "Maybe I'll see you at the meeting tonight."

Melanie couldn't pull her eyes off him as he walked away. "Hey, Brit. What meeting is he talking about?"

"Confessionals. It's a thing they do here. We'll all share our stories."

"I don't have a story. Can I still go to it?"

"Of course, you can. We all have something."

"What's his story?"

Brittany paused. "That's something he needs to tell you."

"Okay, but bed sounds good right now. I'll see you tonight."

Brittany waited until Melanie got on the elevator. She doubted a love connection once she'd heard his story, but Mel was always full of surprises.

Nicole was waiting for her with Mrs Xiang. "We have company, Brit."

"I'm not afraid."

Mrs Xiang didn't laugh. "The three of us need to talk."

Brittany shrugged. "About what? Mom knows my story and she believes me. She knows I wouldn't make it up."

"Nobody's calling you a liar. Your commitment to the story is obvious. Can we talk about your arrival on Earth and the meeting of you and your father?"

"Not much of a story." She thought for a second. "We got here, I met everyone and that included my father. It all went well, and Mom was relieved to hear that I had no intentions of living with him. I had a good visit with Jenny and her kids. When I got home, I had these wild and realistic dreams. Supposedly, I then tried to commit suicide. I'm not sure what the dreams have to do with the suicide, but I'll bet Cassandra does."

"From what I've seen, I believe that you wouldn't intentionally try to harm yourself." She stopped and eyed Nicole again. "These dreams, however, are dangerous. It's rare to dream through another person's eyes."

"What do you mean?" Brittany asked.

Mrs. Xiang looked over to Nicole, knowing she was thinking the same thing. "There are two possible reasons for these dreams. One is telepathic, where someone is sending you these thoughts. That seems to be the version you're both sold on, and that's fine. The more common cause is... schizophrenia."

Brittany coughed. It was like her saliva had gone down the wrong pipe when she swallowed. "Seriously?"

"I haven't seen any signs of a second personality, but you're smart. A second personality would follow suit."

"The other night I dreamt I'd died. If I was her, and I died, then how would I be sending those thoughts?"

Mrs. Xiang leaned forward. "You dreamt you died?"

"I was pushed into the lake and held under. When I sank to the bottom, I saw somebody else there. Then I was pulled out and people were trying to resuscitate me. I remember wanting to render out of there, but I couldn't. What I don't understand is, who was thinking about rendering, me, or her?"

"If you had another personality, she'd know how to render. Did they revive you?"

"I'm not sure. Why?"

"Dreams are strange. A dream of your own death could mean you're going through a positive transition in your life."

"That's a good thing, right?"

"It could also mean there's an alter ego and it's stronger than you. And there's nothing bothering you? Think hard."

"Nothing worth dying for."

Mrs Xiang left Brittany with one more thing to think about. "Who is Cassandra, and is she really dead?"

Brittany was happy to see Mrs Xiang leave. "What if Mrs Xiang is right?"

Nicole had to agree with the two personalities in conflict theory, but what had triggered it? "I have to find this lodge."

"Is she right?"

"I have no idea, but we need answers. There's another lodge that fits the description. It's in Colorado. I need to check it out."

"Okay." She gave her a hug and walked her out. "Do you think I should have told her I read my mother's journal?"

"Nah, you weren't bothered by it."

"It's great that you two cared so much for each other. Are you gonna be back tomorrow?"

Nicole looked surprised. "I'll see you tonight."

"Take a break and get some sleep. Have a bath and relax. You look like crap." She gave her an apologetic smile. "I've got company tonight. Mel and Mathew are swinging by. Manchu might tell his story and we're gonna give Mathew an intervention."

"Maybe I'll take you up on that. I don't need the drama, but I'll swing by for breakfast."

"Breakfast sounds good and hey, I saw you with somebody a day or two ago, before I came up to the crazy ward. I was going to ask about him, but things have been a little bizarre. Who was he?"

"Oh, just the guy that found you. He wanted to see if you were okay, nothing more."

Brittany studied her mother. "Why don't I believe you?"

Chapter twenty-six

The sun was setting in Port-au-Prince, Haiti, as a silver Rolls Royce left the Gomez compound. It was accompanied with a black SUV and two motorcycles. The iron gate closed behind the vehicles. This was Victor's cue to step out from the trees.

Benny dropped his cigarette on the ground and stepped on it with a twist. "How'd you know they'd be leaving?"

"I arranged a dinner party for them."

"Shouldn't you be there then?" Rose asked.

"I wasn't invited, and nobody knows I'm in town."

Benny's jaw dropped as he cuffed Rose in the back. "Why would anybody care if he was there?"

Rose swatted back at him and answered as if her and Victor were long-time friends. "He owns the place."

"What, the restaurant?"

"No. The country, ya moron."

"Huh?"

"This is Victor Wains-whatever." She said as if it might mean something to Benny. It did not. He'd never voted, read a newspaper, or owned a television. He had no idea how politics worked or that a single man could own a country, nor could he believe it.

"If that's what this guy told you then he yanked your chain. I bet he doesn't even own a house. Probably lives in his truck."

Victor let the two argue while he watched the security cameras on the corners of the building. He scrutinised the guards as they passed and studied the man in the rocking chair on the front veranda. If he wanted to get in, he'd need a distraction.

"Okay," Victor ordered, "I need you two to go down to the front gate and put on a show."

"How do you want us to do that?" Benny asked.

"Take your argument down there. Go streaking, have sex, or start playing crystal meth twister in the driveway."

Rose punched him in the arm. "I'm not getting naked."

"Then do something simple. Throw rocks at them."

"They'll arrest us."

"And I'll bail you out. You know I'm good for it. Just make sure it keeps them busy for a few minutes."

Benny liked the idea and crouched down to collect a few rocks.

Rose quickly lit a cigarette. "I don't know about this, Victor."

"You don't get any money if I don't get the necklace, so throw rocks, get naked, or knock out a few back flips. Figure it out and do it now." He turned to Benny. "And you…"

Benny was gone. He'd already moved down to the gate and was ready to throw that first rock. It landed on the veranda and rolled into the front door. That got the one guy out of the rocking chair.

"What you doing, you stupid shit?"

The next rock bounced once and hit the man in the shin.

"Guards! Grab that idiot."

The two guards headed for the gate. Benny started to laugh and hurdled a rock at one of the cars parked by the garage. It hit the trunk of a Volvo.

Rose ran over to stop him. "What are you doing?"

Benny tossed her a rock. "I'll give you a cigarette if you can hit the house. I bet you can't even hit the front steps."

Rose wished he hadn't said that. She couldn't pass on a challenge. She threw the rock and half spun herself to the ground. The rock not only hit the house, but it broke a window.

"Great shot."

"Damn it." Rose grabbed his arm and dragged him to the nearest tree. "Climb!"

Benny did as he was told. It made sense. The gate was opening and the men with the guns were coming out. He'd have climbed faster, had he dropped the rocks. He didn't. Rose was ahead of him and led them to one of the higher branches.

"Why are you climbing so high? The higher we go, the farther we'll fall when they shoot us."

Rose got herself comfortable. "They won't shoot us, not for a broken window."

Benny thought for a second. "Cool."

He locked an arm around the branch and fired another rock at the cars. That one bounced off the hood of a Mercedes. As the guards approached the tree, he threw a rock at them.

"Ha! What are you gonna do about it?"

The one guard picked the rock up and rifled it back at him. It hit him square in the forehead. That knocked him loose and he bounced off a branch as he fell to the ground. The man in the rocking chair jumped Benny and flipped him face down. Then, he threw a fist into his ribs.

"Get down from that tree, or I'll put this shit in the hospital."

Rose thought about it as she heard a siren start up in the distance. What did she care if Benny got knocked around? He was the dumb shit that stole the necklace from her. Then he sold it for a few hundred dollars. How much of that money did she get? "Go ahead and shit kick him."

"What?" Benny tried to look up at her. "I thought we were friends."

"Friends? You smell like a urinal." She held her hands up. "Doesn't he? Smell him."

"We're gonna fuck this guy up if you don't get down from that tree."

"What did you say? You wanna fuck him? Seriously?" She shook her head. "Cause you didn't strike me as the type."

The guy punched Benny hard in the ribs. "I'm seriously gonna hurt this asshole?"

"I don't think you have it in ya. He's too high to feel the pain, but you're welcome to keep trying."

The guy wanted to hit Benny again, but there wasn't much point. She'd have cheered him on. Instead, he grabbed a handful of rocks and started throwing them at her. It was the third rock that took her down. By the time she hit the dirt, the sirens had closed in on them. A police car pulled up and Rose wasn't sure if that was a good thing or bad.

Two officers exited the first car. "What's going on here?"

"These two were throwing rocks at the house, and at the cars."

"You pressing charges?"

The guy from the rocking chair thought for a second. These two would get fed in jail. They'd get a good night's sleep and breakfast. They didn't deserve that. He released Benny and stepped on his hand, accidentally on purpose.

"Opps." He faked a smile. "Just get them out of here. If I see them again, we'll deal with them old school."

They were loaded into the back of the car and taken back to Benny's apartment. Victor showed up in a police car two minutes later. He walked into the place with the necklace, gave each of the officers a couple hundred dollars, and walked them back to the squad car.

Back inside, he held the necklace up. The gaudy purple stone glistened as if alive. "So how does this thing work?"

Benny took it from Rose and placed around Victor's neck. "Feel anything?"

"Not really."

A toothless smile spread across Benny's face. "But you want to, right?"

"That's why we stole it."

"And you're sure about this?"

"Damn it, Benny. I'm sure already."

Benny knew it took more than throwing it around your neck to get the full effect. "Okay then." He walked into the kitchen, opened the cookie jar, and lifted a .44 magnum out of it.

Rose saw the gun and took a step back.

Victor didn't see the gun until Benny pointed it at him and fired six shots into his chest.

Chapter twenty-seven

C hyou and Brittany were sitting in the cafeteria playing crib when Melanie and Mathew caught up with them. They had finished supper and Chyou looked noticeably different. Not overly done, it was a nice change from dreary.

Melanie noticed right away. "Wow, Chyou. You look solid."

Chyou looked over to Brittany. "That's good, right?"

"Five by five." Brittany's earthly slang was a language of its own. "What's new with you guys. Good to see you, Mathew."

Mathew forced a smile after a scolding from his sister on the elevator ride up. "Good to see you too."

"You guys missed supper."

Melanie grinned. "My fault. We had something on the way. Where's Manchu?"

Chyou answered, "he had an emergency."

Brittany looked at her with a cocked brow. "Is he okay?"

"No idea. I just heard myself."

Brittany got to her feet. "Shall we head back to my room?"

They left the cafeteria and nested on Brittany's bed. She decided to start. "I have the chance to be a superhero." She stopped as if waiting for applause. "Seriously. I have a gift. I'm gonna use it to help a girl named Cassandra! She's the one in my dreams."

Chyou cut her off. "Is this what you talked about in today's session?"

"She's sending the dreams to me, or maybe I'm pulling them from her. I'm not sure." She looked over to Mathew whose stare was lost in her words. "What?"

He shook his head. "I'm trying, but you're not making it easy."

"I hope you get over this soon. I'm tired of you thinking I'm some nut job."

Mathew stared her down before getting up and leaving the room. He didn't want to say anything he'd regret. By saying nothing, he'd done as much, if not more. Melanie started to get up and Brittany grabbed her arm.

"Let him go, Mel." She didn't want them fighting on her account. "Give him time. How about we switch gears and turn this confessional into a going away party? It's Chyou's last night here."

Chyou beamed. "That sounds like fun."

Melanie started for the door. "I noticed a store a block down the street. I'm going to get some party stuff. Be right back."

The evening started with chips and dip and ended with a cake that said, 'Happy Birthday Shiro'. Melanie had two slices and, after the sugar had run its course, conked out beside Brittany in her bed. Chyou was in her own bed, and snoring.

Brittany was startled when Manchu popped his head into the room. "Chyou, you sleeping?"

"She's out," Brittany answered. "How ya doing? I heard you had an emergency."

"Oh hi. We can talk tomorrow."

"Wait up." Brittany slid herself out and set a pillow under Melanie's head. "What happened?"

"It was my father. He got beat up in prison." He looked down.

"Mathew bailed, so we celebrated Chyou's freedom with cake. Just a few card games and giggly girl stuff."

"Sounds like fun."

"Hey, do you still wanna play the old spill your guts game?"

"I'd rather talk about space."

"Boring." She followed him out and told him about Cassandra, the gaudy stone and how her eyes had changed colour. She finished up by telling him a bit about her home planet. "You're turn, and a warning, on Alzie we're practical, which means we don't hold back."

"I prefer that." He started, "thing is, I've done some horrible things. I'm afraid you won't understand."

"Were you not listening to my story?" Brittany took his hand and walked him to the window. "You trust me?"

"Sure."

"Gimme a hug."

He awkwardly did as he was told.

The night air was crisp and felt good compared to the stale hospital. Manchu looked down at his bare feet on the damp grass. The blades tickled his toes.

"Wow." He looked up at the window. "Did we just…"

"Climb! Before anybody sees us."

They clambered up to the second branch.

She took a second to catch her breath. "You can talk to me."

He paused. There was no good starting point. "When I was a kid, my father used to beat me. I never understood why. One night, my sister started in on me. He hated them too, so I gave it back to her. She ended up crying. I thought I was a goner, but nothing happened. It seemed to stop my beatings."

"That's so wrong."

"By the time I turned seven, I was quite the shit. My sisters hated me. Vicious cycle."

"Were they ever trying to get back at you?"

"They would corner any girl I got close to… tell them I was too fond of them." He stopped.

Brittany grabbed his hand. "You can stop if this is too hard."

He gripped her hand tight as the first tear fell. "My mother sided with them."

"What the hell?"

"It happened two years ago."

"What happened?"

"I'm not sure. I blacked out and when I came to, I was in handcuffs. My mother was being wheeled out on a stretcher and my sisters were dead. Mom died in the hospital."

"Were you okay?"

"I was, but I couldn't remember anything, other than the voices. In court my father told the jury he suspected I was having sex… with my sisters. It was a lie. You must believe me."

"I do."

"Then, some last-minute evidence put a bunch of holes in my father's alibi."

"So, he did it?"

"Court couldn't decide. Dad went to jail, and I was sent here."

Brittany wanted to push for more but didn't. "I should get you back."

"You don't know what to think, do you?" Manchu asked.

"I don't think you're bad, if that's what you're asking." Although she did have her doubts, and those doubts made her uneasy. But her gut told her he was okay. She pulled him in for a hug and in a split second, they were both inside his room.

"I've never told anybody any of this."

"I appreciate you sharing this with me." Brittany started for the door. "One thing."

"Yes."

"You said you blacked out, but you heard voices?"

"For weeks, in my head. They kept telling me to kill them."

"Your sisters?"

"The voices just said, them."

Brittany made her way back to her own bed and tried to slip into it without waking Melanie. Mel rolled over to give her room and asked, "Where you been?"

"Go back to sleep." She pulled Melanie close and stared at the ceiling. After what she'd heard, she'd hoped for a peaceful sleep.

The distraction had helped her forget about the dreams, but the dreams remembered her.

Chapter twenty-eight

Victor couldn't feel the life draining from his body like he usually did when he'd been shot. Everything happened too fast. So, what was this, a coma? It couldn't be. He had heard multiple shots. Benny had emptied the clip into his chest. Nobody could have survived that. He had to be dead, and since heaven had been ruled out years ago, this had to be hell. And yet, here he was, standing at the edge of a swimming pool, wondering why he was the one skimming the bugs and leaves out of it.

"Hey, Buddy. Can we go swimming yet?"

The man asking was in his late thirties and the bikini-clad woman beside him had to be his wife, or girlfriend. Another woman appeared from the house. She was carrying a pitcher of sangria.

"I made your favourite, Darling."

Darling? Victor did a shoulder check. Was she talking to him? He set the strainer down and couldn't stop staring. She was a redhead, a gorgeous redhead, with blue eyes. Was he that darling? The thought put a smile on his face.

"Honey?" She set the pitcher down on the table beside some glasses that she'd taken out earlier. "Are you okay?"

She walked over to him and put a hand on his chest. Her eyes looked up and fixed on his. They were soft, caring eyes, and they peered into his like he was the only one in the world worth looking at. He couldn't remember the last time a woman looked at him like that.

He gave her a wink, and then looked down at her hand, and then at his chest. Where were the bullet holes?

"Darling?"

Victor shook the thought. "I'm good, Sweetheart. I was daydreaming and got a little lost in it."

"I think somebody needs a drink," she joked. "Just kidding. I hope I was in it with you."

He felt a need to explain but didn't. What would he tell her, that a junkie named Benny had just emptied a clip into him, that he should be dead? Maybe he is, except this didn't feel dead. "I, uh, have been thinking about writing a novel. Maybe something based in Haiti or Cuba."

"That sounds fascinating, Dear. What would it be about?"

He had to think fast. "Drugs, gunfights, and car chases."

Buddy's girlfriend gave a giggle. "Really? What do you know about that stuff? They say you should stick to what you know. Write a novel about accounting."

Her boyfriend quickly weighed in. "Who'd read a book about tax nerds. Nah, I like the drug aspect. Make it about a Canadian who grows marijuana in his basement."

"His basement, Brad?" the girlfriend snapped. "Who grows weed in the basement?"

"They all do up there, Julie." He sarcastically enunciated each syllable of her name.

Victor cut in. "Actually, Brad's right. They rent these huge executive homes under assumed names and gut them. They cut huge holes in the floors for ventilation and the humidity is crazy, black mould everywhere. The houses are write-offs after a couple of crops. When the landlords get the houses back, they have to tear them down and rebuild. A good crop though, can yield a payoff of about a million and a half."

They all stood in silence.

"What? I watched a thing on the news." He paused. "It was very informative."

The redhead walked over to the table and poured the drinks. "I don't care what he writes. I'm going to be his number one fan."

"Thanks, Dear." Somehow, he'd have to figure out her name. His friends were Brad and Julie. He let her pour the drinks and took one. He wasn't sure of much, but he was sure that this was his house, his pool, and his wife, so he gave her a kiss. Her lips were velvety soft.

"Any time, my Hemingway."

"Not Hemingway, Lucy," Brad corrected. "He needs to write like a James Patterson. That guy sells books."

Lucy almost choked on her drink. "Please. You're going to compare James Patterson to Hemingway?"

"Of course not. Hemingway hasn't even penned half the books that James has, right Buddy?"

"I'm going to take her side on this one, Brad. Everyone knows Hemmingway."

"You mean everyone has a James Patterson sitting on the nightstand."

Julie looked over to Victor for approval before pushing Brad into the pool. He lost his balance, started to fall in, and managed to grab her hand. She followed.

Lucy frowned. "Hey. No drinks in the pool."

Victor scooped her up and ran for the deep end.

"What are you doing? I have a drink. Stop…"

The splash of water landed on the dry cement turning it dark. Lucy surfaced and immediately started to round up the stray pieces of fruit floating in the water. "What's got into you?"

Victor laughed. Whatever this was, death or a dream, he liked it. There was no knowing how long it would last, but he'd make the best of it. Just like that, he wasn't a lone wolf. He had friends and a wife, and even though she was drenched and upset, she was beautiful.

"I'm just getting ready for a life of fame as a paperback writer." He swam to the side of the pool. "We celebs get crazy sometimes. Better get used to it."

"Paperback writer, like the Beatles." Brad held up a glass of pool water. "I like it. To the paperback writer."

"I like it too," Victor replied as he scooped up a grape and tossed it onto the lawn.

"Beats our day jobs at the mall, right?"

Victor's smile wilted. Again, another question came up. What was this day job? Something about taxes. "Uh, eight days a week."

"Ha, another Beatles thingy. You're on a roll." Brad was impressed. "Where was this wit on charades night?"

"Sorry. It'll be there, next time. Promise."

"Then you'll be my partner," Brad announced.

"Not a chance." Lucy swam over to Victor and latched on. "This crazy paperback boy is mine, today, tonight, and the next time we play charades."

Victor gave her another kiss. He pressed his body against hers and she eagerly welcomed his touch. Suddenly, he was thinking about tonight. She said he was hers.

"Vincent," she giggled. "I'm not sure what's happening, but I like this new writer persona you've developed."

Victor closed his eyes and fought the urge to throw up. "Vincent?"

Chapter twenty-nine

*W*ith her pants almost dry from the campfire, Brittany
stared into its dancing flames hoping to spark a few
clues. Seven people, that was the count including
herself and she knew none of them, and yet they knew her. A
mission of sorts was the reason for their gathering at such a remote
swampy location and Brittany wanted to know why. Trying to ask
wasn't as easy as she thought. She was Cassandra, and Cassandra
knew everything already, didn't she?

*Just then one of the girls walked up to her and asked. "Are you
mad at Kim. He feels you're upset about something."*

*"No. I can't explain, but I really don't feel like myself right
now. So, what's the deal?"*

*"Kim says his dad can find out who this crazy guy is with the
weapon. If he does, we're all going to stop him."*

*"What kind of weapon are we talking about?" Brittany's eyes
almost popped out of her head as she spoke.*

"What's wrong Cassandra? Hasn't Kim told you everything?"

*"I don't think so. Let's walk and talk." She grabbed the girl's
arm and they headed off into the woods. "What's the weapon and
why?"*

*She gave Cassandra a puzzled look. "Kim says somebody
wants to unleash some wild new creation."*

"In the city?"

*"We're not sure. Maybe the city, maybe the Forbidden Zone.
I'm kind of surprised he hasn't told you this."*

"He has, but I knocked my head earlier. It's there, in bits and pieces." Brittany knew she was supposed to know what this place was, but that wasn't how these dreams worked. Should she ask? They'd likely think something was wrong.

Her friend shook her hand. *"Okay you. Where did you put Cassandra?"* Her laugh was loud. *"Seriously."*

"I'm right here."

She looked over Cassandra's shoulder. He was approaching. *"I'm gonna leave you two to talk."*

He threw the girl a friendly smile as if to thank her for leaving. Brittany had to think fast.

"Hey, so why are you mad at me?"

"Me mad at you? I thought you were mad at me?" He backed the macho down a notch.

It was a ploy that never failed. *"Then... you don't hate me?"*

"Of course not."

"I'm glad to hear." Her eyes softened. *"Did you just see your father? Does he know who this maniac is?"*

"Not yet." He looked at her and smiled. *"But we'll figure this out. We've prevented the extinction of animals and always looked at the big picture. It's who we are."* He rolled up his sleeve to reveal his tattoo. A pair of hands holding a globe had several doves circling above it. *"We're The Keepers, right?"*

She smiled as if she knew what that meant. Just like she suddenly knew there was an identical tattoo on her left hip.

"Brittany. Are you awake?"

Brittany awoke and tried to focus. She muttered under her breath. "Kim?"

Melanie straightened up. "Kim? Who's Kim?"

"Oh, sorry Mel. I was having another dream."

"Do tell."

"I uh, there was something about some halfwit going to use some new age weapon on the Forbidden Zone. I'm not sure where that is, but I heard something about the thinnest part of the planet's crust. I don't know if it's in out future or Cassandra's. Either way, Earth is going to be toast if we don't stop him."

"I've never heard of a Forbidden Zone."

"Me neither, but when Mom gets here, I have a huge lead for her. I was part of some group that protects the world."

"Greenpeace?"

"No. These guys call themselves 'The Keepers'. Ever heard of them?"

"Can't say I have. Hey, your eyes were blue when you first woke up. What's up with that?"

"You saw that?" Brittany gasped. "Those were Cassandra's eyes. The doctor said he saw them too."

Melanie had been humouring Brittany because that was what a friend did, but this was real. What was also real was her interest in Manchu. It was her reason for waking Brittany in the first place.

"Can I ask you something, about somebody, or is this a bad time?"

Chapter thirty

At breakfast, Brittany and Melanie looked like girls with a secret. While Jenny had seen these two in action before, and had become relaxed with their ways, Nicole was put off this time. "What's the joke already?"

Brittany chuckled. "Nothing. I think we're still wired on our good-bye birthday cake."

"Glad to hear, because Virgil needs me to go to Mars today. He's found a way into those hollows. He wants to show me something before he makes his findings public."

Melanie put her fork down. "But we…"

She was immediately cut off. "That's great, Mom. Go and take your camera. Get lots of pictures. They'll be a welcome distraction from this place."

"And you're okay with me taking off for a night?"

Melanie started to put a hand up. "But…"

"Totally fine, Mom. I'm on a better path. Besides, I've got these two to watch my back. When would you leave?"

Nicole raised a brow. "You're overselling. What's up?"

"It's nothing. I was told my eyes were blue when I woke up."

"That's nothing?"

"It's all good. Go see Virgil and say hi for me." She quickly added, "I'll be okay, I promise."

One hour later, Virgil was meeting Nicole at the main entrance. He noticed the camera around her neck.

"Good idea. We can document these crates as we open them."

"Crates?" Nicole asked.

"I've found a warehouse full of them. I might have accidentally done a walkthrough of the place. Sorry." He couldn't help himself.

"An accidental walkthrough? Don't worry." She knew she would have done the same. "Did you open any of them?"

"Not yet, so let's hurry. Hey, what's with that?" He referred to the artifact she was holding.

"I'm killing two birds with one stone. I need to ask Frederich about it."

"Does this have anything to do with Brittany?" He had questions about her being admitted but was waiting for the right time to bring them up. "How's she doing?"

"Better. There hasn't been any drama in a while, but she's got some wild nightmares going on. I need to ask my ghost pal if this thing has any kind of Voodoo powers, or the ability to release some kind of spirit world."

Virgil stood there with his mouth open. He'd have taken a step back except he didn't want her knowing he was afraid of her demonic jewellery. "Uh, good luck with that."

Nicole sighed and offered him the bag she'd been carting around.

"What's this?"

"The second payment for that painting. I figured I'd study it further now that it's framed and hanging in my living room. It really is a wonderful piece of art."

As a partner in crime, he opened his compensation. His eyes lit up as he plunged his hand in for a couple of the sweets and pulled out a comic book. "Nice! Those last ones were intriguing. Such a clever concept."

"I'm glad you're liking them. I've put some Calvin and Hobbs comics in there too. You'll die laughing when you read them."

Vigil carefully put the bag down. "I guess I'll have to be careful then."

Nicole had to wonder how this man could be so brilliant and stupid at the same time. "It's a figure of speech. I doubt laughing could make you croak."

"Of course, I know that. We should go see the hollows."

They wove their way through the caves until they reached the openings. Several hollows had been accessed by a few of the scientists, but not the warehouse area with the crates. He'd kept it off limits. The tunnels had been sprayed with their webbing and were secure. The low ceilings even had Nicole ducking as she walked beneath them.

"We're here."

The size of the room was impressive. Nicole pointed over to some tools. "Grab a pry bar."

Off to the right there was a tool bench. He grabbed two flattened bars and handed her one as they walked up to the nearest crate.

"Let's get started," Virgil said as he dug the end of the tool into the wood.

At first, they were mindful, methodical, and took pictures as they pried the boxes open. Adequate time was taken to document every aspect of their finds. Before long they were opening a little more randomly, and before the hour was up, they were cracking the cases open like children cracking eggs at Easter.

"Medical equipment seems to be the flavour of the week," Nicole deduced, but this wasn't your average equipment. It was extravagant.

"Does this seem a little strange to you?" Virgil asked.

"Maybe a little. Where did all this come from, and what was it going to be used for? It is medical, right?"

"I think this one's an incubator." Virgil was thumbing through some of the packing slips. "A lot of this stuff seems to be research equipment. It's pretty sophisticated." He continued to go through the slips.

"And everything's in English," Nicole had noted.

He started shuffling through the manuals. "That's strange in itself, right?"

"Right, and don't mix those up!" She joked as she gave a nervous laugh. "Just in case we have to send this stuff back."

Catching him off guard, Virgil let out a chuckle. It had been a while since Nicole had shared that dry humour of hers. "Send it back... good one."

"And what should we do with everything? Keep it a secret or invite the masses to help us decipher what it is?" She peered into the lens of what looked like a monster-sized microscope with more dials and controls than a helicopter cockpit. "We'll need some serious electricity."

"You think it requires electricity?" Virgil asked.

"Another good question."

"The manuals are in English. I say we look them over ourselves first." He held one of the books up. "Should we split them up?"

"We could do that." She grabbed one of the bigger books and looked for copyright or print locations. There was nothing. "Do you think any of this could have come from Earth?"

"That might make sense, except the Earthlings aren't advanced enough to get it here."

"Not to mention this stuff is thousands of years old," she reminded him.

Virgil continued to flip through the pages. "It's not only a manual, but schematics, parts lists, troubleshooting sections and a history on how it was invented, explaining why they built certain aspects the way they did. We should do our manuals like this. It even speculates how it might be improved in future versions."

"This one has a list of labs that are working on future models. All the scientists that were in on its creation are listed." She was impressed and then it hit her again, she was on Mars. "Why is it in English?"

Virgil shook his head. There was no way these people could have fluked such a thing as a language. "Could the Martians have visited Earth, like we did?"

Nicole briefly entertained the thought, set the manual down, and eyed the last crate. It was a lot bigger than the others and yet, in all the excitement, they'd almost forgotten about it. "We still need to open that one." With bar in hand, she started toward it. "Maybe the answer lies within."

This crate was well sealed, and they worked up a sweat prying it open. The sweat was worth the effort. They both stared in awe as they moved the front cover off to the side. Nicole looked to Virgil who was slightly embarrassed. "Is that what I think it is?"

"If you think it's a nude woman pickled in a chamber of purple goo, then yes."

Chapter thirty-one

Moral righteousness was the motto that Victor had always lived by, but even he had his limits. That was why he, after a brief struggle within, decided to show Lucy a night she wouldn't forget. He knew this was Vincent's wife, and that he was an impostor in this world, but in the real world, her should-have-been world, Vincent was the impostor. She never should have met him, because he never should have existed. Maybe that was why Victor did it. She deserved a taste of the real world.

Was the guy really a brother, when he was conjured from a book? Was there a special place in hell for having sex with his widow, after you'd killed him? All good questions, Victor thought.

He didn't ponder those questions for long. Instead, he stripped her down and gave her the night that Vincent couldn't. Victor's conjured self was nice, compassionate, and always put others first. He always thought that was what she wanted. The man was wrong.

"Eggs are scrambled, and there's bacon in the pan," Lucy said as she plucked her briefcase off the floor and shuffled her high heels toward the front door. "Gotta run. Last night was…"

She put her free hand up to her head and then pulled it away to recreate a mind explosion. Victor reached for a plate as he watched her ass sashay out the door. Vincent didn't deserve a woman like that.

After eating, he began rifling through every part of Vincent's life for answers. There was the mail on the counter, the study, and the junk drawer in the kitchen. His wife's maiden name was Wheeler. Lucy Wheeler. Like that wouldn't have been awkward for a child growing up.

Victor also found out, from old pay stubs and tax returns, that he was once a teacher. He was now an accountant for an insurance company because it paid better, much better. The mall, that Brad had referred to, was three blocks away, and the company he worked for didn't open until nine. There was time for more snooping.

Shot six times, Victor had become Vincent Wainsworth, and none of this would have been so bad if he was alive, but he wasn't. This was the stone.

In the closet, Victor found brown and blue suits. In the dresser there was more and more drab. How did Lucy ever fall for this guy, unless she was looking for security? From everything that Victor had seen, Vincent was the guy who would never miss a birthday or a mortgage payment. He was the guy who would get up at three in the morning and drive to the gas station to get you a bag of plain potato chips... all because you had a craving and because he loved you more than anything... more than himself.

And then, there it was. Victor found it in his underwear drawer. It was a small business card. That wasn't spectacular in itself, but the name on it was, Dr Terrance Binghamton M.D., Ph.D. Psychologist. There was an address and a phone number, so Victor made the call.

"Dr Binghamton? It's Vincent." Then he added, "Wainsworth."

"Yes, Vincent. How are you?"

"I was wondering about our next meeting." He was ready. Either there wasn't one, in which he would say that he made one and blame Binghamton's secretary for dropping the ball, or there was one and he'd try to bump it up. People get busy.

"You mean the one today at ten? Are you unable to make it?"

"Just confirming. I couldn't remember what we'd agreed on. The one time I didn't put it in my phone, right?"

"It's ten, Vincent."

"See you then, Doc."

Victor hung up knowing that he must have taken the morning off. Guys like Vincent were organised and would have sorted it out in advance. Why go to work if he'd have to leave a half an hour later. That meant he had time to make a coffee and dig up a few more clues, like why was he seeing a shrink, and did Lucy know about this? The card *was* hidden in an underwear drawer.

Nothing else was found, except no-name coffee, bulk oatmeal cookies, and a fridge without beer. Victor took the car and ended up across town at the shrink's office. It was a posh place, and it didn't look anything like a professional building. It looked more like a centuries-old courthouse or some Turkish bath.

Inside there were no numbers on the doors. There was no directory. There was, however, a waterfall inside, three stories tall. Victor knew right away that this was no ordinary doctor. This was the kind of place you went for a debriefing, after a mission. He took a minute to absorb the surroundings. Everything was a clue and divulged the truth. This was government, definitely something to do with the Divine Ledger, and Vincent's adjustment to being here.

"Vincent." The voice came from behind him. The man put a hand on Victor's shoulder.

He turned and did a quick assessment. This guy looked the part of a high-end shrink. The man was a highly trained manipulator, the type who preyed on your every word. Each syllable was a glimpse into the mind and into his next move.

"Hello, Dr Binghamton."

"Please, come with me. Are you hungry? I haven't eaten yet."

"I could use a coffee."

"Good, because we have a lot to cover today. I hope you did your homework."

"My homework." Victor had gone through drawers and found all kinds of things, but no workbooks or journals. "Of course. You know me."

Chapter thirty-two

Nicole stepped forward and touched the glass. It was cold. Not ridiculously cold, but not anything you'd want to go swimming in either. "Do we open it?"

"Is there a manual?"

Nicole fumbled through the stack of books. "It's not here. What do you think?"

"I say no, unless you want her to decompose. She'll rot as soon as she's opened. I'd give her a week." Then he noticed Nicole's amulet. "Your artifact is glowing."

"Could be a power source messing with this thing. Atomic?" Nicole held the artifact a little closer to the glass. Then she thought about how good the girl in the capsule looked. "And you're right, rotting isn't an option. I'll have to figure this equipment out. Whatever it is, it's been doing its job."

"For thousands of years," he added as he moved in for closer scrutiny of the woman in the chamber. "She looks great. I mean..." He blushed. "I mean for a specimen of its age." He looked for cords, wires, or tubes. There were none. "I can't imagine there's a battery this long lasting."

"Can I trust you with this?" Her question was serious, and Virgil knew it. This was a secret that had to be kept from everyone.

"Of course." He tapped on the glass. "I wish we could draw a sample. She's showing absolutely no signs of deterioration."

Nicole wished the same. "We'll have to see if we can figure out why she's in there. Maybe you can check the manuals for whatever power sources they used. There has to be a reservoir. I'm going to snap a few more photos and then head back. I don't want to miss any of Brittany's sessions."

"Okay."

She snapped her pictures and put the camera and manuals by the main entrance. Then she picked up the artifact and headed off to see Frederich. She entered the room and called out for him. She nosed around and kicked open a few boxes while she waited. Nothing caught her eye.

"Miss Nicole. It's nice to see you again. How can I help you? Are you still on your vacation?"

"Not really. I just have a question about the artifact. You said it was a key, but it seems like it's got its own energy. Is there anything else I should know about this necklace?"

"I know you're looking for a planet that started mankind. We believe this artifact is made up of just that. That stone holds the secret to man's origin. Our people tried to uncover its secrets but couldn't. I'm hoping your people will be more successful."

Nicole thought he was kidding. Then she realised he wasn't. "You're serious."

"I have no reason to lie."

Nicole had another question. It hadn't dawned on her until today. "Where did you learn English?"

"I'm sorry, Miss Nicole, but you're mistaken. I know of no, English."

"What?" She took her eyes off the artifact and looked up quickly. Frederich had faded away. "Get back here. What do you mean? Your English is perfect."

As she made her way back to the entrance, she decided to check out the other hollows. Virgil hadn't made a big deal about them. Offices and corridors seemed to be the general theme. There were some papers, but nothing special. There were hundreds of square thin flat glass plates in filing cabinets. They had to be some form of hardened data film. Had the light destroyed them, or perhaps time? When she held one up to the light, all it did was form a shadow. She took it with her when she left. Maybe there was something on Earth that could activate it.

"Hey Virgil, it's time for me to go. Keep an eye on our girl." She casually held up the square disk. "I'm taking one of these. You have plenty."

"Any luck with the artifact?"

"He said it was from Eve but doesn't know any more than we do. Then he ghosted me."

"Ghosted?"

"Earth term, when you take off on somebody."

"Earthlings are complicated."

"They don't do practical." She started to put her suit on for the return trip. "I wish I knew how they came up with their version of English."

"He called it English?"

"No, but he definitely speaks it very well. Hey, thanks again for keeping me in the loop on everything. Sorry I can't give you more."

"Don't be silly. Brittany needs you. I'll take care of things here. I've got nothing but time on my hands."

As Nicole made her way home, she looked down at one of the manuals.

"Why are you in English?"

Chapter thirty-three

Victor took a reluctant step onto the elevator. The interior of this elevator was as white as the rest of the complex. It wasn't hard-on-the-eyes white, like extra clean linen or white snow. It was more an annoying white. It reminded him of a woman he met. She had alabaster skin, sunglasses, and a big-brow hat that hid her from the sun like a huge umbrella. More importantly, it was the kind of white that you'd expect in a medical research facility.

"So..." Victor wasn't sure what Vincent knew of this place, if he knew anything at all. "What's up for today, Doc?"

"Doc?" The man looked back at him as he swiped his card and hit the twenty-eighth floor button. "I think that's the first time you've ever called me that."

"Sorry." Victor felt the elevator dropping, which made sense. The building was only two stories tall. Most of that was for the legit operations. This elevator was a restricted one and had a full bank of buttons. This was possibly CIA, definitely government.

"No. I like it."

Victor studied the man while the man did the same to him. Was his reaction paranoia or were they friends? Victor chose paranoia. "I've been hanging around with Brad too much."

"You seem nervous."

"It's this place. I always feel a little off when I'm here."

The doctor nodded. "I know. We just need a little blood and a tiny flesh sample." He calmly added, "Routine."

When the elevator doors opened, the smell hit Victor right away. It was an oddly sweet smell that he couldn't place. The best he could come up with was a mix of automotive antifreeze, transmission fluid, and perhaps… marshmallow.

A delicious redhead walked by in a lab smock. Victor couldn't pull his eyes off her. As she passed, she shot him a wink. "Hi, Vincent."

"Good morning."

Dr Binghamton kept walking and stopped at the door to his office. He opened it and let Victor enter first. Victor tried not to stop in his tracks or give away the fact that he'd obviously never been here before.

Inside, the office was quite different than the rest of the building. It was dark cherry wood, granite, and smoked glass. There was a wall of floor-to-ceiling windows with a live view of Manhattan being projected on them.

Victor stepped up to them to get a better look. "I never get tired of this."

"So much better than a painting." The Doctor walked behind his desk and sat down. Then he motioned to the couch. "Have a seat and we'll get started."

Victor obediently did as he was told. It was what Vincent would have done, and he wanted to see what this guy wanted, what he knew. Everyone had wanted to know where Vincent had come from. Vinny was an anomaly and, by the way that redhead had looked at him, he was also a bit of a celebrity.

"What's new Vincent? Are you still having those dreams?"

The answer came quick. "Honest? I've been having a bit of a problem with my memories. I'm not sleeping right, either."

"When did all this start?"

"Have I ever been to Russia?"

"No." He started to jot things down. "Why would you ask that?"

"Just forgetful lately, like my appointment. I had to call to get a time. Stupid, huh. I mean, I bet I'm here all the time, right?"

"No secrets, you visit us a fair bit."

"And why am I here. Am I sick? I can't really recall."

"You have a rare cancer, with a name too difficult to pronounce. It doesn't surprise me that you can't remember. Your illness may be progressing."

"What are these dreams I keep having?"

"Pardon me?"

"You asked if I was still having dreams."

"Just a second." The doctor got up, ripped the top page off the note pad and left the room.

Victor got up and took a seat in his chair. The drawers were full of the usual crap: paper clips, pens, scribble pads. The top of the desk was clean, not even a picture of a wife or child. Victor grabbed the note pad. The doctor had scribbled something and taken the top page with him.

There was a pencil in the drawer, and he started to lightly colour the page with graphite. A single word came up. It read Victor. He'd been made.

Victor checked the door, but the doctor had locked it. He started pulling books out from the bookcase hoping for a hidden door, but there was nothing. He'd just put everything back when the doctor returned. "Everything okay, Dr Binghamton?"

He'd returned with a folder and some medical equipment. "We're good. I just remembered the lab really wanted these samples, sooner than later. That's okay with you, right?"

"I suppose."

Dr Binghamton pulled out a vial and drew a blue substance into a syringe.

"What's that Doc?"

"Don't be concerned. This is nothing."

Victor grabbed his wrist to stop him. "I asked you a question, Doc."

A gun appeared in the other hand of the doctor. "I wasn't asking, Vincent."

Victor held up the paper that had his name. "I say we put an end to this game. What is this place?"

"It's not your concern."

"Bullshit." It only took a split second for Victor to get the gun from him. That was because the doctor was more concerned with sticking him with the needle.

There was a struggled and the doctor couldn't get his arm free. "What did you do with Vincent?"

"You wouldn't believe me if I told you. I'm a little grey on what the hell is going on. I need you to start spilling. Why do you want his blood?"

"You understand what he is, don't you?"

"I know there's a Ledger, a chant, and then there's an unwanted person out there, rippling people's lives and rewriting history." Victor held him tight and squeezed his wrist until he dropped the needle. "I can't say I'm okay with that."

"You have no idea."

"What do you want with him?"

Dr Binghamton stopped squirming for a second. And then with a final surge of strength, he shoved Victor, catching him off guard. They landed against the Manhattan skyline. Victor dropped the gun, but quickly slipped an arm around the doctor's throat. He squeezed until the doctor's body went limp.

Then, he looked back at the large pane of glass. It had popped open as if on a hinge, and was that a hidden room?

"Why, Doc. I do believe you were holding out on me."

Chapter thirty-four

B rittany's day had emotionally torn her apart so the sleep she'd fallen into was deep. Her mother had left for Mars and she had preferred to have her consumed with something other than this damn hospital. The idea that this might have been a ploy for attention was ludicrous. She'd had a lifetime of attention. From Grandma's barrage of blood tests and trips to the lab, to Nicole's constant and undivided care, it had consumed her.

Now on Earth, she was the belle of the ball. She had new friends and a father who gave her all the love she could stomach. Brittany enjoyed every moment, knowing it might not last.

Tonight, her and Mathew had hashed everything out. She had fallen asleep in his arms. Melanie had slept on Chyou's bed, which was now empty.

As Brittany's head lay quietly against Mathew's shoulder, her eyes were slowly turning blue as they fluttered toward another adventure.

"Where are we going now Cassandra?"

It was dark and she was... floating? It felt like floating. Brittany had to wonder, was she still in the water? Was that why she couldn't make out anything? She felt safe though, like there was a presence protecting her. She let the dream play out without panic.

The air was musky, and she found it odd that she could sense that in the water. It reminded her of some of the abandoned caves on Earth. Melanie had taken her there and the smell was like some old dank basement. She felt cool, even chilled, and made a mental note to remember that feeling when it came time to wake up.

Would she wake up? Never had her senses worked so hard. Even in the waters of the swamp she had little recollection of the temperature.

Voices floated in and out of her thoughts like people were talking, but she couldn't make out words or even if it was English.

Suddenly, she saw a hint of light, like her sight was coming back. It was slow and steady. Before long she could see shapes. There were squares and rectangles. Blinking didn't clear the images.

This was a new area. Cassandra hadn't dragged her here before. She tried to blink again, clear her vision, but it didn't help. She tried to move her arms, but they felt extremely weighted. Was she still floating?

And then, one of the larger rectangles started to glow and it seemed mystical. It had powers she could feel, but they were foreign. She felt a contact. It felt like nothing she could explain, and nothing she would ever feel again. The temperature spiked upward for a split second and then dropped even lower than it was before. Floating, she thought. I'm definitely floating.

"Talk to me Cassandra. What is this place?"

"Wake up!"

There was a slap that stung her face.

"What the hell?" Brittany put her hands up to stop a second blow and blinked several times.

"You were dead," Melanie cried.

"What?" Her vision had cleared.

"You were dreaming I guess, but at one point you just stopped breathing." She wiped away a tear. "What happened?"

"Relax. I'm totally breathing." She thought back to the dream. She remembered floating but not breathing. "You can't tell anyone, okay?"

"Are you kidding me?" Mel shook her head. "I just sent Mathew for a nurse. He was shitting himself."

"No! I don't want Mom to worry. Do me a favour and act like you made a mistake. You're no doctor. How could you know for sure?"

"Are you sure you're okay?" Melanie was moving in for one of her famous you-poor-thing hugs.

Brittany pulled away. "Don't! Mom doesn't need this. She'll never get on with her life, and that means I'll never get on with mine. Promise me!"

"Okay but... "

She grabbed Melanie's hand. "This is important to me."

"Okay, but we'll need to talk about this."

Mathew broke in with a nurse and they ran to Brittany.

"I'm fine. They made a mistake. Just a false alarm." She jumped out of bed and twirled around. "See. I'm very much alive and well."

The woman sat her back down and started the vitals, first checking her pulse. "This is a precaution." She felt her forehead for a fever and then pulled out her blood pressure tester. After the nurse had checked her over, she gave Melanie and Mathew a dirty look and left. Her coffee was probably cold by now.

"What the hell!" he exclaimed. "You weren't breathing!"

"Relax," Melanie said. "Her mother doesn't need the grief."

"Who cares who needs what at this point? She was dead!"

"I wasn't dead. I was in some kind of chamber, I think. It was cold inside. I was only in it for a minute."

"And you don't plan on telling your mother?" Mathew asked.

"No! I need to make sense of it first."

Chapter thirty-five

That sweet smell returned stronger than ever when Victor entered the hidden room. It didn't stop him. He looked right and saw a very large television screen. It was split into four. In the upper right corner, He could see the unconscious doctor and the office. The upper left held a picture of a woman sleeping. The shot was a little blurred and had a distracting lavender hue. The bottom of the screen had what appeared to be the vitals of this woman. There was a heartbeat, blood pressure, oxygen volume, temperature and...

Victor had a closer look. This girl was cold. The temperature read forty degrees. It was in Fahrenheit. Still, her heart was beating three times a minute and her lungs were drawing two and a half litres of oxygenated goo in that same time. It was shallow, but sustainable.

Over his shoulder he could see the rest of the room. The other side of the area was a lab, complete with titrators, tube rollers, dry baths, a high-performance liquid chromographer, and incubators. In the centre of the room, he saw what he first thought was a counter. As he got closer, he realised he was wrong.

The countertop was a blackened glass top. Victor found the switch and clicked it. The surface cleared, revealing the woman from the monitors. She was nude and had wireless electrodes stuck to her temples, chest, wrists, inner thighs, and neck. Her body was suspended horizontally in a clear liquid. It had the lavender hue. Victor looked back to the upper left of the screen. It was the same woman.

"What the hell?"

Pulling out his phone, Victor quickly snapped a few pictures before heading back to the office. He rummaged through the inner pockets of the doctor's jacket to find the man's key card. With it, it was time to leave. Whatever all this was, it wasn't his problem. He needed to get out of here, and quickly.

The card worked on the elevator and Victor was cordial to everyone he encountered. That got him out of the building. He reached in his pocket for his car keys. There was nothing. They must have fallen out of his pocket in the scuffle. He dialled Lucy.

She answered on the first ring. "Hello, Darling."

"Hey, Lucy. I need you to pick me up. Can you get away?"

"What's going on? You sound out of breath."

"It's been a rough morning."

"Weren't you supposed to see Dr Binghamton this morning?"

"Long story. I'll fill you in."

"Where are you now? I'll come right away."

Victor looked across the street to a park with a lake. There was a sign. "I'm at Dexter Park."

"Are you okay?"

Victor could hear her voice breaking. His wife sounded scared. "It's okay, Darling. The Doctor pissed me off, and I've lost my keys. That's all."

"Okay." She collected herself. "I'm already on my way."

"Not here though."

"Oh?"

"I need to walk, and I don't relish the idea of hanging around this building."

"Okay. No, I get it. There's a dock on the eastern side of the lake. There's also a parking lot. I'll meet you there in about five minutes."

"Thanks, Honey."

"Just stay put when you get there."

Chapter thirty-six

Mrs Xiang walked into Brittany's room and sat down with her and Nicole. "I'm glad I caught up with the two of you today. I was hoping to talk about last night."

Nicole needed to be brought up to speed. "Last night?"

"It was nothing, Mom, and it was this morning. I'm a sound sleeper. You know that. Well, I guess Mathew checked on me and thought I wasn't breathing and freaked out. He even got them to come and check me out. It was nothing more than a mistake on his part. You can ask Mel. Ask the nurse on staff. I'm still breathing."

"What did you dream about last night?" Mrs. Xiang asked.

"Nothing important. I was trying something."

Nicole moved back in her chair. "What would that be?"

"I'm trying to control my dreams. I should be able to, to some degree. Don't you think?"

Mrs Xiang wrote that down. "Why do you need to control these dreams?"

Brittany knew that this was bait. Mrs Xiang wanted her to talk about helping Cassandra. Brittany knew she was no superhero, and she had never claimed to be. She did however feel Cassandra was reaching out to her.

"If I control my dreams, then I control my life. Isn't that right?"

"Do you mean control like manipulate, or control like understand?"

"I mean control like fall asleep without worrying about what happens next. I'm sure that's what Mom wants too."

Nicole spoke up. "This isn't about me."

"It's about all of us, about balance, and about getting everything in perspective. I was talking to Manchu and his issues dwarf mine. And not just him, these poor kids have had it rough. My life has fulfilled all my needs. I'd be the last one to complain about having it rough. I lost Elizabeth, but so did Nicole. I'm sure it's been harder on you. I just want a simple life."

"Well Brittany, that's a positive attitude," Mrs Xiang said as she got up to leave. "And that's exactly what we need."

"Thanks, Mrs Xiang. See you later."

Nicole let the woman leave. "That was quite the performance, Brittany."

"She's super predictable. Now, how was your trip to Mars?"

"Virgil made it into some of the hollows and one was a warehouse. It had all kinds of high-tech equipment, but we're not sure what it does. We even found another body and this one was well preserved."

"That's cool, but..." She pulled the covers back on her bed. "When was the last time you slept?"

Nicole sighed. "It shows?"

"Get some sleep. I'll hang with Mel and wake you for supper."

"But..."

"It's okay to have a nap, Mom."

Brittany put her mother to bed and tucked her in. She woke her up a few hours later with a gentle nudge. "Jenny's here and they're about to serve spaghetti."

"What time is it?"

"It's five."

"What? Crap! I didn't mean to sleep this late. You should have woken me earlier."

"You needed this. We'll do supper and I'll go over those manuals with you tonight. Jenny's taking her kids out to a movie after supper because she said we need a break."

"A break?"

"Mel and Mathew are mad cause I smoked them at Monopoly this afternoon. I did the gloating thing, and it was too much for them."

"Why did you do that?"

"Didn't you hear me? I smoked them at their own game. I kinda like this whole money thing. It's fun fighting for success."

"It's fun only because you won." Nicole tried to fix her hair before heading to the dining room. She was happy the meal wasn't anything leftover or dehydrated. "Are Jenny's kids coming back later?"

"Oh yeah, and I'll apologise for being better than them. Don't worry."

"I hope that's not your idea of an apology."

Brittany smiled.

"And things are good, emotionally?" Nicole asked.

"Mom, things are great. I feel bad for Manchu. He told me his story and he said he blacked out. He doesn't remember hurting his sisters or his mother."

"He doesn't remember?"

"No. And he claims he was hearing voices, inside his head."

"Before he blacked out?"

"For weeks. He claims they were telling him to kill them. How is that possible?"

Nicole remembered something Victor had told her about the FBI and what they were experimenting with. 5G technology wasn't a new thing, like the public had been told. It had been used for decades as a torture and manipulation device. Brittany didn't need to know this. "Not sure, Brit. Do you need anything?"

"What could I need? I have you, my friends, and I've got this whole Cassandra adventure. She's trying to tell me a story, and I'm collecting the pieces. When I get enough of them, I'll start putting them together. I'm making the best of things on my end."

Nicole stayed until Jenny's kids got back. Then she took the manuals and made her escape. She had power sources to find, lodges to check out, and then there was the pickled woman.

Chapter thirty-seven

How long would it be before the doctor came to. Would they come after him? How would he explain all this to Lucy? Her Vincent wasn't the spy type, nor was he all that exciting. That was what Lucy liked about him. He was predictably stable. Today, her husband was finding hidden rooms, attacking doctors, and hiding out from the government. He was endangering her by getting her to pick him up.

He made his way along the trail until he reached the dock. It was quiet. There was an elderly couple walking a dog and two kids tossing rocks at a log that was floating fifty feet off the shore.

Across the lake, Victor could see the building he'd just escaped from. What was the story behind that woman in that fluid? Was she alive, on life support, or was she like Vincent, an abomination conjured from a book? He opened his folder and had a look.

Most of what he saw was Vincent's life. He was told he had acute panmyelosis with myelofibrosis. He was also told there was a cure. That would have been what was in the blue syringe, Victor thought. The truth was likely a lot different. The blood work was them wanting to see what was going on in his body. How was this conjured person different from them, and could they manipulate or replicate him?

Victor saw his wife's car pull into the parking spot nearest the dock and started for it. She was right on time. Then he saw three black SUVs pull in right after her.

Lucy got out of the car, wobbling on her heels as they sunk into the sandy soil. "It's okay Vincent. They're with me."

"No! We need to get away from them. You don't understand what they are. They aren't doctors. He held up the folder. These guys are..."

Lucy cut him off. "We want to help you."

"No, Lucy. They..." It only took a second for Victor to register what she'd said. It was the way she had said we. "You're in on it?"

Her hands went up, a gesture to calm him. "We only want to help you, Vincent."

"Vincent's life is a lie, isn't it?" It made sense. "You're what, FBI, CIA, Homeland. You're not a wife. You're an agent... a handler. Your being his wife is just a part of the job."

"Victor?" Her eyes widened in fear. "Okay guys, the doctor was right. This isn't Vincent. It's Victor."

The guns came out, backing Victor toward the dock.

"Freeze."

Victor could feel the wooden planks creaking under his feet as he inched his way back. He looked over his shoulder. He was thinking what they were thinking. Should he jump? He could only hold his breath for so long and he was Victor. They'd rather bring him in dead anyway.

"You're not going anywhere," Lucy said as she pulled a gun out of her purse. "I'll kill you myself if you don't give yourself up. It's your choice. Dead and wet. Alive and dry."

Victor teetered as his heel hit the end of the dock. He looked back over his shoulder to see water in all directions. He'd never hold his breath long enough to get away. In front of him was the woman that Vincent had fallen in love with. He had fallen for her, believed in her, and he had put all his trust in their relationship. She was probably at his side and holding his hand when he had been lied to about his cancer. She'd likely talked him into trying the trial drug.

"I thought you loved the guy."

She started to lift her gun. "What do you care. You're not him."

"You know he's just a lab rat."

"Oh, he's a hell of a lot more than a lab rat. He's the secret to why we exist and unlike you, he has purpose." She took aim. "Goodbye, Victor."

Victor waited for the lead-to-flesh impact. He'd been shot before and knew how it worked. He also knew he'd used up more than his share of lives. For that reason, he closed his eyes. That was when he heard it. Except it wasn't a gunshot, more a distant humming. The sound quickly morphed into loud squawking. That opened his eyes.

Thousands of birds came at him as the sky darkened. He started to fall backward, but the birds swooped in behind him and held him upright as they started to circle. The humming of wings became deafening as the first few shots were fired. Birds fell as they blocked the bullets from finding their path to him.

Within seconds, Victor couldn't feel the wooden planks under his feet. He couldn't hear the wings flapping or Lucy and the agents emptying their clips in his direction. It was calm, quiet, and he was floating. The last of the light was absorbed and Victor gave into the darkness until the light returned.

He was lying on his back and the birds were gone. The agents were gone. The lake and the beautiful wife he'd trusted were also gone. Instead, when Victor opened his eyes, he saw two people staring at him. Rose was sipping tea out of a cracked cup.

Benny was smoking a cigarette. "He's back."

Chapter thirty-eight

In the room, a low-pitched humming seemed to hypnotise Brittany. She listened to it and wondered what it was. It had to be the old florescent lights. They always seemed to have a hum to them. She opened her eyes and was startled by what she saw.

Again, she couldn't blink to focus and the purple hue from her previous dream had returned. Again, she was floating and quickly understood why. The capsule, or chamber, entombing her was full of a chilled fluid. She reached for her chest. It wasn't hers. Okay Cassandra, she thought to herself, what have you got us into?

Her hand reached out to touch the glass and it was warm. Feeling around the edges, she looked for a latch or some inner control that would open a door or drain off the fluids. There were rectangles and squares on the other side of the glass, but they were badly blurred. What were those things?

I'm not breathing! It was an instant panic that had her gasping for breath. There wasn't any. What did that mean? She tried to make her way to the top of the chamber to see if there was any air up there. She found a small space where she could stick her face, but she couldn't exhale or inhale. She also found a panel but couldn't read it. With only a couple of inches at the top of the cylinder, she couldn't get her eyes out of the fluid long enough to clear her sight.

There had to be either a way out of this thing or a wake up coming. Why had Cassandra dragged her out of her bed? Brittany tried the other route and made her way to the bottom of the *chamber. There was a metal mesh. She imagined she could feel the fluid escaping out the bottom and tried to plug it to see what would happen. She couldn't. If the fluid was escaping through the bottom, then it had to be coming in from somewhere else. She found an infeed at the back of the chamber near the top and tried desperately to hold her hand over it. Maybe she could drain it by stopping the damn thing from filling up.*

The chamber remained full, and her struggle ended. With her energy levels diminishing she slammed a hand into the nozzle. It broke off and the fluid came faster. She swatted at it one last time before letting her eyes close. The fight was exhausting.

What are you trying to tell me Cassandra? With the last of her energy, she drove her heel into the glass. That only pushed her to the back of the chamber.

Cassandra had a story to tell and everything from the housing complex to the swamp had to mean something. For whatever reason, this girl had brought Brittany into her world. Until now it had been more of an adventure than a riddle, but Brittany understood that, for Cassandra, this was serious and even dangerous. She strained to figure out what she was missing as everything started to drift away.

Nicole had been disappointed at her recent trip to the States. Her hopes to find a lodge for Brittany hadn't panned out. She knew Brittany was making the most of her stay in the hospital, but they needed answers.

Nicole waited for the elevator to move. Then she laughed and hit the button for the sixth floor. "That would help," She muttered to herself.

The elevator jerked, and up she went. Maybe, Mrs Xiang would let her take Brit for a walk. How could she say no?

Ding.

The elevator doors opened, and she walked out into the hallway. She buzzed the nurse to let her into the ward and thanked her when she did. It was early and she'd have to wait for everyone to wake up, but she'd brought a manual to go through. She'd hide out in Brittany's room until the kids started to stir.

When she entered the room, she lost her footing on the wet floor and went down hard.

Chapter thirty-nine

Nicole got to her feet and was flustered as she slipped and slid her way across the wet floor. Then she saw Brittany in the bathroom. The sight was hauntingly familiar. The glass door on the shower had been jammed shut and the water was not only spilling through the cracks but over the top of the door. Brittany was floating, limp and lifeless, as the water continued to flow from the broken faucet.

"Brittany!" Her voice cracked as she screamed.

Melanie woke up immediately. Mathew was also a little groggy as he turned toward the scream. Nicole tugged on the stuck door. She thought about breaking the glass but knew that would only cause Brittany to get cut up. Jenny's kids reached the bathroom as the shower door popped open. Brittany's limp body awkwardly spilled out, knocking her mother over.

She scrambled to her daughter's side and, without thinking, reached up and pulled the emergency string right out of the wall. Orderlies were on their way. Brittany was moved onto her back, and she started CPR. Mathew moved in to put two breaths in her for every fifteen compressions.

"Eleven, twelve, thirteen, fourteen, fifteen, breathe!"

Tears ran down Mathew's cheeks, but he flawlessly pushed two deep breaths into Brittany each time Nicole yelled. They were about to go for another round of chest pumps when the orderly showed up. He saw what had happened and got on his radio. On the other end of that radio a man was grabbing the crash cart.

A nurse entered the room and took over for Mathew. The other orderly checked for a pulse. Over and over, they pushed breaths into her and applied chest compressions. Each thrust pushed water out of her lungs and although Nicole could have gone on a lot longer, she wouldn't have to. Brittany started to heave. Water shot out of her mouth and nostrils, and Nicole quickly rolled her over to her side. Brittany coughed out more water, and her supper.

Nicole held her close as her fear turned to rage. "What's going on here. This place is supposed to be safe. How could this happen?"

Nobody said a word. Mathew opened his mouth to say something but stopped. She was right. Her daughter was in trouble, and they hadn't taken it seriously enough. Brittany coughed a couple more times and used her words to break the silence.

"I'm glad I..." she sputtered, "suck at this."

Melanie wiped at her own wet eyes. "Brittany, you scared us."

"What happened?" She tried to pull herself up. She returned her mother's hug like never before.

They watched as an orderly got up and turned off the water. The other continued to hold her wrist and monitor her pulse.

"Everybody out! We need a minute." Nicole pointed to the door. She steadied Brittany as they struggled to get up. Nicole's hip was throbbing from when she fell. "Out!"

Spinning around, Brittany sat on her bed and looked over the room at the chaos she'd caused. "I can't believe this. I thought I was over it."

Nicole grabbed a gown from her drawer and tossed it to her. "Put this on."

Everyone filed out of the room and Brittany watched as they left. "You'll have to help me get dressed. I'm still a little weak... and don't blame them."

Nicole didn't say a word.

"Mom, I'm sorry."

"I know." She sat down beside her. "Was this because of Cassandra?"

"Yes and no." She peeled her wet gown off and put the dry one on. Arms were outstretched for her mother to help.

Nicole grabbed her sweater off the end of the bed and wrapped her in it. "How do you mean?"

Brittany gave her an arm to help her walk. She wanted to get out of that room and let the orderlies mop up the water. Brittany saw the gang down in the cafeteria. "Don't be mad at them. I would be nuts if it weren't for them."

"I'm madder at myself. It was a mistake putting you here." She looked Brittany in the eye. "What does yes and no mean?"

"Promise me you won't get mad?"

"I'm in no position to get mad. Now start talking."

They got to the table in the dining room and sat down. "Night before last I had a dream that I didn't share with anyone. The dream didn't make any sense to me at the time, and I can't say it makes any more sense now, but in it, my sight was all blurry. I saw shapes and they were squares and rectangles." She shrugged. "No big deal, right? That's when I realised, I was in a cylinder. It was filled with a cold fluid. Still no screaming story, right?"

"Wrong." Nicole was hanging on her every word. "Go on."

"Tonight, I dreamt of being trapped in that cylinder again. The fluid was purple, and it was cold. I think she's trapped in it."

At this point Nicole had to come clean. She hadn't told Brittany much about her find because she honestly didn't think it was relevant. This Cassandra that they were looking for, she was supposed to be a woman on Earth.

"What, Mom?"

"Go on."

"Okay. I was trapped in this cold stuff, and I was calm at first. I tried to find a way out of this thing, but the floor was a metal grate, and it was sealed. There was an air gap, but I couldn't breathe the air. My lungs were filled up with the fluid. I was getting frustrated and just waiting to wake up, like in the other dreams, but it wasn't happening."

Nicole started fidgeting through her pockets.

"Mom, what's going on?"

"No. Just a second. I'll be right back." She got up and headed into Brittany's room. The orderlies were still mopping up water. Her purse was on the bed, and she pulled a handful of printed snapshots out and returned.

"What have you got there?"

Nicole dropped the pictures on the table and wasn't surprised at her daughter's reaction.

"Oh, man. That's it. How could you have taken these? Where is this thing, Colorado?" She studied the top photo. Is that a body in this thing? Is that..."

"Yes, that is a body." She moved the top picture off the stack revealing the next one. It showed a better view of the person in the chamber.

Brittany looked at it closely and then shoved it aside for the next and then the fourth and final picture. They were all shots of the person in the chamber. She stared at it for some time in disbelief. "That's her."

Nicole was afraid of that. "Are you sure?"

"I'm gonna go with a definite maybe. Is she dead?"

It was hard to be sure of anything anymore. "I don't know."

"Where is this place?"

Nicole was hesitant. "The hollows on Mars. Those squares and rectangles in your dreams were the crates that we found."

"Mars? What the hell does that mean?"

"I wish I knew. The artifact was with me when I was there. That must have triggered something, but what? Who is this girl?"

Suddenly, a voice came from behind them. It was Mrs Xiang. "I came as soon as I heard. Brittany, are you okay?"

"We found Cassandra," Brittany piped up.

Nicole reluctantly slid the pictures over to her. She spread them out.

Mrs Xiang gave them a puzzled blank stare. "I..." She couldn't find the words. "I don't think I understand. Where is this thing, and what is this woman doing?"

"Mars." Nicole shrugged. "I'll put your questions on the list."

"Is this girl alive?"

Again, Nicole shrugged. "We have no idea."

"But... "

"I'm sorry." Nicole turned to Brittany, wrapped her tightly in the sweater, and consumed her in a strong embrace. They were on Mars in an instant.

Chapter forty

This wasn't Victor's bed from back home, nor was it the bottom of the lake. It was lumpy, as if it had been stuffed with old socks and newspapers. He tried to shake the fog. When it cleared, he saw Rose and Benny. They were staring at him as if he'd returned from the dead.

Victor cleared his throat as he tried to sit up. "What the hell?"

"Wow," Benny exclaimed. "You were only out three days."

"I counted two," Victor corrected.

Rose put her tea down and reached for a cigarette as Victor started to get it together. It was initially meant for her, but she lit it and handed it to him. "You need this more than me, and Benny's right, it was three. Not sure how that works. Maybe there's a travel day."

"Travel day?" Victor asked.

"You were gone and now you're back. Ain't that travelling?"

"I don't know." He shook his head. "If you say so."

Benny tried to hand him a half a bowl of Mac and Cheese. He'd been eating it but didn't want to be outdone by Rose's cigarette gesture. "Here. You must be hungry."

As appetising as it looked, Victor declined. "I'll wait until I can find something else."

"I can cook you something. What do you want? A steak, hamburger, or maybe a big bowl of gumbo?"

Victor took a drag on the cigarette. He half expected the smoke to ooze from the holes in his chest. "What's with him?"

She pointed to the gaudy stone sitting amongst the bullet wounds. "You have the necklace, and he wants in on my million."

"Nobody's getting a million dollars."

"What," they both clamoured in unison.

"Look. Giving either of you that kind of money would get you killed. Trust me."

"But you..." Rose grabbed the cigarette back.

"Don't worry. I'll make sure you each get a house. There's a housing project over on the East End. I'll let you each pick one, and I'll give you a lifetime supply of food stamps, clothing vouchers, and cigarettes."

"And Marijuana?" Benny asked.

It was an instinct to say no, but Victor nodded. "Limited amounts, and don't you make me regret doing all this."

"Cool." Benny pumped a fist like he'd won the lottery. In his world, he had. "And a gaming computer?"

"Fuck off." Victor sat up and swung his legs around and dropped them to the floor. "Hey, did you guys recover this fast when you died?"

Rose nodded. "As long as you keep that amulet around your neck, you feel good. If you take it off, you'll feel like shit again."

"How long do I have to wear it?" he asked Rose.

"Forty-eight hours? It's hard to say. I wasn't shot six times in the chest." She turned to Benny. "In hindsight, that was kinda overkill."

Benny shrugged. "So, I shoot him once, twice, and if he's still standing, I'm a dead man. He's a big guy. I didn't want to just piss him off. He'd have killed me. I wanted to send him on his way, proper like. And wasn't it cool coming back?"

"What do you mean?" Victor asked.

"All those fucking birds." Benny stood up and started to spin with his arms outstretched. "Made me dizzy, but damn that was a rush."

Victor took the cigarette back from Rose. "And you?"

"Lots of birds. They came out of nowhere and swarmed me. I was scared until I realised, they were there to help."

"Help?"

"I was living it up pretty good. The bones didn't ache, the belly was full, and I was happy. My friends were there, and I was working in a little bookstore. Then he came for me."

"Him?"

"I was being followed. It felt scary. Then he attacked me. I thought I was a goner until the birds came."

Benny piped up, "I was being chased by the same guy when they came to me. The birds came from the trees, from under cars and out of clouds. They were everywhere."

"You both saw birds?" Victor exhaled. "What about a man dressed in black? He'd have had a big hat, and a leather coat. His face would have been all pitted and scarred."

"A cowboy dude in a leather coat? Nope." Benny started back in on his bowl of macaroni. "What do you think we are, crazy?"

"Who was chasing you then?"

"Some dude." He turned to Rose. "Regular looking."

"Did the guy have a name?"

"Name? I guess you could call it that."

"What do you mean?"

"It was a name with numbers in it."

"Numbers?" Victor thought about the Birdman's kill list as he pulled it out of his pocket. "Like this?"

"Just like that."

Victor slid his wallet out and took the Alzien card out of one of the slots. "And you're sure about that?"

Benny looked over to Rose and she nodded. "Yep."

Victor held the Alzien card up to his temple and thought of Nicole.

Chapter forty-one

B rittany recognised the area. "This isn't the hollows. This is the main entrance."

"I owe it to Virgil to include him." They found him in the lab. "We have a situation, Virgil."

"Girls. This is truly a surprise. Good to see you again, Brittany. How are you feeling?" He realised how stupid the question was, as soon as it left his mouth.

Brittany stood there, wrapped in a sweater, her hair still wet. "I've had a few eventful days. How are you doing? I hear you found somebody."

He looked to Nicole. "I, uh..."

She noticed the test tubes full of an almost fluorescent purple liquid. "Is that..."

"It's from the you know what. And why is Brittany here? Does she know about the you know who?" Again, he couldn't pull his eyes from the bare feet or the wet hair.

"She had a dream about this capsule. That woman we found, is Cassandra. She's been haunting her in these dreams."

"This is the girl that comes to you in your sleep?" His expression wilted. It was hard to like where this was going.

"Where is she?" Brittany could feel her presence.

Virgil waited until he got the go-ahead nod. "This way."

They entered the room and Brittany started touching all the equipment. Then she noticed the chamber and walked over to it. "It's her. What's that stuff that she's in?"

"It's some organic form of a preservative," Virgil offered. "Mostly natural, it has the perfect resting temperature to prevent the decay of organic tissue. It's also slightly oxygenated, which gives it the purple hue. It's a lot like a supercharged chlorophyll, a synthetic version of course."

Brittany sobered for her next question. "Is she dead?"

Virgil shook his head. "She'd have to be. I couldn't imagine any life left in her after several thousand years of being stuck in that thing."

"I guess." Brittany's emotions stirred as she moved closer. "How do we get her out?"

"Sorry." Nicole put an arm around her. "We need to figure out what this means first, like why are you dreaming about Mars?"

Brittany agreed. "If she's been dead for thousands of years, how am I supposed to help her? And how is she talking to me?"

Virgil was slow to catch up. "Maybe you weren't supposed to. Could it be, she only wanted to tell a story?"

Brittany's ego expelled that notion quickly. "Nah. I was supposed to stop the destruction of a planet. I thought it was Earth, but now I see it was Mars, and I'm way to late. We need to figure this out." She put a hand on the capsule. "And you're going to help me."

The capsule gave off a majestic hue when the purple goo began to glow. Brittany looked closer and could feel the life inside. The others couldn't. Maybe it was because she'd been in that thing and had felt its embrace. The circuit panel on the upper region still danced in her memories, as did the shallow air space and the metal grate that formed the base. She reached out and placed her other hand on it and could feel Cassandra's presence drawing her in.

Her limp body floated in the fluid like it had for so many years. She had remained unchanged for some odd, but scientifically explained, reason. Brittany had to wonder what strange turn of events had cut her life short. The drowning had been one of her last memories.

Brittany leaned toward the glass and blew her hot breath on it causing the glass to steam up. Then she drew a question mark in the glass with her finger. That caused Cassandra's eyes to twitch. It was as if they were trying to follow her.

"Did you see that?" Brittany asked.

Nicole was still trying to figure out the glowing. "What?"

"She's alive."

"I can assure you she's very much dead." Virgil told her.

Then he began pleading his case to open the capsule under a controlled environment. Nicole agreed but needed more answers before making a move that couldn't be reversed. It wasn't like they could just pop her in the fridge.

Brittany was tapping on the glass. "I'm not kidding. She's alive."

Nicole's Alzien phone started to buzz. She picked it up. "Hello?"

"Hey. It's Victor."

"Kinda having a moment here."

"Same. We need to talk. I just…"

"Brittany! Don't you…"

Brittany's eyes had remained locked on Cassandra's. Then, as if being signalled by the girl in the capsule, she took her sweater off and dropped it. The sweater hadn't even hit the ground when she appeared in the capsule with Cassandra. Floating in the fluid, she pulled Cassandra close to her body. In another instant she was out of the capsule and standing with Cassandra's limp body in a puddle of goo.

Cassandra's slimy body immediately slid from her grasp. Brittany didn't even hear her mother yelling at her as she lay Cassandra down on the cold dirt.

"Victor, I gotta go!" Nicole ended the call and dropped the phone.

Cassandra's nude body lay lifeless on its back. There was no heaving chest or colour coming back to her cheeks. "Time for a little help here!" Brittany shouted.

She quickly placed her mouth over Cassandra's and blew a breath into her. She watched as a little of the slime exited her mouth. Then she went in for another breath.

"Why?" Nicole couldn't believe she was doing CPR again. She dropped to her knees and, after the second breath, started with the first set of chest compressions. Each thrust forced more and more fluid out. "What were you thinking?"

"You have to trust me." She leaned forward and forced another breath into Cassandra. The next breath had her lungs filling normally. She moved back as Nicole did another fifteen compressions. The compressions finally stopped bringing up fluids from her lungs, but there was still no life. Brittany forced a large breath into her.

Nothing.

"What am I thinking?" Brittany stopped the breaths, wrapped herself up in her sweater, and rendered off. She was back seconds later with the necklace.

"What are you doing, Brit?" Nicole snapped. "Don't..."

"Call it a hunch." She set it down onto Cassandra's chest. When it touched her skin, there was a shock wave followed by a cough.

Brittany rolled her on her side as Cassandra started to stir. The first cough wasn't that defined, but the next one was. Her first breath was strained as Cassandra's body almost resisted it. Then she wretched more of the fluid out and gasped for another breath. Nicole sat back in awe.

"It's okay. You're going to be okay," Brittany said as she took her sweater off and draped it over her. Cassandra shivered as her body temperature tried to adapt. Her eyes had been open the whole time and they were taking in everything.

As her colour started to return, she laboured to sit up. Nicole helped her, cradling her body from behind. She moved her hair to get it out of her face.

Cassandra coughed again and looked to Brittany. "I was..." She shuttered. "...hoping you'd figure..." she coughed again. "...figure it out."

"Don't talk. Just rest and try to warm up. You're freezing."

"I hope... you can... forgive me."

Brittany had so many questions but settled on one. "Were you trying to kill me?"

Chapter forty-two

The suicides and dreams were explained as Cassandra spoke through the shivering. "Lot... of confusion... glad this is over. Again... sorry."

Brittany let the excitement drain from her body. Not only did they need a quieter approach but also, for the first time in a while, she was alone with her thoughts, and alone with her body. That meant the dreams would be gone. She got up and held her hand out to Cassandra. She took it and let Brittany pull her to her feet. The sweater was adjusted and tied at the front.

"What is this thing?" the young woman asked.

"A sweater." Brittany answered.

Cassandra gave her an impish grin. "No. That."

Brittany followed her finger to the capsule. They walked over to it, Cassandra's steps a little uncertain. She ran her fingers over the glass as if touching an old friend.

"Not sure. It was where we found you."

Nicole was still kneeling where minutes ago a dead Cassandra struggled for her first breath in centuries. She didn't understand, but like Brittany, she realised that overwhelming their new guest was not going to help anyone. Instead, she motioned for Virgil who had quietly stood off to the side, stunned beyond words. He watched as she motioned him to come over and did.

"What are you thinking, Nicole?"

"I'm hoping this means that Brit is free of those nightmares. I'm also wondering how any of this is possible?"

He kept his words to a whisper as Cassandra and Brittany talked. "I've never heard of anything like this in my lifetime and wouldn't have believed it if I hadn't seen it for myself. I know we don't have the technology for this. These Martians were obviously a step ahead in this field. Why do you think those two were brought together?"

"The idea scares me. I was hoping that finding this girl would put an end to the craziness and let us get back to normal. Looks like we've adopted a Martian."

"Tonight's been huge," Virgil told her, "...and I'm guessing tomorrow will be bigger. If I can help in any way, then let me know."

"What do you mean?"

"This is historic news."

"No way," Nicole snapped. "We can't tell anybody."

"Are you saying what I think you're saying?"

"That she's one of Jenny's nieces? That's exactly what I'm saying. We need to run this past my mother first."

"And Brunnard," Virgil reminded her.

"Of course. Did you ever find out what all this stuff was?"

"A lot of stuff dealing with incubation and DNA testing. Even though it looks different, it's quite similar to the kinds of stuff we have."

"Nothing special then?"

"No, just a bunch of commercial grade lab equipment. It does everything we can do, only better." He looked over to the capsule that now only held three quarters of a tank of fluid. "Then there's that thing. I'll keep working on it."

"Keep me posted?"

"Definitely."

Nicole made her way back to Brittany. She was sitting beside Cassandra. They were sharing, which made Nicole nervous. "Can I ask you something?"

No longer shivering, Cassandra calmly nodded. "You can ask. I don't know what I can answer. One day I'm on a dock, the next day some girl brings me back to life in a cave."

"I tried to commit suicide three times," Brittany blurted out.

"There were only two suicide attempts," Cassandra confessed. "That mirror incident was a misunderstanding."

Brittany was confused. "Were you also having dreams?"

"Dreams, nightmares, whatever you want to call them. It was weird seeing myself in someone else's body. I thought someone had captured me. I thought they were doing testing again. I wanted it to end."

Brittany put her hand on the artifact. "Do you know anything about this thing?"

"Yes, it's my lucky meteor rock. It dates back farther than anything we've ever seen. My parents gave it to me. It's rare and they had to pull a lot of strings to get it. Where'd you find it?"

Nicole ignored the question. "Do you know where this rock came from?"

"Somewhere in space. I never got the full story."

"Are you kidding me?" Brittany shrieked. "It's…"

Nicole cut her off. "Enough Brit. We have lots of time to talk about that. We need to figure out a way to get her back to the apartment."

"Apartment?" Brittany wondered. Then she understood. They couldn't render her, nor could they throw her on a pup ship. She likely believed her planet was still alive and well. She also would be thinking they were fellow Martians and that everything was fine. "What are we going to do?"

"I should head home." Cassandra told them. "My mother is probably worried sick."

Virgil was far more practical and blurted, "Take the pup ship." For him it wasn't too soon for Cassandra to see her planet. She'd find out sooner or later.

"What's a pup ship?"

Nicole was too shocked to stop him from saying any more.

"It shuttles us between planets," he added.

Cassandra's jaw dropped. "We can safely travel space? When did all this happen?"

Brittany put a hand up to stop Virgil. "I, uh…"

"Look, if you want answers from me," Cassandra stammered, "then I want them from you. How long was I in that thing?"

Chapter forty-three

B rittany wanted to explain, but Nicole had cut her off. Like Virgil, she didn't see the harm in answers as long as they were honest. Cassandra couldn't be sheltered from this forever. She tried again. "No, Mom. She's right. She deserves answers. I needed answers, and some of them sucked, but I still needed them."

"What's going on?" Cassandra asked.

"Full disclosure," Brittany started, "we're not from here. We're from Earth, but we're friends. We're on your side."

"My side? Why are you on my side?" Then something seemed to confuse her. "And what's an Earth?"

"It's the next planet over. It's one planet farther than this one... from the sun that is."

"The blue one. How did you get here? And how did you learn our language?"

Nicole didn't see that coming, although she had wondered about the manuals. "Is this a Martian language?"

"Martian?"

"We call your planet Mars. Is that okay?"

"Definitely. Does your Earth also speak it?"

Brittany confessed, "We call it English."

Cassandra took a second to wonder how that was possible. They must have learned it from her people. She'd heard that Earth may contain life, and now with space travel, it was only inevitable that they'd learned to communicate. And what had they meant when they said they were on her side. "Not to seem ungrateful, but what brought you here?"

"We're trying to figure out what happened to this planet."

"So, it's true, and you people know about our problems?"

Brittany grabbed her hand. "Isn't that why you came to me?"

"You came to me."

As enlightening as this talk was, Cassandra didn't have time for this. "I'm sorry. Thanks again for saving me, but I must go." She gave a sad-to-leave look, pulled Brittany's sweater tight around her and disappeared.

The three that remained looked at each other, eyes enlarged and jaws open. Had she really just done that? Where would she have gone? There was nothing left out there. Her world had been decimated. They patiently waited for her to return. Seconds turned to minutes.

Brittany broke the silence. "I've got to go find her."

"Whoa. How are you going to find her? She could be buried under a couple hundred feet of volcanic dust." Nicole blurted out.

"But…"

"Look, Brit. I get that this is a tragedy, but there's nothing we can do about it."

"I can still sense her." Brittany tried to look past her mother's fears. These were feelings she couldn't explain. She was right about bringing Cassandra out of the chamber, and she'd be right about going after her. She was almost sure of it. "I'll be back."

Nicole's heart sunk as her daughter disappeared. She was snapped out of her trance by the vibrating card in the dirt.

"Shit timing, Victor. What do you want?"

"Answers, Miss Congeniality." He continued before she could get a word in. "I just died and was brought back by a purple stone that looks a lot like the one you've got. Explain!"

"Purple stone?"

"That's right. I had the stone hanging around my neck when I was shot six times, and guess what, I'm still here. What is this damn thing?"

She held the stone she had up in her hand. "How?"

"I found one in Haiti. I remembered hearing stories about it from a retired prostitute."

"Seriously?"

"About what, the stone or the…"

"The stone, damn it! The other doesn't surprise me. Are you shitting me?"

"You got me. I was bored so I mixed a drink, sat on the deck and decided to make up this big bullshit story." He calmly took a deep breath. "Look. I can send you a picture of my chest where I was shot. Still looks pretty messed up."

"Sorry. Just not sure what to think of this. We just rescued a woman from a glass capsule full of goo."

"What? Where are you? I'll grab the next flight out."

"Don't bother. I'm on Mars."

"You found a woman on Mars? Alive? In Goo?" Victor asked.

"She is now. Says the stone was given to her by her mother."

"Is the stone why she's alive?" Victor asked.

"I'd have to say that's a yes."

"I'd really like to talk to this gal. I mean, I was shot in the chest point blank. I had no heartbeat for three days and then the Birdman's sparrows brought me back to life. And this rock has also resurrected two others that I know of."

"You saw the bird guy."

"Yeah, but I didn't get a chance to talk to him. Where's this girl now?"

"She took off, and Brittany went after her."

"She did what? You're on Mars. Where the hell would she go?"

"I wish I knew."

Chapter forty-four

The shores of the swamp area were calm. Brittany stood there staring at Cassandra as the young woman talked to her friends. What was she thinking? She'd appeared on the shore that she'd imagined in her dreams, but these weren't her dreams. Thankfully, her wet hospital gown had come with her. It wasn't wrapped tight but clung to her body leaving little to the imagination.

Cassandra was now slipping into dry clothes. Brittany yelled out. "Got anything in my size?"

Startled, Cassandra turned around and stared in disbelief. "How did you do that?"

"I could ask you the same thing," she replied as she quickly slipped into a shirt handed to her from one of Cassandra's female friends. "Looks like we have more things in common than just dreams."

Cassandra buttoned up a shirt that could barely hold her. "I know what I am. What are you?"

"Can we go for a walk? I'm afraid your friends would never believe my story, but you've seen my world through your dreams. You might understand some of this."

She handed her a pair of pants. "Sure."

They were slipped on before the two headed into the woods. She was led into a quiet opening where a small stream tumbled over some rocks. "I've been here, but I was seeing it through your eyes. How is this possible?"

"Tell me what you know, and I'll see if I can fill in the gaps. Start with how you got here."

"I'm not sure what you call it, but my mother and I can render. That's re-existence through a non dimension. Basically, I cease to exist where I was, and then I'm recreated where I'm thinking." She looked down at her new clothes. "Anything loose gets left behind. How about you?"

"Same principle, I guess. I know it has something to do with my father, but I'm not sure about the details. He's the scientist."

"My grandfather created my Mom and I'm second generation."

"There's more to it." Cassandra took a seat on a downed tree.

Brittany sat beside her. "What do you mean?"

"Seems like you've just learned how to home in on a subject. I'd have to say that's another part of the gift we have. The ability to find someone by thinking about them."

Brittany had never thought about their gift being more than just rendering. The whole following her here suddenly made sense. "True! And then there's the whole time-travelling thing."

"Time travel?" A smile widened across Cassandra's face. "You'll have to teach me that one."

"Um, you get the credit for teaching me."

Cassandra gave her a bewildered gaze. "Okay. Not sure I understand."

"I'm gonna try to explain this, so bear with me." She started with her story. "You were in a capsule when I saved you. That capsule is on this planet." She waited to see if she was following.

"I'm in a capsule and that capsule is on this planet. Okay. I already had that figured out."

"We found that capsule at what we call a dig site. My Mom, Nicole, was a big part of the exploration. Do you know what a dig site is?"

Cassandra shook her head. "Not really."

"Tombs and fossil stuff."

"Oh, an excavation site."

"Exactly. That's what we were doing on your planet when we found you."

"My planet?"

"We were trying to find out what happened." Brittany looked deep into her eyes hoping that she'd figure things out. "I'm from Earth, one planet over. There's life on that planet."

"There's life on this planet."

"Not anymore," Brittany finally blurted.

"What are you saying? Do our leaders know you're here?"

"It was kind of hard to introduce ourselves. There was nobody here when we arrived."

"Where'd you land, the Forbidden Zone?"

Brittany was done with this game. "You're a true blonde, aren't you? There was nobody here because Mars is a barren planet. All we found was dirt and rocks. No trees, rivers, buildings to speak of, or people."

Cassandra waited for the punch line. "How is that even possible?"

Brittany sighed. "I think I'm from your future. You were in that same future when we found you. Your planet, what we call Mars, was a planet with a huge dormant volcano and a large crack along its equator. We found fish fossils and even remnants of some old houses. In time we found an old high-rise building and a hollow that held some crates. It also had a capsule with a girl in it... you."

Cassandra gave her no reaction.

"I'm sorry. Everything you know, all this, friends and family are gone." Brittany added, "You were in that capsule a very long time."

"You're telling me this planet is doomed and that I've survived it in some tomb of liquid for years?"

"Thousands of years. Sorry." She waited a minute. "Ask me something."

"What would I ask? You can do what I can, and you're from another planet. Oh, and possibly from the future."

"No, definitely from the future. Mars, or your planet, has been barren a long time. You have to believe me."

"That's the craziest thing I've ever heard." She ran over to Kim. "I need to tell you something. It's about our planet."

"What have you learned?" Kim asked.

"This girl says she's seen our future and we're a doomed planet, an extinct volcano and dust." She watched for his reaction. "Do you know anything about this?"

"That mission that I told you about." He looked at Brittany wondering how she could have known. "It's to stop some rogue experiment. My contact found out about it."

"Was it some kind of new weapon?" Brittany asked.

"Don't know. Are you being honest about all this?"

"I can show you." Brittany said as she turned to Cassandra. "Come to Earth. You've already been there in my mind, so you know you'll be safe. I can dig up all the information on Mars and show you what we know."

"Mars? I like the name." Cassandra thought for a moment. "We could go for a short trip. I need to see this future for myself. Can we come back later?"

"Could I stop you?"

She smiled. "I guess not."

"Exactly. And this way you can help me convince everyone back home that I'm not crazy. It's been a tough week for me."

Cassandra nodded. "And you're really from the blue planet?"

"Honestly, no. My planet is spinning around a star five light years away, but that's a story for another day."

Cassandra felt a little unsure, but Brittany grabbed her tight. They were back in the hollows in the time it took to vaporise and materialise. They ended up on the dirt inches from where they left. Not even a minute had passed.

Nicole was talking to Victor and dropped the phone again when she saw Brittany and Cassandra reappear. "You're back!"

"We were always here, but not during the Mars we know," Brittany offered. "It was the one in my dreams, in the past."

"How is that possible?"

Cassandra shrugged. "Sounds like that rendering thing you guys talk about has very few limits."

"Mars was very much alive, Mom."

"Hello?" Victor was still on the phone, his voice coming from the card in the dirt.

Nicole picked the card up. "Sorry, Victor. We'll be heading back to Earth."

Brittany cut in. "Cassandra and I'll meet you back at the apartment. I can Render her there."

"Stay there until we arrive." Nicole managed to get it out before they left.

"Gotcha," Brittany replied as she hugged her new friend, and disappeared.

"Hey Victor. Brittany's going to…"

"I heard. Is that the apartment in Beijing?"

"Yes, downtown. And Victor…" Nicole thought for a second. "Have you still got the other amulet?"

"Yes," he answered. It was still resting on his bare chest.

"Where are you?"

"I'm in Haiti."

"I'll pick you up on the way."

Chapter forty-five

Cassandra played with the light switch while she held a stuffed toy racoon. Brittany was rifling through one of her dresser drawers looking for something to wear.

"Feel free to look around. I just want to get out of these clothes." She looked up from her dresser. "Not that there's anything wrong with the clothes you gave me, but Earthlings have the cooler items. It was one of the first things I liked about this planet. They love choices and spoil themselves with them."

"What kind of differences?"

Brittany pulled out a pair of jeans and tossed them to her. "Hmm. They should stretch over those hips." She ran over to the closet.

Cassandra peeled off her pants and slid the denims on. "Hey these feel good. Are they normally this snug?"

"They'll fit better after a couple of minutes. They're kinda self-adjusting." She pulled a lacy t-shirt out of her closet and handed it to her. "It's cotton. It'll also stretch."

Cassandra put the shirt on, and it was tight. "Is this how it fits?"

"Uh…" Brittany saw her being pushed up through the V-neck and grabbed a different top. "Try this one instead."

The larger t-shirt fit better.

"That's the ticket. How does everything feel?"

Her hands slid over the fabric and she marvelled at how it hugged her curves. "I like it."

"We should go out and get something to eat. The food here in China is also amazing."

"What about the pictures of my planet?"

"Mom will be here soon. You must be starving." She started for the door. "Come with me and we'll get some fresh stuff."

Brittany tried to fill her new friend in on everything she knew about Earth as they got in the cab and rolled down the street. Cassandra stared at the height of the buildings, the kids on skateboards, and the people on bicycles. There was nothing like it on Mars. Their transportation was mainly done on an intricate subway system. They had no tight clothing, and the more Cassandra talked, the more Brittany realised Martians were more like Alziens, than like Earthlings.

"You'll be in for a real treat with the food here." The cab stopped in front of the Golden Palace.

Mrs Lee had the two bags of food ready as Brittany and Cassandra entered. "Thank you, Mrs Lee. This is my new friend, and she's never had food like this before."

"Where you from?" Mrs Lee asked.

Cassandra just stared into her eyes.

"Uhh, she's a Colombian." Brittany grabbed the bags. "Getting late. We gotta go."

The Martian was dragged out of the restaurant.

"What the hell are you thinking?"

Cassandra gasped. "Are you kidding me? Look around. These people are so fascinating."

"You shouldn't stare like that."

"I've never seen anything like it. Dark hair, brown eyes, and they're so…"

"Stop. You're not supposed to talk about people like that."

"Why not?" Cassandra recoiled. "Look at their skin, those eyes, the cheek bones, the…"

"It hurts their feelings if you stare."

"We don't have humans like this on our planet."

"Same with Alzie. It took me a bit to wrap my head around it. Give them another five hundred years and all of Earth will have darker hair, brown eyes, and olive skin, unless they do alterations."

"I know. We did it too. This is like a living history book."

The cab brought them back to the apartment where they ran into the others. Mathew and Melanie were on the deck, Nicole in the kitchen, and Victor in the bathroom.

Nicole helped them with the bags. "Smells like you got Golden Palace again. There are other restaurants."

"I know." Brittany noticed the painting, still on the table. Two corners were held by salt and pepper shakers. A glass and an ornament held the other two. "This is new."

Nicole took a second. "I picked it up before all this happened."

Brittany clued in. "It's from Mars?"

"It is." She looked over to Cassandra. "It was in the rubble of a high-rise apartment. I probably shouldn't have taken it, but it was too beautiful to leave."

Cassandra walked up to it and ran her fingers over it to feel the texture. "It's beautiful, so much emotion."

"Yes, but it wasn't mine to take."

"But someone painted their heart into it. There's no way it should be stuck in a pile of debris." She wiped away a tear as she recognised the building. "This building is where my mother worked. I hate to think of how she must have suffered."

Nicole put her arm around her. "Maybe we can find out what happened."

"Maybe."

Victor came out of the bathroom, slowly made up a plate of food, and joined them. That was the first time he saw her, and she saw him. Victor simply stared. "How the hell did you…"

Cassandra's eyes narrowed. "How do I know you?"

He slowly unbuttoned his shirt, exposing the amulet and the six marks from the bullets that had pierced his chest, lungs, and heart only days ago. "I got shot with this thing around my neck and I had some weird dream about…" He stopped, not wanting to mention his conjured brother.

Cassandra extended a hand. "Can I have my necklace back?"

Nicole interrupted her by holding up a finger. "One second." She left for a minute and returned with the Martian amulet. "This one's yours."

"What?" She took it and held it up to compare. "They're identical."

"They are," Victor agreed. "Has it ever given you dreams?"

Cassandra looked away.

"Cause it gave me a frigg'n whopper. Some crazed doctor had a room with this big glass box in it. The damn thing was full of this purple fluid." He took a step toward her. "Do you know what, or who, I found in that box? I'll give you an easy clue. You'll find her if you look in a mirror. How are you here?"

"It wasn't me. That was a dream... your dream. I don't control what happens when you sleep." She moved over to side-step him.

He cut her off. "Are you saying it wasn't you, because I'd bet a case of hundred-year-old scotch that it was."

She took a defiant turn toward him. "You said you were shot six times, and you died, yet here you are. How are you here?"

"I was resurrected." He patted his amulet. "And before me, a guy named Benny overdosed. He was brought back after two weeks of rotting on the couch. A woman named Rose did the same after being shot three times."

"You're telling me they were dead for weeks?" Nicole asked. "Do you have any idea the level of decomposition that happens in that time frame? Were they at least put on ice?"

Victor knew they hadn't been. "Benny overdosed in his apartment. His buddies weren't the type to even notice, let alone have the smarts to put him in the freezer. Resurrection doesn't care about decay."

"Impossible," Brittany chuffed. "Rotting for two weeks, and then coming back to life? He'd have been one of those zombie things."

"Trust me, Benny's close to that, but that's because of the drugs, not the death." He turned to Cassandra. "This thing brought us back from the other side. It's healed torn, shot up, and rotting flesh. What are you not telling us about this thing?"

"I have no idea what you're talking about."

Victor thought for a second. "Okay. You were trapped in a capsule full of fluid, just like in my dream, and you were freed by the touch of this stone, just like I was. Answer me this. Did you see the birds?"

Cassandra's eyes widened as the amulet slipped from her hand and dropped to the floor.

He sat back on the arm of the couch. "I'll take that as a yes."

Chapter forty-six

An awkward tension hung in the air until Cassandra took the amulet and her plate out onto the terrace. Brittany grabbed her food, shot Victor a dirty look, and followed her. He tipped his head to her. His point had been made.

"You can't trust her," he said as he turned to Nicole. "You know my instincts. They're usually pretty good."

"Give her a chance. What don't you like about her?"

"Where do I start? I found her in a big box of slime, in a dream no doubt. Lo and behold, you also found her in a big box of slime, and she can do this whole beam-me-up-Scottie shit."

"It was a cylinder."

"Whatever." He pulled the front of his shirt open to reveal the stone. "I was brought back to life after days of being dead. It was damn weird and I'm not right. That was three days. She's alive again after a few thousand years? Can you imagine what's going on in that head of hers? I know I can't."

"I uh…"

"I get that she might have answers to your daughter's recent struggles, but she's also in survival mode."

"Survival mode?"

"It's an CIA term. Often, we were on missions that were, to put a positive spin on crime, nationally sensitive. In other words, if we were caught, we'd have to take the black eye for Uncle Sam.

I remember being on a mission in South Korea. We had gone through hell to get this one guy elected. Why, you ask? Because he was willing to go to war with North Korea. He'd been promised tanks, jet fighters, and troops. The only thing he asked was that he didn't throw the first punch."

"So?"

"Imagine all those troops lined up at the edge of this river, ready to fight. Every second that they don't, they're losing their nerve. It starts with bickering about cigarettes. He gave his friend one, two, twenty... When will he ever get them back? From there it goes to punches thrown because somebody said something about somebody's sister. She's cute, she's sexy, or reminds them of a prize hog. You get where this is going. These guys are trained like animals and if they don't get to do what they were trained to do, they go after each other."

"What happened?"

"We went into survival mode and did what we had to do. A few of us made our way into enemy territory and fired on our own troops. When they started firing back, we got the hell out of there."

"What?"

"What nothing. The war was started, each side thought the other was the bad guy, and the animals were released. Because of what we did, they fought the enemy instead of each other."

"That's terrible. Why did the States want the war?"

"To play around with a few military strategies, drop some new bombs, and wipe out North Korea, a communist state. Most of us hate your Alzien communism."

"What if you couldn't get back safely?"

"Our President couldn't get caught up in a scandal, so we were on our own. That often meant being shot or tortured. Desperate times, desperate measures, right? I don't know why this girl was put in the tower of goo, but she's alone right now. That means she needs answers more than you do."

"What do you think she's not telling us?"

"I don't know. Maybe what the link between that goo and these stones are. There's some life preserving energy there and she's not stupid. I also think she knows more about what she is, what her father made."

"Why do you say that?"

"It's in her eyes." Victor focused on Nicole's eyes. "Rapid eye movement, failure to make eye contact, too much eye contact, looking up, down, left or right. It all tells us what the person is really thinking. Cassandra always looks off to the right when she talks to us. There lies the world of make-belief. Her pupils also contract. That's a sign of unease, fear, or she simply doesn't trust us, or maybe it's just me."

"Is all this learning stuff an CIA thing?"

"I took years of beatings, lies, and torture, to make me who I am today."

"You were beaten by your own people?"

"We work at levels where we need to be the best. The alternative is death. Sometimes it's the death of thousands. A war starts or doesn't start. Maybe a cure for some crazy disease isn't found unless there's a population that needs saving."

"What are you saying? You poisoned innocent people?"

"Governments call it motivation." He pulled back. "Most leaders, and their factions, have a history of..."

"I sure hope you're not trying to condone any of this."

"Just saying, the big picture is sometimes more important that the moment. Remember, I'm a righteous man, not an asshole."

"What does that even mean?"

"I'm one of the good guys."

"No. What's the big picture?"

"Right now, this damn stone is the big picture. Cassandra's just the moment. Don't get too close to this one. Find out her story." He started to walk away but stopped. "Hey. Can I ask a favour?"

"You can ask. Not sure I'll help you though."

"I'm looking for someone, and you might know them."

"Got a name?"

"It's an oddball name, letters and numbers. MS01J884236S-66. Maybe you've heard of them?"

"No idea. Why?"

"Just looking." He made a mental note as he walked into the kitchen for an extra helping of food.

He'd noticed that Nicole's eyes had swayed to the right.

Chapter forty-seven

The view from the balcony was spectacular. It was as if she was flying and Cassandra took it all in, but she also kept an eye on Victor. She watched as he slipped into an easy chair to rest his still healing body. She wasn't sure why she thought he was a bad man. It was like a sixth sense. She looked back over the balcony.

"Is your whole planet this busy?"

Nicole had just stepped outside. "Not even close. Earth sits at about four billion."

"Unbelievable. We thought we were over-doing it with one billion."

Brittany tossed a last piece of deep-fried pork in her mouth. "Only one?"

"Our planet is smaller and a lot of it is ocean. And then there are the poles. No one lives there. We also have a huge and uninhabitable section. Nobody's allowed to go there."

Brittany asked, "what is it, desert?"

"Yes, a big one, about fifty million square kilometres."

"Whoa. That's bigger than Canada."

"The crust is thin, and it never stops rumbling. It's constantly transforming itself. Your planet doesn't have anything like that, does it?"

"No," Jenny answered. "We have huge deserts and two frozen poles. Other than that, we're pretty liveable."

Brittany got up and walked over to the computer. She brought Mars up on the screen.

Cassandra gave the planet a quick study. "What's this?"

"Uh, this is Mars, what we call your planet, the way it is now."

Cassandra gave it a much longer second look. "Where's all the water?"

"I imagine it went into space after your atmosphere failed," Brittany answered.

"What are those things?"

"Volcanoes." Nicole tapped on the largest one. "Your planet had a series of eruptions. We figure the venting lasted several years. That destroyed the atmosphere."

Brittany added, "Is that the Forbidden Zone?"

"I think so." Cassandra looked at the next few images and pointed to the deep canyon. I think Capital City was around here somewhere. That was my home. Our purpose was to be the guardians of the Forbidden Zone. "Can I get copies of these pictures?"

With a couple clicks of the mouse, the images started printing. "We can take these with us."

Cassandra gathered up the papers. "You're coming back with me?"

Brittany looked to her mother for the okay.

"I'd feel better if you were here tonight, but you can go. Just remember that this is a group effort. Understood?"

Cassandra answered for them both. "Definitely. I just want to talk to Kim and find out what his father knew. We won't be long."

Victor listened with his arms crossed. He'd definitely seen this type before. She wouldn't cross anybody, as long as she needed them. After that, all bets were off.

Nicole wasn't sold on her either. Skepticism had always protected her, and Victor had a proven track record. "Return as soon as you can. Remember how much I worry, okay Brit?"

"Gotcha." Brittany knew she'd put her mother through a lot these last few days. "We'll be quick."

The two girls rendered to Mars and found Kim and the gang by the fire. He and the others could only stare at the tight jeans.

"Get a good look so we can get back to business," Cassandra scoffed.

Kim was also intrigued by the mascara around her eyes. "That looks... nice."

"What did your father say?"

"Couldn't find him, but I found my contact. Remember how we thought there was some wild weapon being developed?"

"What was it?"

"Not sure, but they're having issues with an energy source." His expression turned grave. "They got thousands of these weapons, Cassandra. It's a part of what's called 'Project Earth'. That's all I've got so far. I'll get more answers from my father tomorrow when I see him, hopefully."

"We'll be back tomorrow then." She handed him the pictures. "Or this is our future. Find out whatever you can. It's important. Really, important."

Victor was sleeping when the girls reappeared. Nicole was standing beside him. "That didn't take long."

Brittany thought they'd been gone longer. "What's with him?"

"Death takes a lot out of you. How'd it go?"

"We found Kim. Turns out there's some kind of weapon."

"Weapon for what?" Nicole asked.

"For Earth. They'd been working on it and had a prototype. They're still trying to find a viable energy source."

"How many of these weapons are we talking?"

Cassandra put her hand on the amulet around her neck. "I'm getting the feeling it's thousands."

Chapter forty-eight

Thump. Thump. Thump. That woke Victor from his sleep. Thump. He looked around. Where was he? This wasn't Nicole's apartment anymore.

Thump. Thump.

Juliet, a young agent, rushed into the room. Victor didn't know her well, but knew of her. Her employment was yet another favour to somebody in the higher ups. Dangerously attractive, she was several beans short of being a lousy cup of coffee.

"Make it stop," she screamed. "Make it stop!"

Thump. Thump.

Victor covered his face with his arm when her head exploded. The body dropped to the floor a split second later. A piece of her skull, long blonde locks still attached, landed on the arm of the chair where he was sitting. That prompted him to his feet.

Thump. Thump.

Where was it coming from? Victor headed for the door. In the next room, two rows of agents sat in chairs facing each other. There had to be a hundred of them, sitting expressionless. Nearly twenty of them were headless and slumped in their chairs. The debris from the faces, the balding heads, and the brains, were scattered amongst the ones that sat patiently awaiting their fate. These were some of the smartest agents he knew and yet, here they sat, awaiting death.

Thump. Thump.

Mrs Steven's head burst. Victor shielded his face as he walked past her. If the order stayed true, Tony would be next, followed by Aubrey, Brian, and Phil.

Thump. Thump.

Being careful not to slip on the reddened linoleum floor, Victor hurried before Tony's head popped. As he made his way past Myrna, she grabbed his arm and stopped him.

Her eyes were distant. "You have to end this. It's madness."

He pulled his arm free, as if she were some zombie panhandling for brains. "I'll try."

Thump. Thump.

Victor ducked a piece of Aubrey's jaw and headed for the door at the far end of the room. Whatever this was, he had no idea how to stop it. It had to be implants, perhaps little explosives on a timer. What was the thumping then? Did he have one of those implants in his head?

Thump. Thump.

"Good-bye, Phil." Victor didn't have to look back to know his and Brian's brains were hanging from the ceiling. Phil had been the one that had talked him off the ledge as a young cadet. He was the one that had taught Victor to see the big picture. Life was a privilege, and that death was just the doorway to the next adventure. We all saw our birth as the beginning, and death as the end. To him that wasn't the case.

Thump. Thump.

Victor opened the door to see two people with their backs to him, a man and a woman. The man was wearing over-sized rubber gloves, a yellow plastic apron, and had a large wooden mallet in his hand. They were both wearing safety goggles. She was alternately handing him the apples and sparrows that she held in a large stainless-steel bowl. The birds sat on top of the apples as if under a spell.

On the floor, in a mess of crushed apples and feathers, fifty or more dead birds lay motionless. Victor stared at them waiting for them to twitch, roll around and come back to life, but they didn't. That was when he noticed the man dressed in black. He was the one who controlled the birds, controlled the souls. The Birdman was hanging in the corner by his neck. Instead of a rope around his throat, his life was being choked out by a live snake.

The woman looked back at Victor. She smiled as if she got the joke before he did. He recognised her immediately.

"What are you doing, Cassandra?"

"Do we have company?" The man turned around. "Oh. Hello, Vincent… or is it, Victor?"

"Dr Binghamton? Why are you doing this?" He noticed an amulet around each of their necks. They wore them as if some cultish badge of honour.

"Why, abomination decapitation, of course."

Chapter forty-nine

Victor jumped up from the armchair as if someone had set it on fire. He pulled the amulet off his chest and tossed it to the first person he saw.

Jenny caught it and quickly called for Nicole. "Victor's freaking out!"

Nicole came running. "What's happening?"

He grabbed for the arm of the chair to steady himself as the life-saving amulet's energy drained from his body. "Get that thing away from me."

"Don't be stupid." Nicole took it from Jenny and tried to hand it back to him. "Put this back on before you die."

"I'd rather take death," he replied as a knee began to buckle.

She tried to slip it over his head, but he swatted at it, knocking it out of her hand.

He struggled to pull strength from every fibre of his being, straightened his legs, and put a hand up. "Don't get me wrong. I appreciate the gesture, because you mean well. I just don't want anything to do with that damn stone."

"What happened?" Brittany asked. "Bad dream?"

"Maybe." He watched as Cassandra reached down to pick it up. "Or maybe it was a glimpse into the future. Either way, I need to get out of here."

He grabbed his coat and slowly made his way to the door. Nicole followed him out of the apartment and over to the elevator.

"What's really going on, Victor?"

"Watch her closely. She's the enemy." Then he remembered the photos on his phone. Sure, he was dead when he took them but was his death real? The photos came up like he knew they would, Cassandra in the box of goo.

"Where did you get these?"

"I took them when I was dead. Not sure what she has to do with that stone, but it scares the crap out of me."

"Where are you going? You can barely stand."

"I gotta find my man with the birds, make sure he's okay. In this last dream, she was killing apples and the birds."

"You lost me."

"Adam and Eve ate the apple. My birdman was being killed by the snake. I've gotta find him."

"You're in no shape to leave. Come back and rest."

"Gotta go. I'm heading back to the States."

"What? Are you crazy? They'll shoot you. Where in the States?"

"I'm not sure."

"How do you plan on finding him?"

Victor shrugged. "I'm hoping he'll find me. Did you bring that Ledger? Maybe we can…"

"No! We're not conjuring anybody."

He pushed the L button and it lit up. "That would make finding him a lot easier."

"Stay safe, Victor, and if you see him..."

"I'll ask." With that, the door closed, and a badly damaged Victor was gone.

Nicole made her way back to the apartment. "You said something about a weapon, Cassandra."

"Is your friend okay? He seemed a little off."

"Victor's a little off on a good day. What do we need to do on our end?"

"I'm not sure." Cassandra settled herself on the couch. "It needs a unique power source, and I can't see it being a threat with Earth as big as it is. You guys have billions of people and you're pretty advanced. They'd be no match."

"Earth has only populated over the last two thousand years. Before then, the population was under two hundred million people."

"Wait." Cassandra shook her head. "Kim said he'd have more answers in a day or two. Why do we have to wait? We're not on a regular timeline. Kim has to follow his course in time, but we don't. What's stopping us from going back two days later?" She looked over to Brittany. "Want to try?"

Brittany nodded. She was ready.

Her mother wasn't. "We don't know how it works for sure."

"Mom, we just did it."

Cassandra stopped her. "Your mother's right. We're only guessing that this back-and-forth leaping is safe. I'll go alone. Stay here and I'll be back in seconds." She checked her clothing to make sure it would stay with her. Then she was gone.

"Damn it, Mom, I'm not a little girl!"

"Enough! And I'm getting tired of telling you to watch your mouth! There's more to this than a little time travelling. I trust you could have gone without incident, but I needed to talk to you without her around. Simply put, we know nothing about this girl. She came back to life after who knows how many years and there's something about her that is sending all kinds of alarms off in my head."

"You mean in Victor's head. You liked her until he showed up."

"I don't know her, and Victor's been on our side the whole time. I trust his judgement."

"What? You were the one that told me about Cuba." Brittany responded, "He was killing people."

"They weren't people," she corrected. "They were conjured from a book. They didn't belong."

"My father was conjured. That means he doesn't belong. I'm his kid. That means I don't belong. You gonna let him kill us some day?"

"You and your father are safe."

"For now. What if the Birdman changes his mind?"

"Victor hasn't seen him in decades," but she knew he'd be looking for him.

"Is that what he told you?" Brittany crossed her arms and gave her mother a defiant stare. "His boss is a guy with a million birds. Where's the vote for sanity?"

"It's billions."

Brittany shrugged. "And yet you don't see all those red flags? How come?"

"Stop it." This time Nicole meant it. "I need you to trust me on this."

"I do trust you. I don't trust him."

"He's on our side. We'll have to be patient."

"Just like we need to be patient with Cassandra. Deal?"

"Fair enough."

Cassandra reappeared.

"You're back early." Brittany put a hand on her shoulder.

The girl was trying not to burst. "Really? It felt like I was gone a while."

"And?"

"This weapon has something to do with rendering. There were other abilities, but the rendering was the big one. It was something to do with armies that could render to different battlegrounds in an instant. It would be a game changer. They'd never get pinned down."

Nicole knew warfare. An advantage like this could wipe out Earth. Earth's population was in the millions, and they fought with spears, bows, and swords. They'd be no match for this new phenomenon. "How did they manage the rendering?"

"Kim's looking into it."

"Earlier you said your father had something to do with your ability. Was he good at manipulating DNA?" Brittany was thinking out loud.

"I went to the housing project to have a visit with my Mom. I asked her about my ability. It was a very interesting talk."

"You never talked with her about it before?" Brittany asked.

"I tried, but she always put me off, and Dad refused to acknowledge what I could do."

Brittany understood how that worked. "What did she tell you?"

"I was born in the same way other kids were, yet I'm a creation of some sort. I asked her if there were others that she knew of and she told me no. I was unique." She had to stop to take a breath. "She started explaining it all to me, but it was mostly over my head. I'm not a scientist."

"What exactly was she saying?" Nicole asked. "Can you remember for me?"

"All I got out of it was mind control, telekinesis, and teleportation, or rendering as you call it. I think the mind control was what Brittany and I were doing, zeroing in on each other." She shrugged. "What's telekinesis?"

Nicole knew what that was. Elizabeth had dabbled with it, with no success. "It's the ability to move objects without touching them."

Brittany gave a fist pump. "Right on! Will I be able to do this telekiwhatever?"

Cassandra nodded. "We should all be able to do it. Mom said it had something to do with the cleansing of our brain. We have the ability because we don't have the clutter. It's like our brains aren't overloaded with our history."

Nicole was starting to feel sick to her stomach. "Could it give us the ability to heal ourselves?"

Jenny had been quietly listening. "Or bring someone back from the dead?"

And what about the birds? Elizabeth had told her about them many years ago, how they'd come to life after being crushed under foot. It made her wonder about who this Birdman really was.

"Mom," Brittany interrupted. "You were born, weren't you?"

Nicole didn't answer.

Chapter fifty

There was no pushing Nicole for an answer when she never offered one. She had to have been born. Nobody had the technology to create someone from scratch. How would it even work? The human body was more than tissue, bones, and blood. It had a soul, emotions, and the ability to think and reason. Humans had compassion and they had a built-in ability to evolve. That couldn't be slapped together like a pizza.

She turned to Cassandra. You're saying we have abilities because our brains aren't so cluttered?"

"Don't ask me how it works or why. The fact is, our souls are fresh and uninhabited. There's a lot more room to expand."

"Is that why I didn't drown when that guy was choking me?" Brittany asked. "I mean it was weird. I felt like I could render away."

"What do you remember from that dream?"

"I sensed an abnormally close connection with the necklace."

"That's because I used the stone as a vessel to get out of my body before I died. It preserved my life. My body died, but my mind, and more importantly, my thoughts, were transferred to the stone. You touching that stone woke me up, and from there I could manipulate you because we were one."

"But I remember being pulled up on the dock. I remember them trying to resuscitate me."

"That was you. I was gone when they were doing that. I was in the stone. You were still sharing the body. I didn't know what was happening until you looked in that mirror the first time. It messed me up. Through your eyes I saw me. I never expected that. I'd heard of experiments being done on humans and my mind began racing."

Nicole wondered. "Experiments on humans? What kind?"

"Everything. It's quite common, but normally restricted to prisoners. My people feel that they have no rights, so scientists are allowed to use them for whatever they want. I had to imagine I was in that category as well. I wasn't a prisoner, but I wasn't one of them either."

That gave Jenny goosebumps. "That's awful."

"Why? These people chose to break the laws. They've done horrible things to people trying to raise families and live good lives. Prisoners can only serve one useful purpose and that is to help science." She looked around at everyone's response. "Oh, come now. They could have made different choices."

Brittany was quiet. She found it hard to disagree, although she wouldn't have admitted it out loud. "So, the shower was different?"

"I was showing you the capsule. At that point, I wanted out."

"How did I know everyone at the little town by the lake?"

"Not sure but that was my favourite place in the whole world, a place where they never judged me for being different."

Then Brittany remembered being yelled at by a man. "Hey, how are we different that the rest of the world? I don't see any difference, but I know it's in the eyes."

"Look into Melanie's eyes," Cassandra told her. "Then look into a mirror. You'll see that her eyes have perfectly rounded pupils. Try it."

Brittany moved over to Melanie and studied her eyes for signs. After a couple of minutes, she moved back to Cassandra and stared deep into her eyes. She could see how the pupils bled into the iris, much like ink on raw paper.

Nicole studied her eyes and then Jenny's. "Why is this?"

There was a brief knock on the door and Nicole's mother entered the apartment.

Brittany hugged her, handed her a plate, and waved her on to the kitchen to load up. "Mom and I have different eyes from everybody else. Did you know that?"

She looked back at the door, suddenly wishing she hadn't entered, but she had, and she was cornered. "Our earliest creatures had to evolve to what they are now. Your eyes are similar to those earliest eyes."

"Why the difference?"

"Sight wise they're very similar, except you have a harder time adjusting to light."

Nicole knew there was more to it. "You're saying I was born?"

"That's a stupid question."

"And yet, I'm asking it."

Her mother's admitting that she was indeed born, came with a stumble. It was hard to miss.

"Why'd you hesitate?"

"Because there's a lot I don't know."

Nicole dropped into the armchair. Her mouth didn't close, nor was she aware that it was open.

Brittany dropped down on the arm of that same chair. "Shit!"

Nicole gave her leg a swat. "Don't swear."

"You were thinking it." She put a hand on her mother's shoulder. The squeeze wasn't a loving one as much as it was a test. She felt normal. "Mom's made of flesh like the rest of you. So am I. How are we..."

Nicole's mother took a seat across from them. "I have no idea how he did any of that. I've already told your mother that."

"You said Mom was a creation. She wasn't made of spare parts, was she?"

"Brittany!" Nicole snapped.

"Well, I have no idea what all this means."

Nicole rubbed her temples. "What was the goo in that capsule, Cassandra?"

"Not sure," she answered.

Brittany scratched her head. "Was that goo keeping you alive, or was it just preserving you? You said you were in the rock?"

"I was. I also think the goo is made from the stone, because I felt a distant connection to my body."

"It's a good place to start," Nicole admitted. "We can compare its structure."

"Mom. What about the ghost?"

"Ghost?" Cassandra asked. "What's that?"

Nicole thought for a second. Against Victor's advice, she'd trust her and take her back to Mars. "I need to show you. Maybe you'll know this guy."

Brittany got back to her feet. "We're going to Mars?"

"We are, but I don't want you two being seen, not until I know more."

Cassandra nodded, but her eyes were dancing in their sockets.

And what would Victor say about dancing eyes?

Chapter fifty-one

C assandra concealed her disappointment well as she stood by the pup ship's console. Was it really a surprise that she wasn't trusted? Nicole's doubts were to be expected. When Brittany shot her mother a look, Cassandra interceded.

"Your Mother's right. I'm just glad you want to find out what happened to my planet and help me change the outcome."

The scenes from the pup ship's monitor mesmerised Cassandra as it carried them over the Martian surface. It was hard to fathom what she was seeing. They hadn't rendered because Nicole wanted the girl to see Mars for what it was. The young woman tried to compare what she was seeing to the topography she was used to. It was quite different without the oceans, mountains, and trees. She admitted that the Valles Mons was definitely a part of the Forbidden Zone. She wasn't sure about the canyons, and it showed in the wonderment of her eyes. When the pup landed, they suited up and took the gondola up to the entrance.

As they entered the small remnant area of the city that led them to the access point of the high-rise, Cassandra got a little spooked.

Nicole noticed. "Does this area look familiar?"

"Really hard to tell. It does and it doesn't. Hard to say when it's such a mess." She looked up at the spider web substance that held the dirt above them.

Again, Nicole felt she was holding back, but opted to let it go, for now. "Yeah, I suppose." She led them through the crack in the wall and up into the building.

Virgil wasn't available. He was sleeping and that was okay with Nicole. He likely wouldn't find any of this funny, or even sane. Thankfully, he still had the lights on.

Cassandra's first views caught her off guard. She'd expected things to be in better shape. The warehouse with the capsule had been well preserved, needing only a good dusting and sweeping of the dirt from the floor. This building didn't have a structural core.

Nicole put her finger to her lips, motioning for them to be quiet. She ushered them up the stairs and into the main room where Frederich had introduced himself. She stopped them at the door and peeked in. He was nowhere to be found, so she searched for a spot to hide them. One of the glass cases would do. It was dark enough to hide behind, and yet give them a perfect view.

She started them toward the case and watched for Frederich to appear. "Hurry!" Her voice was strained. "He could show up at any time."

The two girls nested behind the glass case and Nicole walked up to the spot where the artifact and papers were found. "Hello?"

Frederich appeared like he always had. "Miss Nicole. A pleasure to see you. Quite unexpected, but you've been surprising me a lot lately. How can I help you?"

Cassandra had a flood of emotions as the man appeared out of thin air. He looked and seemed real, as he stood across from Nicole. She could feel her heart beating in her chest and thought it might stop at any time.

Brittany did as her mother had asked earlier and carefully watched for any kind of reaction. She was having a hard time believing what she was seeing. Cassandra looked pale and absent. It was like her heart was about to explode. "Are you okay?" Brittany whispered in her ear.

Cassandra didn't speak. She simply shook her head side to side and disappeared. Brittany was hard on her heels as she also rendered back to the apartment. It was the designated safe zone for this encounter, and it was needed.

"Did you hear that, Miss Nicole?"

She'd heard something like a pair of far away pops, but it was a distant sound, and she was half-listening for it. She'd never really heard the pops made by rendering before, but then she'd never been in a room this quiet. "I'm sorry. What did you hear?"

Frederich quickly dismissed it. "I'm sorry, must have been nothing. How can I help you today?"

"I'm not sure I need help. Life was a little dull, so I came to Mars for a bit of a break from the whole work thing. This place always excites me in ways that daily work can't."

"Why, what is it you do?" He'd got used to her small talk and even started to enjoy it. You never knew what you could learn about a person. "When you're at work that is."

"That's a bit of a tough one. I'm primarily a psychologist, but I also dabble in the other sciences. More genetic manipulation than anything."

Frederich's head cocked to the right. "You know about genetics?"

"My parents did, and a lot of it rubbed off on me. Are you a scientist?"

"I am, of sorts." He was proud to admit it. "I categorised all the different functions of the double helix. We were making great advancements in the field until the leaders opposed our tactics. They tried to shut us down, but this wasn't something we, as scientists, could walk away from. They threatened us, but we weren't afraid. They couldn't stifle our curiosity."

Nicole knew the types. "What did you do?"

"We tried to ignore them, but then they took my wife's life. I took my lab and slipped into a cloak of secrecy. My lab was built with stolen equipment. I'm not proud of the fact, but I did what I had to do."

"That's terrible, about your wife. Did they ever find your lab?"

"No. And it's still fully functional."

"I'm sorry. What do you mean?" That wasn't what she expected to hear. "It wasn't buried in all the ash?"

"No, and it's close by. Do you want me to take you to it?"

Chapter fifty-two

Turbulence rocked Victor's private jet as it made its way toward Mexico. He knew the only way he could get into the States was through one of the drug lanes. From Puerto Palomas or El Paso, they could fly low elevation through New Mexico and on through to DC. There was a small airport run by a friend of his in the Rose Valley area. They could put down there and drive to the city centre, and to the Pentagon. That was the plan. When he awoke, the plane was touching down at what looked like the Jose Marti Airport in Cuba.

He worked his way up to the cockpit. "What's going on?"

The pilot didn't look back at him. He had to watch the instruments. "We've got some real bad weather along the American border. We can still head up the eastern coast, but we need to refuel first."

"Is this Cuba?"

"Yes. Havana, Sir."

"Fair enough. Refuel and get a bite to eat. I'll need an hour or two to run an errand."

"Do you need an escort, Sir?"

"I'll be fine."

Victor left the airport in a taxi and was in Havana in minutes. The place brought back so many memories, the car chases, the tussles with Violet Stormm, and the old lady in the bird shit covered apartment. It also flooded him with a mess of emotions.

There was Bob the Habs fan who only wanted a little freedom from a wife he'd grown to resent, Juanita the girl that had got in over her head with the Russians, and there was Beverly Shipstone. He could have fallen for a girl like her, had she not been on the list.

"We in Havana, now. Where to, Mister?"

"Head to the cemetery."

"*Si*." The driver knew better than to ask which one. This gringo was like all tourists, wanting to walk through the acres and acres of history.

Victor got out of the cab at one of the north gates. He walked in and tried not to think about how he'd shoved Violet Stormm in front of a moving car. She was a good sport about it, and would even laugh about it over drinks, years later.

There was history in Cuba, that was for sure, but Victor couldn't care less about the people buried here. The man he wanted wasn't under the ground. He was alive and, dare he say, and old friend. Sure, they hadn't talked in almost two decades, but they'd been through a lot.

Juan Perez's headstone made a good spot for Victor to take a seat. His chest was still healing, as were his lungs. The air was dry and burnt in his chest like lit gasoline. Still, he wouldn't have wanted that stone around his neck no matter how bad the pain.

A small bird landed on the headstone beside him. It looked up at him like a child might look to a mother when being praised. Feathers ruffled and slowly settled back down. Victor watched as the beak worked away at the feathers, grooming as if readying itself for a date. Seeing the bird made Havana seem like a dream.

"Whatcha up to little guy?"

The bird raised its head. It made Victor think of Robert DeNiro in Taxi. 'Are you talk'n to me? cause I'm the only one here'. That was a good movie. The bird didn't respond like DeNiro. Instead, it chirped once and fluttered off.

Victor watched the bird fly away and looked round for others. There were none. He was stupid to come here, to think that this place still held the magic that it did all those years ago. That was a different time, and that crap no longer existed. Slightly rested, it was time to get going. The plane should be fuelled and ready and he was wasting time.

And why was he wasting time? Did he really want to know more about Vincent, about how that book worked? This was the shit that was behind him now, or was it? Cassandra had brought it all back. Whatever she was, it was dangerous. That, he knew in his heart.

A sudden shade took the sun's heat off Victor's face. As much as he liked the break, it stopped him dead in his tracks. He looked up at the sky to see them, thousands of them. They swirled, dove, and manoeuvred the sky in an aerial display that turned heads. They formed the feathery vortex, like they'd done before, and then shot off in all directions. Nobody, other than Victor, had noticed that the man with the black coat, gloves, and hat, had suddenly appeared from the chaos. They were too busy watching the birds.

Victor saw him and headed over. "I never get tired of seeing that."

The man, who was about six inches taller than the six-foot Victor, watched as the birds left. He didn't speak until the last bird found a perch. "We have a problem."

"The stones?" Victor unbuttoned his shirt to show him the bullet holes. "One of them brought me back."

The man put a gloved hand on Victor's chest. "It isn't right. Dead should be dead."

"What are those amulets?"

"Bedlam."

He summoned for his birds as the first grave burst open. A man, dead for years, clawed his way out of the dirt as if he'd been buried alive. He was dead when he'd been put there. The soil of another grave started to move as a hand breached the surface. The skin hanging on the bones was badly rotted. One by one, people dug themselves out of their graves, each one wanting what the stone had to offer.

The birdman put his arms down, palms toward the ground as if pushing these people back into the earth. The birds began to circle him. Victor watched as the graves became quicksand pulling a few back under. Many continued to claw for freedom.

Victor lost focus as the feathery wings slapped at his face and pulled at his shirt. They circled faster and faster. The man, no longer a man, broke apart, becoming a black dust. He was quickly absorbed by the birds. Then they started for the power lines, trees, and rooftops.

Suddenly, the noise was gone, and he was alone. He stared at the last bird that had perched in a nearby tree. He wasn't sure how he knew it, but this bird was the one that had stood beside him. It was the man with the black coat, gloves, and the hat.

"Bedlam?" Victor uttered as he shook his head. "What do I do about it?"

A hand landed on Victor's calf. It pulled on his leg as the attached body pulled its way up to the surface. It was a woman's body, an older woman. She looked up at him and he could see the bullet hole in her temple. He could also see that the back of her skull was missing. She had been the one in the rocking chair, all those years ago. Her teeth were gnarled as she sunk them into his leg.

Victor woke up as the plane dipped in the turbulence. It had been a dream. He mustered himself to his feet and started for the pilot. "Change of plans. We're going to Cuba."

Chapter fifty-three

Frederich, the no-nonsense apparition, had surprised Nicole by opening up to her about his lab. The man was a lost child in need of something, and Nicole could tell he was baiting her for a favour. He wouldn't be telling her these things if he didn't think she could help him. Thing was, she needed him too, but she'd have to be careful playing this game on his turf.

"Would you like to have a look?"

"At your lab? Definitely," Nicole replied.

"On the main floor, behind a pile of rubbish, you'll find a metal door. I'll see to it that it's not locked. From there, go down the stairs and turn left."

"But where will..." She found herself talking to nobody. "Damn it."

Nicole made her way back down the stairs until she came to the main floor. This area was foreign to her. She'd only searched the upper floors. The dust and scattered bits of debris were littered everywhere, and she had to watch for hanging obstacles. She made her way through the mess of broken furniture.

Frederich's directions had led her to the rubbish pile and a heavy metal door. It wasn't locked, so Nicole slipped into the near darkness. She carefully descended the stairs and shuffled her way along the basement floor. Pipes and cables hung above her like arrant cobwebs as she cut through the disarray. This building was a bit like the ones on Earth as far as the mechanics went. Eventually, the path dead-ended.

"What the hell is this?" She could feel her heart beating faster.

"It's okay, Miss Nicole. There's more." He had reappeared and was pointing to a pile of crates on a pallet. "They're empty. You see I was a good friend of the owner of this building."

Nicole watched as the crates suddenly pivoted at the corner. The massive pile of boxes moved out of the way with ease. An opening appeared, and Nicole looked down into a lit room. For the first time on Mars, she didn't see rubble or ruins blanketed in dust. She saw a technical, fully operational laboratory.

She found herself carelessly racing down the metal steps to steal a better look. "This is incredible. How did it survive the cave in?"

Frederich floundered with his answer. "Let's say, it's sealed up pretty good. Only I can get in or out, unless I invite you."

Nicole started snooping right away. He watched, trying to gauge how advanced she was in that field. The chess game had begun, and she played it better than anyone, except perhaps for Frederich.

"I have to ask, because you seem to disappear and reappear at will. I thought you were an apparition, but…"

"AI Computer. And what you see are holographic images. There are small projectors and cameras in several locations, but I'm triggered by two motion sensors. One is by the crate door and the other is at the history archive, where we first met.

"There isn't one here?"

"No need. Nobody can get in here unless I invite them."

"Good point. And what's in here?"

"This is where I, and a few of my family are."

Nicole slid the drawer open. It was a heavy one that revealed six embryos sealed up in mini cylinders. "These samples are fresh. Are you still working on things here?"

"It's complicated." How could he expect her to understand his situation? "I'm incapable of doing anything other than regular maintenance. These DNA models are ready to go, but I never figured out how to bring them to life."

"Do you mind?" She looked at one of them with a magnifying glass. "This is such delicate work." She took her time and risked his curiosity, but she had to see if it showed signs of origin. She couldn't tell without further testing. "I'm sorry, this is beyond me. What have you tried?"

"All the wrong procedures. As you can see, I have limited samples. Can I ask a favour of you?"

"If I can help, I will."

"I need help finishing this project."

Nicole knew to play ignorant. "What procedure do you need, exactly?"

"I need to know how your people use enzymes to give life to DNA strands. With your advanced technology, I'm sure someone knows how."

"Can I ask who these strands belong to?" The silence was awkward. "You said you were one of them?"

He opted to spare her the details. "To spare you a long-winded story, this is my family. These are parents, a wife and a daughter."

"You realise that this would be replicating the beginning. We'd have to find a way to carry you and the others to term and raise you from infancy. And there's no way you could live here."

"I don't want to be carried to term in a secondary vessel. That would be receiving life from life. I wish for the untainted version of life from creation. I'm also hoping Earth would adopt us and see us as the last true beings of this planet." His look was sincere. "I don't have options. As a computer, I can keep these lights on, but I'm only a beacon looking for help."

"Before we fill out the adoption papers, I have to say, life from creation is difficult." Her eyes softened. "But we won't rule that out. Can I ask a couple more questions?"

"By all means."

"The artifact you gave me holds certain powers. What do you know about it?"

"This may be disappointing, but the artifact is just a key to the box." He added. "I made the box and used it as the key. It was special, but only to me."

"What is that stone? It seems to shimmer at times, like it has a life of its own."

"It was a piece of a meteorite." He didn't admit to any importance. "There were several pieces. My daughter liked them. She was a bit of a geologist."

"I guess she died in the disaster?"

"No. She committed suicide."

Nicole's knees weakened and she felt the blood draining from her face. "Suicide?"

This didn't seem pertinent, yet he told Nicole his story anyway. "She couldn't handle her mother's murder. The stress finally caused her to take her life. It still hurts when I think about it."

"I'm so sorry. How did she take her life?"

"She drowned at the lake. Her friends didn't help matters, wanting her to be a part of their group."

"Group?"

"A group called The Keepers. Just a bunch of kids stirring up trouble. It was too much for my Cassandra to handle."

"Could I see the rest of this lab?"

He thought for a split second and motioned her to one of the other rooms. "The rest is just living quarters and storage, but feel free to look around."

Frederich truly had come close to getting his experiment to work. In that room, Nicole noticed a few plants and several tissue samples living in purple goo."

"You figured out this preserving fluid?"

"I had an associate. He supplied that gem of science."

"An associate?"

"Not important. Can you help me?"

"I can try."

Brittany could only guess at Cassandra's reaction. "You knew him, didn't you?"

Cassandra just stood there swaying like she was about to collapse. She had literally seen a ghost.

"That was my father."

Chapter fifty-four

Nicole's trip back from Mars only took twelve minutes to travel and she rendered the rest of the way once the pup ship had landed. She wanted to get back to the apartment as quick as she could. Brittany had tried to talk to Cassandra, but it was difficult with so many people around. Jenny read this in her usual fashion and took her kids and Brittany's grandmother back to their room.

Cassandra kicked her feet up on the coffee table while Brittany filled a couple of bowls with ice cream. She was reading a book when Brittany returned. "What's this?"

"Oh." She immediately took it from her. "That's my mother's notebook. She doesn't want anybody reading it, even me."

"I was only skimming. The story sounds familiar."

"Probably because I was reading it when I first entered your world. I was horseback riding, walking through a swamp, and... "

"Breaking a mirror and cutting your wrists," Cassandra concluded. "Sorry about that."

Brittany looked down at the bandages. "That's right."

"Where'd the story come from?"

"Mom found some papers on Mars, real weird stuff, all symbols and strange patterns. She's spent years deciphering what few papers she has."

"She never found all the papers?"

"No." Brittany handed her a bowl. "Now tell me about him, your father."

Cassandra took a bite and slowly pulled the spoon out of her mouth. "What can I say. He died thousands of years ago and yet there he is!"

"This is what we call a blind-side." Brittany was calm and almost nonchalant in her questioning. "How do you think he did it?"

"No idea." She twisted up her face. "Imagine seeing your real Mom."

"I would have run up and made an ass of myself."

"Except you're forgetting two things. I never knew him all that well, because he always worked. I also thought we were going to Mars to meet a ghost. I never expected that to happen because they don't exist."

Brittany frowned. "Do you think he had anything to do with this weapon?"

"I didn't know him that well. I also felt an odd presence. It was really strong when he appeared, and even stunned me at first. What is he, and what does that make me?"

Nicole walked in from her bedroom. "I think we all need to talk."

Brittany turned to her. "Bet mine beats whatever you've got. Frederich is her father."

Nicole had already figured that out, but was glad Cassandra volunteered the information freely. "What can you tell me?"

"I have no idea why he's on Mars thousands of years later. He has to be a creation. Think about it. He can disappear and reappear at will."

"That wasn't your father. That was a holographic image. There's a computer running things there."

"So, he's not..."

"Not your father. I imagine he died with the others, a long time ago."

"Maybe we should go see my mother. She'll have answers. She married the man."

Brittany nodded. "It might be the only way. We're at a bit of a standstill."

Nicole, against her better judgement, had to agree. "You'll have to take us with you. We've never been there, and I've never seen Mars, except for the current version."

"I'll take you." She reached over and brought Nicole and Brittany in close.

The three ended up at the housing projects. Brittany was shocked to see how much it was like the dream. Kids played in the streets, gates hung crooked on fences, usually by one hinge. The lawns were dead, and only one house looked like anyone actually cared. Nicole was shocked that this was Mars and needed a second.

"You okay, Mom?"

"Wow." She closed her mouth as she took it all in. "Incredible."

Cassandra opened the door and stepped inside. "Hello?"

Brittany looked over to Nicole. "Talk about being here."

Nicole realised from that comment that Brittany was still living Cassandra's past. "A little weird, isn't it?"

"A lot weird." Brittany gave her a shoulder nudge. "What about you? How do you like the time travelling?"

"It's hard to believe this is Mars."

They entered the house after Cassandra. A woman met them in the kitchen. "Cassandra? Hello. Who are your friends?" She sat down and offered them to do the same. "This looks important. What's wrong?"

Cassandra gave her a hug before taking a seat beside her. "It's about Dad." She wasn't sure where to start but decided on the dreams with Brittany. She eventually told her about the capsule and finished off by confessing she'd seen her father in Mars's distant future, as a computer wanting their help. "How could Dad be a computer thousands of years from now? What was he up to?"

"You must be hungry." It was as if she'd tuned her out.

Cassandra knew her mother had answers. Changing the subject was a dead give away, so she persisted. We're trying to save the planet. We need to know who he is."

"Pardon me?"

Cassandra gave her mother the condensed version of what she'd heard from Kim. "It's important, Mom."

Her mother fumbled her hands. The conversation had come up at least a dozen times and she'd dodged it each time, like a good mother should. There had been excuses when he'd missed birthdays, and she always managed to cover things up in hopes that he'd come around. He never did. "It's a long story."

"These two can do what I do. We need to know what we are, so we can make the right changes."

Cassandra's mother turned to Nicole and Brittany. "You can do it? I'm sorry, my daughter hasn't introduced us. I'm Julie."

"Mom, this is Nicole and Brittany and they're from Earth."

"Actually, we're from Alzie," Brittany corrected.

Knowing there were others that were able to move around by thought changed everything. The fact that they were alien...

"We need to talk."

Chapter fifty-five

Victor walked through the cemetery knowing that his man would show, and while he would have preferred to do this over drinks at one of the local bars, dirt and tombstones would have to do. Each grave seemed calm, no arms clawing at the open air... at least not yet.

After a few minutes, the sky darkened, the birds came. With that, the man soon appeared. He calmly made his way to Victor. Had Victor's feet not been planted in the soil by his weakened state, he'd have met him halfway.

"Why are you here?" the man asked. "You have your list."

"Funny story. I was flying to the States when I had a dream... about you. I've actually had you in my dreams a couple of times, that's if you can call them dreams."

A man of few words, the Birdman said nothing.

Victor started to unbutton his shirt revealing the six marks on his chest. "I was shot a few days ago. I should have died."

"But you didn't." His voice was deep. "Why not?"

"I was wearing a purple stone around my neck. It has healing powers. There was one found on Earth and another on Mars. I wasn't the only one saved either. I was wondering if you had any idea how the damn thing works."

"You actually died?"

"I can only go by what I was told."

"There was no sensing it? You said something about dreams?"

"I only call them that because I don't know what else to call them. I did LSD in the seventies, so I know the difference between dreams and tripping. These were neither. They were more like visions into the future."

"How so?"

"In the first one there was a girl in a tub of sludge. I don't know how I knew it, but the shit was keeping her alive. You were hanging in the corner, a big-ass snake around your neck. Now here's the punchline. A day ago, I saw that girl. She's real, and she's from Mars." Victor showed him the picture on his phone.

The man remained quiet.

Victor continued. "In the other dream, I had met you here and bodies were crawling out of their graves. You said it was bad and that your birds were losing control."

"I don't lose control."

"Well, it sure looked like you were."

The man inadvertently looked to the right as he opened his mouth to speak.

Victor cut him off. "Whatever you were about to say, it's a lie. I don't need lies. I need the truth. What's this stone?"

"You say a rock saved you from death?"

"Me, Rose, Benny, and Cassandra. She's the Martian girl."

"I was worried about this."

"Why would bodies be coming out of the ground? Why would anybody want to see you dead? These rocks, they don't come from around here, do they?"

"They're being used by the enemy."

"You have an enemy?"

"That's why the list."

"The list?" Victor chuckled. "There was only one name on the list, and it wasn't even a name. What the fuck is a MS01J88...uh."

"MS01J884236S-66." He said it with ease. "It's Alzien."

"I don't do that kind of travelling."

"You won't have to."

"Where do I find this MS01J884236S-66 guy?"

"You need to ask your friends."

With that the birds came, flew a few laps, and shot off to the trees. Victor tried to keep his eyes open, but the dusty feathers were too much for him. Once again, the Birdman had made his escape.

"I did," he shouted out, "and they aren't talking."

Chapter fifty-six

Nicole introduced herself before telling her about Alzie, a planet in another solar system. "Our abilities are unique on our planet and Earth has nothing like it."

"Are you sure?" She rubbed her temples. "Frederich, your father, wasn't unique and your abilities weren't inherited."

"How did I get this ability?" Cassandra asked.

"It's complicated. It has a lot to do with genetics and it's not easy to understand."

"I was a creation, wasn't I? Who made me, my father?"

Julie looked to Brittany and Nicole. "You'd all have to be the results of similar experiments?"

Nicole nodded.

"You don't know how it works?" Julie asked.

Nicole's nod was a side to side one. "Not entirely."

"I'll try to explain. If I start to lose you, just stop me. There is one big difference between you three and say someone like me. It has to do with the brain." She paused like a teacher ready to make a point. "The human brain is a capacity driven organ that starts off at about ninety-five percent at birth and ends up at about ninety-eight."

"Okay." Nicole cut her off almost immediately. "You've lost us. We're taught that the conscious and subconscious take up closer to twenty or twenty-five percent."

The Alziens and Earthlings didn't understand the human brain like she did. She had dedicated her life to the study until Frederich had gone against the system, causing her to flee with Cassandra for their safety. "I'll explain a few things."

Nicole and Brittany listened closely.

"The human body is run by signals, but these signals are more than just our thoughts. There's an exhausting process that runs everything we think and do. A lot of these processes are recorded and that takes up the balance of the brain's power and capacity."

"We already knew this," Brittany admitted.

"These signals and processes don't take up one hundred percent of the brain?" Cassandra asked.

"No. We have archives of our evolutionary history saved. As the species evolves, the history becomes clutter. Our capacity to learn more shrinks with every generation."

"How do you know this?" Nicole asked.

"As with everything, it started with theories. We experimented on people to prove our studies."

Nicole wasn't surprised. "These experiments could destroy the human body, couldn't they?"

"Oh yes, and often did." Her frankness bothered both Nicole and Brittany, but they remembered what Cassandra had told them earlier.

Julie motioned for them to be quiet. "You asked how you acquired these abilities. The big difference between your brain and mine is the lack of all that evolutionary data. You see, I have a large portion of my brain dedicated to the steps it took to get me from that basic first human to the highly developed creature that I am today. Try and imagine the countless DNA blueprints slowly morphing me into what you see now. Each generation and every hurdle would be documented in an entirety that you don't fully understand. It's a lot of saved data."

"It would be." Nicole was impressed.

"The downside for you is that your DNA doesn't have a history of errors to learn from." Julie added, "My DNA would never allow a redundant recreation."

Brittany had to wonder. "Does that mean I could become flawed?"

"You seem fine, so if there's no significant flaws, don't worry. In a few thousand years your ancestors will differ a bit from mine. It might be something as simple as eye colour, or perhaps it could be the ability to regenerate a limb. It's hard to say. There's a lot of brain capacity for you to develop. I'd need to lose something to continue evolving."

"So, what happened to your husband?" Brittany asked. "Was he acting weird?"

"When Frederich was a child, he was an angel. He used to push me on the swing, and we never got bored talking. I met him when he was fourteen and within weeks, we were best friends. He'd talk about anything. I never got tired of being with him."

Brittany was confused. "He was a nice person?"

"He was a wonderful man. He spoiled me to the point where I often felt guilty. By seventeen we were inseparable. Cassandra came along shortly after."

"Normal birth," Nicole wondered.

"An insemination. Frederich was very careful with what he shared and with who. Most thought it was a natural pregnancy. He knew you were special because of all the testing he did, but we couldn't figure out what he'd done to you. He was the master of genetics."

"Did he want me as a daughter or a lab rat?"

"Who knows anymore? The man was gifted with intelligence, and they pushed his training. I decided to specialize in the physical mind. Our knowledge complemented each other. After we discovered your lack of evolutionary clutter, he decided to find out more."

"That's why I can do things like rendering?"

"The first time you did it you scared me. It took your father the whole night to explain it to me, and I was one of the smarter ones. He was so excited to show the Leaders that he didn't sleep that night. First thing in the morning he blew their minds and jumped from brilliant to legendary status. He was untouchable and slowly got more and more freedom until it got to the point when I hardly saw him anymore."

"Why?" Brittany asked. Nicole had always had time for her.

"They had to know how it worked."

"But I hardly ever saw him," Cassandra sputtered. "If I was the one with the ability…"

"He took blood and tissue samples from you. He even did scans on your brain. It took all of a day. Then you weren't needed."

Nicole had an obvious question. "He never revealed to anyone that he'd created her?"

"That would have been a jail sentence, maybe death. We're not allowed to do the Creator's job. The rules are strict. No, they thought he'd simply altered her DNA."

"He was trying to make copies of me?" Cassandra interrupted. "Did he ever tell you what this project was called?"

"Never to my face, but I heard him on the phone a couple of times. There were several projects he was in on."

Cassandra asked. "Does Project Earth sound like any of them?"

"I've overheard a conversation about that one the same time the Leaders started shutting him down. They figured he was lying to them about results and about the magnitude of these projects. That was when he started hanging out with people I didn't know."

"Kim had mentioned that Project Earth was a plan devised to invade Earth. They were creating super weapons. Do you think Dad was altering people to be weapons? I mean, if he could cleanse their DNA, that is."

"Very possible."

"Wouldn't people be afraid of being altered?" Cassandra asked.

"No." Nicole thought of the American President. "There are people who would kill for it. It would sure explain why the Leaders were uptight. What else have you heard?"

Julie thought for a bit. "Kim's father was a close friend. Maybe I could talk to him."

"Sounds like eliminating Dad has become a priority with the Leaders."

"He was up to no good and doing it with bad people." Julie looked directly at her daughter. "And he wasn't the only one they wanted to rid from the planet."

Chapter fifty-seven

C assandra couldn't help wondering how this related to the end of her planet, or how her father managed to still be around thousands of years later. "What were the last things you remembered about him?"

"Last things?" Julie spoke calmly as she recounted the day. "Last time I saw him he roughed me up because he wanted to take you away. More tests. I tried to tell him you weren't home, but he wouldn't believe me."

Cassandra didn't remember things the same. "That's not what happened. I came home from school, the place had been ransacked, and we had to flee from the Leaders. He said they wanted to terminate us."

Julie shook her head. "Your father was the one who ransacked the place, not the Leaders. He was looking for you and some folder. He was desperate. I had been thrown down the stairs when you got home. I wanted to yell out but couldn't."

"I never knew. I thought he was taking me to safety."

"We should see what we can find at Mr Bennett's office," Julie announced. "He had some dealings with your father. He'll be at the research library right now, so the office will be empty. Will you two be okay? We shouldn't be long."

"We'll be fine." Nicole watched Cassandra render them away. "Okay, Brit. Take me to that hotel. I want to see what's there."

Brittany wrapped her arms around her.

The inside of the room gave Brittany a shiver as she checked the mirror to see her own reflection. This was where she'd first seen Cassandra and heard her reprimanded by a familiar voice that must have been Frederich's. She remembered a suitcase by the door, but it was gone. The two quickly, and methodically, tore the room apart.

Nicole was almost out of breath. "Nothing!"

Brittany smiled and produced a piece of crumpled piece of paper. "Not nothing."

Nicole read it. "Gerricks Building. This sounds like a military wing."

They made their way through the Martian complex looking for the Gerricks Building. They noticed it at the same time. Brittany looked to her mother. "An Embassy?"

"No, not elaborate enough, but definitely something big and official." She started for the door. "Let's find out, besides I have to show you what's underneath the basement." She thought for a second. That was, if it had been built yet.

The two made their way inside the lobby, taking a brief look before going up a floor.

Nicole looked around the large room full of the familiar glass cases. Brittany tapped her arm like she wanted to ask her something. Nicole nodded. It was the room where they had seen Frederich, the room with the artifact and papers. Nicole looked to the man and smiled warmly.

"Can I help you. Miss?"

"Perhaps a stupid question, but what is this floor?"

"Why this is our Historical Library. Almost every artifact and document relating to our history from this region is here and I would have to assume, because you didn't know that, that you don't have the correct clearances to be in here." His smile looked almost apologetic.

"You would be correct. I'm sorry. It's just that I find it all so engaging, don't you think?" Her flirting was clumsy.

"I do." He took a deep breath and exhaled slowly. "Were you wanting to see anything in particular?"

"I wouldn't get you in trouble, would I? I'd let you escort my every step," Nicole offered.

"That would be nice." He swallowed hard. "Be my guest. I'd be happy to follow you around."

Nicole giggled as she casually made her way to the case where she initially found the artifact and papers. The spot had items, but they weren't anything she recognized.

"You were looking for something specific?"

"I had heard of some documentation pertaining to the beginning of mankind and maybe even some sort of artifact like a neck adorning ornament."

"I know we have documentation that dates back quite a distance, but we've never been able to figure out whether they're from our planet. The language is foreign."

Nicole could feel her heart beating faster. She had to remain calm. "Any chance a fellow history buff could see them?" He was getting her best puppy dog eyes.

"I don't see why not. It's not like you could figure them out."

In a hidden drawer behind the counter the man pulled out a stack of aged documents. He spread them out over the countertop. Nicole was amazed at the aging and the simple looking hieroglyphics. She hadn't seen these pages before. "And have they ever been tested for age?"

"The originals have, and we're talking thousands of years."

"And no translation?"

"You'd think it wouldn't be a problem with these simple figures, but surprisingly, there's no pattern to decipher. There must be some form of elaborate blueprint. We've had our best people look at them. A few theories float around from our ancestors that they're from another planet. It makes you wonder how advanced they are on Earth?"

"There's life on Earth?" Nicole fitted it in for a lead to her next questioning.

"No solid proof, but we've made several trips there. I'd have to say there's something. Why else would they lie about the missions?"

Nicole was running blindly. "You figure they're lying too?"

The man didn't know her, so it was time to backtrack. "Lying is maybe a little strong. It's just odd we've had three missions with no known success. They simply chalk it up as a failed mission and hurry on to the next, like kids with a secret."

"No, you're right. It has always struck me as odd too." So, they had been to Earth. "You wouldn't have extra copies of these documents, would you?"

The man started to round everything up. "Why? They're secret documents. I never should have brought them out." He quickly shuffled them back into the drawer.

"I'm sorry. I just thought they'd look good on the walls in my home. They're artistic, like artwork."

Breathing a sigh of relief, the man nodded. "Actually, you're right. They would look good framed."

"I'm sorry. I've made you uneasy. I never meant to do that, and it was rude of me. Like you said earlier, I could never decipher them anyway."

"That's true. I just don't want trouble." He gave her a wink. "Besides, you don't look like the criminal type."

Nicole gave him a bat of her eyes. "That's so sweet."

Brittany politely interrupted. "Sorry to bother you both, but what are these things?" She motioned to several rocks in an adjacent case. They sat in a pile like eggs in a nest.

The man had been so overwhelmed by Nicole that he almost forgot about Brittany. "These are meteorites. They've come from all over. These ones have been tested and they're organic in nature. I doubt that'll mean anything to you, but it's truly a special feature."

"They're pretty," Brittany added.

Nicole muttered under her breath. "Panspermia."

The man heard her. "Wow. Not too many people know that term. I think I know what your field of expertise is."

Nicole blushed. It brought her back to the days when her and Elizabeth had explained that term to the Earthlings. "Yeah, I'm a bit of a science nerd."

"You'd have to be, to get stuck on this base." He chuckled. "That or a spy." His stare was directed straight at her. It made her uneasy until he broke out in laughter.

"Good one." She shook her head. "We should run. It was nice meeting you."

"Maybe we can get together later?"

Nicole played along with a smile. "Maybe." She wondered what this guy knew. He might get a second visit at this rate.

"We should get back." Brittany knew Cassandra and her mother wouldn't be long.

"Right." Nicole held out her hand in a final flirt to the man and he shook it like a gentleman. She had worked her charm, and it had paid dividends. "Truly a pleasure."

Nicole entered the stairway first. "Those documents are something I'm going back for."

Brittany followed as her mother went down to the main floor and then to a metal door. "Where are you going now?"

"The basement. I have something to show you."

Chapter fifty-eight

Victor studied each bird as he left the cemetery. One of these damn things had to be the Birdman, and he still wanted answers, like how was he going to find somebody without a photo or an address. His name wasn't even a name. By the time he reached the sidewalk, he had the Alzien phone up to his temple. He was thinking of Nicole, but when she didn't answer, his thoughts drifted to Violet Stormm.

"Hey, Vic. Long time no hear. What's it been, ten, twenty years? How many kids ya got?"

He almost hung up. "You haven't changed."

"Are you kidding me? I haven't been shot or stabbed in six months. That's damn near revolutionary."

"What, did you retire?"

"My kid made me quit."

"And you listened?"

"He said if I get shot eight times I have to stop, believed I only had nine lives."

"He knew you weren't a cat, right?"

"I made him a promise back at bullet number four."

"Probably for the better if you're getting shot up that often."

"Why'd you call, Victor?"

"Remember Cuba?"

Violet was still intoxicated from her morning coffee. "We didn't do anything, so if you're pregnant, you're on your own." She barely finished the sentence before laughing.

"You're a real peach. I was given another list."

There was silence. Victor knew she was picking her jaw up from the floor. He waited for her and wondered if she still had it in her to stop him. It had been a few years.

"How many?" she calmly asked after lighting a cigarette.

"One."

"Just one?" That had sparked the detective in her. "How? You think there's another book?"

"Does it matter? I have no idea how to find him... or her."

"Him or her? Are you calling because you need a detective?"

"More like a favour. I think it's one of Nicole's people."

"Really? What's the name?"

"Shit. Just a second." He pulled the envelope out of his pocket and slipped the name out. "It's MS01J884236S-66."

"Where the hell did you get that name?"

"Ah, it is a name. I got it hand delivered, big cloud of sparrows, guy with a black coat and hat. Come on. Keep up. He said it was Alzien."

"That's a hard yes. Why have you got an Alzien on your list?"

"I don't ask questions. You're friends with those people, so I was hoping you could help me find this... whatever. Is it a guy or a woman?"

"It's a guy, and you can't kill him."

"What, is he bigger than me? You know I have training."

"What training? I shit-kicked you back in Havana, but that's not why."

"No, you didn't, and why?"

"The man's already dead."

"Are you sure about that? My Boss doesn't usually make my job that easy."

"He's long time dead."

"How do you know?"

"He's Elizabeth's father."

He thought about Nicole and how she'd acted like she had no idea what he was talking about. "And Nicole would know this?"

"Of course. All you have to do is ask her... Oh wait, you did, and she stuffed you."

"Maybe you could talk to her."

"My fee is a hundred an hour and I make no guarantees. You cover all my expenses, including alcohol, clothing, and hospital fees. I know you've got it."

"You expect me to pay you?"

"You're worth how much? Don't cheap out on us poor folk, Vic."

"I'll pick you up. You still in Vancouver?"

"I'm in Puerto Vallarta with Brad, catching a few rays."

"You're allowed back in Mexico?"

"Kinda, maybe. They don't know I'm here. Passport lotto."

"I'm on my way."

Chapter fifty-nine

As they made their way to the basement, Nicole was thinking about the consequences that might come from saving Mars. If they decided to do it, there'd be ripples. There may not be artifacts or old documents. Virgil would lose his beloved dig sites.

Emotion couldn't be allowed to get in the way of what they were doing. Up until now, it had been about helping Cassandra, finding out about Mars, and helping Brittany sort out the last few days of her life. As Nicole descended the stairs with her daughter, she had to put everything in perspective. Saving Mars and stopping this 'Project Earth' might not be what they wanted.

It was funny how all basements held secrets. One such secret was Frederich's lab. She led her daughter to a locked door. Then she remembered the motion camera. There was no need to trip it. "Quick. Give me a hug."

The lights took a second to come on. When they did, Brittany saw the inside of the lab. "How'd you know?"

"Frederich showed it to me. The man has a story too, and it's nothing like Cassandra's. His story is about the Leaders going after him. They killed his wife, and Cassandra committed suicide."

"Really? I was there. It was a drowning."

"Okay, but what was he told? Maybe he was lied to. We don't know the whole story."

"Who do we trust?"

"No one until we find out more." Nicole looked around. She wanted to go over a few of the rooms.

"What is this place?"

"Frederich needed a lab to continue his work after the Leaders shut him down. He told me that they were after him, so he went into hiding and stole the equipment for this place."

"I think we can agree that Frederich was a bit of a nut job," Brittany deduced. "He lied, stole equipment, and he was an outcast from the scientific world."

"Yeah well, I know what it's like to be thought of as a freak, and to really want answers. You've been spared for the most part, but your mother and I were chased and lied to. Elizabeth was even shot. It's a little much, and sometimes it pushes you into directions you might not normally choose." She had given everything a lot of thought. "I'm not saying Frederich isn't a nut job, but I can't rule out that maybe he is some kind of desperate scientist, willing to do anything for answers."

Nicole slid the custom drawer out to show her daughter the DNA samples.

"These samples are his family and one of them is him. One of these is Cassandra. In the future he wants me to help breathe life into them, without a host."

Brittany leaned against the counter on the other wall to get a better look and felt it shift. "Whoa. His walls are loose."

Nicole found that odd. "Move for a second." She noticed a split in the wall and went in for a closer look. "Help me give this thing a push."

Brittany helped her mother push the wall open to expose a long corridor. It was wide, as far as hallways went, and could have doubled as a long room. They entered it and were surprised to find the walls weren't walls at all but an elaborate series of tiny drawers like the one that held the five specimens. Each one had its own temperature control and small diagnostic screen. Each one held more embryos. "What the hell does he need all these for?"

Nicole estimated that there had to be thousands of drawers, and tens of thousands of embryos. It could only mean one thing. "Let's go!"

They closed everything up and rendered back to Julie's.

"Hey, Mom. Was that Project Earth?"

Chapter sixty

They met Cassandra and Julie back at the house on the little front porch. Nicole and Brittany had beaten them by twenty minutes and were sitting on the front step when they showed up. It took no time at all to get the questions going.

Cassandra started. "How'd you guys do?"

"Your father had shown me a lab in the future, and he told me a story about how he had five DNA strands that he wanted me to help breathe life into. Brittany and I just came from the lab where we found a false wall. There was enough storage to house hundreds of thousands of these embryos."

"Then it's true. Dad was in on it. They were making soldiers!" Cassandra blurted. "Project Earth is an invasion of Earth with these creations. He needs a way to get them started."

To Nicole, it made sense. "But how would he create them all? The only way we can breathe life into all these specimens, is to carry them to term in the womb. Then they need to be raised like children. There's no fast-tracking this."

"We also found out they were trying to bypass the earlier stages of life," Julie offered. "Mass produce embryos, and eventually push fully developed people. They figured they could get it into a three-month process from start to finish. No wonder the Leaders were upset."

"But they have no way to breathe life into them." Frederich's request suddenly made sense to Nicole. That was why carrying them to term wasn't enough for him.

"It has to be stopped," Cassandra muttered under her breath.

Brittany agreed. "How?"

"It has to be permanent," Cassandra added.

Julie's jaw dropped. "This is your father we're talking about."

Cassandra put a hand up to stop her. "I never mentioned this to anyone, but my father was there when I was drowned. I saw his reflection in the water just before the other man pushed me into the lake. I guess I didn't want to believe it, but he was watching while I was held under."

"No," Julie cried. "I can't believe that."

"You mean you don't want to. That bastard watched as the life exited from my body. I'm okay with stopping him, especially if it means saving millions from an invasion."

Brittany was confused. "How would invading Earth kill Mars?"

"Maybe Earth is forced to retaliate?" Cassandra suggested.

"Or there's a backstab." Nicole was thinking out loud. "Earth's still around thousands of years later. That means they never figured it out."

Julie was still trying to grasp her husband's presence when Cassandra was drowned. "And you're sure he was there."

"I saw him. It was like he was controlling the man who had his hands on my neck, although I have no idea as to how."

Julie had heard about other things that her father was working on. "Your father was big into mind control. If you saw him there, there's a chance that the other man was being mentally pushed."

"Which means Dad was trying to kill me, right?"

Julie shook her head. "We don't know that for sure."

"Well, I do. He's paranoid enough to kill me, so if he suspects anything, he'll run, and we'll never find him again. We'll have to get to him by surprise, and that means going back in time before he learned all that mind control or DNA stuff. And I don't think I have it in me to do it."

Julie put her hands up. "Don't look at me. I can't."

"Who then?" Brittany asked.

"I think it has to be your mother," Cassandra said as she looked to Nicole.

Nicole's mind raced for alternatives, but she knew there weren't any. "And stopping Frederich will stop everything?"

"His brilliance is dangerous. If we can get you back in time, we can stop his plans before they start," Cassandra figured. "That's where my mother comes in. This'll be tricky, but you'll have to render into her, a bit like what I did with Brittany. You'll use her residual memories to be able to recall a workable moment."

"I'll be doing what?"

"You have the ability to not just render from place to place, or even time to time, but also from entity to entity," Cassandra explained. "You can render to anything organic. It makes sense if you think about it. The body is just a vessel. That means you can share. That's what I need you to do."

Nicole thought about it for a second. It made sense, but she'd never done anything like this. That being said, she'd never rendered back thousands of years, until now. Could she do it? "How does it work with my body?"

"Your body doesn't disappear, because it's not a complete rendering. You just think of merging and then come back. Everything you need will be there."

Nicole had to think through the mechanics of such a transfer. It would only take a second to absorb Julie's thoughts and history. She thought about how she'd do it over and over in her mind while she paced the floor. Earth could be invaded if she didn't stop them. It was the right thing to do.

"Are you okay with this?" Brittany asked.

"I'll have to be. Just tell me everything, from how you felt, to how you did it." She listened while the two young girls babbled about their feelings and thoughts. After giving them a chance to tell their stories Nicole turned to Julie. "And you're okay with this?"

"No, but I have to think of the bigger picture." She paused. "And about that... I need to see what Mars will turn into if we don't do this. It's a lot to fathom."

Nicole nodded. "Fair enough."

Chapter sixty-one

Victor and Violet showed up at the apartment in China while Nicole, Brittany, Julie, and Cassandra were still on Mars. While they were breaking in, Brad was returning to Vancouver. Mexico had been a chance to clear his head of all the crap that was Violet's life. There was no need to plunge himself back into whatever she was walking into.

"And this is where they were going to meet you?" Violet asked.

"Nope, but this is their apartment. They'll show up eventually."

Violet rummaged through the fridge and immediately found the take-out food. "All good. I'm on the clock."

"I can't believe you're charging me after all we've been through."

"Ya threw me in front of a moving car. My leg was fractured, and I had a limp for three months." She finished loading a bowl and started eating it cold while rummaging for beer. "And what happens if you don't kill the already-dead Elizabeth's father?"

"And you're sure he's dead?"

"Dead as a plantation joke at a basketball game."

"You have such a way with words."

"I'm not a snowflake, if that's what you mean."

"Here." Victor handed her an artist sketch. "I saw this guy with Cassandra and the Birdman when I was in that messed up dream. Is this her father?"

She looked at it. "No idea. I never met the guy. You want me to show this to Nicole?"

"Wait until you get her alone."

She folded it up and put it in her pocket. "Will do."

Just then, four people appeared in the open area of the living room. Nicole noticed Violet first. "What are you doing here?"

She'd just stuffed a large piece of almond chicken in her mouth, so she waved the chopsticks. "Hi."

"And why'd you bring him?"

Violet chewed quickly and swallowed. "He's hired me to find somebody."

"I know. He wants to execute Elizabeth's father."

"Then you did know," Violet stammered. "He said you didn't."

"Did you tell him the man's already dead?"

"I did."

"Again, I have to ask, why are you here?"

"He's paying me by the hour, all expenses included. Who am I to say no to free money?" She added as an afterthought, "Hey, I didn't see any beer in the fridge. Where do you keep it?"

"I don't drink."

"What does that even mean?"

Nicole rolled her eyes. Violet was more Elizabeth's friend than she was hers. "I've got some serious shit going on, so maybe you two could take your circus elsewhere."

It was Victor's turn to chime in. "My guy says he's alive. I don't know your history, but this MS01J884236S-66 guy is on my list."

"Is that a name?" Cassandra asked.

"It's Alzien," Brittany offered as she grabbed the pictures of Mars and handed them to Julie.

"Really," Julie said as she took the photos. "Because that name is riddled all over the documents we found in Kim's father's office. It was confusing because it was used as a third party, or partner."

"Are you sure about that?" Nicole asked.

"Definitely," Julie admitted. "It stood out. We just had no idea what to make of it. These photos are…"

Nicole nodded. "I can't imagine how you must be feeling."

"Shock." She flipped through them. "We need to stop whatever this is."

"I agree." Victor triumphantly put a hand on Nicole's shoulder. "And how could Elizabeth's father be all over those files?"

Nicole pulled away, and again, the eyes rolled. She turned to Julie. "Have you ever seen him with Frederich? I'm not sure what name he'd be going by, but he'd be a wildcard, somebody you've never met before."

"I don't know."

"Hang on." Victor was losing patience. "I need you to finally admit my MS01J884236S-66 might actually be alive?"

"I'll give you a maybe, but if he is, he's being controlled by Julie's husband?"

"Are you talking 5G mind control?" Victor asked.

Brittany had heard about that from Jessie. "And about that…"

"Stop," Cassandra interrupted. "We' were talking about dealing with my father."

"Everyone stop," Nicole growled.

Victor ignored her. "This husband. You all want him dead. Am I hearing that right?"

Nicole nodded. "He's building an army of creations and he's behind Cassandra's murder."

Victor looked at Cassandra before turning his eyes back to Nicole. "Really? She doesn't look all that dead."

"Long story. We need to stop him by going back in time, before he becomes a scientist. His projects can't happen."

"Great," Victor said as he lit a cigarette. "I'll help as long as we can kill two birds with one stone. None of you even need to get your hands dirty."

That brought a silence that even left Victor uncomfortable. "What'd I say? You're the ones who want this."

"We already have a plan," Nicole offered. "I'm going back in time to kill him."

"You? Seriously?" Victor laughed.

"Yes, me."

"You'll never do it. And if you don't stop the real bad guy, this MS01J884236S-66, then Mars is still going to follow the path of extinction. Let me in on this."

Julie and Cassandra knew that Victor, as brash as he was, was right. She looked over to Nicole and nodded. Nicole moved toward Julie and gave her a hug. Suddenly, her body went limp. Julie struggled to keep her from falling to the floor. Brittany was standing close by and helped. Seconds later, Nicole was back, and Julie moved her over to the couch.

"What an encounter." She drew a deep breath and took Julie's hand as she exhaled slowly. "Thank you."

Cassandra took a seat beside her. "How far back did you go?"

Nicole closed her eyes, squeezed them shut, and reopened them. "It's weird. Nothing comes bubbling out, but if I concentrate, I feel like I could pull anything. Try me."

Julie thought for a second. "Try to remember the first time you met Frederich, and then tell me what I was wearing."

Nicole concentrated. "Uh, a red dress given to you by your aunt on your birthday, black shoes, and a handkerchief."

Julie raised her eyebrows. "Can you think of anything else?"

"You had hair clips shaped like butterflies?"

Brittany's eyes danced between the two women. "Yep, I'd say we just nailed a new ability, except, I can't remember all Cassandra's stuff."

"No surprise. You don't pay attention." Cassandra smirked. "I do, however, and that's why I know you read your mother's journal, and how you briefly escaped that hospital with Jessie."

Brittany's mouth hit the floor. "Okay. We can change the subject any time now."

Nicole stood up. "I suppose there's only one thing left to do."

Victor shook his head. "And you think you're gonna end this guy's life?"

"I, uh... I'm going to try."

"There is no try." He got to his feet. "That's why you're taking me with you. You don't have it in you, and you know I do."

"Because you're a righteous man?" Nicole scoffed.

"That, and because I'm good at doing what others can't."

Chapter sixty-two

The walkway skirted the water's edge, along the perimeter of the park. For Nicole, this was the first time seeing this place, and yet, she knew every nook and cranny through Julie's memories. As a child, Julie had spent more time here than anywhere else. These memories came at her hard as she sat waiting for Frederich to arrive.

The occasional jogger ran past them and disappeared off into the distance around the bend. Victor's eyes swept the dense forest where the large cedars towered. It was like a world within a world. By a small waterfall, the water tumbled over the rocks as it made its way to the pool at the base.

Nicole tried to remember when she was fourteen years old. Victor was right. She'd never be able to do this. She looked up at the sky and saw the sun had moved from the high-noon position. It wouldn't be long now.

"Do you have a plan?" Victor asked.

She found herself trembling. "Not really. I don't do this all that often."

"Well, I can't physically kill him in broad daylight. Can you imagine how that would scar young Julie? And has anybody put any thought into Cassandra?"

"Why?" Nicole asked.

"Think about it. There's no Cassandra without a father."

"Oh shit, Victor. Do you think they thought about that?"

"Doesn't matter. It's part of the price tag. But we need to find a method first, and quickly."

"Come with me."

Nicole quickly dragged them off to a little shop just on the outskirts of the park. They sold all kinds of medicines. She knew what it would take to concoct a cocktail of drugs poisonous enough to do the job. It was hard not to think of Cassandra as she worked her way through the store and pocketed what she needed.

Sneaking past the checkout, the drugs and three bottles of juice found their way out of the store. She used a pen to mark two of them as drinkable and left the third unmarked. That one would be loaded.

"How fast does it work?" Victor asked.

"If I had to guess, an hour. We'll have time to get away."

They found a bench and waited with the beverages. Nicole allowed the memories to flood through her again. Today would have been a good day for Julie. She aced a test at school and made three new friends, not including her meetup with Frederich.

Looking down at the juices, she realised she'd inadvertently bought their favorite refreshments. It was odd to know so much about somebody she'd only recently met. She nudged Victor. "Over there."

He glanced over to see Julie appear from a trail. They watched as she stopped at every flower to smell them. The girl looked like she didn't have a care in the world. This wasn't what she needed, especially with an angry father waiting up for her tonight.

Nicole pushed these memories aside. She had to remind herself of what was at stake. Frederich came into view from the left and Nicole pointed him out.

Victor waited for them to find each other. "Shall we go?"

"Not yet."

Frederich took her hand and led her to the edge of the water where they peeled off their shoes and waded in up to their knees. Skipping stones seemed to be a practice on every planet. The two kids giggled and played in the water for what must have been an hour, finding flat stones and splashing water at each other. Julie truly looked happy, and Frederich truly looked sincere. The kid didn't look like the villain from the future that had plans for invading Earth.

They soon moved onto the grass with their pants still cuffed up to the knees. Their fingers were interlocked as they held each other.

He wouldn't kiss her, but it was easy to see that he wanted to. A true gentleman, he'd wait.

Nicole had seen enough as she pried herself from the park bench, took Victor's hand, and strolled toward them. "Excuse me."

The two kids sat up and looked back at them. Frederich spoke for them as they pulled their hands apart. "Can I help you?"

Nicole made eye contact with him and it was intense. She'd never forget that look. Amazingly enough, neither would he, as thousands of years later he would recall a woman just like her with a friend named Elizabeth.

Nicole's voice broke as she spoke. "We were expecting some friends, but we were stood up. I have a couple of extra juices and wondered if you'd like them?"

Julie checked with Frederich like they'd been together for years. "That would be nice, but there's only three bottles and four of us."

"I don't drink the shit," Victor announced as he handed one of the bottles to her. Then he handed one to Frederich. "Sorry. I'm more of a beer guy."

"Thank you." Julie was amused. This man was different, funny. It was indeed her lucky day, topped off with a free drink.

Nicole glanced down the pathway and started to walk away. Victor followed.

She looked back at the two kids guzzling their drinks and tears began streaming down her face. They walked into the trees and when they were out of sight, Nicole gave him a hug. He waited for the surroundings to morph into a living room, but it didn't.

"Hey, Nicole. You forgot to... you know..."

She put a finger to his lips to stop him. Her eyes never left his as he put his hand on her face and wiped a tear off her cheek with his thumb. As hard as Victor tried, there was no reading this woman, that is, until she kissed him.

Chapter sixty-three

Brittany seldom saw her mother this lost. She had reappeared looking dishevelled, like she'd been at a bad party. Nicole tried to say something, anything, but couldn't find the words.

A satisfied, but very confused Victor handed her the third juice bottle. It was unmarked.

"You mean you didn't?"

"We didn't," he admitted as he put a hand on her shoulder. "It wasn't right. I'm not sure who that kid was, or what he might become, but this isn't his fault. My guy is the problem."

Nicole wrapped her arms around him in a hug that lasted longer than it should. Then she opened the drink and poured it down the sink. "We're going to need a plan B. When did Frederich change? Was anything going on in his life?"

Julie shook her head. "I'm just not sure, maybe after that first mission to Earth failed. We all knew it was no failure, but they treated it like one and did an unusual push for a second mission."

Cassandra added, "That was about the same time we were forbidden to ask Dad about his work. Suddenly, he was working on secret projects. He started locking himself in the study and we rarely saw him."

Victor had to ask. "How was that first mission a failure?"

"There was a group of scientists that paid for a return trip and never got it."

"They got left behind?"

"Hard to say. We were told they were slaughtered." Julie had heard that as the rumour but hadn't believed it. "There were too many inconsistencies in the stories."

"I've never heard anything."

"Remember that this would have been thousands of years ago," Nicole reminded him. "Any thing else, Julie?"

"No, but there might be something at the Gerricks building."

"What are we waiting for?" Victor held his arms out. "Who's going to take me there?"

Nicole reluctantly took him in her arms. "You really have issues, don't you?"

"I was getting used to a normal life, before the birdman's return and that damn stone. I can't wait to get back to it."

They were in the building on Mars in a split second. She stood in the room full of artifacts and wondered what Frederich knew of the place. He was no curator, just some computerised lunatic on his own quest. "Find a place to hide. The guy could show up at any time."

Victor crouched behind a case.

She decided to look around before triggering the sensor. She badly wanted to check out the secret drawer, but she knew it would bring Frederich. Could a computer stop her from taking them? Should she care?

"Miss Nicole. How nice to see you." His eyes were different, excited. "Have you learned anything yet?"

"We've had success with embryos implanted, but nothing without a host. My best people are working on it though." That was a lie because she hadn't even brought it up with anyone. No one on Earth or Alzie would be able to help. Earth was still struggling with the whole cloning and DNA mapping. Even if her scientists made a breakthrough, it would be ridiculous to share anything with him. "I'll continue to see what I can find. I promise."

He seemed content with that answer. "I am looking forward to your help. Is there anything else?"

Nicole appreciated the fact that he always put business first. Speak your piece, answer any questions, and then off you go. No need for chitchat. "Well, yes, if you have a minute." She motioned her hand through the air. "So, what is this place? I mean Virgil and

I have been checking it out and it's a nice building, but what was it back in the day?"

Frederich studied her for a second. "Well, it held our archives of history, but you already knew that."

"What else?"

"We had a space program. Three missions were endeavoured, none with any success. Two of the missions self-destructed upon re-entry. I'd like to say that we weren't quite ready to attempt such objectives, but the truth is that there was a group trying to stop us from such accomplishments." He paused. "You have a question."

"Two of them." Her hand was on her chin in thinking mode. "Space missions to where?"

"Earth of course. You are the closest object to us with any formal interest. We could tell you had water and thus life. We wanted to know what kind of life, and more, what kind of environment you were boasting. We knew it was much roomier."

"Really. I guess an upgrade is just something we can't ignore."

"True. You said you had two questions?"

"Sorry, yes. I can't help but wonder who would want to eradicate a space program. It's just that it is such an important venture to find out who your neighbors are."

"I agree. I was all for the program and felt the sorrow of each failure." His look sobered even more than its usual. "A band of kids calling themselves 'The Keepers' had a major hand in some of it. They were doing everything in their power to discredit our leaders, and they were cunning. These kids had informers on the inside keeping them up to date on what the leaders were doing. The space program took a lot of resources and there was no payoff. We took a large hit on this and it didn't take much to get people doubting."

"These kids were pretty important then?"

"No, they were stupid extremists. They started with good intentions but were misguided. Earth wasn't planning on invading us. They were spreading a story that the Earthlings had captured the first two crafts and were using our people for biological testing."

Nicole was surprised at his take on it. "Go on."

"The third craft never made it all the way back. Earthlings had stowed away, and our people heroically destroyed the craft before they could land. Those lost scientists were heroes, and their lives celebrated for years. Meanwhile, our Leaders were accused of running a careless space program."

"Did you know these kids?"

He dropped his head. "My Cassandra knew them. I tried so hard to raise her properly, but she had her mothers will."

"Really. Why would she want anything to do with them?"

"This organization preyed on the innocent." He paused as if emotions were surfacing. His programming was quite realistic. "She was a smart kid, but Kim had swayed her."

"Kim?"

"Kim Bennett. His father was very gifted. He did some great work. I never got to work with him, but he got results wherever they put him." He stopped and adjusted his cuffs. "I'm straying from the question though. You asked about the building."

Nicole smiled. She hadn't remembered her question. Obviously, Frederich didn't see her as any threat and was happy to spill his guts. What troubled her was that his story was very convincing, and it conflicted everything Cassandra had said. Why would he lie? He was a computer. "Ah, that's right, the building."

"Thank you. It used to be an interesting place. This building was a lot bigger than what you see now. This is the data and housing wing. Our scientists are housed on the floors above us. Below us were more data floors but most of it had been destroyed."

"What kind of data?"

"This was a Capital building, so it held the typical data on who was doing what, where they lived and project results. It was more statistics than anything. Other wings had their own data storage. We had a big area in our science wing."

Nicole perked up. "Science wing?"

"Don't get too excited. It was also destroyed. It was our northern wing. There was a space and technology wing, military wing, and a communications wing. In the center of it was the legislative assembly and courtrooms." He looked at her puzzled face. "Where the Council of Leaders held office."

"Sounds important."

"It was our planet's epicentre. Most of the planet's destiny was planned right here in this complex. Both my wife and I worked here. She had an office on the corner in the science wing. It was nicer than mine, but she had a more mainstream status." My work was controversial, and interest was flighty."

"So, what about warehouses and shopping?"

"This building was self-contained. We had several warehouses, all the shopping and food sources required onsite. We had everything here."

"Pretty good security then?"

"Most knew better than to try anything. The military wing saw to our safety. We never felt jeopardized."

"Well thank you for your time, Frederich. I appreciate it. Hopefully, the next time I see you, I can bring some good news."

He smiled. "That would be appreciated. I look forward to your help and would unequivocally enjoy Earth as a new home. I know I could do big things there."

His mood had almost turned fiendish with that comment. It startled her.

Victor waited until he left. "You aren't really going to help him, are you?"

She looked back at him. "Hell no."

"Good, because he sounds more like my man."

"You mean the one you couldn't kill? You had your chance."

"We need to find my guy. MS01J884236S-66 is the one who changed him."

"Your guy?"

Victor nodded. "My guy."

Chapter sixty-four

Victor walked over to the case where Frederich had stood. It was a dusty wooden frame with a solid base and glass top. Some of the glass was broken and had fallen into the case amongst the contents. Nicole had drawn in the dust with her finger. It had been a symbol.

"What is that?"

"That's a Watson-Crick base pair."

"I know that. Why?"

"It was a test for him, to see if he'd react. He didn't." She looked around to see if he was still lingering. "We shouldn't hang out here."

"He's gone." Victor didn't budge. "What is he? I mean, we can't stop a computer."

"We need to go."

"And I need to know more about Elizabeth's father, like where this guy is hiding. He's from your planet, so what do you think?"

"Let's go."

"He's working with this Frederich guy. He turned him into a demonic microprocessor. So where did he end up?"

"I don't know," she snapped. "We need to go."

"We need to figure this out. I've seen the Frederich hologram and the Frederich child. What are the chances of us getting to see the alive grown-up version?"

"Of Frederich?"

"Who else? We find him and we find MS01J884236S-66."

Nicole weighed the pros and cons. Then she stepped toward him and threw her arms around him. They reappeared by the apartment where Brittany had first seen Cassandra, where she'd been dreaming, where she'd first seen Cassandra in the mirror.

Victor took a step back and shook the feeling of being re-atomised. "Damn, where are we now?"

"Same building except in the older version of Mars."

"Good." He looked around before letting his eyes land squarely on her. "Dumb question. Do I look as good as you?"

"What?"

"Every time you do that, you look fresh, like you just stepped out of a spa. Do I look like that?" He stretched the front of his shirt forward. "And I swear these bullet holes get smaller each time."

"There's a bit of a default setting. The process wants that part of you to be original. It can't complete the restoration, but it does help it to get closer." She stared back at him when he wouldn't take his eyes off her. "What now?"

"Nothing." He pulled his eyes away.

"Well shake whatever's going on in that head of yours." She turned and started for the stairs. "We need answers."

"I meant it as a compliment." He hurried to catch up. "You remember Washington?"

"Of course, I do. We met with World Leaders, pitched a proposal and..."

"You had sex with me."

Nicole stopped, shook her head without turning back and started walking again.

Victor continued, "You didn't forget about us, did you?"

She opened a door and exited the stairwell. "There was no us. It was a scientist's curiosity."

"What we did went beyond curiosity."

"You were a lab rat, Victor, nothing more." Her steps were long as she headed across the open area toward a set of glass doors.

"About that..."

She stopped, and this time she turned back to him. He tried to stop but stepped into her. He grabbed her shoulders to avoid knocking her over.

"I'm just saying. I thought you were a lovely woman then. You're still pretty..."

"Pretty what, Victor? Hot? Doable?"

"It was never like that, at least not for me. I just thought we had a little chemistry going on. Is it because I'm older? I think I've aged pretty good."

"You have. You're still a good-looking man and if you must know, you were a favourite lab rat."

"I know. I didn't disappoint and neither did you. I was just thinking..."

"That was your first mistake."

"I'm serious. We made a pretty good team. Did I tell you I've done pretty well for myself?"

"I heard you're some kind of Mayor or something."

"I bought an island and formed my own country. I have four hundred thousand people working for me. Not bad, huh?"

"Normally I'm impressed, but this is a side effect."

"Of the rendering? I don't think so."

"I'm still in love with Elizabeth."

"But you know she's... "

"Maybe, maybe not. I need to talk to the Birdman before I can write off seeing her again."

"Pretty slim chance of that."

"As long as there's a chance, I have to... "

"We wouldn't have to tell her."

"You are impossible."

"Impossible, or irresistible? It's a common mistake."

She headed to the glass doors and gave them a push. They were locked. Victor, knowing that she was still sort of interested, sauntered over like a cat with a mouthful of feathers.

"We're not a hard no are we?"

Nicole rendered to the other side of the glass. She leaned toward the door and gave it a couple of hot steamy breaths. Then, with her finger, she wrote 'hard no' and started to walk away.

He banged on the door. "Very funny. Let me in."

She headed for the stairs and quickly slipped out of sight.

"What the hell, Nicole!"

A man tapped him on the shoulder. "Can I help you?"

Victor turned, gave him a head-to-toe death stare, and walked away.

Chapter sixty-five

A single set of stairs led up seven floors. Nicole found a map of the building's layout after climbing to the second one. The offices were all listed although none of them had the scientist's names attached to the studies. She'd have to go on the hunt for Frederich. In the back of her mind, she was still thinking of Victor.

She didn't leave him behind because he thought he had a chance with her, because if she was being honest, he did. Even older, the man was all man. His arms, attitude, and rugged good looks were as impressive as they were all those years ago. What she didn't need, and she wasn't sure if it was even an issue, was his going on about Elizabeth's father. Even if he was behind this, she couldn't let Victor kill the man. This was her best friend's father. She'd need to know more before that could happen.

The second floor had windows, much like an earthly office building. She briefly peeked through each window. These people were young, likely some form of Martian interns.

The next floor was a physics ward. It was a short stay, as was the fourth. The fifth floor caught her attention and even had her nose against the glass. These people were all about the test tubes and beakers. There were Martian forms of microscopes and incubators, but as with the other floors, no Frederich.

"Are you lost?"

The voice came from the door beside her. A man's head was poking out from the room. He wore a lab coat and held a clear glass plate. There was a hologram displayed across the face of it.

"Sorry," Nicole offered. "I was just on my way to the six floor and I thought I saw somebody I knew."

"Who was it?" he asked. "I can go get them."

"Don't bother. I was wrong."

Nicole ran to the stairs and started up to the next flight. She just made it to the next floor when she was met by another man.

"I need to see some credentials."

"Some cred…" She thought about rendering for a split second but decided against it. She couldn't leave Victor behind. "I was hoping to find somebody."

"And who let you in?"

"I, uh…"

"I'll walk you down."

Not only did he walk her down, but the man walked her to a room not far from the entrance. It had a table in the centre and two chairs, one on either side. "Are you arresting me?"

"Wait here while I get one of our leaders. Maybe you'll be able to explain things better to him."

"I don't think so."

The man watched her from the doorway as her expression went from being confident, to being surprised, and then to being confused. That confusion came from the fact she couldn't render. How did they know?

Back on Earth, Cassandra and Brittany were sharing stories about Victor and their mothers. How often had they been stopped from doing what they wanted, or being with whoever? The stories were endless. Authority sucked.

Violet ignored the teenage whining and played with the amulet that had been around Victor's neck. She could feel the energy coming from the oval stone and couldn't deny the fact that it was powerful. Victor had been shot and he was still here. If she could borrow this thing, she could get back to some serious police work. "What do you know about this?"

Cassandra shook her head. "It saves people."

"Bad people," Brittany added.

"I'm guessing you're not a Victor fan?"

"Not really. He's not a nice man."

Violet ignored her. "How'd it bring him back from the dead?"

Cassandra frowned. "It couldn't. He's lying about being dead."

"He claims he was deader than dead. He took six in the chest. I believe him."

Cassandra thought for a second. "You know him?"

"I do. He wouldn't lie."

"So, you think he actually died?" Cassandra asked again.

"Uh, heart not beating, blood not flowing, and I don't know, cold and clammy." She wanted to put a palm on her forehead. "You have a hard time grasping what people say, don't you?"

A slight popping sound left Brittany and Violet as the only two in the room.

"Where'd she go?" Violet asked.

Brittany shrugged. "I have no idea."

"I thought you two were connected or something."

"We haven't rendered together in a while, so it's faded."

"I guess it's just the two of us then. Do you have any idea where I could get a beer?"

When Nicole left him, Victor didn't head for a safe place to hide out. That wasn't his style. Instead, he found an office and quickly entered it, asking if they'd seen a man. He didn't have the sketch anymore, but quickly started rattling off a thorough description. The people in the office just stared.

A woman, with a familiar voice, stepped into the office behind him and took his arm. "Come with me."

Chapter sixty-six

Cassandra took Victor's arm and turned to leave but was cut off by a man with square cut hair. Even his bangs were cut straight across, running parallel with the third wrinkle in his forehead.

"Who is this man, Cassandra?" he asked.

"He's one of the trial runs. I was watching him for Mr Decker, but he slipped away."

"You know his type are dangerous." He eyed her quickly. "Where's your electro-pacifier?"

She reached for a back pocket, knowing it wasn't there but selling the idea that she actually thought it was. "Oh…"

"You should be careful." He handed her a small black cylinder that was the size of a breakfast sausage. "Take mine."

She reached for it, but before she could take it from him, he shot a small lightning bolt into Victor.

"It's fully charged," the man casually admitted.

Cassandra watched Victor's knees buckle as he took the shot in the meatier part of his right leg. She grabbed the weapon and spun to intercept her newly angered prisoner. The cylinder was brought up to stop Victor from retaliating. "Come with me. Back to the lab."

He let her escort him out of the room. "What the hell was that all about?"

"Think about it. You walked into a secured office asking some very off questions. You're lucky I showed up when I did."

"I was just asking about your father."

"Who is a top scientist that has recently been turned? I can't imagine what they were thinking."

"Why the lab rat story?"

"It was the only excuse I could use. How else would I know a man like you? If anyone asks, you're prisoner FF-192."

"Why do I have to be a prisoner?"

"We don't experiment on good people."

"What kind of experiments?"

"Oh, we do all kinds of trials. But you're too good to do that on Earth, aren't you?"

"Don't kid yourself. We tested the hell out of good and bad people." He remembered all the LSD trips. "How far do you go?"

"Far as we need to."

"You'd do well in the CIA."

She cocked her head.

"Central Intelligence Agency."

"Is that really a thing?"

"Good point. How'd you find me?"

She reached over and pulled a tracker off his collar.

"A girl after my own heart." He took it from her and flipped it around in his fingers. "How does it work?"

"I always carry it on me, in case I have to find people. It's simply a capsule with a bit of my blood in it. I have a very strong bond to the stuff. Nobody else does. It's perfect."

"Makes sense. Now what's your story and don't feed me the same crap you feed everyone else."

"What do you mean?"

"You need to tell me how that stone brought me back to life."

"I don't think it did."

"Uh, I know it did, because here I am."

"The stone didn't do that. It was something attached to these stones."

"Do tell."

"My father did a lot of experimenting on that damn thing. He knew it was special but couldn't crack the code. When he gave it to me, he saw how it affected me."

"Did it take you anywhere?"

"Not at first, but it was trying to tell me something. Then, when I was drowning, the stone invited me inside it."

"Invited?"

"I can't explain it any other way. I drown and the stone welcomed my mind out of its body. When Brittany brought me back, it was like a week had gone by, a week of weird."

"I was out for maybe thirty-six hours and that was close to four real days."

"And was it strange?"

"Very. Why was that?"

"I was hoping you could tell me. And…" She cut herself off.

"Come on. Don't play strange on me now."

"I've heard of the Birdman, the one that gives you lists of people to kill. Why?"

"Why do I get the lists?"

"No. Why do you listen to him? You must have had a reason for trusting him."

"Scared the shit out of me the first time I saw him, and I don't scare easy. Came with thousands of birds. They hovered around him like storm clouds. He told me of a man and then told me what this man was. He has something to do with the book."

"What kind of book?"

"It's some kind of supernatural Ledger. Nicole has them both."

"Both?"

"One was found on Earth, the other one here."

"What does it say?"

"Depends on who's holding it. Men see blank pages. Women see a list of their children, had they had a child every time they had sex."

"Every time? How does it know?"

"It just does. You get to see the names, birthdates, what these children would have excelled in, what education they got, and what they became. You also get the details of grandchildren. And if you are in possession of it, and you know how to do it, you can pick certain children and conjure them into existence."

Cassandra stood stunned. "And one of those books came from my planet?"

"I'm pretty sure."

"This man that you're looking to kill, was he a conjured man?"

"I can't be sure, but that's usually why I get these lists."

"Who conjured him?"

"I'm not sure. The CIA perhaps. They were the ones that tricked my mother into doing it years ago. Then they killed her."

"She made another you?" She swallowed hard. "And did you kill him?"

"I did."

"That had to be hard."

Victor looked away. "It had to be done."

"Because you don't think they belong?"

"They don't belong!"

"Who's to say we do?"

"What?"

"We should be dead, both of us. The stone kept us alive. What's stopping a man with a million crazed spiders or squirrels from hunting us down?"

That wasn't an angle that Victor had looked at. He only saw a brother that wasn't a brother. He, or it, was the motive behind the CIA killing his, their, mother. She was dead because the secret couldn't get out and that was a good enough reason for Victor. "Ever hear of the butterfly effect?"

"There's no such thing. You say you're righteous. Everything happens as a part of God's plan. You're trying to change it because you think it is not a part of God's plan. Which is right?"

"You believe in God? Do you have a Bible?"

"We have stories, and if you believe the stories, you have a God."

He thought about what she was saying. It oddly made sense. "What's your point?"

"I'm saying maybe those people didn't deserve to die."

Chapter sixty-seven

Nicole tried again to render but couldn't. Something didn't add up. What bothered her wasn't the fact that she couldn't render, it was the fact she was taken to a room that she couldn't render out of. How did they know?

She looked around the room. There had to be some new-age electrical force field or some magnetic shield. How would it work? She tried the door. It was locked. No surprise there. She returned to her chair and took a seat. Barely a minute had passed when two men walked in.

"Let's start with your name."

"I'm not sure why I'm here."

"Fair enough. You were found in a restricted area looking for a man who, by some coincidence, we are also looking for. Now, who are you and how did you get in here?"

"What is this place?" She looked around the room.

This got the attention of both men. The one remained by the door while the other continued to ask her for her name.

"It's Nicole."

"That's good. Now where did you come from?"

"You wouldn't believe me if I told you."

"I think you should make it believable, for your own good."

"The truth, you're right. I'm not from around here. First, what's up with this room?"

"We're assuming you know Cassandra, a blonde girl, about eighteen?"

"Why can't I render?"

"Is that what you call it?"

"What do you call it?"

He looked at the other guy, then back at her. "Never really put a label on it. We call it that thing that Frederich's daughter does."

"Is she the only one?"

"She was, until now. That's a problem."

"Why the room, and how does it work?"

"We confiscated his lab and went over his research. Turns out his little girl wasn't born, as much as she was made."

"But she was born, right?"

"Her mother carried her. More a technicality, wouldn't you say?"

"Not at all. Frederich made flesh. Anybody can make the vessel. It's the mind that can't be replicated or created. For that you need a birth mother. Life comes from life. Without it, we're just a package of flesh and bone."

"And you were born?"

"I was."

"But you can render, like Cassandra?"

"I can. I'm not one of Frederich's creations though."

"Did Frederich steal your technology?"

"No, but he is working with somebody who might have the know-how. Do you know who?"

"We know he's working with Mr Bennett. We haven't been able to find him though."

"Anybody else?" Nicole asked. "Maybe odd-named?"

"What does MS01J884236S-66 mean?"

"Where did you get that name?"

"Then it is a name?"

"Trust for trust. Can I see those documents?"

The man nodded to the one at the door who left briefly and returned with a few clear plates. He swiped at the corner and the words appeared. There were formulas and math, lots of math. MS01J884236S-66 was the signature on most of the equations.

Nicole swiped away at the screen to go over the rest of the documents. The name MS01J884236S-66 had come up many times, but not as a co-operating scientist.

"It is a name. He's a scientist." Nicole needed more and she knew they did too. They wouldn't have given her this if they didn't. "Have you ever been to Earth?"

They looked at her. "Earth?"

"One planet over. The blue one."

"We've experimented, with little success."

"You have what it takes. Sadly, you have people undermining you, making you believe these were failures. Earth is attainable and they are moderately safe."

"They attacked our ship."

"You were led to believe that."

"What are you saying?"

"I'm saying your space program was sabotaged from within. It was needed to justify the rise of an army of creations."

"Is that why Frederich was working on these projects?"

"I think so."

"How do you know all this?"

"We need to go for a walk."

Chapter sixty-eight

Cassandra poked her head into Mr Bennett's office first. It wasn't that she was allowed in the area any more than Victor, but people around here knew her. They knew she liked Kim and cut her some slack. Nobody was there. "It's safe."

Victor pushed past her. It was the smell of the room that had caught his attention. That was the smell that he'd remembered from the dream, or nightmare. It was the smell in the waiting room where he'd heard the thumping. People were waiting in chairs and their heads were exploding. They were people he knew. It was the smell of blood mixed with freshly cut apples.

Cassandra walked over to the flask of purple goo. "This is the smell of my home for the last two thousand years."

Victor brought it to his nose and took a sniff. That was the smell all right. "What is this?"

"It's an organic compound made from boiling the stone in water. That's my father's replicated version of the stone. It's a liquid version of what brought us back to life. I'm thinking he was hoping to use it for his soldiers."

"He made this stuff?"

"Either my father did, or that Alzien that you're trying to kill."

"Why make it?"

"Nicole, Brittany, and I were created, but we still needed a vessel with a mind to carry us to term. We need that mind to kick-start our brain waves. Without it, we're no different than rocks. My father wanted a way to cut out the vessel carrying us to term."

She picked up a plate and activated it. After reading it she picked up another and another. They were all boring, simple biometric stuff. None of it had to do with soldiers, armies, or creation.

"What are those things?"

"They're tele-plates, documents, studies, and procedures."

Victor put the flask down. "How common is this shit?"

"This looks like an early version. I'm sure the Leaders don't even know it exists."

"Should we show them?"

"It only maintains life. It doesn't initiate." She quickly panned the room. "How good are you at finding things that aren't supposed to be found?"

"It's one of my many specialties." He went to work, knocking on counters and walls. If there were hollows, or trap doors, he'd find them.

Cassandra started in on the drawers.

Thump, thump. Victor had found something. "Here." He opened the cupboard under the counter. "The shelves don't go back far enough."

"What do you mean?"

"Cupboards go back about eighteen inches. The counter goes back twenty-four." He knocked at the end of the cupboard again and gave it a push. Then he put his palms on it and tried to slide it forward.

"How do you get in it?"

Victor started moving the few items on the counter. Was one of them a latch? Nothing worked. Then he placed his hands squarely on the counter and pushed down. There was a click. Victor let the counter rise up and forward. It exposed the hollow. "Now let's see what we've found."

Cassandra reached in, finding a few clear tele-plates. One of them had been bloodied. "What the… "

"How strong are those things."

"Almost indestructible. Why?"

Victor started looking at the floor, at door handles and started sizing up cubbyholes. He headed straight over to the closet.

Cassandra watched him open the door. She had expected to see a closet full of lab smocks. Victor had expected more.

When the door opened, a body fell out. It was Kim, and that had Cassandra screaming and racing for his dead body. She held him close and sobbed. Victor tried to console her while he looked for the cause of death. It was the edge of one of those plates to the side of Kim's skull. The blow had come from behind and Victor knew the kid probably didn't even see it coming.

"I'm sorry."

"He was worried that they were onto him."

Victor didn't bring up the fact that the kid was killed in his father's office. That meant that either the father, Frederich, or Elizabeth's father was behind it.

"I've got to ask, other than the obvious, who'd want him dead?"

"I'd say it had to be the person who's about to kill me."

"You don't think you're already dead?"

"Not yet. But it will be happening soon." She gave Kim a gentle kiss on the forehead. "Do you think this why they tried to kill me, that I knew too much?"

"That's a very good possibility."

"What's a very good possibility?" a voice behind them asked.

Two men had entered the room. Nicole was with them.

Chapter sixty-nine

Victor took a step back from the closet and passively raised his hands. Cassandra looked up, the tears still dripping from her cheeks. "They killed Kim, Leader Garth."

"They, being Frederich or Mr Bennett," Victor clarified.

Nicole headed straight for Cassandra. She checked for a pulse on Kim and then put her arm around Cassandra. Leader Brad hit a button on his bracelet. It lit a red light and Victor figured that had to mean the Cavalry was on its way. Nicole caught his cue when he raised his eyebrows.

"Victor, I could use a hand here."

"Wait a second." Leader Garth demanded. "What happened here?"

"They killed him," Cassandra sobbed.

"Murder weapon's sitting on the counter," Victor added.

He looked at the bloodied plate. "Why?"

Cassandra started to get up. "We found tele-plates in a hidden compartment. That one was with them. Then, Victor found Kim."

Leader Garth picked up the bloodied plate and activated it. It was studies on a drug to enact a certain strain of virus, nothing that seemed important. Then he activated one of the other tele-plates.

"This is interesting."

This plate logged different scenarios for the space program. Each one was devised to discredit the results. It was propaganda, something the Martian people didn't fully understand or see value in. A third tele-plate theorised different invasions of Earth.

Leader Garth was handed a plate from Cassandra. It had the blueprint for an underground bomb that could defy gravity. The thing was designed to release energy downward and put the lion's share of the damage to the planet. All the plates had Mr Bennett's name on them.

"You think Kim's father killed him?" Leader Garth asked.

Cassandra nodded. "Victor says his people can manipulate other people with some 5G technology. It can get them to do whatever they want them to. Tell them Victor."

"Not just my people, Cassandra. Anybody can do it. I mean your people already know this, right?"

"We are a peaceful species. Who are your friends, Cassandra?"

"They're from Earth."

Her comment came out casual, like there was nothing to worry about, but Leader Brad was already hitting other buttons on his bracelet. Buttons were lighting up and Victor grabbed Cassandra as he threw an arm around Nicole.

"Time to go."

"I agree." She threw her arms around the two of them and they disappeared.

Chapter seventy

The three appeared in the middle of the living room and Victor had to dodge a flying beer bottle. It crashed against the wall behind him, leaving a dent in the drywall. He watched the glass scatter across the room and slowly turned to see an angry Stormm.

"Where the hell have you been?" Violet snapped.

"Good shot," Brittany added. Then she tossed another empty to her. "Try again."

"Are we married?" Victor gave a chuckle and looked around to see if anyone wanted to share in the joke, maybe step in, and add something. They left him high and dry. "Okay. Get mad at Nicole, Stormm. She took me there and then stranded me. Besides, you're paid by the hour and so far, you've made a lot of money, to sit on your ass and drink beer. You're welcome."

Brittany frowned. "Fire two."

"No fire two!" It was Nicole's turn to snap. "This is my apartment. Now clean that mess up."

"But Mom..."

"Not now." She turned to Victor. "I think I've got a plan."

Victor took a seat. "Do tell."

"Those leaders... "

"Leader Garth and Leader Brad," Cassandra offered, not that anyone had forgotten.

"Yes. Those two were going to arrest us, weren't they?"

Cassandra thought about it for a second. "That would make sense. I'd said you were from Earth. That's enough in itself. Sorry about that."

"That means we have to find proof, and I think we have some."

"Does that also mean we're going back to Mars?" Victor asked.

Violet was headed to the wall to clean up her mess. She stopped in her tracks. "Not without me. I didn't leave the warm beaches of Mexico to sit in an apartment."

"Seriously, Stormm." Victor got up. He'd just realised that Violet had beer. It had to be in the fridge. "You're better off here."

"But I can help. That's why I'm here."

"I doubt that."

Nicole interrupted. "You know what? Maybe you could."

Victor and Violet spoke in unison. "Really?"

"Nobody knows you. You have normal eyes and you're a detective. Maybe we could use you as a wild card, but first we need to get that proof."

He cracked a beer and started to guzzle. "We're all going?"

"Yes," Nicole answered. "My walls can't take any more tantrums. Now, everybody gather around. Brittany and I will be picking the spot."

"What spot, Mom?"

"Do you remember the lab, the one beneath the basement?"

"That crazy lab?"

"Which crazy lab?" Cassandra asked.

"How about we go there and maybe, you can tell me."

Brittany put her arms out. "I'll take Violet and Cassandra."

Nicole rolled her eyes. She was stuck with Victor. He set the bottle down and moved in for his hug. The other three had already left.

Victor stopped and took a step back. "What's wrong?"

"What are you talking about?"

"You treat me like I'm a dumpster-diving drug addict."

"I do not."

"What did I do?"

"You didn't do anything."

"Then admit that we were more than just friends at one point."

"We never should have done that. I was mad at... "

"I get the whole angry thing. You were mad at Elizabeth's rejection, and that made you curious about us. Or, were you just mad at her?"

"I was also curious. I enjoyed what we had. It's just that, when she died, the guilt was overwhelming. It was hard to shake."

"But you know she's dead, right?"

"And you were going to talk to the Birdman, remember?"

"About that. He couldn't have had anything to do with that. She didn't have a sparrow, which means he had no say in her fate."

"If not him... who?"

"I have no idea how any of this crap works."

Nicole dropped onto the couch. She had always harboured a little guilt over Elizabeth's death. How could she have been with Victor when she truly loved her? Yet she did. A part of her had loved what he'd done to her, loved what he could have meant to her.

"I'm really sorry for bringing it up. We should get going."

She looked up at him with a tear hanging off her chin. Then she got up, took his hand, leaned toward him, and kissed him. Her eyes didn't close. They remained locked on his. They were lost, hurting, and they needed comforting, the kind only he could give.

"You're a complicated girl."

She brushed the tear away with her sleeve. "I know."

Like a lost teenager, he found himself gawking as she removed her shirt. "What about the others. Won't they be waiting?"

Nicole dropped the shirt on the floor. "You really have no idea how this rendering through time stuff works, do you?"

Chapter seventy-one

Brittany did a double take when her mother and Victor appeared. She couldn't place it, but the woman looked different.

"Where are we?" Victor asked.

"This is Frederich's underground lab."

"Frederich, or..."

Nicole's nostrils flared. "I don't know, Victor. Now focus."

"Are we okay to be in here?" he asked.

"There are no cameras or motion sensors down here." She pushed on the wall, opening the lab to the other samples. "We need to get a few of these capsules back to your leaders."

"We?" Brittany asked. I'm not sure we need everybody going. I mean, what if we need to get out in a hurry?"

"I agree. That's why I want the rest of you to head to the dock after I leave. Victor, you'll be coming with me."

Brittany took a step forward. "Him? Why?"

"Old fashioned muscle, in case I get in trouble. Besides, I need you to fill Cassandra and Violet in on what we know."

"Can't you just render to safety?"

"Not always. They have places with blockers."

"How?"

"No idea." She grabbed a couple of the specimens, before taking pictures of the lab. "Okay go. Victor and I won't be far behind."

Brittany took Violet, while Cassandra went alone. Victor, a little lost at this point, waited until Nicole was ready. She threw her arms around him, and they reappeared in a stairway. Victor knew the spot. They'd been there before.

"I'll follow you," Victor said as he reached for the door.

She put her hand out to stop the door from opening fully. "About earlier…"

"Do I want to hear this? You're a big girl and you don't need to justify your actions."

"I just wanted to say, thank you."

"No need. We're just two people trying to figure our shit out."

"Really?" She let Victor pull the door aside and stepped into the open. "Sounds like you've got your shit figured out."

"I'm the President of an island that's best known for its processed coca products. I'm chasing a guy possessed by one of your people, and I've been killed and brought back by a space stone. I haven't got much under control."

She put a hand on his arm and gave it a squeeze. "That's true."

Panning the area, she noticed the guy she'd seen earlier. He was the one who had arrested her and brought her to the leaders. "Excuse me."

The man noticed her right away and reached for his weapon.

Victor raised his hands, but only as high as his chest. "Easy sport."

"Are you both from Earth?"

Victor turned to Nicole. "You told him?"

"No point in lying to them. We need to establish trust." She held out the specimens. "Leader Garth needs to see this."

"Come with me."

"I won't go to that room. Sorry. I need your trust as well." She held his lost gaze in hers. "Look, I know they've gone over those glass plates. That means they know I'm not crazy."

Victor brought his hands down. "We came to you, so don't be afraid to go get them. We're not going anywhere until we talk to them."

"You have to come with me."

"Not gonna happen, Sport," Victor told him.

"I have a weapon. That means you must listen."

Victor shook his head. "You also have two people that can disappear in the blink of an eye. Even if you get me, she'll be gone with some pretty important evidence."

"And if I shoot her first?"

Victor stepped forward. "Whatever comes out of that weapon, better be able to kill me."

The man studied Victor. Would this Earthling put his life on the line for her? Was that how it was done on the blue planet?

Victor stared him down. "I've never been afraid to step in front of a bullet."

The weapon came down. "Wait here."

Nicole watched the man leave. "You're either crazy or you've got a death wish."

"Or, I believe I have a knack for reading people."

"I'll go with crazy."

"Suit yourself, but it doesn't say much for you."

"You're a good guy, at heart. You're handsome and willing to take a bullet for me. Thanks."

He laughed "You still have that ugly rock handy, right?"

Nicole also laughed. "Okay, time to get serious. They're coming."

Leader Brad wasted no time. "Who are you people? How do you know Frederich, and what do you know about his work?"

Nicole handed him the samples. "We've met his wife and daughter."

"Is Julie okay?"

"You're concerned?"

"She's one of our best scientists. She went into hiding when we pulled her husband's privileges. It was precautionary. Is she okay?"

"She's fine. She tells a different story, one of being an outcast."

"She will always be welcome in our labs. Now what do you know about Frederich's studies?"

"He had help. There's the name MS01J884236S-66 in many of those documents."

"Yes. What kind of name is that?"

"MS01J884236S-66 has to be the one behind this." She pointed to the specimens. "They're planning on bringing thousands of these to life. They just aren't sure how to do that without a hosting body."

"That's because you can't."

"They're getting close."

"How close?" Leader Brad asked.

"I don't know."

"You need to come with us."

"I'm sorry. What?"

"You're an Earthling. I'm guessing he is too?" He lifted his weapon.

"You better split." Victor said as he pushed Nicole aside. "Go! I'll be okay."

As Nicole left, the man took aim and fired. He wasn't sure if Victor could render and wasn't waiting to find out.

Chapter seventy-two

Nicole appeared halfway down the beach. The others had been waiting by the dock.

Brittany noticed her first. "Where's Victor?"

"He stayed behind to deal with the leaders. How much time before you show up here?"

Cassandra shrugged. "Any time now, so how does this work? Do I need to move down to the end of the dock?"

Nicole thought for a second. "No. We need you out of sight, and I know this sounds strange, but it's in case you show up."

"That's right," Brittany answered. "You're future Cassandra. Present Cassandra is the one we need at the dock."

"But she doesn't know she's in trouble."

Nicole started for the tree line. "She'll be in more trouble if she sees you."

From the thick brush they could see present day Cassandra appear from a trail. She had the stone in her hand. Making her way over to the dock, she took a seat at the end of it, just like future Cassandra had done all those years ago.

"This is weird," Cassandra whispered.

"I agree," Violet admitted. "I'm going down there."

Nicole grabbed her hand. "You can't interfere."

"I'm pretty sure you meant to say, I can't let her die."

"We don't know how this will change things."

"You said you wanted to save this planet. Her not dying will change things. Maybe this is the beginning of those changes."

Nicole let go of her. "What are you going to say to her?"

"Small talk. I just want to be close when the killer shows up."

Nicole looked to Cassandra and she nodded.

"Okay go."

Violet got up, looked down the beach and continued down to the dock. She inched closer, did a shoulder check, and quickly assessed her surroundings. It wasn't good. There was no escape.

"Hello. Can I help you?"

Violet turned to present day Cassandra. "Hi. I, uh... what is this place?"

"This is my thinking place," she said with a smile. "Others call it Maramount Lake. You're not from around here, are you?"

"Look at me." Violet took a seat beside her. "Do I look like I'm from around here?"

Cassandra eyed her up and down. The denim was different, as was the shirt and the odd colouring around her eyes. "Where are you from?"

"We don't need to worry about that. What are you thinking about? I mean this does seem like a great place to figure shit out."

"Shit?"

"Stuff." She twirled her hand. "Sorry. We talk a little funny where I come from."

Cassandra laughed. It was rather different indeed. "I have a problem."

"Ha! Just one?"

"Pardon me?"

"It's just that I have so many. One would be a treat."

"Like what?"

"Wow. I've... Nope. I'm not going to start. We'd be here all day." She gave her a playful shove. "That is one ugly necklace. Is that your problem? Cute boy gave it to you, but he's got no taste in buying gifts?"

"My father gave me this, and it's a lot nicer than it looks. It's from space."

"Is that a new store?"

Cassandra pointed upward. "No, space."

"Cool. Can I see it?"

Cassandra reluctantly handed it over. Violet ran her thumb over the stone and could feel its energy. It was a cold energy.

She handed it back. "That's quite the stone. Is it part of your problem?"

"No." She wrapped the necklace around her wrist like a bracelet. "And it's more my boyfriend's problem. He thinks his father is… "

Violet started guessing, "Not his father, a criminal, overbearing, a woman in disguise?"

Cassandra laughed again. "No."

"I'm sorry. I don't do well with guessing. This boyfriend. Is he in trouble?"

"He might be."

"And the father too?"

"No. Mr Bennett is a good guy."

"Then what's the matter with… " She waited for Cassandra to offer a first name.

"Kim. Kim Bennett," she easily conceded. "He's got himself involved with a few others that don't believe our Leaders are… "

Again, Violet waited.

"It's wrong to doubt the Leaders, but he thinks these other people are right."

"What are they saying?"

"I really shouldn't… "

"Look," Violet told her, "I wasn't kidding when I said I have enough of my own problems, so whatever this is, I'm just an ear to bend. I don't need to get involved or take sides. Okay?"

"He thinks the space program is more than just a… "

Again, Violet sat in anticipation. "Don't leave me hanging girl, a what?"

"Hi, Dad," Cassandra said as she looked past Violet.

Two men stood behind them on the dock. "Hi, Cassandra. Who's your friend?"

"This is… "

Violet reached up to shake the man's hand. "I'm Violet, like the colour."

Neither man reached out to shake her hand. Instead, her father stared at it, confused, until she pulled it back. "That's a unique name."

"I'm a unique person."

"Well, it was nice to meet you, but I need to speak with my daughter. I'm sure you understand."

"Of course."

She got to her feet, gave Cassandra a wink, and started to walk away. Her step was quick until she got to the sand. Then she stopped. "Oh, shit."

The birds left the trees and came at her hard. She crouched down and put her hands up to protect her face. Then she looked back at Cassandra and the two men. The one was crouched down on bent knees, one hand over her mouth and the other on the back of Cassandra's neck. He was about to push her in. The father stood watching.

Couldn't they see the birds?

Violet turned back and fought through the fury of sparrows to get to her. When Cassandra hit the water, Violet was at a full sprint. Her shoulder struck the girl's father in the back. She veered off him and struck the other man in the ribs. The three of them were launched off the dock and joined Cassandra in the water. The birds were now swarming the end of the dock.

Birds churned the water as if trying to turn it into butter. Nicole watched from the shore in hopes that Violet would surface. She couldn't see anything in the chaos. Birds that had entered the water were starting to surface, much like popcorn from the oil of a hot pan.

Within seconds, thousands of birds were chasing each other around in a loosely bound tornado.

"Cassandra?" Brittany grabbed at her mother's arm. "She's gone!"

Chapter seventy-three

The bed Victor woke up on was nothing more than a stainless steel table. Foam spheres, no larger than golf balls, were positioned under his head, shoulder blades, hips, calves, elbows, wrists, and heels. They were soft, but remarkably sticky, and they held him in place when he tried to sit up. That bothered him. The fact that he was naked, didn't feel good either.

"Hey. What the hell is this?" he shouted.

An attractive woman hurried to his side. "You are awake."

"I'm fucking naked. Where the hell are my clothes?"

"You are in the Gerricks Asylum. You don't need clothes."

"You're wearing clothes."

She frowned. "I am not a patient."

"Neither am I." He pulled his shoulder with all his might. He couldn't budge it. "Damn it!"

"Please relax."

"I'm naked and I'm stuck to a fucking table. How do I relax?"

"Your vitals are climbing. You need to calm down."

"Then get me my pants."

At that point she realised his angst was from the nudity. She unfolded a small bed sheet and spread it out over his body. "Are you cold?"

He tried to look down but couldn't. "What the hell does that mean?"

She cocked her head. "Pardon me?"

"Cause it can get a lot larger than that. A lot larger."

She shook her head. "What can?"

Victor tried to relax, not that he had a choice. At least she wasn't judging. "Never mind. Thanks for the blanket. Hey, am I a prisoner?"

"That's a hard one to answer. I was told to hold you until the leaders returned. That usually means yes, but I haven't been given any instructions to test you."

Victor was really glad for the blanket now. "Where are they?"

"Now that you're awake, I can summon them."

She walked away and Victor tried again to sit up. The little foam balls held him as if he were a part of the table. And why wasn't he cold? Was the room that warm, or was it the surface above the bed?

Leader Garth was the first to enter, followed by Leader Brad, two doctors, and his nurse. They formed a semi-circle around Victor, leaders on one side and the doctors on the other. The nurse was at his feet.

"You are an interesting specimen," the one doctor announced.

"And you're a free-standing asshole. Let me get up and get dressed. Then we'll talk."

Leader Garth pulled the blanket down to Victor's waist. "That is incredible. What do you make of that?"

The elderly doctor leaned over Victor and took a long look. "He has never been in the chambers."

"What are you saying?" asked Leader Brad.

"These wounds have been healed by the body... from within."

"That's impossible."

Victor tried to pull his head up. "Not impossible. It's quite common. Now let me up and I'll explain."

They ignored him as the other doctor had a close look. "These are recently healed. I would say maybe a month or two?"

Victor laughed. "Try a couple days."

Leader Garth turned his attention back to Victor. "What are they?"

"Gunshot wounds." Then he added, "The one mark that looks fresh is from you guys."

"Remarkable. What about this one?" he touched a two-inch wound on his abdomen.

"Knifed eighteen years ago. Never tell a Mexican his mother blows gophers, even after a forty of tequila. The scar beneath that is a bullet hole from an FBI agent during a drug raid. I've got three more bullet holes in my back as well as several lashes from a man in Kabul. Shrapnel from a proximity mine buggered up my right knee and my left leg has scarring from when I was set on fire in Turkey. Russians love to watch people in pain."

"What's a Russian?"

"Let me up and I'll show you."

"Why have you healed this up on your own when we have chambers that would correct the damage without leaving any of these disfigurements?"

"I like my scars. They remind me that I've lived life."

The younger doctor leaned forward again and tapped the recently healed holes in his chest. "This should have killed you. The damage to the heart and lungs would have been too severe to recover from. I don't even think the chamber would have helped."

Victor remained silent.

"Did something on Earth fix you?" Leader Garth asked.

"It did."

"Is all of Earth this advanced?"

"Are you still planning on invading us?"

"Nobody wants to invade Earth."

"And yet people are dying and I'm a prisoner. Forgive me if I find that hard to believe."

"Why do you think we want to invade Earth?"

"Several successful trips to Earth were deemed failures. You've documented that we were hostile. That is such bullshit. Either you never made it to Earth, or you did, and you think you can invade so you're whipping up a story. In it, we're a bunch of dangerous primates. You lie to your people and tell them you have no choice but to attack us. It's them or us. On Earth, that's called propaganda."

"That's odd," Leader Garth admitted. "That's what we call it too."

He turned and the others followed. Only the pretty nurse stayed behind.

"Is it true?" she asked. She put a hand on his shoulder and gently ran her fingertips down his arm.

"Which part? That they plan on attacking Earth? How about you let me go and we'll talk."

"No," she giggled as she touched his wounds. "That you were healed from these gunshot wounds by something on Earth. We were told you were a primitive species."

"We're pretty hi-tech. How do you think we got here?"

That dipped her brow.

"I'll bet they didn't tell you we number eight billion either."

Her eyes widened. "How many?"

Chapter seventy-four

C assandra surfaced first. Violet and Cassandra's father surfaced a few seconds later. By then the birds had found tree branches. Nicole and Brittany were halfway down the beach and sprinting hard. Nicole reached the end of the dock first.

She reached for Cassandra. "Take my hand."

"He wanted to kill me."

"Take my hand," She repeated.

Cassandra took her hand and let her pull her out of the water. "Why would he do that?"

Brittany was waving Violet closer. "Come here. I'll help you out."

Violet was fished out of the water, followed by Frederich.

"Why, Dad?"

"Why what?"

"You pushed me in."

"What are you talking about?"

Nicole looked around. "It wasn't him. It was the other guy. And where did he go?"

Violet looked in the water. "He got away."

"What's up with the birds?" Cassandra asked.

"I think they were trying to save you." Brittany answered.

Cassandra found them in the trees. "How? They're just birds."

"We don't know." Nicole wanted this girl on a need-to-know basis. And why had the Birdman followed them to Mars? Maybe Victor had the answer to that one, and how was he doing?

"Mom," Brittany asked softly, "where is you-know-who?"

Violet didn't understand at first, but as she rung out her shirttails, she figured out who the, you-know-who was. "Oh ya. We're missing one."

"No, we're not," Nicole explained. "Do the math. We saved somebody, so the future isn't the same. She's gone."

"A ripple?" Violet guessed.

"That's a huge ripple, Mom," Brittany snapped. "Cassandra, what do you remember?"

"Remember?"

"Earth, Chinese food, make-up, blue jeans."

"Who are you, again?"

"You don't remember us?"

"She's not the same person," Violet reminded her. "That's a big-ass ripple."

"But…"

Nicole put a hand up to stop her. "These are ripples. Get used to them, before you make things worse."

"Everything's already pretty bad."

Violet smiled. "Au contraire. Everything's been reset. Can I see you for a second, Cassandra? Alone?"

She nodded. Violet was the only one she trusted at this point. The other two women were crazy, and her father had wanted to kill her. Violet had been there for her, saved her life.

"There's a lot of shit you aren't gonna understand and I get that. What I need is for you to listen to my crap, for like two minutes."

"Okay."

"No going poof, got it?"

"Poof?"

"Doing that transporting thing where you zap from place to place. Just stay with me and listen for a couple minutes. If you still wanna go once I'm finished, then I can't stop you."

"How do you know about that?"

"Oh, do I have a story for you. Ya ready?"

"I don't know."

"Too bad. Here goes nothing."

While Violet told Cassandra of her alternate ending, complete with the destruction of Mars and her computerised father, Nicole worked on Frederich. He didn't recall knowing her or ever giving her any documentation. He did however know about the book she was talking about and of the gaudy necklace.

"And you don't remember wanting to drown your daughter?"

"I can't even imagine. That being said, I'd been hearing voices for weeks. They get in my head and I… I don't know who to trust."

"Really?"

"When they leave, there's a fog that lifts, and then it's like they were never there."

"But it's subliminal. They're always in there somewhere."

He shook his head. "What is?"

"Never mind." She knew the fog, and the voices, were gone. "I need to know about the space program?"

"I wasn't on that project."

"But you were making soldiers, in order to invade Earth."

"Invade Earth? No. I made copies of Julie, Cassandra, my parents, and myself. It was to save humanity. You see we're years away from a catastrophic event. The Forbidden Zone is going to erupt, and I don't think we can stop it."

"What about venting it?"

"That might have worked, had we started years ago. We're venting now, but it's not enough."

"You need to increase the venting."

"Our Leaders say it isn't safe. They aren't willing to take the chance."

"Some damage spread out over years is better than a mass extinction."

"The Leaders claim that's not possible."

Violet was reading between the lines. "Is that why they're ramping up their space program?"

"It would make sense," Nicole added.

"Where is this venting area?" Brittany asked.

"It's out in the middle of the Forbidden Zone."

"Can we get there without alerting the Leaders. This needs to be kept quiet."

"I have the clearances to get us there. First, I need to go to my place and grab a folder. It has all the venting progressions. We'll have to meet up after I get that."

"Where do you want us to be?"

"I'll meet you at the transit junction. You'll have to get Cassandra to show you where that is. I could explain, but it's hard to find, and even harder to get through security. She knows an easier way."

"By teleporting us?"

"Yes."

Nicole let him run off before turning back to Brittany. Cassandra and Violet were finishing up their conversation. Then the young woman disappeared.

"What? No!" Nicole cried. "Where the hell did she go?"

Chapter seventy-five

Victor watched the nurse as she worked her way around the room, cleaning and polishing. Every few minutes she would look over at him. It wasn't the usual, is he still alive, glance, but more a what-makes-this-guy-tick one. Who was he and why was his body so marked up? She wasn't sure why she was feeling what she was feeling, but Victor knew. It was primal, something that was embedded into her DNA thousands of years ago. Women wanted rugged and strong, like men wanted soft and curvaceous. It was the hardwiring that centuries of refinement couldn't overcome.

"What's your name?"

"Excuse me," she replied, far too eagerly.

"I'm Victor. Victor from Earth. Actually, I'm from a little set of Islands in the Indian Ocean. The Isles of Corvus. I own them."

"You own an Island?" She moved in by his side.

"Islands. There are several."

"How can you own land?"

"That's how it's done on our planet."

"But you said there are eight billion people. Do you all own islands?"

"No. I'm considered well off. I have many people living on my islands, and they work for me. I pay them well and give them homes to live in, much like your Leaders."

"You are a Leader?"

"I am, but only on my islands."

"I must apologise. I did not realise you are a Leader. Have you mentioned this to Leader Garth?" She raced over to a compartment and retrieved his clothing.

"I hadn't."

"On our planet we have the highest respect for all Leaders. I have to believe that it doesn't matter the planet. A Leader is a Leader. You really should have told them."

There was a swipe of her hand over the control panel at the foot of the table and Victor could feel the foam balls suck him down for a brief moment and then release.

She handed him his shirt first, as it was on top of the pile. She held the rest of his clothes while he dressed. One piece at a time he went from naked to feeling a lot more comfortable.

"You have a question?" Victor asked.

She had watched him dress, studied his body. "No. I'm fine."

"No, you're not. What do you want to know?"

"How does your body heal?"

"It had help. When I was stabbed, I had the wound sewn closed. I would have bled to death otherwise. Gunshots are different. You need to remove the slug, make sure you fix the inner damage, and then sew the hole shut."

"You were recently shot six times in the chest. Tracking these bullets, you would have had fatal wounds. The heart would have stopped right away, and the lungs would have collapsed. How could you have survived? Even if doctors were there when you got shot, I doubt they could have fixed you in time."

"You're right. No doctor would have been able to fix me."

"Then how?"

"I'd rather not say." He quickly added, "Not that I don't trust you to keep my secret, but I doubt you'd believe me."

"After seeing the damage to your body and analysing it, I'd believe anything."

"Have you ever heard of a scientist named Frederich, a bad egg, banished by your Leaders?"

"I worked with him, but I wasn't involved in his studies about creation. That is a strictly forbidden topic here."

"How did he plan on breathing life into them?"

262

"He and his partner were brilliant scientists, but for whatever reason, they thought the key to life was in that stone."

"The stone like the one he gave his daughter?"

"He only gave it to her to throw off the other scientists and the Leaders. They originally thought it held the answer. Isn't that crazy?"

"Not at all. When I was shot, I was wearing that stone."

"You were shot here?"

"No, on Earth."

"I don't understand. There's a second stone?"

"There is. It was around my neck when I was shot."

"And you felt it?"

"I did."

She smiled. "Can I run a test on you?"

"A test?"

She was already heading for the cabinet with the syringes and vials. It was like she wouldn't be taking no for an answer. "To check for a remnant from the stone. It's a quick test. I'll need some of your blood."

"Uh, sure, But I'll draw it, if you don't mind."

The syringe was handed to him and after a brief inspection, he jabbed it into one of his veins and took some blood.

She took the syringe and headed for a computerised glass cube. It was a three-dimensional microscope of sorts. A few drops of the blood landed on top of the cube and slowly bled to the centre. Then she hit a few buttons, and everything came to life. The cube enlarged and the blood was magnified within the cube. Eventually, it was displaying a near atomic structure of the sample.

"There. Do you see that?"

"What am I looking at?"

"You've got red and white blood cells, and you've got plasma. The plasma contains proteins, carbs, enzymes, and other stuff, while the red cells define your blood type."

"With antigens."

"That's right. Now look closer at the antigens."

Victor saw the anomaly right away." What does that mean?"

"That means that Frederich was right about that stone."

"What do you call this blood type?"

"He called it the MS01J884236S-66 type."

263

Chapter seventy-six

While Brittany and Violet walked up the beach toward the lodge, Nicole stood at the end of the dock, staring at the birds that had swarmed the trees like angry bees. They were here, which meant he was here.

"Come on, Mom. We need to find the Transit Junction."

"Change of plans." She had spotted him in the shadows.

Violet turned around and started back to the end of the dock. That was when she also saw him. "What the hell is he doing here?"

"Then that is him, isn't it?" Nicole asked.

Violet remembered the man from Cuba. "It is."

"I need to talk to him."

"I'm not sure it works that way."

"He owes me an answer."

"Come back here and stand beside me."

Nicole backed away until she was standing beside Violet. "You don't think he'll talk to me?"

"He might have a question or two of his own." She cupped her hands to her mouth. "Hey! We need to talk!"

Silence, but the man moved out from the shadows.

"Do you want to help these people or kill them?" Nicole asked.

The man didn't stir.

"We can leave and let them die. It'll only wipe out the entire planet. Is that what you want, or do you want us to stay?"

The man moved up to the shoreline. They had his attention.

"We can leave."

With that, the birds left the trees. They started circling the man and chattering a chaotic chant of shrieks and chirps. Nicole took a few steps back and Violet followed suit. The cloud of birds rose up into the sky, leaving the shoreline vacant. It swirled, dipped, and approached as if angry.

It came at the dock with a fury. Violet and Nicole squinted as the birds flew past them, many glancing off their shoulders, hips, and arms. Then the birds raced across the beach, past a terrified Brittany, and into the trees behind the lodge.

When Nicole and Violet opened their eyes, the man was standing at the end of the dock. "You understand this isn't my doing."

"I don't understand anything. You wanted Victor to come here and kill Elizabeth's father. We believe the man is already dead."

"He's very much alive."

"Is he behind all this?"

"The man wants the secret."

Nicole took a second to consider this statement. "Where is he?"

The man continued. "When Victor was shot and brought back to life, the secret of life became a part of him."

"But that didn't happen until after he got your list."

"That's right, but the secret was used to bring Cassandra back to life before that. She is gone now, as is the secret that was within her. Now I need you to take care of Victor. Eliminate the secret."

Violet sputtered, "What? You want us to kill one of your soldiers?"

"He holds a dangerous truth. The secret must die. Then you need to eliminate those stones. They're dangerous."

"Why not just take away Victor's bird, like you did with Elizabeth?" Nicole asked.

"Victor's bird has been replaced. He visited me in Cuba. When I found out what he was, I tried to stop him. I couldn't."

Violet stepped forward. "I won't kill him."

"You really don't understand him, do you?"

Violet shrugged. "The man had a bird. He was one of us."

"No. Vincent was one of you and Victor killed him. At that point I made him one of my soldiers. He was a good soldier, but now he's dangerous."

A sudden numbness overtook Violet's body. "Hold it. Vincent was the normal one? That would make Victor an… "

The man finished Violet's sentence. "An abomination? Yes, he is. That skull you found, that was the real human. Vincent had a bird."

"Elizabeth wasn't an abomination," Nicole snapped. "Why'd you kill her?"

"I couldn't let Brittany enter this universe without a price. Abominations should never mate."

Nicole turned to Violet. "Sparrow for sparrow."

Violet took another step toward the man, upsetting the birds. "You're a long way from home. Can you render?"

He looked down at her. "I have no limits."

"Good. Then you should be able to bring Elizabeth back, for Nicole and Brittany."

"Too many years have passed. She would have a hard time adapting."

"You said no limits. Is that a lie?" Violet taunted.

"I don't lie."

Violet chuckled. "I'm thinking you have limits."

"You are such a fool."

"And yet you came across the lake in a flurry of feathers to talk to us. You need us. Now, I'm no stranger to how this works. You bring back Elizabeth and we owe you. What's your price?"

The man stood there pondering her offer. Maybe she could help him. "Leave now. Go back to Earth and let this planet cleanse itself. That is the proper course of fate."

Violet looked over to Nicole.

Nicole was smiling. "We could do that. We'd just need to find Victor."

"I'm here to see that Victor stays," the man grunted.

"What?" Violet snapped.

"He's served his purpose. I have no more use for him."

"Ya, well he's a friend."

"He was also conjured, and his body holds a secret. He needs to stay and perish with the others. MS01J884236S-66 cannot have that secret, and Victor cannot seem to kill him."

Nicole took a step forward. "There has to be another way?"

The man raised his arms. That brought the birds from the trees. "You need to leave, now… Victor for Elizabeth."

Again, the birds dove, swirled, and flew a chaotic aerial dance around them. When they left, the man was gone.

Brittany came running over. "Is it true? We get her back if we leave. I'm game for that. Cassandra's gone so that means we've made changes. Maybe this bird dude's wrong and we've done enough."

Violet shook her head. "We're not going anywhere. We need to find Victor."

"What? Screw Victor." Brittany took her mother's hand. "We need to leave, Mom, before he changes his mind."

Nicole took a deep breath and exhaled slowly as she thought of Elizabeth. "We've got to go."

"Help me find Victor, first," Violet pleaded.

"No. You have to come with us, or you'll be stuck here."

"And it's okay to leave Victor behind? No way."

"He's just a damn abomination," Brittany chuffed. Then she disappeared.

"You slept with him, Nicole," Violet reminded her. "How can you leave him?"

A tear rolled down Nicole's cheek. "I need Elizabeth. I want her back. I've made my choice."

"It's been almost twenty years. Her life would be impossible. The guy is lying. He won't bring her back for you, or anybody."

The tear was followed by another. "He's the one in charge of souls. He's not lying."

"Well, I'm staying."

That second tear was angrily brushed away. "Suit yourself. I can render you to the complex, but you're on your own after that."

"Whatever."

Chapter seventy-seven

The nurse's name was Adirra and she'd loved Victor's stories of being shot, stabbed, and beaten. She also loved his stories of Earth, how he'd acquired the Isle of Corvus, and that bad boy attitude of his. There wasn't a man around that aroused her like he did. He had surfaced primal feelings that she never knew existed in her.

"Are you going to get in trouble if you let me go?"

Adirra smiled. "I shouldn't think so. You're a Leader."

As she held the door open for him, he kissed her. Knowing she was married, it wasn't a kiss that would lead to anything, but he made sure it was enough that she wouldn't forget him.

"Thank you."

"Stay safe, Victor."

"You as well."

He made his way around the corner and was looking for a crack to crawl into when he saw Cassandra. She looked like she was on a mission, and he wanted to know what that was.

"Hey, wait up."

She stopped and took a defensive stance. "Excuse me."

"It's me, Victor."

"Do I know you?"

Victor studied the eyes. They never lied. "What did they do to you? Are you okay?"

"I don't understand."

He looked down at her clothes, still damp from what had to be an unscheduled dip in the lake. "Let me guess. Father tried to drown you. People from Earth showed up. Now you're off to see your Leaders and tell them the story about the planet's doom."

"And about the birds."

"Birds?"

"Violet said they were trying to kill me."

"I don't believe that. What else did she tell you?"

"Do you know the Violet woman?"

"We go way back. We're on the same side."

"And what side is that?"

"The one that stops Mars from being a deceased ball of dirt. Now what about the birds?"

"I don't know. I was pushed in the lake and then your Violet knocked everyone into the water. She saved me. That was when thousands of birds flew in and out of the water. Where did they come from?"

"Did a man come with them?"

"I don't know."

"And your father?"

"He didn't remember trying to kill me."

"He wouldn't. Your father was being controlled. This Violet woman, did she come with you?"

"I left them at the dock. I must talk to my Leaders. They need to… "

He looked down at her wrist. "You have the stone."

She pulled her hand back. "My father gave it to me."

"So, you know how it works?"

"Works? It's just a meteor rock."

"And yet it's why everybody is dying."

"Dying?"

"What do you know about Project Earth?"

"I have a friend who's helping me, but I haven't seen him in a while."

"I'm sorry. You meant Kim?"

She didn't like how Victor had known the name. "What about Kim?"

"He was found in his father's office. He was dead, and I'm thinking the father will be found the same way. Now what is this Forbidden Zone?"

"Why?"

"Seems we have two problems. Someone is trying to invade Earth, and this planet is doomed unless we can stop some planet ending catastrophe. And stopping the destruction of this planet seems to be the only way I'm going to get back to Earth."

She half-ignored what he said about Kim. How could he know? "I need to see my Leaders."

"Hard no on that one. How about we head back to the dock, before we lose the others."

"The Leaders need to know."

"They already know. They're okay with the idea. We're on our own."

She stared into Victor's eyes, studying them. He knew that was a good sign. She wanted to trust him, wanted to save the planet. Hell, maybe she even wanted to get him back on Earth as much as he wanted to be there.

Then she disappeared.

"Shit."

"I think somebody's losing their touch."

Victor turned around to see Violet walking toward him. She was alone. "She had no idea who I was. What did you guys do to her?"

"Long story short, the Cassandra we knew is gone. That happened when we saved this one's life."

"That was present day Cassandra?"

"Yep. We also saw the Birdman. He did the feathery tornado thing and told Nicole and Brittany they could have Elizabeth back if they left."

"Left as in… "

"Back to Earth and not looking back."

"Are they actually contemplating it?"

Violet laughed. "They're already gone."

"How the hell are we getting back?"

"Unless you got a spaceship in your back pocket, we aren't."

"And you didn't go with them?" Victor asked.

"Friendship's a pretty stupid thing, eh?"

"That means if we want to survive, we better save this planet."

"That would be my take."

Chapter seventy-eight

Victor started for the area where he'd been stuck to a bed by little foam balls. Other than Violet, that nurse was his only friend on the planet. She was just leaving the office when he and Violet got there.

"Hello, Adirra."

"Leader Victor. Hello. Who's your friend?" Then she whispered, "Is she also from Earth?"

"I'm going to say yes, but honestly, I can't be sure."

"Screw you, Vic. Yes, I'm from Earth." She wasted no time getting to the point. "Do you know where we can find the Transit Junction?"

"I'm going there now."

"Can you take us?" Victor asked.

"I cannot. It is forbidden to citizens, level three or lower security, and I'm sure Earthlings. You don't have a CommonPass, do you?"

"CommonPass?"

"It's a bio passport that holds your information, immunisations, security clearances, travel restrictions, biometrics etc."

"Why the hell do you need all that just to travel?"

"It was all put into place years ago after the Reorganisation," Adirra told them. "You don't have anything like that on Earth?"

"You did a reset?" Violet asked. "Was it because of a war, or a pandemic?"

"Pandemic, and it was a complete restructuring. It happened before I was born. They couldn't get a handle on resources, population, or the plague. Before too many people died, our governments changed the laws, rewrote our finances, and brought in the CommonPass. It gave the Leaders complete authority. Best thing that ever happened because we were failing the planet."

"Build Back Better," Violet joked.

"Build Back Better," Victor repeated. Then he shook his head. "Let me guess, before the outbreak, people could travel freely, gather when they wanted, choose their jobs, own property, have opinions?"

"That was a broken system. Most are irresponsible. There was poverty, global trade disorder, and disagreements between regions on politics and laws. Some areas were deep in debt and sinking further and further. Others were doing well. We couldn't continue that way."

"And a reset fixed all that?" Violet asked.

"It did."

"It didn't," Victor snapped. "It's a knee-jerk reaction and nothing more. It allows the government to take over. Before you were born, you had freedom, and you weren't monitored like cattle. How is this system better?"

"I'm not treated like cattle, and the system works."

"That's because you've never known freedom. Imagine being able to think for yourself,"

"I make my own decisions."

"Then take us to the Travel Junction and help us get through. Wasn't it you who said you were looking for a little adventure? Or is that not allowed?"

"Enough, Victor." Violet stepped in front of him. "We need your help. Your planet will die if we don't get to that Transit Junction."

Victor grabbed her shoulders and pulled her aside. "Telling her that isn't the answer, Stormm. She's convinced her Leaders have everything under control."

"I disagree. She's a big girl. She can handle the truth."

"Stop," Adirra snapped. "What is the truth?"

"The Forbidden Zone is close to an eruption. We know the force will crack the surface and lava will spew for months."

"Months?"

"The pyroclastic cloud will devour your atmosphere."

272

"What'll happen to us?"

"You will die," Violet continued. "Everyone you know will die. We want to help, but we can't do anything unless we can get out there."

"Okay. I'll take you."

Adirra took them through the upper area and down a level. Now below the complex, they travelled a series of tunnels to a train station. The subway didn't look like anything on Earth. The tunnels were rounded and no more than ten feet in diameter. The cars were only big enough for four people and hovered over the grooved track like a string of pearls running through a glass straw.

"Do you see Frederich?" Violet asked.

Victor panned the platform. "Was he supposed to meet us here?"

"He's over there," Adirra said as she pointed.

"Excellent." Violet led them down to the platform. "Frederich. We made it."

"Where's the rest of them? And who's this?"

"This is Adirra and… "

"I know Adirra. Who's the man?"

"This is Victor. He's with me."

"What happened to Nicole?" he asked.

"Birdman promised her a miracle and she bit," Victor snapped. "She went back to Earth with Brittany."

"And my daughter?"

"She took off." Violet shrugged. "She didn't say."

"She was adamant about going to the Leaders," Victor answered. "Truth, remember?"

Frederich turned to Adirra. "Thank you for bringing them here. I never would have thought you to do something like this."

"Then it's true?" she asked Frederich.

"It is. Before I came here, I talked to Julie, my wife. She's been to Earth, and she's seen our future. It's disastrous."

"Oh, now I feel terrible," Adirra admitted.

"Why?" Violet asked.

She pointed to the guards that were closing in on them. "I thought you were lying."

Chapter seventy-nine

It was a split-second decision. Victor shoved Violet and Frederich toward the front of the pearls and stepped between them and the security guards. It was more a reflex than anything. He knew Stormm could get the job done.

Violet grabbed Frederich's arm and dragged him with her to the lead pearl. "What now?"

When he put his hand on it, a door opening appeared. Violet shoved him inside and without looking back, followed.

"Hit whatever you gotta hit to get us the hell out of here."

Frederich put a hand on the display in front of him and the door's opening closed. The pearl began to roll in its groove and out of sight. Inside the pearl Violet watched as a map came up on the screen. The destination was quickly put in, the Forbidden Zone Station. Frederich had the clearances.

"How does it work?" Violet asked. "Are we rolling? I don't feel dizzy."

"It's a double walled shell. The outer shell rolls, the inner is a gyroscope. We're sitting flat."

"And the ball knows where to go? How?"

"When I put my hand on the display, it read my thoughts."

"Oh shit. That's so wrong."

"It's convenient."

"Having your inner thoughts stripped from your brain by a machine is bullshit."

"How would you do it, type a destination into one of those old-school keypads? That's how diseases are spread."

"Hell, ya." Violet stammered as she looked down at the map. "Looks like we have time for a couple questions."

"What do you want to know?"

"Thousands of years from now, when the planet is dead, computer you is still here, hanging out at the complex with an underground lab with a whole mess of embryos. How?"

"That's not me, and I only have five specimens in my lab. Besides, I'll never live through such an eruption."

"But you're a computerized hologram."

"Amazing. What else did you want to ask?"

"What are they gonna do to Victor?"

"They'll fire a charge at him. It's an energy ball that stops the heart for a few seconds."

"They know he's an old guy. It'll likely kill him."

"He seems strong enough." He held his hand over the screen and thought about a front window and one appeared. The tunnel was flying past them.

"Did you just think that?"

Frederich grinned. "The wonders of technology."

"No. The blasphemy."

"You don't approve of an easier life?"

"I don't agree with anything being integrated into my body. It's bullshit. Keep it natural, I always say."

"It's that bullshit that separates us from the animals," Frederich told her. "We don't just embrace our evolution, we control it."

"More like sabotage it." Violet looked down at the map. "Are we almost there?"

"We are there."

The pearl stopped and the door opening appeared. Frederich exited first. Two guards were waiting for them.

"You're under arrest."

Violet put her hands up. "First things first. I won't put up a fight if you let us tour the facility. I mean, we made it this far and you've got the gun thingy."

Frederich added, "I'm a scientist. We only need a couple of minutes and then we'll let you take us back, without incident. This is important."

"I'm not sure I understand."

"Please, ask Leader Daniel if I can check the venting in the Forbidden Zone. Tell him I'm asking as a favour and that I will report my findings directly to him."

The guard had his partner watch the two fugitives while he made the call. When he returned, he gave an affirming head nod. They quickly toured the facility. Starting on the main floor, they checked the visual of the venting pools.

"Doesn't look like much," Violet noted as she watched the fifteen pools on the monitors.

"No, it doesn't," Frederich agreed. "Are these the only thermal outlets?"

"Active ones," the plant manager admitted.

"And what is the output?" Frederich asked.

"The venting is regulated at about 300 degrees Celsius."

"What? That's not near enough."

"I can assure you that our Leaders have our best scientists on this and they're telling us that this is sufficient."

"I've seen the future," Violet told them. "This is definitely heading for disaster."

"You've what?" the guard asked. "Who are you?"

"I'm from Earth. The Earth in the future." Violet waited for a response that didn't come so she continued. "You have a planet-ending incident, and everything shows this area as ground zero."

"Frederich quickly cut in. "What she's saying is true. As you know, my daughter has abilities. She's somehow brought the future to us."

"Good thing too, because as long as I've been alive, Mars, your home, has been nothing more than a dead planet," Violet added. "The whole surface is barren and orange from the rusted iron."

"But Leader Garth and Leader Brad have assured us that we are venting a satisfactory amount."

"How are the other factors?" Frederich asked. "The surface temperature and seismic readings, are they stable?"

"Seismic are climbing, but the surface temperatures are fairly steady."

"You're a scientist," Frederich told the plant manager. "You know how important these readings are. If anything is on the rise, we're in danger."

While everyone was calmly huddled around the monitors, Violet took it upon herself to throw a fist into the throat of one guard, before driving a heel into the groin of the other. They both dropped. She jumped on the first guard and hammered her fist into his cheek. That punch rendered him unconscious.

"Get me a rope."

"What are you doing?" Frederich asked.

"I feel bad for these guys, but you've got a corrupt system here. These guys answer to it. Now grab me something to tie them up with."

Frederich pulled a box out of his pocket and took two stickers out of it. They were round and thicker than paper and yet when placed on the temple, dropped the recipient into a deep slumber. "We don't tie people up here. it's barbaric."

"Shit. How long will they be out with those things?"

"An hour or two, or until we take them off."

"Sure as shit beats handcuffs."

"Handcuffs?"

Violet waved a hand as she started for the plant manager. "Never mind. Can we turn the venting up?"

He looked down at her light frame. The woman had just taken out two well-trained guards. "We can, but everything can be monitored by the Leaders at the Command Centre."

"That's back in the complex?"

Frederich nodded. "I'm sure they've already seen their guard's vitals and realised they've been subdued. They will be sending more, many more."

Violet looked down at the two men. "How would they know that?"

"We're all monitored for heart rate, anxiety, vitals, remember?"

"Then all your Leaders may be corrupt. They would have known Kim was dead, or that you were being controlled. That means they were the ones doing it. At the very least, they knew about it."

"What? Why would they do that?"

"Look. This planet is more advanced than Earth. That means you have a successful space program."

"We've had serious difficulties with… "

"Nope. Not buying it. Your space program is fine."

"Why would our Leaders lie?"

"You said you went through a reset, that everyone allowed your governments to buy your homes, pay off your debts, and biometric the crap out of your asses. Your new species status is sheep, or cattle. Now imagine going to another planet and taking it over."

"I see the benefits of exploring another planet, but why would they want to kill us off?"

"Someday you'd want to follow them. Let's face it, Earth is bigger, better raw resources, and a lot more malleable. And who's to say that, down-the-road, events don't corrupt this planet. But this is their Earth? I don't see them wanting to share."

"We'd promised them that we'd never… "

"Desperation kills promises like a hungry lion in a bunny farm. When push comes to shove, all bets are off, and you'd do whatever is needed. Your technology is far too superior. They couldn't let you live. Your Leaders, and their elite, need a fresh start, and a clean getaway."

"I cannot believe they would do such a thing."

"And yet, here we sit watching these thermal pools doing nothing while the end draws near. You guys were manipulated into a reset, and now you're being manipulated into extinction. You need to change these venting settings before it's too late."

"It's no use. They'll just eliminate us and change the settings back."

An eerie grin spread across Violet's face. "I have a plan."

Chapter eighty

The immobiliser, Martian weapon of choice, packed a hell-of-a wallop the first time Victor was shot. This last time was just as bad. That being said, he'd only blacked out for ten minutes and there wasn't near the fog there was before. They were still dragging Victor to the infirmary when he came to.

"Wait, where are you taking me?"

Leader Garth was walking ahead of them. "Are you trying to blow up our planet?"

"No. We're trying to stop you from doing it."

"Why are you here, really? I don't want to hear any more of these saving-the-planet lies."

They entered a room where Nicole and Brittany were already sitting. On a table in front of them there was a spilled folder full of pictures. They were shots of Mars, taken by the Hubble telescope and by Nicole when she was at the dig site.

"You couldn't stay away, could you?" Victor chuffed.

"There was no Elizabeth, like he promised. We waited for a week before rendering back. Your Birdman is a liar."

"Are you surprised?"

"Maybe a little. Maybe just disappointed."

Victor walked over to the table under his own steam. He fanned the pictures with a clumsy sweep of his hand. "You told them?"

"They don't believe us."

"So, beam them up."

"Huh?"

"Show them the future."

"Already offered. They refused."

Victor turned to Leader Garth. "Why don't you want to know, unless…"

Nicole waited for him to finish. "Unless what, Victor?"

"Unless they had a plan. My question is why?" He paused knowing Leader Garth wouldn't divulge anything. "I'm going to make a guess. Stop me if I'm wrong. You have decided that Earth is the better prize. At just under two hundred million, it's an easy mark. With your technologies, you'd have no resistance. How many of you are going? I'm guessing most of the Leaders, a few elite, and a handful of friends. Maybe a few hundred?"

"How would they get there?" Nicole asked.

"Don't think for a second that they don't have ships ready for the journey."

Nicole seemed confused "But everyone we've talked to has said the space program was a failure."

"They've either lied or were too stupid to know any better. I have no doubt they're ready to make the trip. They've already checked out Earth and they've found a spot." He turned to Leader Garth. "I've noticed you haven't stopped me yet."

"You're entertaining. Please, go on."

"What I can't understand is why would you let your planet die, or don't you believe us? I mean, we have pictures and you're not stupid."

"We don't need your pictures."

"You can stop it," Nicole offered. "We can help you."

"Why would we want to stop it?"

Nicole shrugged. "Millions of lives are at stake."

"Millions of lives that wouldn't be able to function without us. What are they going to do when we're gone? Do you think they'll be able to keep everything running. We're doing them a favour by giving them a quicker death."

"What if they try to follow you?"

"They all know that inter-planetary travel isn't possible."

"But it is."

"Yes, but nobody believes it."

"They'll wonder where you went."

"Not when they find our bodies, charred beyond all recognition at the Forbidden Zone Station." He added, "your friends are there as we speak, and it's not like you Earthlings don't have a reputation for aggression. You attacked us when we reached Earth on our last mission and now you've come to this planet with a purpose. There'll be no doubt to how we died or what they'll need to do to protect the planet."

"A frame job," Victor assessed. "And we walked straight into your plan."

Just then a man walked into the room and whispered in Leader Garth's ear.

"Looks like Frederich and your friend just moved our cause forward," Leader Garth said as he got up and headed for the door. "There was an explosion out at the Forbidden Zone. Your arrest has just become official."

Chapter eighty-one

The collars put around Brittany and Nicole's neck were to prevent them from rendering. They worked as good as the room they were taken from. The detention centre didn't have a non-rendering room, but it was locked down. Victor had never seen a place like this. Yes, it was a prison, but it didn't feel like one. The furniture was nice and there was a fridge.

"Anybody hungry?"

"Seriously, Victor?" Nicole fidgeted with her collar as she took a seat. "You think that explosion was Violet?"

"Who else? She probably went out there, saw it wasn't venting like it should and blew the place up."

"How would that help?" Brittany asked.

"Even if she forced them or tricked them into venting the planet at a higher level, these assholes would find out and set the levels back down. She blows it up and the place is venting properly, and there's no turning back."

"Think she saved the planet?"

"Maybe, but she killed us in the process. These idiots just had everything they needed dropped into their lap. Now they simply drag a few cadavers out there. These jokers make it look like they went out there to talk some sense into us and everyone was killed in the process. We'll be convicted and they'll be free to ship out."

"We'll tell them the truth," Brittany chimed.

"And they'll believe us because… "

"He's right," Nicole admitted. "We're Earthlings hanging out with a rogue scientist."

They sat in silence while Victor raided the fridge. Most of the food looked like something you'd find on Earth and tasted even better. After an hour of incarceration, they were joined by Violet and Frederich.

"How bad is it out there?" Victor asked.

Frederich shook his head. "We've got a slow lava flow, but the pressure is still too great. We've bought this planet a little more time, but it's still doomed."

Violet shrugged. "They want the planet to die. They're fucking off to Earth and don't want these people to follow them."

"We know," Nicole told her. "We're going to be the scapegoats for killing their Leaders. Cadavers are being shipped over there as we speak."

Violet nodded. "Sounds like we all got the same script."

"And we played our parts perfectly," Brittany added.

"Except instead of an Academy Award, we get jail."

"Jail," Victor laughed. "They're going to off us as soon as they get everything set up, likely make it look like a foiled escape. There's no way we'll be allowed to tell our side of the story."

Just then, Cassandra appeared outside the window of their apprehension room. She held up the gaudy stone and closed her eyes. They all watched as she held the stone against the window and squeezed her eyes shut.

"What the hell is she doing?" Nicole asked.

"Open the door," Victor snapped. He walked over to the window and banged on it until she opened her eyes. "Let us out."

"I can't open the door, or it will trigger alarms. Now be quiet. I need to concentrate."

"Concentrate on getting us out of here then."

"I am. Stand back." Again, she tightly closed her eyes and concentrated as she held up the amulet.

Victor, thinking she was trying to blow the glass window, took a step back. The gaudy stone started to pull itself from her hand and vibrated against the glass. It was as if a magnet was trying to rip it from her hand. Then she let go and the stone jumped through the window and landed around Victor's neck.

"What the hell?" He grabbed for it and started to pull it off.

She continued to stare at him through the unbroken window. "No! You need to leave it on."

"How? Why?"

"I teleported it to you because I need you to follow me."

"What the hell are you talking about? I can't... "

She slammed her eyes shut again and put her fingers to her temples.

Victor started to feel dizzy. He also put his hands up to his head and dropped to one knee. "Stop it. It hurts."

Cassandra continued.

"Stop it," Nicole shouted as she watched Victor drop to both knees. "You're killing him."

"Uhhh..." Cassandra started to grunt. There was no turning back.

Nicole raced to Victor's side and grabbed for his arm. Her hand went through him as if he were a ghost. A split-second later he was outside the room slumped beside Cassandra.

"Holy shit," Violet whispered under her breath.

Victor quickly got to his feet, banged at his chest and held his arms outstretched to look at them. "What did you just do?"

"Long story," Cassandra answered. "But there's no time for it."

She took his hand in hers and squeezed tight as he fought to pull his hand free. She calmly closed her eyes again.

"No way. You're going to explain this before I go any... "

Before he could finish that sentence, the two of them had disappeared.

Chapter eighty-two

Victor didn't recognise the swamp or all the trees. It wasn't an area he'd ever been to. Looking around, this could have been Earth or Mars. Oddly, he didn't give a damn about that. He wanted to know how he was pulled through a wall.

"What the hell just happened?"

"I think you Earthlings call it rendering."

"I'm talking about that thing with the wall. Normally I get a hug and don't feel like I was ripped apart."

"But you're a…" Cassandra stopped to study him, his eyes, and his reaction. "What do you think you are?"

"I'm a human, a regular guy."

"There's nothing regular about you anymore. Yes, you're from Earth, but only sort of. We can talk about that later. Did one of you people blow up the thermal pools?"

"Violet and your father probably did it. The planet is building up too much pressure and your Leaders are unwilling to vent it off properly. Now let's talk about… "

"That actually makes sense, but why aren't the Leaders venting it?"

"They want the planet to die."

"I don't buy that. If we die, they die."

"I'm betting that they've got ships waiting to take them to Earth. Long story short, Mars dies, they get Earth, and we get blamed, not that it matters because there won't be anything left of us when your planet erupts."

"Then we need to go back to the Bureau."

"The Bureau?"

"It's the area where the Leaders hold their daily meetings, store their files, and strategize our future. It's close to where you were held."

"You think we'll find a few dirty little secrets?"

"I do."

"And you've been there?"

"Once or twice, when I was young. My father used to be a highly acclaimed scientist."

"We need to walk there though, because that weird shit you're doing to me is… "

She reached over and grabbed his hand. "Sorry. No time."

The building was grand, with an atrium full of trees and plants. They re-appeared behind a shrub that had purple flowers. Again, Victor didn't care about that.

"What is this?"

"Shh. It doesn't hurt as long as we're making contact."

"I thought the only way I could travel like that is with a hug."

Cassandra shrugged and gave him an awkward hug. "Feel better?"

"No."

"If you're advanced you don't need the contact, but the less contact, the more painful the de-atomising is."

"Tell me about it. And what did you mean earlier, when you said I'm only sort of from Earth. I'm an Earthling."

"We have to keep moving."

"Not until I get my answers."

"Here's the thing. What I need to tell you is big. It will distract you, so how about I tell you later, and I will. You're a very unique individual."

"Trust me. I can handle it."

She frowned as she studied him. "Okay. You were conjured from a book and that, combined with being killed and brought back to life with the stone, makes you… "

"Whoa. Stop. I wasn't the one conjured. Vincent was, and he's been taken care of."

"What do you mean, taken care of?"

"I killed him. I killed all the abominations."

"No! Tell me that's not true."

"Decapitation and a ritual with the skulls. They had to be stopped."

"Vincent wasn't one of the conjured ones. Who told you he was?"

Victor thought for a second. No one had told him. It was the way the whole thing had happened. His mother had been lied to by the CIA. She had picked the name and chanted the verse. Vincent had come into existence. It was the only logical explanation.

"I am not the abomination."

"I know. You were conjured from the Ledger. You are anything but an abomination. Earthlings are the abominations. They share their souls with birds."

"Well, what do you... Never mind. I don't want to know."

"Can we talk about all this later? We need to stop these guys first. Then we can argue which version of humanity is right."

"Which version? There is only one version... God's version."

Cassandra stared him down. "I sure hope we get a chance to talk before one of us gets killed. Come on. We need to bring our Leaders to justice."

"They're not my leaders."

Cassandra panned the area. There was nobody around. "Something is wrong."

"You mean with your Leaders?"

"Yes."

"They're off staging their deaths. They plan on being charred by that explosion out in the Forbidden Zone. The bad Earthlings will be blamed for killing them. Then they can board their spaceship and invade Earth. Nobody here will be the wiser and the Earthlings will be blamed and executed."

Shut it already. The fact they aren't here gives us a huge advantage." She ran out into the open. "Come with me."

Victor still needed a second to let everything absorb. Had he killed a human? The Birdman had told him to do it. He ran to catch up. Why would the Birdman have lied to him?

"Hurry up. I knew it was a mistake to tell you anything."

Victor started to follow. "How do you know all this stuff?"

She opened a door and entered a boardroom. "When I found out I could do that thing you call Rendering, I knew I was unique. It bothered me at first until I did some digging. I was created and given life by a nurturing body. That means my life is actually a portion of my mother's life. Much like cell DNA replicates from a mother cell, I am a replicate, except my vessel was man-made in a lab. You, however, were conjured from a Ledger. Neither your vessel, nor your life, is man-made. It's more like a blueprinted clone, but it's real. There is a third type of life. That's the Birdman's system. Somehow, he can give a bird's soul to the universe and the body follows. Not very natural if you ask me."

"And the stone?"

"I have no idea how that works, except it is the purest form of energy. There is no bias or umbrage. Now help me find some files."

"How do you know this?"

"I've spoken to Kendall."

Victor tried to keep up. "And who's Kendall?"

"She told me I couldn't tell you, or your friends."

"What?"

"You'll meet her in the future. That's all I'm allowed to say. Can you please look for something, before it's too late."

"Why not." He needed to refocus. "What are we looking for?"

"Anything that might incriminate our Leaders; any space documents, venting predictions, timelines on our demise."

Victor started looking but soon stopped. "Actually, I have a better idea."

Chapter eighty-three

Victor took a step back from the counter. He looked around the room and wasn't seeing what he wanted to. "What are you thinking?" Cassandra asked.

"Hear me out. These guys are at the venting stations, right?"

"Or they've been there, staged their death, and moved on."

"Is there a way to track them?"

Cassandra's eyes widened as she bolted for the door. "Great idea."

Victor was right behind her as she entered the Analysing Station. It was a large room with comfortable chairs and monitors on the one wall. Cassandra quickly entered the names of the Leaders. Several clusters of dots were grouped in several subway pearls.

"That's them," she told him.

"Who's in the other pearls?"

"Probably their accomplices," Cassandra admitted, "friends, and military. Do you want me to bring up their names."

"Not important. Where are they headed?"

"That, I don't know. According to the public records, this line doesn't exist."

"How long is it?"

"Looks like its about eighty miles. I can't believe they've managed to keep this a secret."

"I'll go out on a limb and say they're heading for their great escape. Can you shut them down?"

"Yes, no problem." She started tapping away at the console. "I just need to type in a few things."

Victor watched as she tapped on the glass console, and yet the pearls kept moving. He gave her a minute. "Not working?"

"No, it's not. Maybe I can overload the system. If so, we can trap them before they reach their destination."

"Hands up."

The voice came from behind them. Victor looked back to see a guy that looked a little more official than the usual security guard. Cassandra saw the highly decorated General but continued tapping. She had seen him before at one of the galas, when her father was still in good standings.

"What are you doing in here?" he asked.

Cassandra finished up and motioned to the screen. "Watching our Leaders trying to escape the planet."

"Pardon me?"

"Look at the monitor. Those red dots are our Leaders, in pearls on a secret track. Have you ever seen that one."

"Pearls?"

"Sorry. That's what Victor calls them."

"Our Leaders are dead. I just got word that they perished in an explosion at the Thermal Facility."

"They're alive and well." Again, she pointed up to the monitor. "They double-crossed us and tried to blame it on the Earthlings."

He stepped up to the monitor and studied the dots. They were indeed the credentials of the leaders. The track was one that he'd never seen either. At least forty pearls had stopped in a tunnel, thirty miles short of their destination. The system had overloaded.

Victor started to inch toward him.

"No, Victor. We don't need to use force. He sees what we see. He just needs a moment to process it."

"I don't understand," the man almost whimpered. "Why would they do this?"

"We can explain, but first we need the military to round them up."

"Do we arrest them? I mean, they're our Leaders."

Victor walked up to him and put a friendly hand on his shoulder. "I'd think real Leaders wouldn't pretend to be burnt up in a staged explosion?"

Chapter eighty-four

Seven pearls arrived at the thermal pools, shortly after everyone was released from their holding cell. While Victor and Violet had already seen a win, Nicole and Frederich wouldn't admit a win until the thermal levels and pressures had started to decline.

The pools began to bubble ferociously, spewing lava, rock, and venting steam. It looked violent and out of control, but this was what was needed. Eventually, there would be more pools added for better management.

"It will take a few minutes, but that should do it," one of the scientists admitted as he maximised the venting on the few undamaged thermal pools."

Nicole turned to the plant manager. "We need to always meet or exceed these levels. There can be no exceptions. It may include evacuating Capital City some day. Do you understand?"

"I was following the direct orders from Leader Garth."

"Fair enough, but not anymore," General Henderson told him. He was the man who freed Nicole and the others. He was also the one that put out an arrest warrant for the Leaders and anyone associating with them. He was a dedicated soldier but had no problem adjusting his focus when corruption reared its ugly head.

"And these Leaders are being rounded up as we speak?" Violet asked.

"We'll be getting an update on that soon." He turned to the plant manager. "Do you have an office I can borrow?"

"Right this way."

Cassandra was standing beside Brittany. She had watched everything with a child's curiosity. "That's it? Our planet isn't going to end up like those pictures?"

Brittany was equally captivated. "Pretty unbelievable."

Nicole put an arm around her. Although saving Mars was an amazing accomplishment, she was still thinking about the Birdman, and what he had promised her. He had reneged, muddying the victory. She reached for Victor's hand, and he took it.

Nobody saw the interlocking of fingers, or the uncharacteristic smile on Victor's face. "Best part about all this, Violet didn't get shot. That's gotta feel pretty good, eh Stormm?"

"Fuck you, Vic." She half-raised a middle finger. "Question. If this is all kumbaya again, can we get going? Brad's probably getting worried."

"He's likely enjoying his freedom," Victor joked, "throwing a party, or watching football with a pizza on his lap."

"Nah, I got him trained."

"You ain't there. Trust me, we can resort back to cavemen in minutes."

Violet let that comment go. "You owe me a shit-ton of money for this, Vic. And I don't take cheques."

"That depends on when we get back. The way I see it, you'll be getting nothing more than a couple of days wages and travel time."

"What? We've been at this for… "

"I only pay for real time, not whatever this was."

"Then I want mileage." She knew that would amount to a suitcase full of cash.

General Henderson interrupted. "We have news. Seems my men managed to arrest the Leaders. We also have just over two hundred accomplices in custody. They're being brought in and will await trial. We've also seized a large space craft, loaded with equipment and weapons."

Nicole sighed. "Great work."

"Not really. We've received word that a smaller craft has left."

"Do they know who was in it?" Victor let go of Nicole's hand and looked up at the monitor.

"No idea. We're investigating."

The lead scientist interrupted. "General Henderson. We are seconds away from a stabilized Forbidden Zone."

They split the screen and watched the monitored surface pressures drop to the acceptable ranges.

"It looks like we've reached stability, General."

"That's fantastic," Nicole said as the muscles in her neck finally began to relax.

"It sure is," Elizabeth sighed. She put an arm around her friend.

The oddly familiar voice cut Nicole's breath short. She looked over and almost jumped out of her skin. The shock was quickly overcome by joy as she drew the woman in for a hug. A haze of questions rolled through her mind as she held her close.

Elizabeth pried herself free. "Are you okay? You look like you've seen a ghost."

"Are you kidding me? We've... " She smiled as she stared. "Look, Brittany. It's Elizabeth."

Elizabeth tried to follow her eyes. "Brittany? Who's that?"

"What? She was right here." Nicole looked around but couldn't see her. "Where is she? Brittany!"

General Henderson was equally shocked. "I don't see her either, or the other two, for that matter."

"Brittany!" Nicole panned the room. "Violet! Victor! You remember Victor from Cuba, right Elizabeth?"

"Of course." Elizabeth was staring. "We haven't seen them in quite some time."

"Okay. You remember them." She looked back over her shoulder toward the transportation deck where the pearls were. "Brittany!"

"You're scaring me. Who's Brittany?"

"You dated a man named Greg, saved him from drowning. He got you pregnant."

"I don't remember it quite like that. I saved him, but..."

"You had a daughter. She was right here." Again, she looked around and her eyes finally fell on Cassandra. "She was here, right? I'm not crazy."

"No, you're fine. I, uh, she was here. Same with the others."

"I have to go find them."

Frederich stepped closer. "Who is this, Nicole?"

"This is my best friend." She studied her for a second before adding, "but she's been dead for almost twenty years."

Elizabeth cringed. "What the hell are you talking about?"

Nicole took her hand. "It's true. You got pregnant and died giving birth, to Brittany."

Elizabeth pulled her hand away. "Why would you say that?"

"Because it's true." She noticed the purple ring but didn't say anything.

Elizabeth scrunched her face and stepped back. "No... we..."

Nicole continued to hold her hand out. "You remember something, don't you?"

"I... I remember a hospital. It felt so... I was shot."

"Yes, but that didn't kill you." Nicole reached for her hand again. "Months later, when you were giving birth... It all went so very wrong."

"I don't remember dying."

"Maybe they're back on Earth, at the apartment. I'll have to render us there."

"The apartment?" Elizabeth stared off trying to remember. "Why is everything so fuzzy?"

"I'm not sure." Nicole, in fact, had no idea. She turned to Frederich and Cassandra. "We have to go."

"Of course." Cassandra held up a hand. "Give me half a second. I have something for you, for all you've done for us."

The woman left and returned with a hand full of papers.

Nicole took them from her. "What are these?"

"I can't be sure I'll see you again. Brittany told me you didn't have this set of documents. These are the ones we cannot decipher. This is not all of them but it's a start."

Nicole took the papers and shuffled through them. The symbols and abstract patterns were the ones she'd seen while flirting with that caretaker. Did she want this right now? "Why are you giving this to me?"

"I had a dream, when I was in that chamber." She dropped her eyes. "In the dream, you were standing at the base of a volcano. There was a boy. He's supposed to help you understand them."

"A boy?"

"I also remember rain, but it wasn't water. It was like a fuel of some sort, and it was burning. Victor was there."

"They're still alive?"

"It was a dream." She paused. "They must be somewhere. The dream was so real. I also saw a large city of death. It was massive."

"Anything else?"

"Not that I can remember."

Nicole tried to stop herself from trembling. Something in her believed Cassandra. "Thank you."

Cassandra gave her an assuring smile. She wanted to tell her all about a woman named Kendall but didn't. It was too risky. "You've done so much for us."

Nicole took Elizabeth in her arms and tried to render. When it didn't work, she tried again with a different location. Again, she had no luck.

Elizabeth shrugged. "What's wrong?"

"I'm not sure. It's like the destinations aren't there."

"But you can still render, can't you?"

"I think so." She disappeared and reappeared across the room. "Works fine."

"Maybe Earth has changed. I have a spot that might work." Elizabeth raised an eyebrow. "Do you want me to try rendering us there?"

"Can't hurt." She looked back at Cassandra and held the papers up. "Thanks."

Nicole was half-expecting a beach in Cuba, but where they appeared was anything but. It was the ledge of a cliff.

"What's this?"

"Not sure. There should be writing on the cliff wall behind us."

They looked over and sure enough, the stick figures were there.

"This is good. What else do you remember?"

"If we climb up to the top, there'll be a house. It's Greg's."

They climbed along a trail to the top. There was no house.

Elizabeth turned and looked out over the vast wilderness. "That's not right. Where is everything?"

Nicole studied the lay of the land. It took a second to see it. The buildings, roads, and monuments were missing, but the river and lands were the same. This was Washington DC, but it wasn't.

"I think we can call this a ripple."

Chapter eighty-five

Violet, Victor, and Brittany stood at the end of the dock staring at a shoreline that wrapped around a small mountain lake. The dock, shore, and trees looked familiar to Victor. So did the lake and the building off in the distance. Brittany and Violet were completely in the dark as to where they were.

The amulet, still around Victor's neck, was warm against his skin. "It's okay. I know this place."

Violet saw the stone glowing. "Did we get sucked into one of your dead stone thingys?"

"I think so." In the distance he could hear the thumping. He immediately imagined the hammer, the basket of apples, and the crushed birds. "We've gotta go."

"Why, Victor?" Brittany asked. "What's going on?"

The first bird landed on a branch that hung low off a distant tree to their right.

Brittany saw it first. "Oh shit."

A second and third bird landed on a branch ten feet up on the same tree.

Victor started for the shore. "Run!"

Twenty or so birds quickly swooped down to the ground at the shoreline. By the time Victor was halfway down the dock, the birds on the ground numbered one hundred, with more on the way. They swirled and swarmed the end of the dock, making Victor, Violet, and Brittany the hunted.

Stopping them halfway down the dock, the birds started to break away and head for the forest. The noise slowly eased as they found branches to perch on. Now standing at the end of the dock, his boots firmly planted in the soil of the shore, stood the Birdman.

"You failed me," he told Victor.

"You lied to me," Victor replied.

"I did not. The man exists, and I still want him dead."

"Not that. Was I conjured from that book, or was it Vincent?"

With that, the trees released the feathery darkness, and the dock was swarmed once again. They pecked and slapped the three with their wings and beaks in a relentless attack.

Victor sprinted for the shore and the other two followed. The Birdman had vanished into the cloud of feathers as the three headed for the parking lot. Above them, the squawking was deafening. In the distance the thumping noise echoed.

"What the hell is that, Vic?" Violet asked.

"That's the sound of death." He spotted a moving car through the maze of feathers and beaks. "This way."

The window on the passenger's side was partially rolled down and the man inside was yelling at them. "Get in!"

Violet opened the back door and jumped in first, dragging Brittany behind her. Victor followed and slammed the door. In seconds they were speeding down the road and away from the chaos. A few stop signs were ignored as they tried to make their escape.

Brittany lifted the left cheek of her butt. She'd sat on something when she was pushed in the car. It was a book, her mother's journal. She ran her hands over the embossed cover. It read, The Gift of Distinction.

"You can slow down, now," Victor told the man.

"Hey," Violet added. "Thanks. I thought we were goners."

Brittany held the book up. "Uh, where'd this come from Mr…"

"Name's Vincent," the driver offered.

"Vincent?" Violet asked. "We were sure lucky you showed up when you did. You sure look a lot like…"

Victor grabbed her leg and squeezed hard.

"Ouch. What the hell, Vic? The guy looks just like you."

"That's because this is my brother," he whispered.

Ripples

Book Four in the Eve of Humanity Series

(Sneak Peek)

Kevin Weisbeck

Chapter one

Wen Nicole and Elizabeth arrived in Washington DC, the city had been replaced by a vast wilderness. It was clear that a price had been paid for what they'd done. Although Mars was safe, the ripples of the past few days had created quite the change.

Elizabeth looked out across the valley. The answer to why they couldn't render to the Davis house was now obvious. Had China also been changed like this? That would explain why they couldn't render back to the apartment.

"It's beautiful," Nicole admitted out loud.

"It's horrible." Elizabeth had to look away. "We did this."

Nicole didn't feel the guilt. There had to be a simple explanation. Suddenly, she remembered the older temples in China, one in particular. China could hold the answers, that is, if it still existed. There was one temple that stood out as a good rendering choice. It was the oldest, and hopefully, it was built before the day they changed Mars.

"Give me a hug. I'm taking you to China."

China?" Elizabeth gasped.

Nicole pulled her close and rendered the two of them to the Luolong district. The White Horse Temple was quiet when they arrived. Usually flooded with tourists, it was surprisingly desolate. They stepped out into the courtyard.

Elizabeth saw the statue of the horse and walked over to it. "I forgot how simple this place was."

"I'm just glad we made it here, and that there's some form of civilisation." She looked past her friend and pointed. "And people. Let's hope one of them has answers."

Two men were walking toward them, obviously Mr Cheng's guards. It wasn't until they were closer that Nicole noticed they had their guns drawn.

"Wait!" She put her hands in the air. "Don't shoot. *Bùyào kãi qiãng.*"

The guards said nothing. Instead, they handcuffed and forced them into the back seat of a patrol car.

"What's happening here?" Elizabeth looked to Nicole. "Should we render back to Mars?"

"I think I'd rather find out where they're taking us. Mr Cheng could be on the other end of this drive. Try thinking of this as an adventure."

"I'm no longer a fan of adventures."

Nicole squirmed to get comfortable. The cuffs had been cinched tighter than they needed to be. "I get what you're saying, but aren't you curious as to why they don't do the tourist thing anymore? I mean, did you see anybody back at the temple?"

"Who'd come if they get treated like this?" Elizabeth looked out the window as the car wove through the streets. Before long, the pavement turned to dirt. They were heading for the mountains. "I'm going to ask them where we're going. *Wómen qù nâ?*"

The guard in the passenger seat looked back, more than a little surprised that she spoke the language so well. "You make mistake. You must pay."

"Good. You speak English. What did we do wrong?"

"No one allowed in China unless you Chinese! You speak, yes. But that not make you Chinese!"

He seemed agitated, but it was more bark than bite. Elizabeth could tell he wanted to ask her how she'd learned the language, but his discipline wouldn't allow it.

"Where are you taking us?"

"You are being taken to the house of detention." He paused. "Where you will be sentenced."

Elizabeth glanced over to Nicole. "I think he meant to say, where we'd await trial."

Nicole knew that wasn't what he meant. "We're not Chinese, so a trial would be a waste of time. Call it practical."

"I'll call it something alright." But it was true. The whole time they were driving through the city, they hadn't seen one person who wasn't a local. "We should ask them about Mr Cheng."

Nicole was more concerned with Brittany. Where had she ended up? "Knock yourself out."

"Can we speak with Mr Cheng," Elizabeth asked. "We know him."

"Who?"

"Your President, Mr Cheng."

"The only Cheng I know owns the produce stand in the market. He always has the freshest celery. I can assure you he won't be able to help." The two guards laughed. "But if you need fresh cabbage, I'm sure he is your man."

Nicole sighed as she stared at the passing countryside. Brittany had to be in a different time. It made sense. She was in the correct time, probably eating Mrs Lee's take out in the apartment. Would she have gone back to the apartment? "What year is it?"

"Why you ask?"

"I'm just a little confused."

"It's 2002."

"That was a stupid question," Elizabeth chuffed. "I could have told you that."

Chapter two

Nicole sat back. They had ended up in 2002 and not the 2020 as expected. They had rendered to the present and missed the mark by damn near twenty years, and oddly enough, none of this had registered with Elizabeth as wrong.

A lone guard opened the compound gates, allowing the small car to enter. They pulled up to a small building on stilts. The two men pulled them out by their shoulders and escorted them into the shack. It was a modest single room with nothing more than a filing cabinet, a desk, and an air-conditioner that hung out of one of the windows.

They were shuffled in front of the lone desk where a larger woman sat, staring down at the papers she'd just been handed. She looked up at them. Her eyes made deliberate contact with each of them before returning to the papers. Nicole and Elizabeth remained silent while they awaited their fate. Finally, the woman spoke as she scribbled in her notes. "Put them in two."

Elizabeth wanted to ask her a few questions. "*Duibùqi.*"

The woman recognised Elizabeth's ease at speaking their language but held a single finger up to her lips, hushing any further words. "Now is not the time for you to make mistakes that might influence your stay here. We'll talk when the time is right. First, you get settled into your new home."

Elizabeth bowed in respect. This woman didn't need a reason to make their lives miserable. Nicole dropped her head as well, but not out of respect. She couldn't let this woman see her animosity. The guards moved in and hurried her and Elizabeth outside. She didn't look back, meeting the summer heat with a fire of her own.

Nicole leaned in close to Elizabeth. "I'm ready to render out of here now?"

"Don't let them get to you. They're not the big picture." She smiled as the guard gave her a shove to shut her up. She wouldn't let him get to her either. "You wanted an adventure."

Across the compound they saw their new home. It wasn't fancy and right away they knew they wouldn't be able to stay long. A thirty-by-thirty foot square of cement made up the floor and four posts held up a dilapidated tin roof. Chain link fencing ran from post to post with a missing section to be used as a doorway. They looked back to the guards who pointed to the opening.

"In!"

Although the shade was welcome, a breeze would be needed to bring the sweltering heat down a few degrees. The other women in the building watched as they picked a spot to sit. Elizabeth returned their gaze, trying to figure out what their stories were, but it was pointless to guess. This wasn't the China she remembered.

The cement was harder than they imagined. At least it was clean. They'd likely have to sweep or hose it off daily as part of their chores. Nicole was imagining what the food might be when a rolled-up blanket hit her in the side. She looked up in time to see the second one coming and caught it. "Stupid asshole!"

Elizabeth chuckled. "You really need to relax."

"Two blankets and no pillows! Seriously?" She watched the guard leave. "What time do you think it is?"

Elizabeth motioned with her eyes to the broken part of the fence. A guard was arriving with a few trays. "It's supper time."

The food was being brought in. Elizabeth got up and checked it out, more out of curiosity than necessity. She grabbed two of the trays and passed one to Nicole. As she started to lower herself down, her knees buckled.

Nicole grabbed her by the arm to steady her before she could fall. "Elizabeth?"

"I'm okay. Just a little woozy."

Nicole spread one of the blankets out. Then she helped Elizabeth shimmy over, leaning her against the fence. "You sure you're okay?"

"All good. I just need to eat something." She bit into a bun and motioned for Nicole to sit. "Eat. We need our strength."

Three women sat across from them and they'd been watching. They saw the two newcomers get dropped off, and they'd seen Elizabeth take the stumble. They grabbed their trays and headed over.

"Hey."

Nicole stopped eating. "Hi."

"What's you story?"

"We were caught at one of the temples. They arrested us on the spot."

"Does that surprise you?" She asked. "My name is Sandy, and this is Paula, and Andrea. We were caught at the border."

"I'm Elizabeth and this is Nicole. We're not from here and didn't know the rules."

"Really, because the rules are simple. No outsiders allowed. You're either Chinese or you pay the price. What brings you here?"

"You wouldn't believe me if I told you," Elizabeth grimaced. "I wouldn't believe me right now."

"Try us! We're good listeners and we love a good story."

"We're not from around here and came to fix things." Nicole blurted the words out before looking over to Elizabeth. "What? I say we rip the Band-aid off and see what we've got."

"Did I hear you right, that you're planning to fix China? I'd say you're off to a rough start, and it won't get any better if you try and tell this story at your sentencing, but that's okay. You'll have a few weeks before you have to worry about that."

"Weeks?" Elizabeth stuttered, "This, this is China, isn't it?"

"Exactly." Paula answered. "What rock have you been hiding under?"

"It's just that the China we remember was much kinder and gentler. It was a country that allowed foreigners."

Sandy threw her hands up. "I find it hard to believe that China was ever like that."

"Why are you here?" Nicole asked.

"We're underground. We were in Australia and got out before all hell broke loose."

"All hell?"

The woman cocked her head to the right as she looked at her. "Seriously, where have you been hiding?"

Nicole shrugged.

Paula continued. "Years ago, Australia was wiped out, everyone dead. It all happened so fast. Since then, all borders were shut down and the countries aren't allowed to mingle."

"What are the other countries like?"

"Don't know. We can't get out."

"What happened in Australia?" Elizabeth asked.

"We heard it was a man-made virus, but we didn't wait to see it firsthand. Word has it, there were no survivors."

"No, that can't be," Elizabeth replied. "We were monitoring…"

They all watched as the expression drained from Elizabeth's face. It was immediate. Her eyes remained open as she fell back against the fence.

Nicole gave her a gentle shake. "Elizabeth?"

Chapter three

The red 2006 Grand-Am slipped and slid as Vincent continued to race it down the street. Birds, crushed under the wheels, took their time coming back to life. As they did, they rejoined the chase.

"I thought you were friends with this guy, Vic," Violet teased.

The car jerked right as Vincent slammed a curb. Violet was thrown across Brittany's lap and onto the floor at Victor's feet.

"Sorry!" Vincent shouted as he tried to get the car back on the road. "Hard to see with all these feathers. Where the hell did they come from?"

Victor tried to pull Violet up from the floor, but she was wedged in pretty good. "Birds are my problem, I guess. They belong to this guy, and I've pissed him off. I'm guessing he wants me dead."

"I heard you stopped by my house." Vincent asked, "What were you doing there?"

"About that… "

Violet had taken Brittany's hand and was almost pulled free when the car bucked again.

"Damn it. Can't we stop for a second so that I can get the hell out of here!"

"No!" Victor snapped as he yanked at a handful of shirt to free her. "Put your damn seatbelt on or pay attention."

"Like you're wearing yours," Violet snapped.

x

"Don't need to. I'm... "

Feathers had kept Vincent from seeing the corner and the car left the road with a thud. Victor and Violet slammed into the back of the front seats, while Brittany was launched through the opening between the seats and onto the floor by the glove compartment. She quickly recoiled and pulled herself up into the front seat.

"Sorry again," Vincent said to her. "I can't see anything."

Brittany tried to peer through the mass of black feathers. "Go faster. Maybe we can outrun them. We're on a straight stretch, I think. Pin it!"

Vincent planted his foot on the gas pedal. The birds slowly lost ground and the windshield cleared. "It's working."

"Just don't slow down again," Victor shouted.

On the last impact, Violet had taken the headrest of the passenger seat in the face. She wiped the blood from her nose onto her sleeve. "And where is it that we are going?"

"I'm just trying to lose the birds."

"Damn, you and Victor look alike," Brittany noted while she stared at the man behind the wheel. "Now I'm even curious. What were you doing at his house, Victor?"

Again, there was no answer. He also didn't cuff Brittany in the head for asking, although he wanted to. Who was she to be stirring it up?

"You met my wife. The love of my life. What did you think?"

"She was nice, for an agent."

"Pardon me? She's an elementary school teacher."

"And you've got some freaky rare cancer."

"That's not funny. I could die without my treatments."

"Except you don't have cancer and your wife isn't a school-teacher."

Vincent had inadvertently slowed, and the birds were overtaking them again. "You lie."

"I have no reason to lie. And keep your foot into it."

"I can't. The car is handling a little odd."

"The birds don't give a shit."

"What do you want me to do, run us off the road?"

"Use the sidewalk," Violet suggested. "Always works for me."

Vincent could do one better. He crossed the sidewalk, broke through a fence, and headed into a park. Large trees allowed him to drive beneath the canopy. That split the birds up. While a few followed at ground level, the majority soared high above the trees.

Brittany smiled. "This also works."

Vincent wove the car between the trees while he kept his foot mashed on the accelerator.

"Where are we going," Victor asked.

"I told you, I don't know. We're trying to lose your friends."

"I mean, where does this park end. Are there any tunnels?"

"No. Just an ocean."

"What?"

The last of the trees thinned out and suddenly the birds were back. On the horizon, the blue of the sky met the blue of the ocean. Vincent cut a hard left and found the road that ran along the shoreline.

"I can cut back into the trees."

Violet looked over her shoulder and, through the back window, the cloud of wings and beaks looked angrier, if that was possible. "I say we stay on the road and keep your foot into it."

"Can do."

The road was straight, and at this point the closest bird was a good fifty feet back. Vincent glanced down at the fuel gauge and gave a relieved sigh. He had three-quarters of a tank.

"Why were you at my house?"

"Your house, your wife, your damn cancer. None of it is real."

"I beg to differ."

"Differ all you want. It's no more real than this car chase."

Violet shook her head. "You say'n this isn't real, Vic?"

"Ya." He paused. "You have no idea where you are, do you."

Vincent guessed a car chase and the others agreed, all except for Victor. He knew better because he'd been here before.

"I was shot a few days ago. Six slugs in the chest."

"My God," Vincent gasped. "How are you here?"

"This is why I'm here. I died. That's why you're here, Vincent. You also died, years ago."

"Bullshit. How."

"Decapitated," Violet chimed in. She figured Victor could use the backup.

"How the hell can you say that? I'm here."

Victor hesitated. "I was the one who killed you."

"Look out!" Brittany screamed.

Victor's confession had Vincent looking at him in the rear-view mirror. When Brittany yelled out, his eyes returned to the road just in time to see the woman.

In the middle of the road stood a beautiful blond in a white dress. She looked lost, like she had no idea where she was, or how she'd got there. Vincent cut the wheel hard to the right. The front wheel caught the curb and pulled the steering wheel out of his hands.

A guardrail, made out of rotted lumber and chicken wire fencing, didn't even slow the car down. The red Grand Am cut through the barricade, shot across the wide walkway, and was launched twenty feet into the water.

Victor tried to open his door but couldn't. They were deep in the water and sinking fast. He tried the door's electric window, but again, with no luck.

In seconds, the car had touched down, twenty feet below the surface. Water was leaking in through the dashboard and doors, but it was only a heavy trickle. Still, they'd be neck-deep in water soon enough.

Violet lightly tapped on the window with her knuckle. "At least the birds aren't chasing us anymore."

Kevin Weisbeck

Other Books by Kevin Weisbeck

Madeline's Secret

Madeline suffers from amnesia when she wakes from the car accident that killed her sister. Her parents, husband, and small child are all strangers. As she accepts these people into her new life, she uncovers a secret, one so dangerous that it could ruin her if it ever got out.

Johannes

A Madeline's Secret Companion Book

In the days that followed the death of his parents and girlfriend, Johannes is visited by a pair of friends he hadn't seen in over a decade. Fast Eddy Cruiser is the one that used to look out for him when he was a teenager. Heidi, his high-school sweetheart, was the one he needed that protection from. Having these two people back in his life could only mean one thing. Trouble would be as certain as the emotions of a relationship that didn't end well.

The Darkness Within

A victim of his own bad choices, Johnny Pettinger is stranded following a plane crash in a remote mountain wilderness. His injuries are serious, but they're not the only factors preventing him from getting home. In order to do that, Johnny needs to shine a light on the very reason for his being there, the ***Darkness Within***.

Lockdown

When my wife and I went on a ten-day vacation to Peru, we didn't expect trouble. It was a country with zero cases of the Corona virus. But our holiday soon turned into a three-week lockdown, and we weren't alone. Thousands found themselves fighting to get home, as the Corona virus became a global pandemic. We had originally hoped that our Canadian government would get us get home, but other factors were at play. We weren't just fighting the governments of these two countries. We were fighting the Colombian Cartel. This is the fictional story based on a real event, and it's the story the newspapers didn't tell you.

About the Author

Kevin Weisbeck is a Canadian author, born in Kelowna, British Columbia and currently living in Okotoks, Alberta. He's had several short stories published in magazines and newspapers, and currently has one in McGraw-Hill's iLit Academic Program.

He can usually be found on the couch with his laptop in front of him and his Ragdoll cat, Franklin, on his shoulder. It's not an ideal writing set up, but Franklin doesn't mind. Otherwise, Kevin enjoys hiking, kayaking, camping, photography, and golf (when the weeds and water don't get in the way).